A GIRL IN TIME

A GIRL IN TIME

John Birmingham

GWC

For my Dad.

PART ONE

CHAPTER ONE

In twenty-nine days, she would be rich.

Cady was almost dizzy with the thought, although it might have been sleep deprivation, too. And maybe a little hunger. That was her own fault, she knew, as she leaned forward into the glow of the iMac.

But it didn't matter.

Because in twenty-nine days, she would be rich.

She shivered in the cold. The tiny studio apartment was unheated except for the valiant efforts of a cheap, Chinese fan heater plugged into one of three power boards under her desk. It was also dark, except for the computer screen and the small constellation of status lights on various pieces of equipment.

Cable modem. Power boards. Macbook Pro. Mister Coffee. A big ass Beoplay A9 kicking out The Funkoars "What's Your Malfunction?" at half volume.

Still loud enough to shake the building.

It was a gift, the A9. Or maybe a bribe, or some sort of enticement. She wasn't quite sure. But she did know she couldn't afford that level of awesome. Some guy from Electronic Arts had sent it over when the game hit number one on the paid App Store.

And stayed there.

And stayed there.

She rubbed at the gooseflesh on her upper arms, warming herself with the friction and the satisfaction of staring at her Sales and Payments pages on iTunes Connect.

Murder City was still number one.

"Suck on that, Pikachu." She smiled, and her mouth formed an attractive bow, but there was nobody else in the one-room apartment to see it and smile back.

Cady McCall did not much care, because in twenty-nine days, Tim Cook would back a truckload of money up to her front door, and she would be rich.

She checked her watch, her Dad's old Timex, a wind-up piece of analog history. He'd worn it to the factory every day until he retired. Almost time to get going, but she thought she had just a few minutes to check her reviews. Never read the reviews, they said, and they were right. But most of Cady's, like ninety-five percent of them, were four and five stars. Mostly five. And the gimps giving her the one-star write-ups were universally hilarious. Mouth-breathers, all.

She'd made a Tumblr out of them. It was hugely popular, and the affiliate ads linking to her app on iTunes were unexpectedly lucrative.

Suck on that, gimps.

The Funkoars closed out their rap. They gave up the A9 to Tony Bennett getting his groove on with Michael Bublé, a duet of "Don't Get Around Much Anymore".

That was the good thing about living alone, one of the many excellent things about living alone. She could play whatever the hell music she wanted, as loud as she liked to play it. And she liked it loud. Her studio was on the top floor of a four story warehouse, an old cotton mill.

Solid brick. Bare wooden floors. Big picture windows overlooking Puget Sound.

Cool, right? But apart from a sweatshop on the ground floor, she was the only occupant. The brickwork badly needed repointing with mortar, the wooden floors were scored and dangerously splintered in places, and you couldn't see out of the windows. They'd been painted over sometime in the 90s. The building was marked for demolition, the whole block for redevelopment, which was how she could afford the space. She had no lease, no security of tenure.

Again, didn't matter.

Twenty-nine days.

Her phone chimed. A message from Georgia.

Already here. BuzzFeed guy 2. Where r u?

She quickly sent back a canned response.

On my way!

Cady stood up from the desk, closing the windows on her reviews without bothering to read the new ones, but pausing with her hand hovering over the mouse before logging out of Connect. She couldn't take her eyes off the estimated amount of her first payment.

Georgia responded to her canned reply with an emoji. A skull and a flame.

Die in a fire.

That broke the spell. Cady smiled. She could afford to smile. In twenty-nine days, four and a half million dollars would drop into her bank account. They would probably invite her to WWDC. She might even demo.

The phone rang while she was throwing on a leather jacket and scarf. It was cold outside, and probably wet.

Because Seattle.

The call came in on her landline, giving her the excuse she needed to bust out an epic eye roll. It would be her mom. Only her mom called her on the landline. She only had the landline because of her parents, who were convinced her Uncle Lenny had died of a brain tumor from his cell phone, which he was always yammering on when he was alive, God rest his soul.

Uncle Lenny also smoked two packs of unfiltered cigarettes a day and liked a shot of rum in his coffee.

He drank a lot of coffee.

Cady totally would have answered the call, but she was running late, and Georgia was half way gone to getting pissed at her. And that was why she had an answering machine anyway, because she just didn't have time, and her parents trusted voicemail about as much as they trusted cell phones not to shoot death rays directly into your head.

And the idea that they might just send a text? You know, something efficient?

Forget about it.

"Hi, Cadence, it's your mom."

The old familiar voice, a little tinny through the cheap speakers. Cady dropped the volume on Tony and the Boob, but did not make the mistake of picking up. That could delay her by up to half an hour, and she had people waiting.

Better to call back in the morning.

"Your dad clipped another couple of stories for you today. He's sending them in the mail tomorrow."

A pause. Probably waiting to see if Cady picked up. But if she picked up, she'd get in trouble for screening the call, because her mom knew how small the apartment was, and she had no excuse for not answering already. Best to pretend she was already gone.

An almost inaudible sigh.

"You should call your dad, Cadence. He's not been well. I think some days searching the google for stories about you is what gets him out of bed in the mornings. He's very proud of you, darling. You should call."

She almost picked up then, but Melville started yowling for dinner, and she didn't have time for him either.

"Go catch some rats," she said, using the toe of her Doc Martens to push the protesting tabby cat out of the front door.

There were always rats. Hence, Melville.

Her mother's voice was lost in the rumble of the heavy steel door sliding in its tracks. The cat looked up at her as if to say, "Well, where's the beef, bitch?"

"Rats," she said. "I mean it. Earn your keep, pretty boy."

The landing outside her apartment was dark. The bulb had blown months ago and was too difficult for her to reach. It hung on a wire over the stairwell. She could almost reach it, if she was willing to risk a broken neck. There was no point calling the building owner. They weren't coming out to change a light bulb. She wondered sometimes if they even collected the rent from the account she paid into.

Cady didn't care. She used the flashlight on her iPhone. She juggled the phone and the padlock on her front door with practiced ease.

The cat yowled again, suspecting the worst.

It was even colder in the stairwell. Maybe cold enough to freeze the water in the pipes again.

Twenty-nine days.

Four and a half million.

Her boots sounded louder than usual on the concrete steps and she wondered if something about the temperature of near freezing air amplified sound waves. It made sense, but that didn't mean it was right.

She would've made a note to ask Jeremy the next time she saw him. He was a sound engineer at Square Enix. He'd know, and not knowing was bugging her now that she'd thought about it.

She didn't make a note though.

She had the phone in her hand, but only an idiot would hurry down a darkened staircase in an empty building, thumb typing on her phone. For sure she'd trip and break her neck or something and then who'd spend all her money?

The sweatshop was closed up and quiet as she swung around the landing on the first floor. That was unusual. Russians ran that place, and they normally worked those Asian women until late at night, seven days a week. She checked the time on her phone. It was still early, although she was now more than a few minutes late for dinner.

Maybe the Russians had moved on. Maybe Immigration had caught up with the women.

Unlike the question about whether cold air amplified sound waves, the fate of the sweatshop wasn't something likely to keep her up at night. She'd be gone from this dump soon anyway.

Her phone buzzed with another message from Georgia.

BuzzFeed guy is cute! Don't hurry.

That was good then, she thought, as she hit the street and pulled the main door of the building closed behind her. The deadlock engaged with a loud click. She put the phone away and started walking toward the restaurant. It was a couple of blocks away, not long if she hurried. She was trying to kick the habit of staring at a phone while she walked. She'd seen a guy slam into a telephone pole doing that, and in this part of town you needed your wits about you anyway.

"Cady, I don't like you walking the streets at night the way you do," her mother said pretty much every time they spoke. Another reason for not picking up that call a few minutes earlier. "You live in such a rough part of town, dear."

And she did, but Cady McCall was not a victim in waiting. She had a can of mace in one pocket of her leather jacket, and she'd packed a small but sturdy LED flashlight in the other. It threw out a wicked bright beam, enough to blind anyone she light-sabered with it. And held in the fist, it made a great improvised weapon. The sort of thing douchebros called a "tactical" piece.

The rain she had feared was less a drizzle than a really heavy mist. She'd be damp, but not soaked, by the time she walked the few blocks to dinner. Cars drove past every minute or so, going in both directions, their headlights lancing into the darkness like searchlights in old war movies.

Some women, and a lot of men, cannot help but look vulnerable when caught on their own. Moving through an empty landscape, they seem to invite threats. Cadence McCall was not like that. She was not overly tall, but long legs and thick hair that fell halfway down her back made her seem taller. She carried herself through the night with a confident stride, her boot heels thudding and squelching on the wet sidewalk. It was real confidence, too, not just a show for anybody who might've been watching.

She was somebody who felt at ease on her own.

And anyway, she wasn't worth mugging.

Until her iTunes money dropped, she had sixty-three bucks to her name.

CHAPTER TWO

Georgia had argued that sushi was not a great choice on a cold, wet night in November. She wanted Greek, of course; her last name was Eliadis. But Cady loved sushi. They had hot dishes, too. And BuzzFeed Guy was paying.

"Matt. His name is Matt, not BuzzFeed Guy," Georgia stage-whispered. He was away from the table when Cady arrived. "And you're going to give him a great interview, because he's going to be my new boyfriend, and he's going to give it to me six ways from Tuesday."

The restaurant was about ten minutes from being crowded. The seats at the sushi train were all taken, and all but a couple of booths were full. They were in one of the booths, because you never ate from the train unless you wanted to catch an express ride to food poisoning. Four empty beer bottles on their table spoke to how well Georgia and BuzzFeed Guy—Matt—were getting along.

Cady made herself say his name five times so that she wouldn't forget. She would make herself say it at least twice in the first couple of minutes, just to fix it in her memory.

"Stop saying his name," said Georgia, digging a knuckle into her ribs. "He's mine. You were too late. So don't think you can come in here with your sad little Jessica Jones look and steal my future husband away from me."

Cady squealed and laughed and tried to slide away from her friend, and completely forgot the name of BuzzFeed Guy when she looked up and found him smiling at the pair of them from the end of the table. He was good-looking. Movie star good-looking. And even though she had promised herself she would remember his name, because that's what grown-ups did, one look at this guy and all rational thought climbed aboard the sushi train and choofed away, possibly never to return.

"Hi, BuzzFeed Guy," she said.

"Hi, Murder Girl," he volleyed back, sliding into the booth across from them, carrying three beers.

"Matt," said Georgia, emphasizing his name, "this is Cadence McCall. Cady, this is Matt Aleveda. He will be your BuzzFeed journalist tonight."

They shook hands while Cady struggled to think of something to say other than, "Oh my, you're cute." She could see why Georgia wanted to rush him out the door and into bed. All of her strategies for this interview, all of the carefully prepared little pull quotes she had already imagined featuring on the front page of the site between "Tay Tay and Beyonce's Cage Match" and "37 Pictures of Dogs Who Just Can't Even Anymore" . . . they all flew right out of her head.

"You want to order?" he asked, saving her from the vast embarrassment of staring at him and saying nothing, just grinning like an idiot.

She nodded and swigged at her beer, mostly to hide behind the bottle for a couple of seconds to regain her balance. She felt Georgia kicking her under the table as if to say, "See, see, I said he was cute."

"I like the hot ones," she said, before hurrying on. "The hot dishes, I mean."

A bright hot flush bloomed somewhere beneath her tee shirt and spread to her face. She knew it was coming. Knew it was going to be bad. And that just made it worse.

"That's why we should've had Greek," said Georgia. "Do you like Greek food, Matt?" she asked.

"My grandmother was Greek," he said, his smile completely authentic. "She was a cook on a big cattle ranch down in Arizona. That's where she met my granddad. He was a vaquero, a cowboy from Mexico. So yes, I do like Greek food."

"Then next time we go to Lola, and moneybags here pays."

"Hey, I don't get paid for another month, you know," said Cady.

"Okay then. Yanni's, and then Lola."

"So you haven't made any money off the app yet?" Matt asked. "That seems almost weird. It's been number one for weeks now."

"It takes a while to confirm the sales," she said. "Sixty days, usually."

Talking about her game, Cady started to recover her poise. It was as though the earthquake which had threatened to knock her on her ass stopped, leaving her shaken, but suddenly surefooted. The restaurant was getting noisy as more people came in to take the last seats, and the patrons who were already there raised their voices to talk over each other.

"Do you mind if I ask what sort of a payday you're looking at?"

She didn't mind at all.

"Four and a half million dollars initially. It'll fall away after that, after *Murder City* drops off the front page and then the best seller lists. But I can probably make do."

She felt Georgia's foot tapping her ankle again.

What? Was she being a jerk? This was why her friend had come along with her. Cady wasn't always the best judge of what to say in these situations.

"Sweet," said Matt, clearly impressed. "Explains all the clones."

"They're garbage apps," said Cady, and Georgia kicked her. Hard. Matt noticed.

"It's true," Cady insisted. "They are. And I feel really strongly about this. I spent a long time working on that game. I maxed out my credit cards. Ate grungy rice and fish heads. I slept in a cot in front of my computer. I did the work. It paid off. I'm not going to be modest about it."

"No reason to be," Matt said as a waitress appeared to take their order. "If you were a guy, it wouldn't be an issue."

Georgia dug her fingers into Cady's arm.

"Mine," she whispered.

Matt reminded them he was picking up the tab, and they over-ordered. Cady doubled up on the tempura seafood platter with an extra serve of Dungeness crab.

"Rice and grungy fish heads, remember?" she said when Georgia gave her The Look.

They discussed the games industry: "Nintendo should just give up on hardware."

Sushi trains: "Most of the time they're like, 'This is what comes back on the train line from the toxic waste factory.'"

And the latest superhero movie, another failed Green Lantern reboot. A particular hate-favorite of Cady's.

"The love interest dragged. Again. The super villain was more sentient smog bank than relatable nemesis. Again. And while you have to love the idea of the green man's powers—your flight, your mad awesome combat skills, a workable indestructibility, and that whole of energy-into-mass conversion thing—they just didn't sell me on the Lantern having any chance at kicking Superman's ass, which is the gold standard in these matters. One star. Would not even torrent."

Matt was recording the conversation by then.

"So, you guys. You're besties, right? Where'd you meet?"

"College. At a self-defense workshop," said Georgia.

"Seriously?"

"Seriously. Have you seen the data on campus rape?" said Cady, using a pair of chopsticks to awkwardly move a large piece of fried crab meat into her bowl.

"So you're like unstoppable killing machines of death?" he asked, with poker-faced sincerity.

"Worse," Georgia answered. "Female game devs."

"Our superpower is ruining everything," said Cady.

"So, Georgia, did you help Cady on *Murder City*?"

"Nope. It's all her own work. She doesn't play well with others."

"It's true," said Cady. "I'm just a girl with mad coding skills, but no people skills."

"And your diagnosis," Georgia prodded. "Don't be modest. You're a high functioning sociopath too."

"According to 4Chan."

Matt took out a Field Notes reporter's notebook. It looked to be about half full already.

"According to Reddit," he said, flipping through the pages, "you're an insufferable lesbian, and every boy you ever dated died mysteriously after placing five-star reviews of *Murder City* in the gaming press."

"The technical term is 'corrupt gaming press'."

"I stand corrected."

"You're actually sitting down," Georgia teased. "This is why nobody trusts the media anymore."

More food arrived. More food than they needed.

The restaurant was uncomfortably hot and noisy with the crowd by then. A family moved into the booth behind Matt, a single dad and three daughters. They looked young, the oldest possibly not even in school yet, and they were hideously excited. Their father looked pained as the girls launched themselves at the moving buffet.

"Choose careful, girls. I only got thirty bucks to get us through. Maybe some avocado rolls?"

Cady was looking directly at him when he spoke, and his eyes locked on hers, his voice trailing away at the end, the three hungry children ignoring him completely. She felt herself blushing again. Without asking Georgia or Matt, she grabbed the plate of hand rolls which had just arrived at their table, stood up, and walked them back to the next booth.

"We over-ordered," she said. "You should have these."

The girls fell on the food.

"Rocket ships!" the oldest one cried out.

Their dad started to say, "That won't be necessary—"

But Cady spoke over him.

"Yeah it will. We ordered too much. Chill. It's all good."

She spotted their waitress a few tables over, and before anyone could stop her, she marched over, pointed out her booth and the family next to it, and explained she would be paying for the little girls and their dad. Satisfied, she returned to Georgia and Matt. He was smiling crookedly at her. Georgia was not smiling at all.

"What?" she asked, slipping back into her booth.

"Nothing," said Georgia, in a tone of voice that said everything.

"I'm gonna just . . . go the bathroom," said Matt.

"What are you doing?" Georgia whispered fiercely when he had excused himself.

The embarrassment Cady felt when the girl's father had caught her looking at him returned, doubled in strength. She dared not look in his direction.

"Shut up," she said, in as low a voice as she could and still be heard. "I was just helping."

"You're not," said Georgia. She flicked her eyes over the back of Matt's seat. The guy was still sitting in the booth, his daughters oblivious to any disturbance in the Force.

But even Cady could tell now there was a great disturbance in the Force. The man was concentrating fiercely on his food, staring at the hand rolls—"rocket ships!"—as if defusing a time bomb. The three girls feasted merrily, but he did not eat at all.

"We'll talk about this later," said Georgia, "but promise me you won't do anything stupid to look good for Matt again. Anything else," she added.

Embarrassment threatened to flare into anger then, but Cady got a hold of her temper before it broke free.

"I don't know what you mean," she said.

"Yes, you do," Georgia shot back. "You were being selfish in that very special way you have, Cady. When you don't think about anyone else. Just yourself and what's best for you. But I said we'd talk about it later."

"No, we'll talk about it now."

Her anger was returning, like a wrestler who had been pinned suddenly finding a way out of the hold down.

"I wasn't being selfish. I was thinking about—"

Georgia leaned right into her personal space.

"You were thinking about how it would look when Matt wrote you up as the most generous girl in the world. But that's not how it will turn out, trust me, because that's not how it is."

She almost left then.

Almost stormed out into the cold.

She could even see herself slamming her last sixty-three dollars down on the table of the booth next door. And it was only that image, of a crazy woman throwing money and shade at three little girls and their poor single dad which brought her up short.

Maybe she *had* been a jerk?

Maybe she *was* insufferable?

Considering the possibility was enough to drain her foul temper. It was like losing herself in the effort of solving a really complex coding problem.

She took a sip of her beer.

"Okay," she said, quietly, being even more careful not to catch the eye of anyone in the next booth. Not the children, and certainly not the father she'd probably embarrassed.

Humiliated, even.

"But now I gotta pay for their dinner, too," she said quietly, knowing Georgia would understand what she meant. Georgia knew her better than she knew herself. "Can I borrow some money? Or do you think we can hit up BuzzFeed Guy for it?"

CHAPTER THREE

It wasn't a total disaster. Matt really was a good guy, and he made nothing of the awkward break between Georgia and Cady when he returned from the bathroom. They didn't ask him to cover the extra check, though. Didn't even mention it. Georgia slipped the waitress her corporate Amex.

"I'll tell Bungie I was trying to recruit you," she said in a discrete aside before Cady left. "They'd wet themselves if they thought there was a real chance you might work for them, or even consult. Their augmented reality guys are a bunch of ass-clowns."

Cady agreed to meet up with Matt the following day. He wanted to watch her at work, but she said that would be as boring as watching him type up a story. Worse. She wrote in Swift, not English. Georgia suggested she take him on a tour of all the local software houses she'd been fired from before opening her own one-woman code shop and writing *Murder City*.

Done deal, they said. A date.

The three little girls and their dad left an hour before Cady. They weren't hanging around for beers with BuzzFeed guy. The oldest of them stopped at the table and gave her a note.

"I drew you a picture of unicorns," she said, without explanation.

"Unicorns are awesome," Cady smiled, "and so are you. Thank you."

"What was that about?" Matt asked, although he totally knew.

"She had the best kill streak of everyone in her kindergarten," said Cady. "She just wanted to say thanks. Happens all the time."

And it did. Not the kindergarten thing. That was an outrageous lie, which would probably read well in his final story. But it did happen that, on the rare occasions she left the apartment, she was sometimes recognized, and people did come up and tell her all about their latest hit or longest kill streak in the game. You saw people playing *Murder City* all the time. There had been think pieces about it. And hot takes. So many hot takes.

That was going to get more intense after Matt's story ran on BuzzFeed. Two thousand words, he said. A major feature. The publicist she'd hired said she should get ready to do some TV after that. Maybe even the morning shows. Cady wasn't entirely sure how she felt about that. Her idea of breakfast TV was Netflix with a microwave burrito lunch. But she knew her parents would be thrilled after years of trying to explain to their friends and neighbors what the hell it was she did for a living, and why she kept getting fired.

Her dad would probably start sending her VHS tapes of her appearances.

But it would sell more copies of the game.

She shivered inside her leather jacket and pulled the scarf tighter around her neck. She had an update she wanted to get ready by the end of the week, and she already knew she was going to work through the night on it. She had warned Matt not to come looking for her before lunch time.

The streets were much quieter on the way home. The rain had stopped, and the clouds had broken up in patches, letting through the light of a handful of the brightest stars. But only the brightest.

Her phone buzzed. A message from Georgia. Despite her earlier resolution that she would not stare at her screen while walking along the street like a phone-zombie, she pulled it out and read the series of blue bubbles as they popped up.

Sorry.

U know I only want the best 4U.

Cady, all artists r selfish and selfishness will take u a long way, but it won't get u where u need 2b.

We only get there by helping each other 4 real.

Also

The skull and flame emoji popped up, this time with Edvard Munch's *The Scream.*

Translated?

Die screaming in a fire.

Cady smiled before she could get angry again.

L8r, bitch.

Another canned response, but a genuine one. Georgia had been right. She'd been wrong too. There was a part of Cady that had honestly felt the pain of that dad in the restaurant. She knew what it was like to have to get through a whole week on a handful of carefully hoarded cash. She had no idea why he took those girls out to eat when he was so broke. But he had his reasons, and she was only trying to help.

Georgia was also right, though, because she'd known exactly what she was doing when she made a show of paying for their dinner.

She was making sure that Matt Aleveda got a good look at her being Robin Hood, or Cady from the hood or whatever. Taking money from the rich—and who was richer than Apple?—and giving it to three poor little girls sentenced to avocado sushi.

It was in that exquisitely awkward moment of self-realization, when she was dying on the inside at just how transparent and obnoxious she had been, that they came for her.

"I don't like you walking the streets at night the way you do," her mother said.

"Be in the world, not on your phone," the aiki-jutsu guy at the self-defense class said.

"I'll be fine," Cady McCall had protested when Georgia and Matt insisted on walking her home after dinner. But they didn't insist very hard. They had just ordered more drinks, and it was obvious where that was going. Her need to get back to the 0.1 update had finally got the better of her, and besides, she had all those self-defense classes and her trusty can of Mace, and it wasn't like she was some retard who walked along the street, alone and lost in Facebook when she should have been "in the world."

Was it?

The first she knew of the danger was when one of the men grabbed her arm. She did exactly the wrong thing, trying to pull away instead of going with the flow of the attack as she had been taught. Or to be more accurate, as she had been told, because she hadn't been taught, had she? She had learned nothing.

She dropped the phone, and the screen shattered. Strangely and stupidly, that was what she cared about, a broken screen on a two-year-old phone, and not the man who had just grabbed her forearm and was dragging her into an alleyway.

She tried to scream, then.

Screaming was good, the self-defense instructor had told them. Screaming was a natural response to the horror of an attack, and you should not underestimate the horror, the pure, organic fear and loathing you would feel when another human being laid hands on you with hostile intent.

Use the fear, they said.

Scream, but scream with intent.

Turn it into a war cry. A fearsome shriek into the face of an attacker will stun him. Not for long, but it will interrupt the momentum of the attack just long enough for you to respond. It would disrupt him.

You work in digital, Cady. You should know all about disruption.

A war cry would take his balance.

They were very big on "taking balance" in the self-defense class. "Take a man's balance, and you take ninety percent of his strength," the instructor told them. He said this with the smooth confidence of somebody who knew themselves to be right.

Take his balance psychologically with a fierce *kiai*, the warrior's shout. Take his balance physically with *kuzushi*; when he pulls, push. When he pushes, pull. Do not resist with strength. Meet hard with soft. Be water around the rock.

It was just a stupid campus self-defense class. Twelve weeks. But those twelve weeks were based on thousands of years of experience in the combat arts. It should have counted for something.

Maybe it would have, if any of the training had come back to her. Maybe if she'd kept up her training, like Georgia, who still attended classes three times a week.

But Cady hadn't, and so none of it counted for shit. Not her twelve weeks of messing around in class. Not the millennia-long history of actual combat and intense training which underlay the ancient fighting art.

Cady screamed and seized up and struggled and fell to the ground, where her knees hit the edge of the gutter, and she lost even more of her balance, dragging the first man down on top of her.

A rush of images and sensations.

Pain in her knee.

More pain in her arm and shoulder as the man holding her wrenched them, hard.

Skin scraping off the back of her fingers on the wet surface of the road. The electric jangle of impact running up through her funny bone.

A harsh, unpleasant smell, like burning motor oil.

Silence.

They said nothing to her. Made no threats. No demands. They didn't even breathe heavily.

Crying pitiably, she tried to twist out of the grip on her right arm, but it was like trying to pull a limb out of a piece of farm machinery. More pain, and no sense at all that she could escape.

And then she was free.

She felt the nearness of some great impact, like a car hitting a tree down the street or a heavy load falling out of a high window and landing behind her. And then she could see the stars again, those few, lonely diamond points which managed to peer through the broken cloud cover and the glowing cloak of the city's light dome.

It wasn't silent then.

"Leave her alone, you sonsabitches."

A man's voice, a deep and rolling thunder in the night.

And then the dull, concussive pounding of fists on flesh.

They made some noise then, the two who had come for her. One cried out like an animal, a dog with its tail caught in a slamming door. The other grunted and snarled and said something she could not make out in the chaos and fury of the fight.

She was in a fight!

The realization struck her as a solid blow, solid enough to knock her from her feet had she not already been sitting on her ass in the gutter, curled into a ball as three men sailed into each other with fists and boots and elbows and knees.

And when it couldn't get any worse, it did.

"Look out, girly!" the big voice called out, the one which had broken over her and her attackers like the opening thunderclap of a summer storm. "Knife!" he shouted.

And she did move then. She rolled away as best she could from the frenzy of three homicidal maniacs who seemed to be fighting over her.

A thought occurred to her, or maybe only the fragment of a thought, because it was small and broken, and it flew through her mind far too quickly for her to hold on to.

Did she do this?

Was this her fault? Something to do with the game? Murder City.

But it really wasn't the most important thing right at that moment, was it? She let the question go as she rolled like a log out into the middle of the road.

Jesus Christ. She was gonna get run over.

But if she didn't move, she was going to get cut.

With that little bit of distance, she could see what was happening for the first time, could finally start to arrange it into some sort of coherent form.

Two men versus one.

The duo looked like . . . well, like nothing and nobody. Unremarkable men, unremarkably dressed. One of them in a pair of jeans and a plain hoodie. The other in chinos and a Seattle Mariners rain slicker. You could stand behind them, waiting for a burger at Red Mill or Zippy's, and two minutes later you wouldn't be able to recall a thing about them.

Hell, they could have been sitting in the next booth over at sushi tonight.

The other guy, the cowboy, she thought because . . .

Because he looked like a goddamned cowboy.

Not the sort of heroic idiot who wades into a mugging out of some archaic sense of manly moral obligation. But an actual cowboy. With cows and stuff.

Of course he had no cows with him right now, but he was wearing a big hat.

A cowboy hat.

And a belt full of bullets. And a six-shooter at his waist. And his brown suede jacket looked like he'd cut and tanned the hide from one of those cows of his that she couldn't see right then. And his jeans didn't look fashionable, they just looked old and dirty.

And he smelled.

Like cattle dung, wet leather, stale sweat and cigarettes.

He was holding a knife.

Which was kind of weird, since he'd been the one who'd shouted the warning about a knife. But the other guys were also holding knives, so Cady supposed that made sense of a kind, although her head was swimming, and she wanted to vomit, and her vision was greying out at the edges.

Probably best not to take her word for what made sense at that moment.

The cowboy was holding a knife that looked big enough to carve up a bison. She wondered why he didn't just shoot the two men, and then the entirely rational thought occurred to her that she wasn't actually in a video game, and you couldn't just go around shooting people.

Apparently sticking twelve inches of sharpened steel into them was perfectly acceptable, however, because she had no doubt this guy would do exactly that if he got the chance.

"No, don't," she said weakly.

They all ignored her.

Her would-be muggers—

If that's all they were, Cady.

"I don't like you walking the streets at night the way you do, Cady."
—whatever they were. Mad fans. Muggers. Rapists. Whatever.
They looked like they'd be cool putting a few holes into young
Rooster Cogburn here with their own knives.

With their *stilettos.*

An assassin's blade. Not like his.

She'd worked freelance on enough Ubisoft titles to know the
difference.

They tried to circle around him, and she realized with renewed
horror that they were still intent on getting to her. He seemed
equally intent on not letting them.

Desperate to know what she'd got herself into, Cady asked in a
high, keening voice, "Who are you? Why are you doing this?"

But nobody answered.

It wasn't like the movies. There was no banter. No witty back-
and-forth. Just three men with knives intent on killing each other.

She tried to scramble away from them on her butt.

Water soaked through the seat of her jeans.

It was weird that she noticed, but she did.

There was a quiet, drifting moment where the three men were
obviously attempting to maneuver into the best position to attack
or defend, and then the cowboy attacked.

She was so surprised she gave out a little, "Oh!"

He bellowed.

He roared.

Roared like a bear.

And he charged the man closest to Cady, slashing wildly at the
air with that crazy, big-ass knife of his. Her eyes bulged, and then
she scrunched them shut because everything was wrong. The
knife wasn't just cutting through the air; it was cutting through
the man. It was inside the man.

Inside him!

Oh, God.

And the other guy was coming at her.

She scrambled to her feet, or tried to, but something slammed into her, driving her back down. Knocking all the air from her body. Cracking her head on the pavement.

Putting out the little diamond lights of the stars, but filling her head with hundreds more.

Just before the world turned black.

CHAPTER FOUR

She awoke in a bed, but Cady knew she hadn't dreamed it. She knew that before she knew where she was. Cady slipped from a nightmare, where tongueless dead men sliced at her with knives, into a waking panic. In a bed not her own.

Not a hospital bed either.

She opened her eyes and wanted, more than expected, to see her room, even though everything was wrong. *Because* everything was wrong.

And he was there. The cowboy.

The bed was an old single-size with a lumpy mattress, a thin, filthy blanket, and his coat for a pillow.

It smelled even worse than the blanket.

Her panic forced her upright, but nausea and dizziness dropped her right back down. A headache came riding in on the back end of that, a huge pain, sharp and dull all at the same time.

"Whoa there, missy. You took a mighty crack on that purdy little head of yours. Best you be lying still for a ways down the trail yet."

He stood and took a small bowl from a wooden table.

"For if'n you need to be sick."

Cady realized it was nearly as big as a punch bowl. It just looked small in his hands. She flinched away, and he nodded and set the porcelain bowl down carefully on the bed, where she could reach it. He stood over her—loomed over her, really—like a giant redwood, but made no other move in her direction.

"Had m'self knocked acock like that more'n once," he said. "If'n yer eggs ain't scrambled fer good by it, best thing is a sip of old Adam's Ale and some gentle time in your roll."

Cady stared at him, uncertain that she was hearing him clearly. He had a well-modulated voice, with an accent that sounded like a smooth blend of two or three old whiskies. But the whole effect was archaic, rather than charming.

He had not slept. She recognized the watery, red-rimmed eyes and the dark smudges beneath them as the badges worn by the all-night crew.

Her crew.

She recognized worry in those eyes, even fear. But there was no obvious threat to her in them. They seemed to look in on a kind, if troubled soul. His shirt cuffs, though, were stained with dried blood. He wore a waistcoat in a dark paisley design, and she thought she could make out a few drops of dried blood in the swirling patterns there, too. The knife was still at his hip, the giant blade he had slashed at and pushed *into* that other guy.

Cady had seen him run a man through with it.

And he wore a gun, and an old-fashioned belt strung with bullets like Chinese firecrackers.

And a hat.

Still with the hat.

"Oh, my pardon," he said when he saw she was staring at it. He whipped off the Stetson—she supposed it was a Stetson because weren't they all?—and held it to his heart as he sketched a small bow that reminded her of the way they had bowed to their instructor before those worthless self-defense classes.

The smug asshole taught them that at least, if nothing else of any use: how to bow.

The cowboy came up out of his bow and introduced himself.

"Deputy US Marshal Titanic Smith, ma'am."

She was still staring at him. He was handsome under the grime, the unruly mustache, and three days' worth of unshaven stubble, but the relief that flooded through her like a cool mountain stream when she heard the magic words, "Deputy US Marshal", washed every other thought out of her head. Except for one.

"Titanic? Seriously?"

He seemed a little put out that she would ask.

"Christened John Titanic Smith, ma'am," he said, "by the holy hand of Reverend Nolan in Purdue County. But I have found, as I made my way through the world, that many folks don't cotton to dickering with a John Smith, so Titanic I am by reason of convenience."

She shook her head . . . very . . . slowly. Her neck was stiff and the pain behind her eyeballs was ballooning out to fill her skull. She took in the room, but it gave her no reason to feel any better. A small, mean space, it was dark, with only one window, obscured by a curtain that looked to have been fashioned from a hessian sack. It filtered what little daylight could get through the grimy window glass. At first she thought the window had been painted over, like back at her apartment. But, no, it was just dirty.

Really, really dirty.

She could hear the city outside and wondered where she was and why she wasn't in hospital. The whole deal was starting to creep her out; the peeling wallpaper, the smell of mold and damp and unwashed feet.

"Do you mind showing me your badge?" she asked and regretted it as soon as she spoke. If Smith was a psycho, she had just put him on the spot.

"You're lying on it, ma'am," he said.

What?

She didn't understand.

"My jacket," he nodded at her. "Your pillow, such as it would be."

"Oh, sorry," she said, and reached around behind her, being careful not to turn her head too fast or to strain her neck muscles.

The coat was heavy and fashioned from brown suede. It would have been an oddly stylish choice for a cop, were it not for the stains and the stink. She heaved it around from behind her with some difficulty. Smith stepped forward to help.

"You're all tangled up, ma'am," he said. "Here, allow me."

He took the coat and held it in front of her. Cady expected him to search the pockets for his wallet, but instead he pinched the shoulders as though he was a tailor displaying a dinner jacket for sale. She saw a large, slightly tarnished metal star pinned to a lapel. When she squinted, Smith held it so she could read the old fashioned typeface.

DEPUTY US MARSHAL.

He gently folded the jacket and gave it back to her. Cady wasn't sure she wanted to lie on that thing again. It smelled like the animal it had been cut from. But it was the only place to rest her head.

She gave up, replaced the coat behind her, and leaned back against the iron bedhead.

Time for a cut scene and some exposition.

"So, those guys. Who were they? And where are we? And why here? I should get to the ER. Get scans. I need to call my parents. And my publicist."

She was starting to babble, her words running over each other. The marshal held up one giant hand and shook his head.

"Hang fire, there, missy."

"My name is Cady, not Missy. Cady McCall."

"All right, Miss McCall."

She sighed forcefully, but let it go. The headache was getting worse.

"You're safe," Smith assured her. "That's the first thing you need to know. And those varmints? I can't rightly say who they were, although I am sadly familiar with the type. I will testify they meant to ventilate you with them Arkansas toothpicks."

She started to WTF him, but Smith had already turned away and shuffled back to his chair by the window. It was more of small wooden stool, really, and it looked like it might collapse under his weight. The guy had to be six-and-a-half feet tall—he had to stoop to avoid scraping his head on the ceiling—and he was built like something out of *Gears of War*. But he also looked exhausted and . . . what?

Uncomfortable, she thought, with a glimmer of insight. He was reluctant to tell her something because he was embarrassed or self-conscious about it. Intuiting the source of his unease was enough to confirm it for her.

Marshal Smith was in some sort of trouble, and now, maybe, he'd dragged her into it.

Awesome.

"You could have shot those guys last night," she said. "Raylan Givens would've shot them. They were armed. You're a marshal."

"Can't say as I know this Givens feller, but I can set with that," he replied in that weird, archaic way of his. "I'd have dug for my cannon, Miss McCall, 'cepting that you were in my line of fire."

He said it like "*larn o' far.*"

"No sense to be putting a bad plum in you, were there?" he finished.

Wa thar?

"Are you from some backasswards part of Arkansas," she said, "because man, your dialogue."

"Purdue County, ma'am, as I did tell."

Quiet fell between them, but it was not a companionable silence. Cady was waiting for him to explain what the hell was going on, and Smith seemed less inclined to explain anything the longer he went without doing so.

"You should take a sip or two of water," he said, nodding at a chipped, ceramic mug on the small table next to her bed.

"You should tell me what the actual fuck is happening," she replied.

Smith reared back as if struck.

"Don't know that there's a call for such language, young lady."

She almost laughed then.

"Don't "young lady" me, *pardner*. Under all that grime you're not that much older than I am. But I'm getting older, fast, every minute I lie here listening to you. So give it up, Raylan. What've you got me into?"

He sucked at his mustache as if pained by the very question. It was a hell of a mustache. Some hipster barber probably toiled over the thing for an hour getting it just so. It seemed pretentious, even a little bizarre for a police officer, but then so was the hat and gun belt and even the silver star pinned so ostentatiously to his lapel.

Ooh, look at me, I'm a Federal Marshal.

Rather than answering her, Smith took out a pocket watch—another prop, another affectation—frowned at whatever he found there, and put it away. It struck Cady that she had no idea of the time. Could be early morning or late afternoon. She might have been out of it for a whole day and night. She looked at her watch. 12:40 p.m.

Matt!

She was going to miss her BuzzFeed guy. He was probably looking for her right now, ringing her phone again and again.

Her broken phone, she remembered, and started casting around, searching anxiously under the covers, her eyes quickly scanning the small room. All of her shit was on that phone. She was an unperson without it.

Man, she hoped Smith had picked the thing up.

"My phone," she said, a statement that was a question, too. His frown grew cavernous for a second, a deep rift valley between his eyes.

"Your . . . phone," he said, as though trying out the word for the first time. "You dropped it."

"Well, duh! Did you get it? All my contacts, my appointments. *Fuck*, my banking apps! I don't have a PIN code on it."

Again, the frown.

"Look," she said, "my Touch ID was flakey 'cause of a salsa incident, so I turned it off. I know I should have put the PIN back on, but I'm only ever at home because I work all the time and . . ."

His head tilted to the side and nodded slowly like somebody who understood, but thought her an idiot. It was like talking with an especially slow child, except she was the slow one, and she was having trouble making herself understood.

"I'm sorry, Miss McCall. We didn't have time. More of them came."

"It's Ms. Not Miss. And back the fuck up. More of them? More . . . of . . . them?"

"Afraid so, ma'am. We had to get gone quick."

Her head was really pounding now, and she could feel a nervous twitch tugging at the corner of one eye.

"Enough," she said harshly. Raising her voice sharpened the spike in her head, but it also felt so good on an existential level that she raised it some more. "You better start talking, Marshal, or I'll be talking to your bosses when we get out of here, and to my Congressman, or woman, or whatever, and to the press right after that. Maybe even before. I know a guy at BuzzFeed you know. He's doing a story on me right now, in fact. Do you even know who I am?"

She knew how much of a superdouche she sounded, but it felt good to let go, to lash out at this guy, even if he had saved her ass last night, because he hadn't done much for her since, and to be honest, she was starting to freak the hell out.

"So, you tell me right now, mister. Where am I? And what time is it? I have places to be."

Marshal Smith did a fair imitation of man backed into a corner. He blew out his stubbled cheeks, scuffed his boots on the bare wooden floor, and nervously reached for the stupid fob watch again.

He swallowed.

Amazingly, he looked a little like a man too frightened to speak. Instead, he reached into his back pocket, and took out a few thin sheets of folded newsprint. He unfolded the paper and appeared to read the front page, searching for something.

"You're in London, Miss McCall. It's a little before ten in the morning on November 9th, in the year of our Lord, 1888."

CHAPTER FIVE

She might have screamed if she hadn't swooned. That's how Smith described it when she regained consciousness a few minutes later.

"You swooned for a moment there, ma'am."

"I don't swoon," she said, pushing away the cup of water he offered. Half of the contents splashed on the bed. She didn't care. "Nobody swoons. This isn't *Downton Abbey*," she said in a shaky voice.

She really was frightened now.

This lunatic was no law officer. He had kidnapped her. Killed those other men. And now he had her in his little murder box where he was looking to play out some whack-job, swoon-lady fantasy.

She had to get out of there. She moved quickly, without thought.

Cady leapt for the far side of the bed. The door was just a few feet away. She wasn't restrained, so there was that. But she was still handicapped by concussion or shock or whatever, and as soon as her feet touched the ground, the room started spinning, and she pitched over, crying out in alarm as she fell to the floor.

"Oh, hell fire," said Smith, but he made no effort to pursue her. "Watch out there, or you'll do yourself a mischief, woman."

Cady was surprised to find she was still wearing her jeans. Figured he'd have stripped them off her. Probably would have given them a good sniffing, too. The hairy pervert. But her jeans were exactly where they should have been. Her leather jacket hung on the back of the door, her scarf draped over it. Her boots were lined up underneath.

Ignoring Smith, or whatever his name was, she launched herself forward again, scrabbling across the floor on her hands and knees. The dizziness wasn't as bad this time. The pounding of her heart was flushing the fog from her brain, but she didn't make it much further.

"Look," said Smith, in a loud voice. "Just look."

By some magician's trick she didn't understand, he whipped away the dimness of the room. She looked over her shoulder to find he'd simply pulled aside the hessian sack covering the window. The wooden sash rumbled up in its frame as Smith pulled at a small handle, and the weak, grey light of day poured in, fixing her in place like an animal caught in the headlights of a car.

"Look," he said again, not unkindly this time. His tone seemed almost apologetic. "If you can walk, you'll need to see this."

Squinting a little into the light, she could already see that something was terribly wrong with the roofline across the street. Everything was misshapen, crooked. Wrong. From what little she could see from her perspective on the floor, there wasn't a straight line or a good right angle anywhere out there. She could make out sagging gutters, crooked windows, and slumping chimneys. Thick black smoke poured out of half the chimney stacks. The roof tiles, many of them broken, were thick with bird shit.

But it was the chimney smoke that undid her. No way the EPA was letting that happen.

The smoke and the noise and the smell of the city.

The stench of it.

She was no longer in Seattle.

She was nowhere that she knew.

* * *

When Smith stepped away from the window and came to offer his hand, she took it. He lifted her gently from the floor and led her over to the open window.

"Probably best that you set yourself down a spell," he said. "I find what's a-coming for you to be a powerful tribulation."

She did as she was told, dropping onto the stool where he had been sitting. Her mind retreated to childhood wonder and confusion, and to fear, as she sat and marveled at all that Smith had revealed.

Their room was on the top floor of one of the tallest buildings for miles around, but that did not lift them high above the scenery. She was peering out of a dormer window set into a steeply-pitched roof. The room was small because it had to fit within the confines of the attic space. Marshal Smith's head scraped the ceiling, not only because he was an unusually tall man, but because the ceiling itself was set low so that the walls could meet it at the perpendicular. Her room was a little box, hidden inside a triangle of roofline. A city stretched away before her, but not a city that she recognized.

Her eye found none of Seattle's seven hills. The distant ranges were so far distant as to be invisible, and the cold waters of the northwestern Pacific found no ingress here. Puget Sound, Lake Washington, the peninsula, the mountains had all vanished, plowed under a vast grey-brown plain of tumbledown brick and fetid smoke. Here, a dark labyrinth of dense and winding alleyways; there, a giant iron scab of mills and factories, spewing toxic waste into the air, pissing foul chemicals and poison onto the streets and into the waterways.

There was a river, she saw now. A wide, slow moving sewer, crowded with sail craft and steam boats. Not the jaunty paddle steamers of Deep South mythology and modern tourist trap, but working vessels of bizarre mashed-up topology and tech. Mast, sail and smoke-blackened funnel all crammed in together on the same deck.

Small patches of greensward struggled to breathe under the crushing weight of vast slums and dark factories. The smell of it was choking, a strong hand squeezing her throat as she gagged involuntarily to deny the foul miasma. The uproar was a constant assault upon her ears, yet so different in tone and color to the traffic hum and jet roar of a modern city that Cady could not help but listen. She heard the crunch and shuffle of a million feet, actually heard them, in amongst the clip-clopping of horse shoes on cobblestone, the rumble of wooden wheels and the shouts and curses of a language which she spoke, but did not understand.

And what she didn't see was even more important that what she did.

There were no cars anywhere, but hundreds of horse drawn carriages, most of them two and four seaters, and some weird-ass conveyances as big as buses.

"Oh, shit," she whispered. A shiver turned into a shudder and became a series of deep body tremors like the uncontrollable extremes of late stage Parkinson's.

Smith pulled down the window and let the tatty curtain fall back into place.

"Ma'am," he said, "will you be in need of some assistance to return to your bed? It will help you reconcile yourself to the hard truth of this if you are to take a spell off your feet."

She slumped against him and swore again.

He did not scold her this time.

"I do understand," he said. "It is a most surprising and unsettling experience, believe you me. I have had the misfortune of it more than once."

Smith gingerly helped her back to the bed, letting Cady lean against his arm, but not supporting her in any other way. Her legs were weak, the muscles rubbery, and waves of hot flushes followed by chills rolled through her body.

She was certain she would vomit and reached for the porcelain bowl he'd given her earlier, recognizing it this time as an old-fashioned bedpan.

Last night's sushi and beer came up in a loose, sour rush. When she thought she was done, that there could be no more, she heaved again, her stomach muscles convulsing to expel the last few drops of yellow bile.

"Oh, God," she croaked, and this time took the cup of the water when he offered it, using a mouthful to wash and spit.

"I'm sorry," she said weakly, passing the pan to Smith, who took it without complaint.

"Ma'am, you have no need of an apology on my account. It is I who am in debt to you and fear I cannot repay what I have taken."

Still shaking, and now snuffling through a snotty nose, she folded her arms and rubbed her hands against the goosebumps which ran up to her shoulders.

"You'd better explain," she said for the second time that morning, but this time no aggression or faux menace inflected her words. Cady McCall's voice came from far away and sounded small and lost.

Marshal Smith refilled her drinking cup from a small jug of water. He looked like a man in need of something a good deal stronger, but handed her the heavy mug and returned to his ridiculous little stool.

"Look, no, stop," said Cady as he was halfway seated. "You look like a rodeo clown on that thing. Just . . . sit at the end of the bed. I trust you. That thing looks like a terrible sight gag about to go wrong."

Smith appeared to consider the invite.

"All right then, Miss Cady. I do appreciate the consideration. This little milking stool sits about as cozy as a big old dab of prairie coal."

She rubbed a thin, greasy film of sweat from her face with a shaking hand.

"I have no idea what you're talking about. But sit down, please, and tell me what's happening."

The mattress sagged, and the metal bed frame squealed in protest when Smith lowered himself. If possible, he looked even more uncomfortable sitting on her bed. He fetched that old, gold watch out of his vest pocket and made another face at it, as if he too had a BuzzFeed guy waiting on him somewhere.

"I do believe this here timepiece to be the source of our perdition, Miss Cady."

He held it out for her.

"Ms.," she said absently.

The pocket watch was obviously an antique, but so was Titanic Smith. The gold casing was dull and scratched, the glass face—she almost called it a screen—not much better. It was a working man's device, used hard and oddly heavy, but then it was made of gold. Or she assumed so. Cady hefted the piece in her hand, turned it over, looking for an inscription, but found none.

There were no complications on the face.

Everyone knew about complications these days because of the Apple Watch. This thing had none. No date. No calorie counter. Nothing. It didn't even have a minute hand. Just a crown for winding and one very ornate-looking hour hand, which was coming up on ten. Her mind slipped back to Seattle, to Matt and Georgia, and she had to drag herself back into the here and now with an effort of will.

Suspend your disbelief, Cady. Hear him out. Then deal.

"Looks like an old watch," she said, passing it back.

Her nausea was backing off, and with it the headache.

"That it does," he conceded.

Smith took the watch and carefully replaced it in his vest pocket, fastening it to a small, but sturdy chain. For it being the source of all their "perdition," he seemed neurotically attached to the thing.

"So, where'd you get it? The TARDIS?"

He digested the question, chewed it over as though there might be some real protein to it, before shaking his head.

"No, ma'am. And do not haze me as a tenderfoot. I have this infernal device from the Indian Territory. From a Chinaman in some distress I happened upon there."

"Go on," she said. The discomfort she had felt upon waking was gone, as if she'd washed down a couple of aspirin with vodka. As improved as she may have felt in body, however, her mind was still circling the drain.

Marshal Smith's eyes roamed over the hills and valleys of her crumpled blanket, but he was not scoping her out. It was as though he were searching an internal landscape, reflected in the world in front of him.

"All righty then," he said, as though preparing to lift a heavy load. "Best I start my tale at the beginning of all this. On the say so of Judge Parker, Marshal Fagan had hired on more'n two hundred deputies to clean out the western district and the Territory with it. That's where I was, tracking the Buford twins, when I chanced upon my Chinaman waylaid by road agents."

Smith was an easy man to listen to, she found, in spite of the odd turns of phrase. He had one of those voices that was a pleasure to hear.

"My oriental friend was, I am afraid to tell it, not long for our world, being two or three good bootlicks from pleading his case to whatever slant-eyed captain of the gate guards the heathen heaven for the yeller devils."

Okay, maybe not so easy to listen to.

"There was three of them and one of him, but they were so busy with kicking him to actual pieces that I was able to walk right up with my Spencer rifle and do for them."

"You shot them?"

"Dead," he confirmed with a satisfied nod.

"Wait. When was this?"

"I would call it four and a half weeks passed, ma'am."

"No, when did your Marshal . . . what's his name?"

"Fagan."

"On what *date* did Marshal Fagan send you after the evil twins."

"The Buford boys?"

"Yeah, them."

"I rode out of Fort Smith on June 3rd, 1876, ma'am."

Cady closed her eyes and took in a deep breath, holding it for three seconds, and releasing it slowly.

Gather your data. Do not make assumptions.

"All right. Go on."

Smith returned to his tale.

"There weren't much I could do for Wu; that was his name as he told it to me. They had been fixin' to annex his gold, Wu said; all Chinamen, like leprechauns being known to have a stash of it about them."

Cady could not tell if he was being serious, but she let it pass.

"I nursed him for a day and promised that I would inter him when the time came, which seemed more of a consolation to the man than my having done for those who did for him. He was delirious, or so I thought, most of that time. He told me of travels so peculiar that I could not credit them with any plausibility, even though as a Chinaman so far from home, he must have covered some strange and foreign miles to fetch up dead in the territories."

Smith, who had fallen into a sort of reverie in the telling of his story, returned from it then, looking up at Cady with eyes so haunted she had to suppress a grimace.

"I tell you true, Miss Cady, I do not doubt his tales now."

"Go on," she said, in a quiet voice.

"Well, those road agents might have been meaner than cat meat, but they were not entirely stupid with it. Mr. Wu was indeed possessed of some gold and sundry valuables. A short time before he passed, he bid me to fuss at the roots of a nearby tree. There I found his swag."

He patted the vest pocket where he kept the watch and unhooked a small leather bag from his belt, opening it to show her a handful of gold nuggets.

"The time piece, Mr. Wu explained, was very special, and dangerous, with it. He was far gone by then, and I misapprehended him, assuming that he meant it was a danger to a man like him to carry that quality of precious trinket. For myself, a sworn and well-armed regulator of hard won experience, what danger might there be in having such a handsome fancy? Even on the frontier," he added with a small, bitter laugh.

Cady waited for him to go on, but he didn't. He seemed lost within his thoughts again. Finally she prompted him by tapping his knee with her foot.

"So what? The watch. It's like a time travel thing?"

He needed a moment to consider that before answering.

"Yes, ma'am, I suppose it is. That and more. A time traveling thing."

CHAPTER SIX

INTERLUDE

Small fissures and cracks opened on the face of the mountain two days before the eruption, and from them poured hot streams of ash and smoke. Birds and mountain goats fled from these signs and survived, at least for another day or so. Tainted air, hissing from the same ruptures in the earth, settled into some of the valleys overlooking the blue-green waters of the bay, poisoning a small flock of sheep and one young boy who had been watching over them.

The boy, the third son of Marcus Luvenalus of Misenum, was the first person to die in the eruption of Mount Vesuvius, but his passing was not recorded. A day later, his remains were entirely destroyed by a pyroclastic surge of superheated fluidized gas and rock fragments that burst forth from the ground, rolled over the tiny corpse, and raced away toward the coastline at a speed of nearly three hundred miles per hour.

Having rumbled, shuddered, and groaned as the very armor of the planet cracked beneath it, the mountain finally exploded in the middle of the day with a roar that was not merely akin to the ending of the world; it was the end for many thousands in its shadow. A gigantic column of smoke and ash thrust up miles into the sky, throwing off sheets of flame and long arcs of blue-white lightning. Night fell hours before its time, and with it, a rain of fire. The countryside and the tiny Roman settlements around the Gulf of Naples suffered bombardment by white hot pumice stones and suffocation by ash and smoke. Again and again the earth tore itself apart, eventually firing monstrous boulders into the heavens, giant fists of hot rock shot through with veins of magma that landed like the hammer blows of the gods.

Through the early moments of this cataclysm stole two figures who were not gods, but who seemed just as little perturbed by the destruction and carnage. They had arrived in the town of Pompeii a day earlier, well before dawn, without attracting the attention of the city watch to their presence.

They looked like . . . well, like nothing and nobody. They were unremarkable men, unremarkably dressed. You could stand behind them, waiting for a punnet of sardines at the marina gate or a piece of fruit from vendors along the Via dell'Abbondanza, and two minutes later you would be unable to recall a thing about them.

The minutes before the first major eruption found them enjoying the sun while they could, across the street from the house of Julius Polybius. There were thirteen people resident in the rather grand villa: seven family members and six servants. The thunder of the mountain tearing itself apart brought some of them out into the street, where the other residents of the town were already starting to gather and point and excitedly discuss the event. The first small, hot flames of fear were already racing through the streets of Pompeii, preceding by a few minutes the initial fall of real fire.

The two men, who were apprentices, did not announce themselves when they followed the occupants of the house back inside. They moved through the building as though they were as intimately familiar with its passageways as any of the inhabitants. They did not cross paths with anyone, making their way by 'a circuitous route to a small nursery at the rear of the dwelling. A child, not yet old enough to walk, slept in a cradle there.

The men entered the crèche, took the sleeping infant from its bed, and disappeared. Quite literally. They winked out of existence, all three of them, and the child, who would grow up to follow them into apprenticeship, was perfectly excised from human history. All that remained was a harsh, unpleasant smell, like burning motor oil.

That is how it always is when the apprentices arrive. They come in the moments just before the ship sinks, or the earth cracks open, or the deep space platform catastrophically disintegrates after being struck by a microscopic black hole. They snatch a cradle from beneath the hooves of the Mongol horde, rescue a newborn from the great black wave of the tsunami, pluck a lone and lucky soul from the ovens of the death camp.

The apprentices replenish their ranks in such a way that the life edited from the long and bloody narrative arc of humanity is never missed.

But that is not all they do.

CHAPTER SEVEN

How could she not believe him? She had the evidence of her own eyes, the testimony of her senses. She could hear and feel and smell the truth of it. The only thing stopping Cady from believing everything Smith had said was the objection of her rational mind to so much crazy piling on to her all at once.

She plucked at the thin and probably unwashed blanket. It felt sticky. Verminous. She looked at his hands as they lay in his lap, his fingers rubbing at each other as though he were rolling invisible dice in them. She took a breath. The room smelled no better than it had before. It was moldy and stale. She started to feel gross just because she was sitting in it.

Cady tested her injuries again. She had deep scratches on the back of her hands. They stung when she made a fist and cracked open the scabs. Of her headache and her nausea, however, there was no sign. They had passed in something of a miraculous recovery. She looked at Marshal Smith again and at the vest pocket where he had tucked the watch away. The sick, free-floating nausea she had felt on waking in this room had disappeared when she took hold of the watch.

"Can I see it again?" she asked. "The watch, I mean."

"Most certainly," Smith said, before going through the elaborate procedure of unchaining the thing to hand back to her.

Cady took the timepiece from the Marshal and turned it over in her hands, paying much closer attention this time. But there was nothing to it that she had not seen the first time around. Only the absences were noteworthy: the lack of complications, the missing inscription by the watchmaker identifying the work as his or her own—his own, most likely, she had to concede—and no keyhole or latch or mechanism for opening the face or the body. That seemed strange.

"Man, I wish I could get an iFixit teardown on this," she muttered before addressing Smith directly.

"How do you change the time?" Cady asked. "I mean, when it runs down. I imagine these old things needed to be wound every day. Maybe even twice. What is it, the crown? Is that how you wind it?"

"No!" he cried out when he saw she was about to do just that.

Cady flicked her thumb away from the mechanism as though burned. Smith held both hands up in a stopping gesture.

"I would really appreciate it if'n you did not go fiddling with that thing, ma'am," he said. "No good ever comes of that."

She smiled in spite of herself. "So, how do you wind it up? Or change the time when it stops?"

Smith shook his head.

"It never stops. It never runs down. And as best I can tell, wherever you are, that's the time. If you are of a mind to change the time, though, and I mean that in the literal, you turn the crown. But please don't," Smith hurried on to say.

She frowned at him, but let the expression slide from her face when she remembered there was so much more to be skeptical of here than a watch which adapted to time zones and datelines.

Smith took the watch back from her.

"So, we have a piece of technology, an artifact of some sort, that you say is able to interface directly with the space-time continuum."

"That is what I would say, were I some pointy-headed professor given to such talk, Miss Cady, yes."

"Ms."

"Fair enough."

Cady tried reframing this insanity as a technical problem. It helped her deal with the feeling of vertigo that wanted to sweep over her again. She propped herself up a little straighter in bed. The iron bedhead wasn't especially comfortable to lean against, but she wanted to talk with Smith on equal terms, not as an invalid.

"Okay, so talk me through the past four and a half weeks. That's how long you've been on the move with this thing?"

"As best I figure it, yes, ma'am."

She wished she had a notepad and pencil, or a laptop, something to take notes with. The room was bare of any such conveniences, however, and Marshal Smith did not look the sort of man to bother himself with such things.

"So, how did it happen?" she asked. "When did you go from looking after your mysterious Chinese friend to roaming up and down the timeline?"

The Marshal made a show of folding his arms and letting his chin fall onto his chest, as if in deep thought.

"I buried Wu late in the morning of my second day with him," said Smith. "I put him under the earth near the tree where he had hidden his valuables. Carved his name into the trunk, for what it was worth. I cleaned up camp, saddled up, and rode out, heading deeper into the Indian territories. I still had those Buford boys to bring in. Judge Parker wanted them dancing from the noose a'fore I moved on t'other concerns."

"So you took his watch, his gold, anything else?"

"He had some rice which was not too wormy. Otherwise I buried his things with him."

Smith seemed not at all embarrassed by having robbed a dead man.

"And you had no idea there was anything special about the watch at this point?"

"None at all," he said. "I had played with it some, thinking that it might need winding. But otherwise, no. Chester and me, Chester being my horse . . ." It came out as "*mah hoss.*" "We were two days on the hunt for the Bufords when I had occasion to check the time, wondering whether I might lay up for the evening in a fair stretch of bottomlands where the grazing was good and the water sweet."

That haunted look stole over the cowboy's features again.

"I do not know that I intended to trigger the infernal mechanism the way I did. But I did just that. One moment I am atop old Chester, on the banks of a wide but shallow river. It was late in the day, the sun was fixing to lay herself down for the night. Next thing, old Chester is bucking like an unbroken colt with a chili pepper jammed into its fundamental, if you will excuse the allusion. He nearly dusted me."

"I think I get the point," she said. "So, what, you're no longer in Kansas? You're in downtown Seattle, or something?"

"Weren't in Kansas, ma'am."

"Weren't my point, sheriff."

"Marshal, miss."

"*Ms.*, Marshal."

"Done and done, then. Point was, we weren't where we was supposed to be. I would hazard a silver dollar that we weren't *when* we was supposed to be, either, if you get that point as well."

"I do. But you couldn't tell?"

Smith shook his head, looking forlorn.

"We had exchanged one wilderness for another. That was more than enough confusion for man and horse to be getting on with. Chester started bucking. I was a-hollerin' at him, and then just hollerin' because I could tell he had come apart for good reason.

The sun, which had been setting, was rising, and that dawn was breaking over a field of dry tangle weed, not green pasture land. The river was gone. The hills had flattened themselves all out like a bedroll. Everything was catawampus."

"Cat-a-what now?"

"All messed up, Ms. Cady," he explained, getting her name right for once. "Took me some hairy minutes to get Chester calmed down, and when he was finally settled, I will confess to you that my own condition was catawamptiously chawed up."

Cady nodded. "I'm gonna go with the Google translation. You were messed up, right?"

"Righteously so, ma'am. Now, a man in my line of work, on good open range, he might find himself taking a nap in the saddle, if'n he trusts his mount. And I did trust Chester. But that's not what happened here. I did not fall asleep and wake up a ways down the trail. That poor horse and me, we was snatched off'n one place and just dropped smack dab into another one."

"Any idea where?" Cady asked.

"Not at all, not even to this day," said Smith. "We were in the Badlands, I will credit that much. But none that I have endured. It was a flat landscape, bare but for one or two trees, and them of a type I had not seen before. We rode for a day, looking for some sign of where we had miraculously arrived without the intervening inconvenience of having traveled there. The whole time my mind was of a fever, and Chester, he weren't much better. Normally a placid beast, it was like he had the demons in him."

"Did you see any animals? Anything that might place you somewhere?"

"Only at some distance, ma'am. Giant birds. As tall as a man, and ugly as original sin. They made a sort of gulping noise. I managed to shoot one, but it was poor eating."

"How long were you there?" Cady asked.

"Day and a half," said Smith, seeming more distressed as he got deeper into his story. I had food and some water, but there was no grazing for Chester, and not so much as a muddy puddle for him to drink from. This howling waste went on forever. I believe we would have died there," said Smith. He sighed. "I do believe my poor friend did die there."

"Chester?" Cady asked.

"Yup."

Marshal Smith gave the impression of preparing himself to do something difficult. Squaring his shoulders and taking a deep breath.

"We were coming up on our second night there and I was getting close to having a conniption fit. I did not think myself in my right mind. We had made camp under a small tree, the only tree on a vast plain. I set to digging among the roots looking for what water I might squeeze from the damp soil. I kept at that fruitless task for some hours, until well after nightfall. There was a full moon out, bright enough to read by if you had your letters, and I checked the Chinaman's watch, idle in my wondering at how long I had been digging. Well, my hands were shaking. I guess I triggered the mechanism again, which I now know to be a double press on the crown."

He had fallen to talking to his hands, but he looked up at Cady then.

"Poor Chester," he said, his voice twisted by grief. "I abandoned him in that howling waste."

"Oh, Marshal," said Cady. "I'm sorry." A silence fell between them. "But you didn't abandon him," she said, softly, when the quiet became too uncomfortable to bear. "It was like you were, I don't know, like you were swept away in a flood or something."

The look he gave her spoke eloquently of just how little he thought of that excuse.

"At least I do know where I landed next," Smith said. "Africa."
That surprised her.

"Seriously? How? I mean how do you know it was Africa?"

"Elephants," he explained. "I could see elephants and I know they are in Africa."

Could have been India, Cady thought, but she did not want to interrupt him.

"So, what happened then?"

Smith put aside the loss of his horse and concentrated on the story.

"I fetched up in grasslands. I guess there must be plenty to go around. Anyway, I knew I had done it again, because although it was dark, this place smelled very different, and there were a lot more trees. Not a forest, or a jungle, mind you. More like open rangeland with small clumps of trees here and there. Of course, I couldn't see that at first. I just knew it had happened again and I had lost Chester. I had also lost my possibles bag, my teepee, and all of my vittles."

"Your camping gear and your food?"

"You would call it so. It was back with Chester, for what it was worth to him," he said bitterly.

"Please go on, Marshal. It's important."

She'd learned that the trigger mechanism for the device was a double push on the crown. He probably knew even more without knowing what he knew.

"I did try to get back to him," Smith said.

"How?"

"Just kept pushing that little doodad on the watch. But it made no difference. I know now that you only get one go every day."

Cady sat up in bed.

"Every twenty-four hours? So it recharges once a day?"

"Figure as much."

"And how long have we—"

"We got here at two aught nine in the morning," he said, anticipating her question. "You still have the better part of a day cached up here a'fore we can move on."

"Okay. That's useful data. Keep talking. Is there anything else you've been able to figure out?"

"Nope," he said, straight up. "Only that most places and times are skeersome bad and best avoided."

"Except your own time?" she asked. "Because we're almost there right now. Ten years out, but close enough."

Smith stared at her for a moment before speaking.

"Not nearly close enough, Ms. Cady. I had me a little girl a-waiting on my return," he said. "Still do, I would hope. I left her with the nuns as was my custom when I rode out. I have to get back to her. Her Ma died bringing her into the world. Elspeth is all I have, and I am her only kin. I could take sail for the United States. I still have enough of Wu's gold. But she would not remember me. Her father went missing in the territories twelve years ago, and she would be a woman of seventeen now. Old enough to have wed and delivered me of a grandchild, if'n the sisters did not take her into the nunnery of course. They do that."

He paused, and to her surprise and not a little embarrassment, Cady saw he was close to crying.

"I fear, if I do not get back soon, that is exactly what will come of my absence. They will take her east and put her into cloisters as their own."

"And you've been . . ." Cady searched for words he might understand, "you've been jumping around history every day since? Hoping to somehow luck into the right time and place?"

He shook his head, not in denial, but in shame and frustration.

"Ms. Cady, I am a simple man. I have my letters and arithmetic from schooling, but not much more than that. I am not an academic. I do not understand the scientifical wonders of Mr. Morse's telegraph. And I most surely do not understand this infernal device."

He held up the watch.

"I have been lost on an ocean of time for more than a month now and I do not mind telling you I am desperate for help. Any help."

"I'm sorry about your daughter," said Cady. And she was. But she was mostly sorry for herself. If this guy couldn't get back to his own kid, how the hell was he going to get her home? She felt the first stirrings of anger as it dawned on her she might have been dragged into this on purpose, rather than by accident.

"Is that why you brought me? To help you?"

"Oh, no," he said. "I would never presume upon your consideration. No, ma'am. I brought you here because of those scalawags that bushwhacked you."

She felt the heat banking up beneath the coals of her flickering resentment and anger.

"Well, thanks for that but I'd just as soon have stayed. You looked like you had them handled. Why did I have to get caught up in this?"

"I surely do apologize," said Smith, "but them fellers you saw were not the only ones. There were more. There's always more."

"What do you mean always?"

Smith chewed at his lip, sucking in the tips of his mustache.

"Call themselves apprentices," he said, "and they been chasing me since I got caught up in a willing frolic with some continentals."

"What does that even mean?" she asked, exasperated.

"I'm afraid I got into a fight," Smith explained, "and I had to kill a man. I guess they must be marshals, too, because they been chasing me ever since."

CHAPTER EIGHT

"Oh man, time cops? Really?"

"No," said Smith, "or at least I don't reckon as much. They don't act like lawmen to my understanding. Never identified themselves. Never tried to talk to me. After the business in the marketplace, they just started turning up, looking to plug me."

Cady stood up from the bed. The walls felt very close. She walked to the window, careful not to catch her feet on any nails or splinters. The cracked and rotting floorboards offered an abundance of both.

"And they call themselves what? Apprentices?" she said, twitching aside the burlap curtain and peeking back out through the window. It was caked so thickly with grime that it was like peering into a fog, but the scene was still recognizable.

Totally not Seattle.

Totally not her time or place.

She saw details which had escaped her before. Strange red brick buildings, climbing three and four stories above the crush of tumbledown shanties and slums, giving the appearance of lighthouses in an endless leaden grey sea. Miles and miles of thick black telegraph wire strung from teeter-tottering wooden poles, like the web of a giant alien spider colony. And across the street below, impossibly dense with foot traffic, a shed of rusted iron and rotting wood with a flat roof on which dozens of children, all filthy and dressed in rags, huddled close together like a litter of abandoned puppies. They looked as though they might freeze out there, but none did anything to improve their position. They simply lay, as if drugged, occasionally moving against each other, perhaps burrowing into the mass of bodies for warmth.

Cady grimaced and let the curtain fall back, striding over to where her boots stood by the door. She tried to forget the image of the freezing children.

"Apprentices. Yeah, I heard them address each other by that title," said Smith. "They ain't never identified themselves to me. They just come at me when our paths cross. Usually with blades and fists. Once or twice with guns."

She dressed while he rambled. It felt good, pulling on her boots. It felt normal. Next, her jacket and scarf. Smith's frown grew deeper as he watched her.

"I hope you ain't fixin' to wander away from camp," he said. "We get too far apart, and you could find yourself stuck here. Like Chester."

Cady walked determinedly back to the bed, picked up Smith's jacket, and tossed it to him.

"Then you had better stick close, Marshal. You got me into this mess. You better not leave me here."

She stood in front of him, her boots planted shoulder-width apart, her hands jammed into the pockets of her leather jacket. She could feel the can of mace in there. It was reassuring, but not much. A tenuous link to another time, and a little equalizer she intended to keep to herself.

"I will help you get back to your daughter," she said, "because figuring out how to do that is the only way of figuring out how to get me home as well. But understand this: you're not calling the shots. This is a partnership." She waved a finger back and forth, metaphorically tying them together. "We work as a team and we might just get out of this. No, screw that. We will totally get out of this."

"I am mighty relieved to hear that, young lady," said Smith in a voice that betrayed his absolute doubt in her promise, "but you really don't want to be walking out that door."

She fixed him with a defiant look, challenging Smith to contradict her.

"That's exactly what I'm going to do, Marshal, and you're going to come with me. You're gonna stick close. You're gonna tell me everything about what has happened to you the last month. You're going to give me the data I need to analyze this problem. And while we're doing that, we're gonna pick up some supplies, because it's obvious to me you have no idea what you're doing, and a little bit of preparation now could save us a hell of a lot of grief 500 years ago, or a thousand years from now, depending on where that crazy-ass timepiece of yours takes us next. So, let's roll."

Titanic Smith grumbled, but he did not put up much of a fight, not once Cady explained what she intended to do. He agreed it was a better plan than he had yet conceived. Pulling on his heavy suede jacket, Smith rolled his shoulders until it sat comfortably on his massive frame. The coat was long enough, she noted, to fall over his six-shooter and the giant knife strapped to his other hip. The cowboy hat went back onto his thick, unwashed hair completing the perfect picture of a frontier lawman. Which, she supposed, he was.

"Ma'am, you will need to prepare yourself a'fore we head on down," he said.

"Yeah, I know," she said. "The past is another country. I got it. I played a lot of *Assassin's Creed Syndicate*, you know. I probably know this city better than you do."

He favored her with the sort of disapproving look she hadn't seen since the last time she'd tried to work in a team environment.

"I meant your appearance, Miss Cady."

She rolled her eyes, but gave up on correcting him. He was only being polite, she supposed. A polite, sexist ass.

"What? You think I'm gonna draw more attention than you, Buffalo Bill?"

"I would wager it as a righteous certainty, yes ma'am. You have your hair out like a San Francisco harlot, and you are dressed in a fashion to excite attention you do not need."

Cady wanted to push back, hard. But she bit down on the feminist tract she was about to unload in his face, took a deep breath, and let it go in a long exasperated sigh.

"Okay, let's play the tutorial."

She watched him translate the phrase inside his head. It was like watching the gears grind in there.

"Womenfolk round these parts, they just don't look like that," he said, nodding at her outfit. She checked herself, up and down: boots, faded blue jeans, black tee shirt, black leather jacket, dark blue scarf knotted loosely around her neck. She was also wearing thermal underwear—it had been cold in Seattle—but nobody could see that.

Cady supposed he had a point. Recalling the street scene she had spied through the window, the women all looked like extras in some bullshit *Oliver Twist* musical. They didn't look like Dickensian cosplayers; they were hard-core actual Dickens bitches. They all wore dark heavy dresses, with some kind of bird-cage arrangement strapped to their asses under the folds of their depressingly drab Victorian hijabs.

"Fine," she said, doing her hair up in a loose bun. "Give me your hat."

"Well I don't know about—"

"Just give me your hat, Smith."

He handed it over. It sat a little awkwardly on top of her bundled mass of hair, but it gave her a boyish appearance that would have to do for now. Cady was not frocking up or strapping herself into a corset. In the hat, she could at least try to pass for a teenaged boy.

"Jesus Christ, we look like a couple of freaks," she said. "Come on."

As soon as they left the small room, she could hear the roar of the crowd downstairs. It echoed up the bare wooden staircase at the end of the cramped and badly lit hallway. A man was asleep on the floor, legs splayed out in front of him. He looked like he'd wet his pants.

"What is this place?" Cady asked.

"A saloon, The Spotted Goose," Smith told her. "Not the best and not the worst either. Needed a place to camp out where they wouldn't ask questions of a man carrying a woman over his shoulder."

That gave her something to think about as they trooped down the rickety staircase. The noise of the crowd grew louder and more intimidating as they descended.

"How did you pay for the room?"

"Some of Wu's gold."

He shook his head, dismissing the concern that appeared on her face.

"Weren't much of a pebble. Still plenty more where that came from."

"You probably got ripped off," she said as they turned onto the landing and descended the final set of steps. The scene that confronted her was a steampunk vision of fratboy hell. Although the marshal had told her it was late morning, the main hall of the tavern was already crowded and roaring with hundreds of men. Had she not already lost all of her dinner, vomited into the bedpan in the room upstairs, she would have painted the floor in front of her with it, so foul and overpowering was the stench. Hundreds of unwashed bodies, bad breath, cigarette and pipe smoke, rancid farts, and rotting food, all assaulted her sinuses. It was almost impossible to see across the room, so thick was the unfiltered fug of smoke.

She had stopped dead at the sight and the stench and only started moving again when Smith took her by the elbow and dragged her along, using his own body as a battering ram to clear a path through the press of filthy drinkers. Their voices, their accents, it was all so harsh and alien that she had trouble understanding a word of it, although that was as much a matter of the volume as the dialect in which they spoke. She bumped into somebody, knocking half his drink out of the enormous, greasy glass he was clutching. A horrible face, a fright mask of bulging eyes and yellow, rotting teeth—what few there were of them— loomed up in front of her.

"Eren't yer got no fuckin' eyes," the man roared.

He made a grab for her, his fingers brushing her breast, and she swatted his hand away.

"Cor, that's a fuckin' bit of jam," he shouted over the general uproar of the room and reached for her again. Smith's fist crashed into his face, and the man went flying into the rabble. Cady flinched and cried out, expecting a brawl to erupt and engulf them, but instead, only laughter and cruel mirth chased them through the room. Within a few steps, the heaving crowd had closed behind her and she lost sight of the man Smith had punched out.

Cady had to clamp her free hand down on top of the marshal's hat to prevent it being knocked off and lost. Her other hand held onto his arm. She did not dare lose contact with him in this chaos. So tightly packed were the hundreds of drunken revelers that she was buffeted by pressure waves passing through the mob. More than once she had to struggle to stay on her feet. It was as bad as any mosh pit she'd ever been in. Smith kept them moving at a pace that prevented her being dragged under, but she became aware of more and more of the men beginning to focus on her. Strange curses and shouts followed them across the room. Hands pawed at her, first her shoulders, then all over her body.

It was horrifying.

And then it was over. The marshal shouldered through a pair of swinging doors and out onto the street. A new miasma of toxic odors rolled over her, but this was more redolent of a barnyard. Body odor and tobacco smoke gave way to horse manure, although they did not give way entirely. The sidewalk, such as it was, was not nearly as crowded as the tavern, but it still heaved with throngs of Londoners muscling their way past, and sometimes into, each other. There were more women out here, and she saw immediately that Smith had been right. She did not fit in.

But he had also been mistaken in thinking they would stand out. The massed humanity on the streets of London seemed to have arrived from every corner of the globe. Perhaps it was their proximity to the docks. She had glimpsed the masts and funnels of hundreds of ships just a mile or two distant on the river, and although the locals were all of a sort—sallow faced, stoop shouldered, thin and loud—they did not have the city to themselves. London was the capital of an empire and it seemed that, if she cared to look, she could find amongst the throngs of poor English men and women visitors who had sailed up the Thames from every corner of the globe. In the first few moments after their escape from the tavern, Cady spied turbaned Sikhs, African-Americans, a Chinese man in a bright silk dressing gown, and an

Arab-looking dude in a fez selling monkeys from a hand drawn cart full of bamboo cages.

She had no time to stop and take in the menagerie. Smith propelled her along the street, gently but forcefully steering her away from the inn they had just left.

"Thank you," she said, meaning it. Her heart was still racing. "That was pretty intense. This is pretty intense. I didn't expect it to be like that. I just thought . . ."

She trailed off because she didn't really know what she had thought. Did she really imagine a couple of hours spent in the open world of Ubisoft's digital London would prepare her for this monstrosity?

"It is a helluva thing," said Smith. He stayed within arm's distance, shoving and knocking aside anybody who tried to get between them. It was like being escorted down a football field by the offensive tackle, a monster truck intent on ploughing through all opposition. The men here were crazy macho, stomping about like pro wrestlers on angry pills. She got used to it though, and even began threading aggressively through the crowd, like a salmon swimming upstream, but always staying close to her companion.

"I was a goodly while finding my seat on this particular bronc," Smith said as they passed around a crowd gathered outside a storefront where a carnival barker invited all comers to "witness the horrors of the Burmese Ape Woman."

"Have you been to London before?" she asked, quickly having to qualify the question, which sounded a lot dumber than it had in her head. "I meant, like, you know, the normal way?"

They made it past the crowd outside the freak show—Cady assumed it was some sort of freak show—and crossed an intersection where a couple of alleys meandered away into a medieval-looking streetscape, which seemed even more crowded than the wider thoroughfare along which they were moving. The dogleg alleyways were thick with foot traffic. Small knots of window shoppers clustered around the sooty panes of stores, much to the irritation of men in top hats and women in flowered bonnets who waved umbrellas about as if to threaten a whipping. Cady craned her head around Smith's obscuring bulk to see what might have drawn such attention, but all she could see were a few small signs identifying the storefronts as bookshops.

"I have passed through here twice before," Smith said, distracting her from the scene, "but not as a conventional traveler, no. I laid low not far from here when everything was much smaller, but more dangerous. Another time, there was a war."

His voice was grim and he did not elaborate. Cady did not ask. Maybe he'd been here during the Blitz? He'd probably have trouble understanding it. Must have been terrifying.

They made their way across the intersection, hurried along by the curses of a London bobby who blew a loud whistle and waved them out of the flow of traffic. For a city without motor vehicles, London's traffic still heaved and roared like a storm-tossed sea. There seemed no pattern she could recognize to the torrent of horse-drawn cabs, carts, and omnibuses. She was pretty sure that's what they were called, the double-decker carriages drawn by teams of horses which snorted and pissed and shat all over the cobbled road surface. Hooves and steel shod wheels trampled and mashed the droppings to a thick brown paste that lent the outdoor air the fetching bouquet of an industrialized sewage plant.

"Come on," said Smith. "Let's keep moving. This is your plan."

They walked for hours, but the day refused to grow brighter or warmer. In fact, Cady became convinced it was much later than Smith had said. The watery grey light of late autumn lost the timid luster it had enjoyed when they first emerged into the street, and she could feel the biting chill on her exposed skin as what little warmth remained of the day quickly leaked away.

"Fog," she said, at last. "Look."

They had been striding up a wide avenue, keeping to themselves, talking quietly. Smith looked up, his eyes following where Cady pointed.

"Reckon as much," he said. "Seen the like of it in San Francisco, too."

The city was disappearing, as though beneath a shroud. The Londoners seemed to pay it no heed, even though the fog bank was denser and heavier than anything she had known in Seattle, which was saying something. It had an evil color to it, a malarial yellow-green tinge, suggestive of pus and contagion. Cady could feel the cold leeching in through her leather jacket and even through the thermal top she wore beneath her tee shirt. Gas lamps were sparking to life, lit by swarming teams of men and boys with long tapers. The light was soft, even beautiful, a rare contrast with the seemingly infinite ugliness of the greater city.

"What's the time?" she asked Smith.

He checked his mysterious pocket watch, holding onto her arm as he did so, presumably in case he twitched and winked away in time. The idea made her nervous. What if he triggered that thing while they weren't in contact?

"It's gone a little after one o'clock," he said. "Be getting dark in a few hours anyway, I reckon, this time of year. Best hurry on."

They resumed their journey. Cady's attention was torn between the gaudy, fascinating spectacle of late Victorian London and the information she was intent on getting out of Smith. He was not a stupid man. Far from it. She could tell he was possessed of a sharp native intelligence, and he was streetwise in a way she would never be, in spite of having played at living in a loft on the waterfront in a "bad" part of Seattle; "bad" meaning that property developers were at least six months away from making a killing on redeveloping the whole neighborhood.

She wanted to know how many times he'd jumped.

That was the term she'd settled on when he had nothing better. *Only to be expected*, Cady thought. She came from a time and had been raised in a culture a hundred years descended from H.G. Wells. As much as the reality of time travel had put the zap on her head, the idea of it was not inconceivable to Cady McCall. The theory of relativity was old news.

So, she wanted to know, how many times had he "jumped."

"Can't rightly say, Miss Cady," he said, his tone apologetic. "First couple of times, I did not know what was happening and I could not rightly say, at least once or twice, whether I made passage from one time and place to another or not. I may have passed from one dark wilderness to the next without being aware of it. I haven't always fetched up in places like this," he said, waving one hand around to take in the city.

They were moving from the slum district in which they had arrived, through a commercial area of warehouses and light factories. There were still tightly-packed residential neighborhoods surrounding the industrial estates, supplying the workers for the mills, but she thought the houses themselves were growing larger, less ramshackle. They were still obviously given over to slum housing, with many families living under the one roof, but the change in architecture seemed to speak to some progress in leaving the worst part of the city behind. Or at least, she assumed it was the worst part.

"Try to remember, Marshal. It's important. To get home, we have to figure out how this thing works. It's a piece of technology, the watch, the machine. It has gears and sprockets and little wheels inside. They're doing something weird, but they will be doing it according to a set of rules. I can work those rules out. I'm sure of it. It's like code. You just have to understand the language and apply the rules. So think. How many times have you jumped?

If you recognized the time and place, that would be good to know. And if you even half suspect you see a pattern in the way you've moved around, that would be even better."

The fog was rolling in so heavily it had become an almost physical presence by then. It muted the sound of the city. The clip-clop of hooves, the squeak of carriage wheels and somewhere in the distance, the blast of a steam engine whistle, all felt much more distant than the earlier clamor of the day. Millions of people were still constantly in movement around them, though. If anything the traffic grew worse, slowing to something less than walking pace in the impenetrable thickness of the cold and sickly pall.

Smith had taken hold of her again, but there was nothing creepy or douchey about it. Cady was glad to feel his strong hand gently wrapped around her upper arm. She did not want to be separated from him and trapped in this fairytale hellhole.

CHAPTER NINE

Whenever they had to ask for directions, which was frequently, Cady let Smith do the talking. He seemed comfortable with the locals, which made sense. He wasn't that different from them. She didn't trust herself not to say something stupid. When possible, he sought information from uniformed police officers, bobbies, dressed in capes and those stupid little hats they wore. They invariably asked him about his sheriff's badge, or marshal's star, whatever it was, and he told them he was with a traveling Wild West show. It never failed to impress and endear.

Mostly, though, he simply asked some street hawker or dark-coated gentlemen in a top hat. Employing this pathfinding technique, they moved slowly toward the old center of the city, which was now barely visible around them. Cady was very hungry and starting to shiver with the cold, but there was nothing they could do until they cashed up. Smith still had a handful of Wu's gold, and she intended to get as much value out of it as she could before he frittered it all away.

Between these occasional stops to ask for directions, she interrogated him about his movements and the watch. She would make proper notes later on, but for now, as best she could tell, he had jumped at least two dozen times, moving up and down the timeline, even landing somewhere that sounded like the far future.

"Found myself in a city," he said, "but not like this." The marshal waved a hand to take in the city, and the fog was so thick it was as though he had stirred a thick pea soup with a big wooden ladle. "Weren't no one living in the city," he explained. "It was mostly flooded. Looked like it had been that way for a long time. Most of the buildings, they were empty, some of them toppled over, but I do declare, when they were built you could have plucked the stars from heaven away up on the highest of them."

They had come to a large roundabout where the traffic had ground to a halt. Unseen carriage drivers cracked whips and cursed at each other. Bells clanged on horse-drawn vehicles, and pedestrians threaded their way through the misty chaos, ignoring abuse from the drivers and the warnings of a single, overwhelmed police officer who feebly blew on a whistle while Cady and Smith worked their way around the tangle.

The pavement, which had been laid down in cement or slabs of stone or something, gave way to a long stretch of broken gravel. It was muddy underfoot and sucked at her boots as she trudged through the mire. One benefit of the all concealing fog was the cover it afforded them as they made their way through the crush of foot traffic. People loomed up out of the mist and disappeared back into it in mere moments.

"Have you taken any baseline measurements, done any testing to benchmark outcomes and compare . . ."

She could see from his expression that he had not, or more likely that he had no idea what she was talking about.

"I am a practical man, Miss Cady," Smith said, "but I am no professor of mechanics. Nor did I spend much of my school days with my head in the history books. I'm afraid I just cannot answer what I take to be your questions."

The pavement resumed, and with it, the clicking of ladies' heels and the crunch of gentlemen's boots on the solid footpath. She was almost dizzy with hunger.

"You're right, sorry. It was a stupid question."

"No, ma'am. It was a good question. It gives me some hope that you may be possessed of the wherewithal to untangle this knot. I spent some days in the era from which you hail, and although much of it was vexing to me, I did notice that your womenfolk are not backward in pushing themselves to the fore and claiming those ranks and privileges previously reserved only for their brothers and fathers. I wonder, then, are you some kind of learned mechanic or even a professor of the scientific arts?"

She snorted in laughter and then felt badly for it because of the look on his face.

"I am sorry if I have made a mistake," he said. "But—"

"No, no, you're good," she said. "Hell, you're doing better than I would. To answer your question, no, I'm not a mechanic or a professor. It'd take more time than we have and more patience than I've got to explain what I do for a living. But, a sort of combination of mechanic and professor is close enough."

Smith seemed satisfied with that, and they resumed their trek. Cady had no idea where they were, and could not shake the compulsion to reach for her missing phone and open Google Maps.

Of course doing something like that in Victorian London would probably end badly. She wouldn't be burnt for a witch or scooped up in some black ops extraordinary rendition program for walking around with alien technology, but she could imagine getting mobbed and beaten to death.

"These guys who were chasing you, these apprentices," she said trying a different approach, "do you have any idea where or when you ran into them? You said it was in a marketplace or something?"

"I believe it was in Florence, ma'am. In the country which has lately taken to calling itself Italy."

Cady took a moment to process that. It had been a couple of years since she had done Western Civ in high school history. When had Italy become a thing? Not Rome, but the modern nation state, the home of pasta and Lamborghinis. Sometime in the 1800s, she thought. That would make it "lately" to Smith.

Visibility was improving, not because the fog was thinning out; if anything it was growing thicker and harsher on the throat. She could actually taste a sulfurous essence to it. The system of street lighting was simply becoming more orderly and well-maintained. The elegant black lamp posts with their gently glowing gas lights were close enough together in this part of town that you could navigate from one lamp to the next without losing sight of either. The crowd, too, was less of a mob and more considerate of her personal space. The gentlemen in their long black coats and top hats, and the women rugged up against the chilly fog in capes and flowered bonnets smelled much better by virtue of not smelling of much at all.

"Why Florence?" she asked. "I mean, why do you think you were there?"

Smith grinned, happy to have a quick answer for her simple question.

"Because I asked them."

Cady frowned, not satisfied with the response and for a moment, not sure why. And then it struck her.

"Do you speak Italian? Or Florentine, or whatever they were talking?"

Smith tipped his head to one side as if considering the problem for the first time.

"I do not," he said. "I suffered through the Latin mass in my younger years, but these folks were speaking good American."

"No they weren't," said Cady, her excitement returning. "No way they were speaking . . . American, or English, to be a language nerd about it."

She pulled him out of the main flow of foot traffic into the entrance of a taxidermist. The interior was more brightly lit than the street outside, and she could see what looked like a small private zoo in there: stuffed tigers, a lion, even some sort of bear standing tall on its hind legs. Every wall was covered in mounted trophies and animal heads.

"I guarantee you, Marshal, they were not speaking English," she said, "or American, or whatever. They weren't even speaking Italian, not the way a modern Italian would."

Struggling through the crowds had kept them warm, and Cady shivered as the fog and the bone-chilling cold wrapped itself around her again.

"The people in this city, in Florence, could you describe how they were dressed? Did you see anything like machinery? Steam-driven or gas-powered or anything like that?"

Smith shook his head, but he did not look frustrated or disappointed.

"I could not place the year and I'm sorry that I did not think to ask. My head was still not right at that time. I was confused and thought myself ready for the asylum. There was nothing like the newspaper I picked up in the tavern with today's date helpfully printed on the front page."

"Did you see any printed material?" Cady asked. "Anything like books or pamphlets or magazines or journals?"

"No, nothing like that. And to answer your question, the folk I encountered were all dressed like players in a pantomime. It was like they wore costumes from the Middle Ages, the men in tights and curly boots, the women in ball gowns. The rich ones anyway. Beggars and vagabonds seem to dress in the same rags no matter what the year."

"Marshal, they weren't wearing costumes from the Middle Ages. They were just clothes, everyday clothes from that period. So, you were able to talk to them?"

Smith nodded. "Like I'm talking to you. Like I spoke to the celestial merchants of Shanghai when I fetched up there once."

"And it never occurred to you that it was a little strange, everybody speaking your language?"

He shrugged.

"Everybody's always spoke American to me, and I've met plenty of continentals and celestials and Arabs from the Holy Land. Back in my own time and place, I mean. Frontier draws folk from all over, and it's a terrible handicap to them if they can't speak a word of our lingo."

"Yeah, but they learned it. I'm guessing everyone you've spoken to since you met Mr. Wu has spoken perfect English. Am I right?"

"No," he said, "not everyone." He seemed very satisfied with being able to say no. Smith grinned at her as though he had caught her out with a marvelous prank. "Not you, Miss Cady. There are times I can't rightly make head nor tail of your fiddle faddle."

Her eyebrows knitted together as she tried to think through the significance of that, but she was too cold, too hungry, and it seemed a trifling concern for them to waste time on right then. Much more significant was the new data point she had.

The watch wasn't just a time machine, it was some sort of universal translator.

CHAPTER TEN

"I'm afraid this is most irregular," the jeweler protested.

You don't know the half of it, pal, thought Cady.

They had chosen the store because it looked respectable without being ridonkulously exclusive.

Hamilton and Sons, Goldsmithing and Fine Jewelry enjoyed a prominent street frontage on the edge of the financial district, but not too prominent. Entry was negotiated via a door in a side street running off the main thoroughfare. The windows were clean, polished every day to afford an unrestricted view of Hamilton's chosen wares, but they were not the grand arched display windows of the larger and more notable dealers on the main stem. Hamilton himself, a stooped and balding man with a permanent squint in one eye received them in a small, private office away from his main showroom.

"Mr. Givens, you say?"

"Deputy US Marshal Raylan Givens, Mr. Hamilton," Smith corrected him, giving Cady reason to grin with delight and not a little admiration. The marshal impressed her recalling that tiny detail from their conversation back at the Spotted Goose. Surprised her too. She wasn't expecting him to use an alias.

She did not introduce herself, and Hamilton did not seem to care.

"Marshal, I do not question your credentials," Hamilton protested, although he had done just that a few seconds earlier, "but you have arrived here under a misapprehension. We do not buy and sell commodities. I deal in refined artifacts, sir. Gold, certainly, and silver, and gemstones too. But I do not trade in raw materials, only the finished objet d'art."

Cady worked hard at containing her annoyance, but all of the jeweler's objections and arguments seemed to flow over Smith like fresh water in a mountain stream. He smiled at Hamilton as if he knew the man was perfectly happy to make a deal, rather than professing outrage at the very suggestion.

"And I am not proposing, sir, that your establishment should do anything other than the fine work it has carried on, lo these many years, and surely will for generations to come. I merely offer you the opportunity to continue your good work, which is spoken of, even in the salons of New York, as the very zenith of perfection in these arts."

Hamilton turned his squint on that statement with such a fierce air of scrutiny that Cady expected him to screw in one of those little eyeglasses these guys used and give Smith's bullshit an even closer going over.

"New York, you say?"

"And Chicago, sir," Smith assured him. "Which, by the by, is how I come to your door seeking consideration. My sister married one of the largest cattle merchants in that city and seems determined to spend his fortune on frippery and ostentation. She has spoken fondly to me of her wish to one day visit England and to place within her possession such trinkets and baubles as she assures me can only be had from the house of Hamilton and Sons."

The old jeweler gave him a look that testified to his deep skepticism of the story, but also his appreciation of the effort that went into telling it.

"I suppose I would not wish to incur the poor opinion of such a lady," Hamilton said. "I cannot make any promises, Marshal

Givens, but I suppose I might do you the courtesy of appraising your offer."

They left the jeweler a short time later, two nuggets lighter and three pounds richer. Smith also carried a hand-drawn map, courtesy of the jeweler, directing them to their next stop. It was late in the afternoon by then, getting on to four o'clock according to Smith's watch, and Cady had never been more appreciative of a thermal base layer.

With real money to spend, they were able to accelerate their passage through the city. Smith offered to split the money with her.

"Weren't mine to lay claim to, anyway, and you should have a roll, less'n we get separated. If'n we do, get yourself back to The Spotted Goose in Aldgate. That's our rendezvous."

She took a handful of confusing coins from the marshal and stashed them in the zippered pocket of her leather jacket, tucked in next to the can of mace. The marshal had probably seen his fair share of makeshift currencies and barter economics on the American frontier. Dickering with Victorian money didn't seem to bother him all. He considered three pounds a good deal.

"Cool," she said. "But why the fake ID? Raylan?"

She playfully dug a knuckle in his ribs. He shooed her way, but gently.

"Just taking due precautions, Miss Cady. Apprentices will be likely looking for us soon, if not already. No reason to make it easy for them. I would not have identified myself as a marshal either, 'cept for old Hamilton back there catching sight of my badge a'fore I could hide it away again."

Setting their course for the London docks, they first hailed one of the horse-drawn omnibuses that added so much congestion and manure to the city's roads. There was no bus stop. Titanic

Smith simply strode into the slow moving scrummage of traffic and whistled loudly at a conductor hanging from the rear entrance of a towering green bus. The driver veered the horse train toward Smith, ignoring the shouts and curses of the passengers and pilots of a dozen hansom cabs and even more commercial carts and wagons. As the bus drew closer, it seemed likely to topple over on the uneven road surface, leaning over Cady at such a precarious angle she was reluctant to approach it. She had to stay with Smith, however, and he had no qualms about bounding up the steps.

She followed him quickly, judging it better to be inside when the thing fell over, rather than standing under the hammer when it crashed down. The floor was covered in straw, and all the seats were taken by men, some of whom glared openly at her, and some who stared as though she was the Ape Woman of Borneo, or Burma, or whatever. Cady could tell they were confused and even affronted by her appearance. Up close, she was obviously a woman, and they were probably meant to give up their seats. But she was dressed like some rock-chick biker-bitch, a little too fashion forward for this crowd by about eighty years or so.

She flipped them the bird, and followed Smith up top.

"Come on, we'll sit on the knife board," he said as he climbed the little spiral staircase to the top deck. They found seats on a bench that ran down the middle of the roof, the passengers there sitting back to back. It wasn't pleasant in the cold and damp conditions, but Cady did appreciate getting a load off her feet. She groaned quietly as she sat down, the feeling of moving without walking a delicious treat. They must have covered miles on foot since they'd left the tavern.

The Spotted Goose, she reminded herself. The rendezvous point if they should be separated. Her heart beat faster at the idea.

As fascinating as this little open world adventure was, she had no desire to be stranded in 19th century London. She'd never been the sort of weenie who worried about micro-aggressions or demanded trigger warnings every time somebody busted out a sick fart, but Cady was getting a definite old-school douche-bro vibe from this place. Like she'd stumbled into some sort of primeval beta of Gamergate where all the men looked like evil beard fags.

At a guess, this was not a happy place to be a woman. *But then,* she thought, *where was?*

"So, tell me about Florence," she said, "and these guys who've been after you. The apprentices."

"It's not always men," he said. "Sometimes they're women, too."

"It's nice that they have an equal opportunity employer," said Cady. "Do you know anything else about them? Who they work for? What their issue is with you?"

The bus moved slowly, never exceeding the pace they had managed when they were walking, but at least this way they weren't burning energy she didn't have. Cady had already complained to Smith of being hungry, and he had produced a few strips of dried meat wrapped in wax paper for her to chew on. It hadn't helped. They needed to eat, but first they needed to stock up on some other supplies.

"They don't always find me," said Smith, keeping his voice low, and inclining his head toward hers. "Especially not if I keep my head down." None of the other passengers were talking to each other, but she didn't think it would matter if they were eavesdropping, or trying to. As much trouble as she often had understanding the local vernacular, they would be at a similar disadvantage listening in on her conversation with Smith. Even with the fog lying like a blanket over London, the city was still a constant, turbulent storm of noise—the clanging, pounding, steam-driven machinery; the endless destruction and construction of building work; the raised voices of the Londoners themselves; and the surprisingly harsh din of traffic before the era of rubber tires and internal combustion engines.

"First place I happened on them, as I said, was Florence. I shook 'em off there, found myself in another wilderness for my trouble, but an agreeable wilderness with fair weather and a stream in a forest where I could take clean water. I believe I was somewhere in the vicinity of home that time, for I was able to shoot a turkey and have him for my supper."

He pulled the wax paper package out of his jacket again, grinning.

"That jerky I gave you before could well be a thousand years old, Miss Cady."

"You're killing me, Marshal. Let's circle back to the A-story, the apprentices. When did they show up next?"

Smith thought it over as the omnibus swerved to pick up another passenger.

"Next time I saw them, I was in the Far East," he said. "A barbarian city swarming with such a sundry collection of human-ity that I hardly stood out any more than the next fellow. Would have thought I might pass discretely through such a place, replen-ishing my supplies, waiting until the timepiece would allow of another departure, but no. This was the first time I encountered a lady apprentice, and I speak true to tell you that she was a hellcat I would not care to tangle with again. Came at me in a bathhouse while I was soaking the dirt out of my creases. Hell of a thing."

"Were you alone?" Cady asked.

"It is my preferred choice when taking a bath, ma'am."

"And in Florence? You said they threw down in a marketplace."

He was a moment considering that before nodding.

"Yes. They 'threw down,' as you say."

"And you weren't alone there?"

"Damnation, no. There was an all-fired brawl. The whole town was going at it full split, like Kilkenny cats."

"Alone in a crowd then?"

"If'n you wish, I'd allow that, yes. You have a point you're riding up on, ma'am?"

"Not yet," she said. "Still collecting data."

She collected more as they left the crowds of the dark, fog bound streets behind for the even darker, more crowded Underground. Cady was surprised to find the Tube already in existence, but it was nothing like the mass transit system of the 21st century, or even the 20th, and the locals did not call it the Tube. The bus conductor looked at her as if she was a crazy foreigner when she asked. Smith did better inquiring which line of the Underground would get them closest to the docks. He paid for their tickets as they left the omnibus, a complicated exchange of coins that Cady was glad to play no part in, and they alighted near steps outside the entryway arch of the Mile End Underground station.

She recognized the building, or its type, from *Assassin's Creed*. In the game, it had the name of a different station and it wasn't interactive. You couldn't use it to fast travel around the map. Here, a billboard promised frequent services and cheap tickets. "Discounts For Seasonal Passes!"

They joined the throngs pushing through the arch and bought second-class tickets from an attendant at the booth inside.

"We should roll like Kanye," she said, only half joking. "First class all the way." Cady didn't care to imagine what second class would be like in this giant seething slum.

"No need to waste resources," said Smith. "Middle of the locomotive gets there right after the front."

She didn't mention that they could have gone third class if they were really cheaping out. Didn't want to give him any ideas. The passengers were immediately segregated by class when they arrived at the platform. The wooden planking and hard ceramic tiles created an echo chamber for the footsteps of hundreds of commuters. It was louder, closer, much hotter, and even fouler smelling than the streets above. Steam, smoke, and soot hung like burning smog in the air, stinging her eyes. The advertising posters which covered every flat surface were so covered in grime as to be unreadable. Many of the poorer travelers were drunk and keeping themselves topped up from a series of bars up and down the platform serving "spiritous liquors" and "miraculous potions." She wondered if she could score cocaine legally here, or even opium.

Probably in first class.

Sherlock Holmes hit the pipe like a boss, Cady recalled. She imagined he'd be sitting up front with Watson amongst the gilded mirrors and buttoned leather door panels, not on the bones of his ass in the altogether more Spartan surrounds reserved for B-listers like themselves. Their train announced itself with a screeching steam whistle that caused the entire crowd to surge before the engine had arrived, let alone come to a halt. She pressed herself into the protective embrace of Marshal Smith's sheltering arm, letting him be buffeted by the human pressure wave.

It mostly just broke and flowed around him.

"Saw a feller go under the wheels in Chicago once," he said, bending to shout into her ear over the cacophony of screeching steel wheels, slamming doors and shouting drunks. "Hell of a mess."

They had a bench to themselves in the second-class carriage, but Cady resolved the next time they did this, they were rolling with Sherlock and Kanye up in first. Their fellow passengers soon filled the carriage with tobacco smoke, which she could not escape because the windows had been closed against the fumes, ashes, and sulfur from the engine. It was hot enough that she was sweating in her thermals inside of a minute, and she stared long-ingly at an advert for "Metropolitan Mixture" cough syrup, a "thaumaturgic elixir for sufferers of the Underground Cough."

Probably more opium.

Smith did most of the talking while they rode under the city. He had worked the coal mines of Kentucky as a younger man, he told her.

"Only for a spell, but it inured me for life to all but the most noxious fumes," he said. "This might help," he added, offering her a handkerchief.

Cady shook her head vigorously. The smoke might kill her years from now, but that disgusting viral trap would probably put her under before the end of the week.

"The thing I have found about the apprentices, Miss Cady," said Smith, "is that the more aggressive I am in pursuing my interests—my principal interest being to get the hell away and gone home again—the more likely they are to track me down. It makes sense," he said. "A fugitive with even half of one-tenth of a lick of sense will get himself to ground while I am looking for him. Every time he raises his head, he has a very good chance of getting it shot off."

"So that's why you wanted to stay back at The Spotted Goose. To stay under the radar."

She could see him playing with the word *radar*, rolling it around in his mouth like a hard candy. For a moment, she thought if he had been in London during the Blitz, he would surely know what radar was, but then she realized she was using the hindsight plug-in. Any geek worth their pocket protector knew that radar had saved the RAF during the Battle of Britain, but it had been a top secret technology at that time. Cady wasn't sure when it been declassified.

Smith surprised her by nodding.

"Yeah. Under the radar," he agreed.

He was holding the pocket watch in his hand, stroking the glass face with his thumb.

Cady was already convinced it was some sort of translator as well as a time machine. But now she had to wonder whether it translated concepts as well as language. Another thesis to test. More data to collect.

She filed the question away, though. She would come back to it later. There wasn't much she could do to investigate it while they were riding around in public.

"I need to know about how you've moved through space, as well as time," she said discretely, leaning in to him. "We need to map out where you've been, and see whether it's somehow connected to *when* you were there."

"I'll do my best, ma'am," Smith said. "But sometimes I fetch up in a wilderness. And others in places I never heard of, not even in school."

CHAPTER ELEVEN

Back up on street level, the suffocating miasma of fog and factory smoke and the increasingly familiar stink of horse manure was a blessed relief after being closed up in the Underground for half an hour. The shocking chill of emerging into late afternoon was likewise a pleasant change after the hot, cramped confines of their second class carriage; for a few minutes, anyway, until the cold began to sting her exposed skin. Smith consulted Hamilton Sr.'s hand-drawn map and announced they were only five or ten minutes' walk away from their destination.

It was full dark by then, and the crowds were thinner in this part of the city, although there were still hundreds of people shuffling past each other on both sides of the street. Visibility did not extend much further than that. As the travelers moved from the heart of old London into the newly industrialized docklands neighborhood they found the gas lamps spaced much further apart. The roads, although still heavily used, were trafficked mostly by commercial haulage. Giant horses pulled enormous wagons piled high with barrels of beer. Simple carts dragged by smaller teams carried mystery loads between warehouses and factories.

"I reckon this would be our feller," said Smith, removing his Marshal's badge and pointing to a flat fronted, two-story building with an enormous red sign surrounded by dozens of small electric bulbs. They were the first electric lights Cady had seen since arriving in London.

They had arrived at Bumper Harrison's Colonial Stores.

Light spilled out of the shop through two enormous arched windows. Inside, the store looked like a cross between a gentleman's outfitter and an army surplus depot. A bell chimed over the door as they pushed through the entrance. A young man and woman, browsing racks of—what? Safari outfits?—gave them a cursory glance as they entered, lingering a few moments longer over Cady's outfit than Smith's. He was probably the sort of character they expected to see in here.

The double-height ceiling created the impression of a much grander, vaster space than Cady had been expecting. A walkway ran around the second story, creating a sort of mezzanine effect. Thousands of hardback volumes filled bookshelves on most of that level, although some of the space was given over to dark wood cabinetry with old leather handles. She couldn't help wondering what was filed away in those drawers. Mounted butterflies? Shrunken heads?

Smith, who seemed as much at home here as he had on the omnibus and Underground, strode across the bare wooden boards, his boot heels clicking and thumping, his big wide American voice booming out, "Good day to you, sir."

A small man with an enormous mustache came to attention behind the counter.

"And good day to you, sir. Harrison is my name. Bumper Harrison, late of the 24th Regiment, and now proprietor and lord of all you see. How might I be of service?"

Cady joined Smith as he approached the counter. She had taken off her borrowed hat as she entered, and now she pushed her fingers through her hair, which was coming loose from the bun she had tied hours earlier. Her long dark tresses felt greasy and gross.

"And good day to you, too, young lady," smiled Harrison, the first genuine smile she had seen all day. Smith was a dour character whose natural expression seemed to be a frown.

"Hey," she said, before catching herself and adding awkwardly, "how do you do?"

"I do very well, thank you," said Harrison, as his grin grew wider and his disposition sunnier. "Is there some way I might be of assistance to our cousins from across the seas? If you were off to America, I might assume you need outfitting for the frontier. Since you have arrived from the New World, I can but wonder what brings you to my Emporium."

"Well, pardner," said Smith, catching Cady's attention because he sounded like he was playing a character now, rather than simply being in character, as he had been with her. "You done caught me out. I will indeed be returning to the goldfields soon with my fiancée, Miss Jane, here, and I thought, while we were in London, we might avail ourselves of the finest frontier outfitters in the Old World. Hickok is my name. William Hickok."

She suppressed a smirk at being introduced as the wife-to-be of Wild Bill Hickok. She assumed Smith was simply being cautious again, not giving his real name. She didn't imagine the apprentices would be canvassing the city, going door-to-door looking for a displaced game coder and time traveling US Marshal, but Smith had been at this a while longer than her, and he'd warned her that they tended to show up whenever he raised his head.

"Well, you have come to the right place, Mr. Hickok. I have outfitted settlers and colonists who have traveled to the four corners of the British Empire, and I am certain I can provide you with whatever you seek."

What we could really use, thought Cady, *are antibiotics, painkillers, water purification tablets, a GPS system, decent Internet access, and some sort of flux capacitor to get us the hell out of here.* But she smiled sweetly and kept her opinions to herself, as was the fashion at this time.

"I'm sure you can help us, Mr. Harrison. Our needs are simple, just a few possibles. I will take whatever you have in the way of bedrolls and blankets, one of each; a three-man tent; two water canisters; salt pork and dried beans, say three days' worth; a compass; binoculars; one rawhide rope, thirty feet with a softened eyelet; a fire steel; two large dry bags; and a box of shells for my Colt .45, the 1878 model. Should you have one, I would not be averse to having from you a repeating rifle and a box of ammunition. A Winchester model '73 would do nicely."

Harrison nodded slowly and approvingly. The young couple who had been browsing the safari suits and pith helmets had wandered over a little closer while Smith spoke. They both regarded him in the same way they might admire a really fine cow or draft horse.

"Honey," said Cady, "if I could get a long, waterproof coat, something warm, that'd be awesome. Oh, and a notebook, too, and some pencils. For my studies."

Harrison turned his lopsided grin on her again.

"Young lady, I may have just the thing for you. From the Antipodean colonies, a cattlemen's duster. If your fiancé would allow me the impertinence."

Cady smiled back at him.

"Allowance got nothing to do with it," she said, in a reasonable imitation of Smith's wide, flat drawl. "I dig my own gold, I have my own money. I wear my own pants."

She took out a handful of heavy coins, anxious at the thought it might not cover the cost of the coat. She would look like a bit of an idiot then, wouldn't she? But Harrison looked to Marshal Smith, whose sanguine expression testified to all the damns he did not give about the matter.

"If it's trifles and such like you'll be supplying us, sir, you might as well throw in one of those mouth organs I see on yonder counter and a neck rack for holding it, if you have one. I'll take some pipe cleaning wire, if you do not, and fashion a holder myself."

"I believe I might be able to provide satisfaction," said Harrison and he shuffled away to begin filling the order.

"Sorry for spending your money like it's my own," Cady said in the least apologetic tone of voice she could conjure up. "But I'm cold and wet and tired of everybody looking at me."

"It's because of the pants," he said. "But as I told you before, ma'am, I don't count this as my money either. I don't know where Mr. Wu had his gold from, but he put me to a considerable inconvenience passing off that infernal watch of his, and I have dragged you into the bramble thicket in much the same way. Whatever you want, whatever you think we need, add it to your shopping list. I have no doubt Mr. Harrison would be just as amenable to dickering over gold nuggets as the jeweler was. Probably even more so. He could put a tasty nugget under glass on his counter, a promise of guaranteed riches to his clientele should they invest in the finest and most expensive of his wares before taking sail to the New World."

Smith's eyes never left hers, but she saw his hand open his jacket and rest lightly on the polished wooden handle of his pistol just before she heard the voice behind her.

"Hello," said a woman.

"We could not help but overhear your conversation with the proprietor," said her male companion. Cady turned around and discreetly moved out of the line of fire in case Smith decided to start shooting. Harrison returned at that moment, his arms full of cardboard boxes and paper bags.

"'Ere you go, then," he said. "Just give me a few more minutes out the back and I will see to the rest of your order, Mr. Hickok. Young lady, I have included two notebooks and a complimentary box of pencils to encourage you in your studies and as a token of our appreciation for your having come so far to do business with us."

"Thanks."

"Is it possible that you are the famous Mr. Wild Bill Hickok?" asked the young man as Harrison left.

Cady was aware of Smith's outline softening just a little bit, as though the tension which had tightened him up had been eased off, just a notch.

"Not even in my most fevered dreams," said Smith. "I share a moniker with the man, but very little else, sir. Last I heard of Wild Bill, he was off to seek his fortune via Deadwood."

"Oh, but you do so look the part!" exclaimed the woman. Her eyes were sparkling, her cheeks flushed a bright pink, and Cady thought it a distinct possibility she might just have a proximity orgasm right there in the middle of the store.

"You'd be surprised how often he gets that," she said. It was the young man's turn to come over all a-twitter then.

"And Jane, was it?" he said. "You certainly look like you are dressed for the open range and riding the Bighorns."

"Are those a pair of Mr. Strauss's famous denim britches?" the woman asked, her excitement increasing. "I have heard so much about them. Why, I have heard that a team of horses is not strong enough to pull them apart. I wonder where I might find some?"

Her boyfriend, or whatever he was, chimed in at that point, lest her pretty little head float right off her shoulders.

"We are away to the diggings in Western Australia," he explained, "to seek our fortune without the weight of family and expectation to hold us down, and it would be marvelous to hear a talk from a couple of old hands such as yourself about what capers and adventures might await us."

"And where I might find a pair of your magnificent britches!"

Harrison reappeared with more goods and a long, brown coat draped over one arm.

"I have everything you asked for, Mr. Hickok, and if you'll allow me the indulgence sir, I'm going to suggest you consider a field surgical kit. I have a small one here issued to the medical staff of my very own regiment, sir, the storied 24th."

Harrison opened a small leather pouch containing a collection of wicked looking scalpels, scissors and hooks, two lengths of rolled bandage and various packets of powder.

"Good idea," said Smith without hesitation. "Add it to my bill and pack everything into the dry bags. One for me to carry and one for Janey."

"Oh, this is very exciting," said the young man. "You absolutely must dine with us at our club tonight."

"I'm afraid—" Smith started, but Cady rode in over the top of him.

"Your club, you say? The two of you?"

"Why yes, of course," said the woman. "I understand that to be a radical departure from established norms, but we of the Frontier Club are all committed to making an abrupt break from our established lives, and I am sure you would testify that life on the frontier has a salutary effect on old-fashioned hierarchies and roles such as that between man and woman."

Smith's expression had gone from that of man facing a potentially lethal threat to one of a man confronted by a potentially lethal bore. Cady's response, however, hovered between amusement and enchantment. She had never before met such earnest doofwads, and she'd done a whole semester of women's studies before switching to comp sci.

"So, we could get something to eat at your club?" she asked.

"Of course," said the young man. "But our manners! Please, I'm Bertie Roxburgh, of the Cambridgeshire Roxburghs, and this is my betrothed, Miss Gracie Worthing of Duckmanton on Wye."

"Wye, indeed," Cady smiled. For the first time in many hours, she did not feel as though she was desperately windmilling and free falling through the day. "Come on, Wild Bill," she teased Smith. "We need to eat and these folks have been kind enough to invite us all to a hoedown at their campfire."

She pronounced it "*far*."

Smith did not look pleased. "We must be away before dawn," he said.

"I shall see to it that a hansom delivers you to your rooms in plenty of time for bed," said Bertie. "Come, come, we shall help with your luggage."

"That's mighty obliging," said Smith, "but we'd best be carrying our own loads."

He handed the smaller of the two dry bags to Cady, who took it, but stood her ground.

"Don't bother wrapping that coat, Bumper," she said. "I'll wear it now."

He came around from behind the counter to help her into the duster. It fell to her knees, conveniently hiding most of her outfit. There were plenty of pockets to stash equipment and minor stores. "Possibles," as Smith had called them. It felt warm and the material looked as though it would hold out moisture for a couple of hours.

"Looks good," Cady said. "We'll take it all."

"And you'll come to supper and talk at our club?" enthused Bertie.

"I don't know about talking," said Smith. "Never been much of a talker."

"Luckily I am," said Cady, "and we'd love to."

CHAPTER TWELVE

Bertie whistled up a carriage out on the street. Smith was the last to climb on board, his massive frame causing the springs to squeak loudly as they absorbed his weight. The driver offered to take their baggage into a wire basket on the roof, but the marshal insisted on keeping both of the large canvas sacks inside the carriage with them. The rifle, discreetly enclosed within a soft leather case, sat propped between his knees. Young Bertie had trouble keeping his eyes off it.

Feeling a lot less conspicuous now that she was hidden away within the folds of the warm, dry cattleman's coat, Cady returned Smith's hat to him. He kept it in his lap while they rode to the Frontier Club, his fingers picking at the brim. He was subdued, but agitated, his face a relief map of furrows and creases. Cady took his hand at one point, as a young woman might do with her fiancé, but he did not respond in character. His fingers continued to pluck nervously at the brim of his hat as he peered through the windows of the cab as though expecting to be set upon by Apaches or bandits at any moment.

"You must tell me all about your adventures in the Wild West, Jane," said Gracie. For a moment, Cady was caught out, having relaxed a little for the first time in hours and forgetting that she was still playing a role.

"What would you like to know?" she asked.

Gracie leaned in as if to impart a secret. Her fiancé mirrored the gesture and all three of them met in the middle of the carriage like conspirators.

"We have heard that all of the old certainties and hierarchies and ways of doing things fall away on the frontier," said Bertie.

"I have been told that women in the colonies enjoy much greater standing thanks to the responsibilities they must carry out on the frontier," said Gracie. Her eyes positively shone with excitement in the light of a passing gas lamp.

"We are great believers in the equality of the sexes," said Bertie, unconsciously imitating Smith's wary scanning of the streets outside the carriage, lest someone should overhear such radical views. "Have you read the works of the Marquis de Condorcet? *Sur l'admission des femmes aux droits de cite,* perhaps?

Cady sketched an apologetic expression.

"I still haven't got to that last Harry Potter yet."

"I'm not familiar with him," said Bertie. "Is he a student of John Stuart Mill?"

"Albus Dumbledore," said Cady, and Smith did squeeze her hand then. Hard.

"Ow! Honeybunch, remember your strength."

"And you remember not to tease people here, Jane. It will be noted and you will be found out."

"I'm sorry," Cady said, but to the young London couple, not to Smith. "Wild Bill here is right. But so are you, Gracie. You should go to the New World. You should help *make* a new world."

She looked out of the carriage window. The fog had closed as leaden and grim as a funeral binding, but Cady could tell they were rolling through another slum, or what she thought of as a slum; row after row of closely packed terraces, mean little hovels, overcrowded and grimy.

"This world sucks," she said, mostly to herself, as she watched a thin man, barely clothed, and covered mostly in bruises and scabs, dragging himself through the crush of foot traffic, one hand waving an empty bottle, the other grabbing at a wrought-iron railing to hold himself up in the final extremes of what was probably mortal drunkenness. If he fell asleep on the streets tonight, he would not wake up tomorrow.

"What a delightfully expressive turn of phrase," exclaimed Gracie. "The Old World does indeed suck, doesn't it, Bertie?"

"It does, my love, and that is why we will make a new one, far from here. It sucks," he said, trying the phrase out for himself.

"It sucks, it bites, it blows chunks," said Cady, stopping only when Smith kicked the side of her boot.

The Frontier Club met in a couple of private rooms above the ground floor of a popular ale house in Aldgate, not far from their own room at The Spotted Goose. Cady had been expecting a clubhouse, an old sandstone building perhaps, full of stuffed animals and looted artworks. But the Frontier Club was an association, not a building, and the F-word spoke more to the member's gently radical politics than it did to geography. Bertie and Gracie were not unique in hoping to find more freedom beyond the shores of England, but most of the Club's patrons dreamed of changing the world, not their home address.

The meeting rooms were unheated, save for one small fireplace in the corner of the larger room, and Cady was happy to stay in her duster. Most of the two dozen or so club members were rugged up against the chill and remained wrapped in their scarves and greatcoats even as the room warmed up with their body heat. Supper was a potluck affair; sandwiches, thick soups and heavy mugs of warm ale. Bottles of gin appeared from nowhere. She fell on the modest buffet, inhaling half a loaf of bread and a bowl of pea and ham soup. It was mostly pea. The ham was a couple of scraps of pig fat stuck to the bottom of the pan, but she was so hungry by then that she didn't care.

Smith stood guard over their luggage in one corner of the room, but soon found himself surrounded by an audience hungry for stories of the Wild West. His fans were mostly men, Cady noted, while she soon attracted a circle of mostly young women who, like Grace, were easily impressed by tales of her adventures with the legendary archaeologist, Doctor Indiana Jones, and the even more legendary artifact hunter, Miss Lara Croft.

"And is it true," asked Gracie, who had assumed the role of MC for their small group, "that women on the frontier are not just required, but expected to do everything a man can do?"

"Going backwards in high heels," Cady said with a wink to appreciative laughter.

A thin faced man with a prematurely receding hairline, the only male in their group, laughed along with the women, but said, "Surely you don't do everything, though? You would not be expected to fight off savages, would you? I cannot imagine myself getting the better of a Zulu warrior or a Comanche brave. By what deviltry would you do such a thing?"

His question elicited a round of feminine dissent and protest.

"Oh pooh-pooh to you, Chumley!"

"Don't you bother with him, Jane. He's new to the Club."

"He's only been here a month. The cheek of him!"

"I'm only asking out of curiosity," protested this 'Chumley'.

Cady smiled disarmingly at him. She was feeling generous. "Don't let them tease you, Chumley," she said. She was well fed by then, full of soup and sandwiches and half a pint of increasingly tasty ale, and she felt more comfortable and in control of her circumstances than at any time since waking up in that grim little attic room with Smith. "Tell you what," she went on, "why don't you try and strangle me, like a big bad Comanche, and I'll show you how I'd get the better of him."

A brief flight of excited giggles broke up and disappeared in gasps and cries of surprise at her challenge. Chumley—had she heard them right, was that even a real name?—smiled uncertainly, but his expression really turned rubbery when Cady took his hand and placed it on her throat.

"Oh, my!" said Gracie, her pale cheeks blushing bright pink. The other women cooed and gulped and fanned themselves, and Chumley looked as though he might faint at the skin-on-skin contact.

"Go on," said Cady, gently. "Strangle me."

She felt the merest tremor in his fingers. Maybe he was about to close them gently around her throat. Maybe it was just a nervous twitch. She moved before he had a chance to tighten his grip.

It was one of the first techniques they taught at that class on campus, the self-defense course she'd taken with Georgia that had been such an epic fail when she'd actually needed it. Here, with no pressure, she executed it without a problem. A simple hip rotation and wrist lock. Cady shifted her stance, turning her body side-on to the attacker, as she had learned. This had the effect of taking most of her vulnerable areas off-line and, more importantly, of opening a gap, just a small gap, between her throat and her very gentle, very compliant attacker's hand. Her own hand snaked in over the top, took a firm grip on the fleshy mound below Chumley's thumb, and peeled off the one-handed strangle as she turned her body back toward him.

Even as she performed the maneuver, Cady silently chastised herself. She had forgotten to take his balance, to extend his arm out straight and pop his elbow against her upper torso. She hadn't distracted him with a shout or a soft tissue strike. She'd basically done it all wrong, again. But this time it didn't matter. Poor

Chumley had no idea what was happening as she bent his hand back against the wrist, forcing the joint into hyperextension. He cried out in alarm and began to collapse under the pain. Cady held up the little finger of her other hand.

"Ladies," she said as though giving instruction, which was exactly what she was doing. She laid the tip of her pinkie against Chumley's locked up hand and pressed, ever so lightly. He fell to the floor. Her admirers clapped and cried out their appreciation as she hauled him back to his feet with a strong two-handed grip.

She gave him a peck on the cheek for his help.

No hard feelings.

Chumley blushed almost as feverishly as Gracie.

"Oh, my word," he said. "Where did you learn to do that?"

"Fort Apache," said Cady, "in the Badlands of Deadwood, from Marshal Raylan Givens."

The small circle of women burst into applause, while Chumley gazed at Cady with the moon-faced, cow-eyed intensity of a newly converted true believer.

A deep voice growled just behind her.

"My dear, a word if you would, please."

Smith.

She felt him take her elbow in a strong grip, a hold she had no chance of breaking no matter what little parlor tricks she might care to try.

"Of course, darling," she trilled as the marshal drew her away, out of the meeting room, into the dimly lit hallway. Behind her, the Frontier Club came together and responded as a whole to the excitement, the gentleman members now hazing poor Chumley about having allowed a mere woman to get the better of him, the mere women testifying that "Miss Jane" would be back presently to turn them all into feather dusters, just you wait and see. The atmosphere was convivial, good-natured. It was all in good fun.

But not out in the hallway.

"What the hell were you doing?"

Smith's hand tightened around her upper arm, and she did move then, turning slightly to dig her shoulder into his body and jerk her arm out through the gap between his thumb and the tips of his fingers. The move worked as it should have, but only because he let it. Cady did not doubt that if he wanted to, Titanic Smith could crush her tiny bones without effort.

"Nothing," she protested. "I wasn't doing anything."

"I saw what you did to that barber's clerk," Smith growled, his voice low and threatening.

"How do you know he's a barber's clerk?" she started to ask, but stopped herself when she realized Smith was just using some Old Western slang. Back in her day, he'd probably have called him a fag.

"It was nothing," she said, less guiltily, more forcefully this time. "Just a little aikido, a self-defense move that, quite frankly, these women could do with learning. We might have fallen in with the world's most liberal adventurers' club here, and it still feels like 4Chan to me."

Smith looked at her as though she was speaking in Fortran or C++, which to him, she guessed, was about right. Maybe there were limits to his universal translator or maybe . . .

"I told you we had to keep our heads down," he said through gritted teeth. "I told you we had to lay low, like fugitives. Because that's what we are. We got to belly through the brush here and you need to get that through your pretty little head. Because every time you poke that head up, you make increasingly short odds of having it blowed clean off."

"Listen, you," she said, hearing her mother in her voice and not liking it much, but plunging on anyway. "I know what total surveillance looks like. That's the world I live in. Or lived in, until you dragged me out of it. Remember that? When you dragged me out of my perfectly acceptable life into your personal shit show? Well, that place? Where I came from? An all-powerful all-seeing spy state isn't a paranoid delusion. It's Facebook and Google and Edward Snowden. And long story short, I know what being watched all the time feels like. I. Fucking. Monetized it," she said, stabbing her finger into his chest to emphasize each word.

"And this," she went on as she waved her arms around at the upper floor of the ale house with its dank peeling wallpaper and the smell of wet feet, "this is not it. So chill out. We'll eighty-six this bitch just as soon as your not-so-goddamned-smartwatch reboots. But for now I've had it, okay? I want to get another drink and a sandwich and spend a little time hanging with my home girls here who could do with some mentoring on how to dejunk the patriarchy so that, maybe, just maybe if I ever get home, Gamergate is a fucking historical footnote and not my own personal reality show."

Smith folded his massive arms and slowly straightened up, looking down upon her as if from a judge's bench.

"I have apologized for the necessity of roping you into my troubles. I have done so more than once. We have reached the end of that particular trail, missy, and the time is nigh for you to be removing the cloth from your ears."

He leaned down toward her again, getting right into her grill.

"This here, what you are doing, this is exactly what will bring the apprentices. I do not know how, I do not know why, I just know that this will do it."

"You don't know much, do you?" Cady shot back. She refused to cower under his glare. And it was a real glare, too. This was a harder, meaner side of him that he had not allowed her to see before. As far as she was concerned, that just made it all the more important she stand her ground.

"Everything alright out here?"

It was Gracie, surprising them both when she put her head around the corner.

"Yes," they answered in unison, but with such force that the words landed like fists, knocking her back where she had come from.

"Good-o then," her retreating voice cried out from inside the room.

Cady's hand was inside the pocket of her leather jacket, her fingers stroking the can of mace. If this guy so much as laid a hand on her, she was going to hose him down. No way was she going to be dragged through the past by some Lynyrd Skynyrd, stupid-hat guy in manheels and a belt buckle as big as a fucking football.

"Do you even know what a temporal paradox is?" she said quietly. "An alternative timeline? A stable time loop? A butterfly effect?"

She could see from the way his expression softened from an angry scowl into something that looked like deep thought, that perhaps she wouldn't have long before he actually did. His hand, she saw, had reached into a vest pocket to stroke that damned watch again. Seizing the moment while she could, Cady pressed on.

"Well, I do. And I got some good news and some bad news for you, Marshal. Good news is that you have grabbed up somebody with half a chance of understanding what the hell is happening here. The bad news, for you, is that you are going to have to cowgirl up and accept that I am the smartest guy in the room, and if anybody is going to get us home it's going to be me. Not you."

She could see by the look on his face that he was less offended than interested. But he was still a little offended. Ugh. Men.

"I got no doubt you were really good at what you did back in 1870 or whenever it was. But that's not what you're doing now.

You don't even have the language to describe what's happening. The theory of relativity is like fifty years away in your personal future. For me, it's old news. Wormholes. Quantum entanglement. Superstring theory, it's all old news."

Cady had no idea what actual role any of those things had to play in time travel. But she'd wasted enough time on *iO9* and *Boing Boing* to know they were sort of relevant.

Sort of.

And she was certain that as soon as she could get online again, she could quickly cram enough study to offer a Masters-level explanation of the phenomenon compared to anything Smith had offered.

He seemed to reach the same conclusion after a few seconds digesting her bite-sized rant.

"All righty then," he said, with obvious reluctance. "But remember . . . You don't belong here. You are a pebble skipping across the surface of this pond. Ripples follow you. Try not to be a damned boulder."

CHAPTER THIRTEEN

A barmaid ringing a school bell broke up the meeting of the Frontier Club a few minutes before the alehouse downstairs closed its doors. By then "Bill Hickok" and his betrothed had been inducted as honorary members of the club and "Jane" in particular had become fast friends—besties, as she insisted—with Gracie and the other ladies, the "Frontier Grrls," as she also insisted on calling them.

At one point, she had half a dozen of these drunken, Victorian proto-feminists falling about laughing as they growled at each other that they were all "frontierrr grrls" now and their gentlemen had all best watch out.

"Grrr, grrr."

Smith did relax, but not much. He told more stories about life on the actual frontier, stories which Cady supposed were mostly true, unlike hers. The gentlemen of the club, most of whom had never been closer to a frontier than the wilds of Cockfoster, gave up plying him with pints of ale in the face of his continued refusal to drink them. But they happily hung off his every word about prospecting in California, marshaling in Tombstone, and scouting with the cavalry.

"He is a seriously handsome brute of a man, your Mr. Hickok isn't he," Gracie breathed into Cady's ear, along with enough gin and ale fumes to power a small ride-on lawnmower.

She caught herself before she said, "Seriously not."

Instead . . .

"*Sherioushly . . . hot,*" she said, slurring her words a little as she breathed her own highly concentrated fumes back in the face of her new best friend.

Nineteenth century beer, it turned out, packed a hell of a punch.

Smith said nothing about her being drunk when he came over with their bags, handing her the smaller satchel with all of the lighter items in it, including her notepads and pencils.

Chumley appeared, as if he had beamed down from orbit. He was still grinning uncomfortably, but also sweating now with the small room having heated up over the course of the night with all of those bodies packed in together. Like Smith, he looked sober.

"Please, allow me," he said, reaching to take the bag from Cady. She was drunk enough that he caught her by surprise and had managed to pry the sack out of her hands before Gracie intervened.

"Come now, Chumley. Our Jane is not the sort who needs to be fetched and carried for. You of all people should know that."

He handed the bag back to Cady as the room emptied, and Bertie joined them, standing next to Smith, looking eager to continue the night's festivities.

"But my rooms are very close to The Spotted Goose," said Chumley. "It would be a discourtesy if I did not offer to escort them home. It's very easy to get lost in the fog, as *you* would know, Gracie."

Bertie chortled at that. Some inside joke, Cady supposed. Grace wiped the grin off his face by pulling on her gloves and back handing him in the solar plexus.

"That will be enough of that, Bertram Roxburgh, if you ever wish me to become Mrs. Gracie Roxburgh. And after talking to *Ms.* Jane I'm not entirely sure that you should not become Bertie Worthington."

Both Bertie and Chumley laughed, but neither of them seemed entirely sure that she was joking.

"You run along, Chumley old man," said Bertie, recovering his sense of worth by having a swipe at Chumley's. "We don't require your presence any more. You must have some dreadful trade to be seeing to, and we must take a carriage through Aldgate. It will be a matter of no moment to see our American cousins safe home. I'm afraid the cab will not comfortably seat five. Not with this colossus of a chap trying to squeeze himself in. I don't suppose you could afford it, either."

Bertie slapped Smith between the shoulder blades and bellowed out a hearty peal of laughter, which fooled nobody, least of all Chumley, who had been given his marching orders. Cady had not seen someone so deftly dissed and dismissed like that since high school. It was quite an uncomfortable reminder of how stratified this society was, even amongst these radical egalitarians. She wasn't sure what Chumley did for a living, but the fact that he worked at all placed his station far below Bertie and Gracie, whom she had come to understand were funding their adventure in the New World entirely from the proceeds of their respective family fortunes.

"Of course, of course. You're right, of course," said Chumley, first blanching then blushing with embarrassment at being reminded of his lesser rank. Smith regarded the interchange with his usual expression, mournful and unmoving. Possibly uncaring. You never could tell what was going on behind that granite facade.

Cady could not help but feel Chumley's humiliation burning her own cheeks, but if she was being honest with herself, and the beer helped with that, she no more wanted to spend the rest of the evening with him than Gracie did.

"I will thank you for a m-marvelous evening," he said, beginning to stutter as the social horror got the better of him, "and I w-would w-wish you all the b-b-best."

"And all the b-b-best to you, old man," said Bertie.

Cady gave the poor bastard a peck on the cheek to send him on his way, feeling both awkward and relieved at his exit.

"Ugh. He means well, but honestly, he's such a podsnapper," said Gracie. "I'm surprised his mother lets him out of the house."

"I do rather think she throws him out with the night soil every morning," said Bertie, and they chuckled with the enjoyment of sharing a small moment of cruelty. Cady had felt herself adrift on the seas of time all day, but she had not felt as lost as she did right then. She liked Gracie, genuinely liked her, and hanging out with the Frontier Grrls for a couple of hours had gone a long way toward chilling her out to a point where she might even be able to deal with the total insanity of what had befallen them. Of what had befallen her, because although Smith was in the same boat, for twenty-first century Cady, he was as dead and buried as all of these guys. She was the only one who was really lost, when you thought about it. After lots of really strong beer.

She felt Gracie's hand on her arm, squeezing softly.

"And now we must all go out for supper and drinks. Real drinks. Our treat."

Cady pulled herself back into the present, the past, whenever the hell she was, and found her friend—her oh-so-ditzy, oh-so-pretty, cruel little golden-haired friend—hanging on to her arm, dragging her toward the door, grinning and giggling as though she hadn't just been an unspeakable bitch, and in an exquisitely self-conscious moment of clarity, Cady thought, *this is what it's like for Georgia, being friends with me.*

Remembering her friend and how far she was from home unsettled her again, and she allowed herself to be led away. Only the low rumble of Smith's voice did anything to halt her progress.

". . . Jane . . ." he said carefully, obviously having to remind himself of the cover story he'd thought it necessary to use, "are you forgetting that we have travel plans? We have to leave on the morrow, at a very particular time and place, if you will recall. Indeed, I do believe it was you who insisted on the arrangement."

"Dash my wig!" Bertie exclaimed. "We'll have none of that. Wherever you need to be, whence ever you are required to be there, put yourselves in my care, sir. But for now let's be away to tickle our innards."

"That's very kind of you, Mr. Roxburgh," said Smith, "but my fiancé was most insistent that we adhere to her itinerary."

"Oh, do come along, chuckaboo" said Grace, actually dragging Cady toward the door. "When are you leaving? In the morning? By locomotive, or hansom cab, or do you plan to rope and ride a couple of bison over the horizon."

And then she fell about laughing at the unintended rhyme, and Cady, who was realizing just how drunk she was now that she finally had to start moving, was laughing along with her. There was a slightly jagged, hysterical edge to her laughter, but that simply amplified Gracie's high spirits.

"Jane?" Smith said again. "We have to take that carriage in a couple of hours. We leave just after two in the morning, if you recall."

She did. Even through the haze of alcohol and hysteria, she did remember that. She had insisted they make their first jump together as close to the moment when they arrived here, and from the same place.

"Well, that settles it then," declared Bertie. "We shall none of us visit the Land of Nod this evening. We'll give old London town a jolly good seeing to, and pour you directly into your chosen carriage."

Their destination, a supper club called The Old Persuader, was a three story palace, faced with shiny plate-glass windows decorated in gold leaf rosettes and gilded cornices. Illuminated, bright colored adverts for THE NO MISTAKE CORDIAL and THE FAMOUS KNOCK ME DOWN MIX covered the facade. Cady could hear a piano tinkling and raucous voices raised in loud song. Bertie led the way, tipping some guy in a top hat who took their coats and hats before taking them in hand and carving a path through the crowd to a booth in a corner where waiters cleared away the remains of a meal and laid out cutlery and crockery and a plate of bread and butter.

The atmosphere was thick with cigar and cigarette smoke, the fumes of heavy drinking, and the smell of cooking fat. Cady was hungry again and fell upon the plate of buttered bread, surprised to find the slices so white. She'd always assumed white bread was a modern thing. Jugs of ale arrived, and water for Titanic Smith, who insisted on it.

Titanic Bore more like it, thought Cady.

Food arrived. A haunch of beef surrounded by steamed greens so vivid in color they might have been touched up in Photoshop. Roasted potatoes, honeyed carrots and some kind of savory pudding or soft biscuit followed with boats of gravy, a pot of mustard and more bread. Cady didn't think she could fit it all in, but surprised herself, with unexpected encouragement from the marshal, who put aside his clear preference to be somewhere else.

"Don't know when we might eat again on the trail," he said, forking a couple of thick slices of beef onto his plate, "so believe me when I say that I am mighty appreciative, Mr. Roxburgh."

They passed a couple of enjoyable hours in this fashion, eating, drinking and talking with Bertie and Gracie. Even Smith loosened up a little—agreeing to stop calling Bertie, 'Mr. Roxburgh'— and then a lot, taking a turn on the piano in one of the lounges, later in the evening. He had a remarkable ear for music and a surprisingly beautiful singing voice, a gift from his mother, he told them. He was able to pick up a tune, having heard it hummed for a few moments, and could improvise his own arrangement after just a few bars.

"A man has to entertain himself on the frontier, ladies," he explained, as he pulled a harmonica out of the possibles bag in Cady's care and added the mouth organ's bluesy wailing to the tinkling keys of the piano.

A rowdy, appreciative audience gathered around him while he performed a set list of tavern favorites from the Old West and took a few requests from the locals. Cady found herself relaxing as Smith played, allowing herself to imagine that maybe this would all work out. He too, visibly relaxed as the night went on. It was hard to think of any real harm coming to them while they had such a pleasant time. Gracie taught her to sing along with a couple of music hall numbers, and she and Cady scandalized and delighted the room by tweaking the lyrics to "Our Lodger's Such a Nice Young Man" as the clock ticked over to midnight.

She was tiring and about to return to their booth when Smith stopped her in her tracks with opening notes of a song she knew well, the first piece of music she'd actually recognized that evening.

As he banged out the first bars of "Louie Louie" on the piano, a devilish grin splitting his usually sombre features for the first time, she actually screamed in recognition and grabbed Gracie by the shoulders.

"I love this song!" she cried out.

Which wasn't exactly true. Back home, she would have flicked radio channels or wondered what was wrong with the algorithm that had caused Spotify to serve up her grandfather's music. But here, the familiar, brutally simple, repetitive riff was an unexpected and welcome shout out from an old friend in a room full of strangers. And then Smith added the harmonica and his own vocals to the mix.

Cady recognized the rhythm and the form of the lyrics, but not the words themselves. They sounded the same, but different. Something about missing a little girl across the sea. Still, the crowd soon picked up the chorus, and like a college dorm full of drunken students, they started roaring it out while Smith hammered at the piano, blew hurricanes through the mouth organ, and added his own, weirdly old-fashioned but powerful vocals to the mix.

Cady hauled Gracie out onto the dance floor—or the small space between a couple of potted ferns next to the piano that she declared to be the dance floor—and gave her new bestie an impromptu lesson on how to dance like nobody was watching. Grace had drunk even more than Cady and had no immunity to the timeless appeal of rock-n-roll—especially not as interpreted by the honky-tonk stylings of "Wild Bill" Hickok. Soon she was twerking and grinding like a stripper on double time.

More people joined them on the floor, and Cady wondered if Smith might have picked up some other tunes on his travels, but he stuck with an extra-long version of "Louie Louie," which was fine with the drunken rabble in the piano bar of the Old Persuader.

Groans of dismay and protest greeted the final notes of the song and "Wild Bill's" announcement that was he was "all played out." They met back at their booth, where hangers-on were hanging on, madly keen for more tunes.

"You absolutely must teach me that delightful fancy," one young man insisted. He was nattily dressed in black-and-white striped trousers, a daffodil-yellow shirt, and a bright red tie. He carried a cane for effect and tapped it against a half-empty champagne bottle to draw everyone's attention.

"I am the *lion comique* at the Empire," he announced. "At Leicester Square!" he added, when Smith shrugged as though it meant a bit less than nothing to him.

"You come on back here tomorrow night, and I'll teach it to you," Smith promised, which was enough to mollify him, and gradually the crowd broke up and the background roar dropped back to something less apocalyptic.

"And with that, we have to mosey," said Smith, who like Cady, looked happy for the first time that day.

CHAPTER FOURTEEN

"When it's time, we just dig in our spurs and get gone. You understand?"

Smith was helping her up into a cab. Bertie and Gracie were already fussing about inside, settling themselves for the ride back across town.

"Sure," said Cady, even though she wasn't quite sure why he needed to tell her. And then the thought occurred to her through the haze of the night's drinking. "Even if they're watching?"

"Yeah," said Smith. "Just hold my hand and our baggage. But don't be touching or holding onto nobody else. Not less'n you plan on making a whole wagon train of this."

The imminence of departure helped sober her thoughts a little.

"Okay. Got it," she said.

"Come along, you two," crowed Bertie. "The night is but young."

"You sit next to me, Jane," said Gracie, patting the faded bench. The whole carriage settled and groaned as Smith climbed in and took the seat next to Bertie. He had both of the dry bags full of possibles and equipage on his lap and he hugged them to him like sleeping children.

Back in her long, concealing coat, Cady was grateful for the warmth of the well-sealed oilskin. It was bitterly cold outside now, and the fog made it worse, stealing in to draw the heat from their bones.

"The Strand, my man!" Bertie shouted to the driver, and they rattled away on the rough cobblestone road. Although the crowds and traffic had thinned out noticeably, Cady was still impressed by how busy the city was so late at night. London was like New York. She never slept.

Cady found herself wondering what New York would be like right now, in this time.

Awful, she decided, if you were anyone less than a railroad baron or heir to some banking fortune. But then, New York in her time wasn't much better, was it? Not if you weren't rich and famous.

And then she remembered. She was very rich now and internet famous, but not here. She caught Smith's eye across the dark confines of the cabin, and she could see that he was anxious to be gone. He checked the pocket watch every few minutes. He did have his kid to get home to, but that didn't make her needs any less valid. She had family, and friends, too, and a life she hadn't asked to be dragged out of.

"Wild Bill," she said, adopting the nickname Bertie had taken up, in spite of Smith's insistence he wasn't *that* Hickok. "That was some impressive work, tickling the ivories back there. I thought you didn't like that sort of attention. You always told me you liked to keep your head down when you were in a new place."

"Oh, Bill," said Gracie. "You shouldn't hide your light under a bushel. You are a wonderful singer and quite the devil on the pianola. Why would you not want people knowing?"

Smith looked at Cady while he considered his answer, but turned to Grace when he finally spoke.

"It was my ma, learned me the piano, ma'am. She was a music teacher. Playin' is all I have of her now. I like to keep it for myself. As for not wanting all the attention, Jane, you are right. I did say that and I do believe it. But I thought you might like to hear a tune that was more familiar to you. We are a long way from home."

"We are," Cady said quietly. "Thank you."

"And we are almost done here, anyhow. We will be gone very soon."

"My word, Bill," declared Bertie. "You sound like a man on the run."

"All our lives we're either running toward something, or away from it," said Smith. "You and Miss Gracie are lucky to be running toward better days, with your grand adventure ahead of you."

And that was enough to set both of them off, excitedly talking about their dreams and plans for life in the new world.

Cady just wanted to get back to her old one.

On Smith's instructions, the driver dropped them a block down from The Spotted Goose.

"We get a carriage here for the next leg of our journey," he explained, "in sixteen minutes," he confirmed after checking his watch.

"Well, you have more faith in the punctuality of the coach company than I, Wild Bill," said Bertie, "especially in this part of town. Are you sure you are to be picked up here?" Bertie looked around, unconvinced.

"This is where we came in, and this is where we leave," said Smith, directing his answer more to Cady than Bertie, "in fifteen minutes, now."

"How thrilling!" said Gracie, still high from the night's adventures and doubly excited by a countdown . . . although, it occurred to Cady that Grace would have no idea of what a countdown was. The space program was a long time from here.

"It's so sad you're leaving us," she said, suddenly reaching the maudlin drunk part of the evening. "We've only just become such good friends."

She hugged Cady, who returned the embrace and found herself reluctant to let go. Regardless of how mean Grace had been to Chumley, there was an innocence and even a sweetness to her that Cady found compelling. She was like a child. It was weird to think this young woman was probably more than a hundred years dead.

"Oh, don't cry," Gracie said, when she found Cady's eyes wet with tears. "We'll stay in touch. Write to us the very moment you reach your next stop. The post will find us at either of our parents' estates."

Smith insisted on paying the cab fare, in spite of Bertie's earlier promise. It appeared an unselfish gesture, but Cady figured he was just emptying his pockets of travel shrapnel. She still had her local coinage. It'd be worth something on eBay, for sure, like a rare stamp or a first-gen iPhone still in its original wrapping.

Or maybe she'd just keep it as a souvenir of a very weird day and night she could never tell anybody about. Not unless she wanted to spend the rest of her life in a straightjacket or the interrogation cells at Area 51.

It wasn't like she needed the money, she reminded herself. Not if she could get home. Her heart started to beat a little faster at the prospect of departure. She walked a little away from the carriage, her arm draped around Gracie's shoulders. Her new friend, soon to be lost forever, leaned into the embrace.

"I'll miss you, Janey," she said in a quiet voice. "You are the most fun I have ever had."

"Backatcha," Cady replied. Grace seemed to understand what she meant.

Cady didn't imagine they'd make it home on the first attempt. But there was always a chance. Always some hope. Likewise, she wasn't quite sure how they were going to get rid of their new friends, and was beginning to suspect Smith intended to jump right in front of them if necessary. The fog was so thick and the night so dark that it wouldn't take much to disappear. Just a few steps into the murk and they could be gone forever.

"So, where exactly is this mystery carriage to collect you?" Bertie asked. They had alighted from their cab near the winding alleyways Cady had noted earlier in the day. Lit by a few scattered gas lamps, they looked even more picturesque in the gloom. The scene was something closer to Shakespeare's London in Cady's imagination, half-timbered houses with slumping bay windows and gables almost meeting over the middle of the muddy cobblestones. It was much less crowded now, but a few lone souls still drifted about, peering into the windows of the old shops.

"Would you like to have a look?" asked Grace, in a surprisingly conspiratorial tone. "You can't visit London and not take a quick looksy-dooksy at Holywell Street."

"Oh, no, Gracie, you wouldn't," her fiancé protested. "*The Times* says it's the most vile street in the whole of the civilized world."

"*The Times* can go toast their blooming eyebrows," she shot back. "Come on!"

She had her arm through Cady's and dragged her out into the scrummage of traffic before Bertie, or Smith, or even Cady herself, could protest.

"Miss Ca—Jane!" the marshal cried out. "Jane, don't go missing. We have to leave."

He sounded genuinely helpless, the first time she had ever heard that note in his voice. Cady almost turned back, but a wagon, piled high with potatoes, all but ran them down when she tried to reverse course.

"Open yer fuggin' eyes, you dim strumpet!" yelled the driver, adding a crack of his whip as an exclamation point. It seemed easier, then, to just carry on over the road and get turned around on the other side. But Gracie was having none of it.

"Come along," she said when they reached the relative safety of the footpath.

"But Smith and Bertie!"

"Smith who?" said Grace, still tugging at Cady's elbow. It was like fighting with a bargain hunter on Black Friday; Grace knew what she wanted, and nothing was holding her back. She forgot about this mysterious "Smith" almost immediately. "Come on, Janey. Just a quick look."

Smith's voice boomed out of the fog and darkness, searching for her. "JANE!"

It sounded much closer this time. And then the marshal was there, with a bemused-looking Bertie in tow, dodging and weaving though the wagons, carrying all of their luggage in the two dry-bags. His face was thunderous.

"Now is not the time, Jane—" he started.

"But it's the perfect time," Grace said, giggling with excitement. For her, the night was just a long and fabulous adventure. "Come on."

"Don't you get away again," Smith warned.

"I won't," Cady promised, and she meant it, "but we've got a little while yet, don't we?"

"Nine minutes."

"My word, you Americans are punctual," said Bertie.

The group of four friends, reunited again, walked a little further into the alleyway. Now that she was there, Cady thought the scene was more Harry Potter than William Shakespeare. It looked the sort of place a young wizard might go to buy his first wand. A faded half-moon, once painted gold, hung over the door of the nearest shop. Droopy eyelids and pouting lips painted in red gave the face of the moon a sulking expression. In the window lay piles of books and china plates.

Interesting business synergy, thought Cady. *Content and crockery.*

Gracie was giggling uncontrollably now, and Cady finally understood. The next few stores were also bookshops, but of a very particular sort.

Ye olde Victorian porn merchants.

One of the shops, although closed, was still lit by gas lamps inside, allowing her to pick out titles such as *Captain Stroke-All's Pocket Book* and *Gay Girls of New York*.

Cady burst out laughing, which sent Gracie into peals of hysteria and drove away the few lone window shoppers, all of them men in long, dark coats and top hats. Having protested the idea of venturing into the most vile street in the whole of the civilized world, Bertie pressed his nose up against the glass of the bookstore to get a better look. Cady smiled as she watched the two long-dead lovers twine their fingers together. She carefully stepped backwards, away from the window, finding Smith waiting for her. He placed a hand on her shoulder.

"Best you not stray, ma'am."

"So we're back to ma'am, now?"

"I'm just about done with all this play-actin'. I got me a headache just from keeping my own name straight, let alone yours, *Miss Jane.*"

His tone, which had been stern, was softening. She could tell he was relieved to be all but gone.

"That was your idea, not mine, buddy."

Bertie had slipped his arm around Gracie's waist, which Cady assumed would be a terrible scandal were anyone to see them. But the alleyway was all but deserted now. They had driven off the last of the lonely perverts and the night and the fog shrouded them so completely that nobody more than a few steps away could have made them out as anything more than indistinct shapes.

Part of her wished she could take her new friends along with her. They had already declared themselves outsiders of a kind in their own world, and Cady felt certain she could help them find a place in hers. She'd have the resources to do so, just as soon as she got back there.

Gracie giggled as Bertie nuzzled at her ear and drew her further into the gloom, away from the time-travelers. Smith linked his arm through Cady's, juggling the two sacks as he did so.

"Ya have to let them go, Miss Cady. I know it's hard. But it is the only way. See? We are gone in four minutes."

With her arm tucked securely into his, Smith held out the pocket watch for her to see. It looked as unremarkable as ever. He put it away in his vest pocket again, and squared his shoulders.

"Does it hurt?" she asked.

"Nope," he said. "You get it right, you won't even notice. Come this way. We arrived a little ways down Half Moon Passage there."

He nodded to where an even smaller alley cut away from the backstreet with all of the bookstores. It smelled strongly of urine and vomit, even more so than the rest of the city. She resisted the urge to call out goodbye to Gracie. In a few moments she would be long gone, long dead and—

Cady heard a scream. A terrible scream that sent waves of gooseflesh up her arms and made her shiver.

The marshal stiffened beside her, and she could sense him wanting to draw his pistol, but he was encumbered holding onto her and all of the baggage.

Another scream, ending in a grunt and a horrifying sound. A sort of wet, ripping noise.

"Goddamn it," said Smith, and he did reach for his gun then, while awkwardly keeping Cady's arm tucked into his. He had the gun out in one hand and the watch in the other, with the neck of the possibles bags bunched into the same fist, when Chumley emerged from the fog with a knife.

His arms were covered in blood.

He wasn't grinning maniacally. He wasn't cackling like a fiend.

His face, which had been so animated earlier in the night—by excitement, by fellowship, by nervousness and at the end by humiliation—was now as blank and expressionless as a blackboard washed clean.

Cady screamed Gracie's name, but nobody replied.

She lost her footing as she gripped Smith's arm, pulling his aim off when he fired. The bullet meant for Chumley shattered the window of a store somewhere in the creeping dark.

The killer came on, not pausing, not even flinching. The long blade of his knife, painted with blood, seemed almost black in the weak lamplight.

His eyes were fixed on Smith, who had set himself to receive the attack and get off one more shot.

He never got the chance.

Before he could pull the trigger, Cady grabbed at the watch and squeezed. Twice.

CHAPTER FIFTEEN

INTERLUDE

The Watchmaker leaned over his workbench. He seemed too elderly to still be doing such fine work. His eyes were milky with cataracts, his fingers long and hooked into claws, the joints and knuckles inflamed with arthritis. The skin on the back of those pale hands was paper thin and dark veins crawled over them between liver spots and fine grey hairs.

The bench was long, disappearing into darkness beyond the fitful candlelight in which he fussed at an ornate time piece. Hundreds of mechanisms, tiny pieces of carefully crafted silver and gold, twinkled in the warm glow: pinions and pivots, balance springs and safety crescents, repeaters and meantime screws, all of them laid out on a large square of black velvet, weighted down at each corner with silver ingots.

The Watchmaker bent low to his toil. Lost in concentration, his breath wheezed heavily through his open mouth. His hands did not shake, however. The tools he took up, the calipers and stakes and files, he wielded with infinite precision and surety of purpose.

The chronometer in his old, gnarled hands was complicated. Such things always were. This was not the first occasion on which he had been required to tend to the piece. A small fault, uncorrected for too long, was threatening to turn into something of much greater moment. He shook his head, disapproving, but he was barely conscious of the movement, so fierce was his concentration on the problem. Long, grey hair, which fell in lank strands over his bristled, sunken cheeks, brushed the back of his hand.

He peered deeply into the works, resisting the lure of losing himself in there. Even flawed as it was, the timepiece was a construction of peerless beauty; its depths completely unfathomable to any not trained in the art. Whole worlds lay within when one knew where to look for them. So, too, though, the flaw which required his attention.

There could be no doubt of it. He'd had his apprentices searching, but perhaps that had been a mistake. Perhaps the real fault was his in not maintaining the piece properly.

He grunted, dismissing the idea. He had ever been the very model of industry and diligence. He would apply all necessary rigor and prowess to this present difficulty, teasing and probing and bringing to bear the hard-learned lessons of his long service to the chronometric arts and science.

The old Watchmaker rummaged through his tools, selecting a brass loupe with three quite particular bespoke lenses, affording him the magnification needed to peer into the works at the scale necessary to detect such an infinitesimal discontinuity.

PART TWO

CHAPTER SIXTEEN

It were a hell of a thing. Every goddamn time. Titanic Smith never did reconcile himself to it. There a man stood, in one particular time and place, and then there he did not.

He understood what'd happened of course. He and Miss Cady had traveled in an instant from Queen Victoria's London to . . .

Well, for a wonder, it looked awfully like her home town. If "town" weren't too meager a word for the vast and gaudy cordillera of colorful lights that climbed into the dark night sky down yonder way. He was certain he recognized that particular tower, the one that reminded him of a spear or an arrowhead pointed at the heavens. He'd seen some wonders the last thousand years or so, and that was one of them.

"Home," she confirmed, her voice shaking. "I'm home."

"Maybe," said Smith, who was a cautious man to begin with, and who had learned to give full rein to that native caution on the long, strange trail he had traveled since crossing paths with the Chinaman Wu.

And then the shock took his companion and she slumped against him, shaking.

"Oh, God, Smith. What happened to them? Why was Chumley there? What did he do?"

Smith thought she might utterly collapse and take to howling in the manner of an hysterical woman, but Miss Cady pushed away from him, standing a little apart in the night, her arms wrapped around herself as if to wrestle directly with the fear run wild inside of her.

"He killed them," she said, her unsteady voice almost, but not quite, wailing. "*Why?*"

"I do not know, Miss Cady," he returned, "but I fear now that Chumley may not have been as he represented himself. I fear that he may have been one of them that have been hunting me."

Her hands made a harsh whispering sound as they rubbed at the oilskin coat she had bought, either to warm herself or to calm the tremors that had seized upon her.

He could see it all contending on her delicate features. The distress and surprise of unexpected violence, the guilt of escaping, both of them at odds with the need to go back and help a friend, and the rational, intelligent mind recalling their greater predicament. When she spoke, her voice was brittle.

"But why? Why would he do that? Why would he pretend? Why attack Grace and Bertie?"

"I do not profess to know, Miss Cady. I am as unsettled as you by the incident."

"Incident? God, Smith! He killed them!"

"Figure as much. Don't know why."

"Can we go back?" she begged. "Is there some way we can help?"

It sounded less a genuine question than a desperate plea with no expectation that his answer would satisfy. Before Smith could even get going on a reply, Miss Cady had thrown one hand up as if to stop him wasting the effort.

"I know, I know. We can't, can we?"

"Not for twenty-four hours," he confirmed.

She shivered then, with a full body shudder that appeared to arise from deep inside.

"Oh, God," she said in a small, frightened voice, "Gracie, I'm sorry. I'm so sorry."

"Ma'am?" said Smith, unsure of how to handle her. She was obviously not given to the sort of frailty he might have expected from a citified young woman, but neither was she hardened by the experience of life beyond the boundaries of civilization, like so many frontier women of his acquaintance.

"Twenty-four hours," she repeated, looking around to take her bearings. "Right. So if I can figure this out, we could, like, step back a day from now and make it right?"

"Go back to London, you mean, from when we just left?"

"Yeah."

Smith shrugged in a gesture which committed him to no promises and testified to his paucity of comprehension.

"If you can figure to do that, Miss Cady, you will have set me on the true and certain path to my Elspeth, and I would do whatever you asked in the way of setting right those things we may have done wrong by our very presence."

She took a moment to stare into the distance where the city lights of Seattle blazed under the stars. He thought he could see tears in her eyes.

"What's the time? Right here and now?" she sniffled. "We should have noted that as soon as we arrived."

She was still upset, but he could see her choosing to dig in the spurs and ride the wild horse of her emotions into submission. He checked the watch, squinting a little under the moonlight.

"I would estimate we arrived here at a quarter of ten in the evening."

"All right," she said, through clenched jaw muscles, struggling to take control of her feelings. It was like watching her stuff one item after another into a crowded saddle bag. Guilt, fear, shock, confusion. Jam them all way down in there. "We need to check the date," she said, "and get a fix on exactly where we landed."

They were stood on the edge of a forest, by the side of a road, one of the wide, gloriously smooth stretches of black macadam he remembered from her world and a few others like it. The city was some distance away. Uncertain of the scale, Smith would not hazard a guess at how many miles. Those twinkling towers, he knew, were so much taller than the tallest building he had ever known before losing his way through the years that he dare not even speculate.

Miss Cady wrote something down in one of her notebooks, before hauling the binoculars out of the same bag. Her hands shook as she raised them to her eyes.

"Looks like a gas station just up there . . ."

The words fell away and she let the glasses drop.

"Look," she said, suddenly pointing and yelling. "Hey! Hey, you two!"

Smith peered in the direction she had indicated and after a moment he picked out the form of two figures, trudging away in the dark. A man and a woman, it seemed. Miss Cady cried out again.

"HEY!"

They turned. First the man, and then the girl, and Smith felt his testicles crawl up inside his body. It was exactly the same reaction he'd had the morning he'd woken up with a rattlesnake coiled at his feet.

He was certain he recognized the twin figures.

It was them. His own self and Miss Cady.

And then they were gone. Disappeared into a darkness as black as the feathers of a carrion crow. Miss Cady called out again and ran a little ways up the road, using the binoculars to search for them. Smith followed her, carrying the two bags, making sure he could get to his pistol quickly if needs be. He could see the tension in her outline as she searched, saw it ease off when she gave up and turned back to him.

"You saw that, right? That was . . . that was us."

"I believe so," Smith agreed. He passed her the lighter bag and she put the binoculars away before returning to the exact spot where they first arrived and making a small cairn of stones she collected by the side of the road.

"What was that? Some kind of reflection? Or echo or something?"

"Can't rightly say, ma'am. Never seen that or the like of it a'fore."

She shuddered as though feeling the same queer sense of revulsion Smith had just experienced. It passed and he saw the young woman gather her resolve.

"Right. When we leave next time, we leave from here and we wind the watch back by one minute on the hour. As soon as the twenty-four hours are up."

"Okay," he said. "You care to share your thinkin' on why?"

She stood up from where she'd made the small tower of rocks. Her knees were slightly muddy and she slapped away the wet dirt.

"My thinking," she said, "is still pretty basic, but here's a basic thought. You wind the watch forward to go forward in time. You wind it back to go back? Sound reasonable?"

He considered it.

"I believe you may be onto something, ma'am," he said. "Can't say as I have applied myself in any regularized fashion to such a formula. For a good long time I had not the foggiest idea of what was happening or even what role Mr. Wu's damned watch played in it, if you will excuse my cussing."

She afforded him a thin, strained smile that would have to make do as regards her forgiveness.

"I can't promise it'll help, Smith," she said. "We might try this on the next jump, and still end up explaining ourselves to Starfleet or running away from hungry dinosaurs. But that thing only seems to have two control mechanisms." She nodded at the watch in his vest coat pocket. "The hour hand and the crown. It's a pretty simple UI. Let's try the simplest affordances first. See where it gets us."

His comprehension of her meaning, the translation of the unfamiliar terms, seemed almost instant here. He knew what she meant by UI and affordances, even though he had never heard those words used in such a fashion before. Starfleet, too, he understood, as the name of fictitious space mariners from a story set in the far future, out among the stars. The watch told him so, but it helped that he'd been there as well.

They were nearly ten minutes walking to the gas station. Two horseless wagons happened past in that time, neither of them stopping or even slowing to offer a ride. Smith had some experience with these "cars" now. He could not drive one of course, and he had not yet ridden in one of the machines, but he was past jumping out of his skin when he encountered them. Miss Cady, naturally, thought nothing of the remarkable contraptions, cursing the two that passed by only because the drivers refused to pull over and allow them to climb aboard.

The stretch of road curved gently, but not so far that they ever lost sight of the small, single building toward which they walked. A gas station, it was called. A version of the stations where he had stopped for a fresh mount and supplies back in the Territories. The night was warmer than the cold, fog bound evening they had left behind in London, but it was still uncomfortably chilly, and once or twice, he felt light drizzle falling.

Miss Cady fell silent for some time after the unsettling experience of first seeing themselves, and then seeing themselves disappear into nothingness. Smith was willing to wager that she was lost in her thoughts on the significance of the matter, and for his part he was content to allow the young woman her ruminations undisturbed. It had taken her mind off the awful scare they'd had back in London and the terrible fate that had almost certainly befallen the couple she had befriended.

For his part, Titanic Smith had learned not to make friends during this whole forsaken misadventure. Such connections rarely broke even or well. Indeed, Miss Cady was the first person with whom he had even spoken for the better part of two weeks, other than brief exchanges to effect some necessary transaction while securing supplies or to seek information. Two weeks and many hundreds, possibly thousands of years. He had only intervened to protect her when the apprentices who had been tracking him suddenly turned their malign attentions to her. And having drawn her into a hell of his own making, how could he abandon her to whatever fate awaited the poor girl in the London of her past? It was a revelation and a blessed mercy to him that she had proved out so strangely well-educated on matters scientific and even resourceful on matters of a more practical nature.

It was no inconvenience, either, that she was right pretty to behold, even if immodestly dressed and somewhat difficult of temperament. Smith was man enough to confess that she had adapted to her situation noticeably quicker then he to his, and unlike him, Miss Cady seemed to have the scholarship required to apply some manner of method to unraveling their troubles.

A persistent drizzle settled over them as they reached the station. Signage proclaimed it a 'Texaco'. It was so very different from the remote depots and commissaries of his time, and yet there hung about it the same funereal lonesomeness. He fell in behind the local girl as she navigated her way through the mysterious installations and equipage of the place. But he also readjusted his grip on their travelling baggage to allow him rapid ease of access to his weapons. In Marshal Smith's experience, often as not, men were like to fetch up hard and angry against each other in a frontier terminus such as this.

"Just be cool," said Miss Cady as she pushed through the glass door into the harsh, white light of the building's interior. Everything smelled wrong to Smith, but then, everything always did in these places where he was not meant to be.

A bell rang over the door, taking him back to Fort Smith, where Thompson's General Store had enjoyed an identical convenience. But the man behind the counter was no Thurgood Thompson. He looked to be an Indian, in the original sense of the word. A dark skinned fellow with a towel wrapped around his melon. He was reading a book, making notes in the margins, and his tired watery eyes regarded them with blank indifference.

Miss Cady walked down an aisle piled high with brightly colored foodstuffs. Some of them he recognized as cookies and the sort of sweet treats a lucky child might find under a Christmas tree. A good deal of the merchandise was a complete mystery to him, but not as much of a mystery as the strange machine to which his travelling companion addressed herself. First, she fetched out her wallet, and then, from the wallet, a small rectangle of hard, brightly colored material. It looked to be about the size of a calling card. She fed it to the machine, which appeared to wake up at the prospect of the meal.

Smith watched as the young woman did something akin to playing a pianola, eliciting from the contraption a series of strange sounds. The next sound, which emerged from her, was even stranger and more unexpected. A series of curse words so voluble and foul he might not have expected to hear them from the worst sort of degenerate.

"Is there something wrong, ma'am?" Smith asked, and she surprised him again by laughing.

"Are you kidding me?" she laughed again. "No, nothing is wrong. In fact I think we got our first lucky break."

She held up a handful of banknotes, fanning them out like a card sharp on a paddle steamer.

"I'm rich," she said. "Like, crazy stupid rich."

She was shaking her head as though to deny it.

"I didn't know if my card would even work. I didn't . . ."

Another thought occurred to her, and she lost interest in explaining herself to him.

"Hey," she called out to the shopkeeper. "Hey, man, what's the date today?"

The attendant lifted his bloodshot gaze away from the book he was annotating and stared at her as though he did not understand. Smith wondered if he spoke English. Miss Cady folded away her money and the magical card which had conjured it up from the strange machine. She put both in her wallet, which she carried in the pocket of her tight fitting dungarees.

"The date?" she said again, then, "Don't worry."

Instead she plucked a magazine from a rack, drawing Smith's attention to it for the first time. He hadn't noticed the display in amongst the visual clutter of all the unfamiliar color and merchandise. His eyes went wide. More than half of the publications decried from their lurid covers the most confronting filth he had ever seen. It was a world away from the illicit reading matter they had spied back in London. Here, no quarter was given when giving offense. Smith actually stepped back into the shelves on the opposite side of the aisle, as though recoiling from a rabid dog.

"Thunderation!"

"This the latest copy?" he heard Miss Cady ask, as she waved one of the few periodicals not explicitly given over to depravity.

It was entitled *Who Weekly*.

"Yes, just in yesterday," the clerk assured her. He spoke with a natural American voice, at odds with the dark tint of his skin and the alien cast of his features.

She placed the journal back amidst the smut without so much as a blush. She noticed his discomfort and snorted with amusement.

"Don't pretend you haven't done worse," she said. "I've seen *Deadwood*."

Miss Cady›s demeanor had passed from shock and distress into something more adjacent to excitement. She took a small utensil from a rack next to the journals. It was encased in a hardened see-through shell of the wrapping material you saw everywhere at this place and time.

Plastic, as he recalled.

"I'll take the phone and whatever SIM you got with the most data on it," she said. "And if you could open up the blister pack for me, that'd be awesome."

Their transaction occupied the next few minutes, with Miss Cady asking a series of questions which could only be related to her new 'phone', a sort of personal, walking-around telegraph apparatus. He had seen their like in a number of times and places, but knew himself no more qualified to operate a phone than he was to control one of the horseless carriages. He had even seen the "cars" driving themselves around at one time and another—in a year far into Miss Cady's future, he presumed—but he had not the courage to climb on board for a ride. It was like this everywhere he went.

So much of his energy and concentration was devoted to avoiding catastrophe in the pursuit of the most simple aims, such as finding food and shelter, that he had not dared experiment with the local conveniences, lest they bring him undone. This was as true of his travels into the distant past as it was when he found himself adrift many years from now.

"Come on, Smith," Miss Cady said, her business done. She waved the phone at him. "We're catching a cab to my place. There's no Ubers anywhere out here."

Again, now that they were back in her native time and place, the translation of her meaning was instantaneous.

They were to take carriage to Miss Cady's lodgings.

CHAPTER SEVENTEEN

The accommodations were more pleasant inside the station, but Smith understood the reason why she had them wait outside in the cold rain. Their conversation would have drawn the attention of the shop clerk by reason of its insanity.

"We overshot by two and a bit years," she said. "We landed in February 2019 and about fifteen miles from where you time-tunneled us back to London. But, that's pretty good for my first spin at the wheel of the TARDIS, don't you think?"

"It is remarkable, Miss Cady," he said. "I don't cotton how you achieved such an end. I just been jumping around like a steer with a freshly-branded behind."

"Like I said," she explained, or tried to, "I just broke down the affordances on the user interface and worked backwards from there. Not perfect. We're still in the wrong place and time. But this is a hell of a lot better than hanging out with Queen Victoria. We can do this, Smith," she said, her voice bright with hope as she slapped him on the back in a remarkably mannish way, "I'm gonna get home, and you're gonna get home, and I think we can even restart the level with Gracie and Bertie."

The marshal nodded without conviction as he took in what she was saying and what all the strange words meant. She had certainly proved herself more adept than he at winkling out the correct usage of the Chinaman's watch, but she seemed to be discounting the interference of its guardians, the apprentices. They had not taken kindly to his employing the magical chronometer, and he did not imagine for a second they would approve of her gaining mastery over it. But Miss Cady was so transported by the success of her experiment and the theory behind it that Smith was not inclined to discourage her.

"So, we have twenty-four hours until we can try again," she said, thinking out aloud, "or a bit less I guess. What's the time now?"

He started to reach for the watch, but instead she consulted her phone, which turned out to be a timekeeper as well.

"Forty-seven minutes since we arrived," she mused, more to herself than to him. "That leaves us . . ."

She pressed at the glowing glass window, which constituted all but the entirety of the strange handheld telegraph machine. Her thumbs danced over the brightly colored illustrations as she cursed and muttered to herself about the "stupid android."

He wasn't quite sure what she meant. That small, quite amazing piece of glass was nothing like the robots he had seen in her future. Miss Cady ignored him as she worried away at the . . . phone.

"Okay," she announced at last. "I've set a countdown clock. We have 23 hours and 13 minutes . . . mark!"

Satisfied with whatever plan she had set in train, the young woman put away the device.

"I can't deal with explaining any of this to anyone right now," she said. "I wouldn't even know where to start or how much to tell. So I figure we can crash at my place, if it's still there, and if it's not, we'll just grab a couple of hotel rooms somewhere. I can afford that kind of thing now. Benefit of an enforced savings plan."

"You'll have to explain, I'm afraid, ma'am. I'll take your advisement that the watch translates most things, but sometimes you still leave me pondering your true meaning."

She smiled, and although it was a little ragged around the edges, it appeared sincere. She brushed a few stray strands of hair out of her face with a still shaking hand.

"Sorry," she said. "It's just so much, all at once, you know."

"I am the choir here that you are preaching to, ma'am. Yes. I understand."

She took a couple of calming breaths, leaning forward to look up and down the dark and quiet road as she did so. Keeping an eye out for their carriage, he figured.

"When I left, like, a day ago for us, but a couple of years ago for these guys . . ." She waved her hands airily, as if taking in the store clerk, the gas station, the whole world. "Oh, man, my parents are going to be pissed! I wonder if I should tell them, or just roll this timeline back? Anyway, a couple of years ago when I left, I had just finished . . ." She paused and seemed to consider how best to tell her story. "Let's say I had just finished a job, and I was due to be paid. Well, I've been paid, here, you know and . . ."

He watched as she struggled to come to terms with whatever had happened. It seemed absurd to him that she could so readily adapt to the madness and impossibility of traveling through the ages, and yet have difficulty accepting that she had been paid for a job of work. An errant gust of wind blew cold rain across them, and she shivered inside her oilskin coat.

"Anyway," she shrugged. "There's nine and a half million dollars in my account."

"Damnation!" Smith exclaimed, unable to catch himself before the curse left his lips. "Do please excuse me, Miss Cady," he followed up quickly. "It's just I have never heard of such a sum of money being piled up in one place by any one of my acquaintance, is all."

She seemed to regard his apology with wry amusement, and he remembered how unaffected she had been by the display of wanton carnality on the covers of the station periodicals. Smith reminded himself that this young woman might not be weathered by the standards of the frontier whence he had come, but she had grown up in a different world and it had obviously rubbed away at her in very different places. Given the curses he'd heard dropping from her pretty mouth, he was probably safe to suppose she was not much ruffled by his idea of strong language.

"That's cool," she said. "It gave me a hell of a shock, too."

And there she went, cursing again, although to be fair, invoking the name of Satan's playground was a mild sort of cussing compared to the way she had previously sulfured up the air.

"Anyway," she went on. "My cards haven't expired yet, and it doesn't look like anyone froze my accounts, so we have access to funds. As much as we need. We're gonna be good, Smith. We're going to work this out."

She punched him on the arm this time. Her spirits were lifting by the second. It was a most remarkable turnaround for a young woman who had been confronted by a homicidal maniac just a short time ago, and who had lost a friend, however recent of acquaintance, to the said same fiend. He could only put it down to Miss Cady's indomitable belief in her own abilities. She did seem convinced she could set everything right.

Smith chose his next words carefully. He did not much want to say them, but honor demanded that he give voice to the thought which had just occurred.

"You know, ma'am," he said, and she picked up on the somewhat formal tone of his address.

"Yes, Marshal?"

"Well, it seems to me, that unless you are all fired up to get back to the exact moment when you left, you have no real obligation to me, and good reason to bring our connection to an end."

She tilted her head to one side and examined him with a calculating detachment he had previously seen only on the face of one or two especially punishing defense attorneys.

"What do you mean, Smith? And remember, I don't have the universal translator. So keep it simple."

He shifted the heavier of the two bags from one shoulder to the other.

"I'm just saying, Miss Cady, that if you find yourself amenable to the current circumstance, I would understand if you were to decline the opportunity to resume a long and dangerous trek through the centuries with me. I did not intend to get you involved in this and I cannot in good conscience expect that you would extend your involvement were it no longer necessary for you."

Her expression was unreadable, but she did not dismiss him out of hand.

"Marshal, you take a hell of a long way around getting to your point, don't you?"

He smiled at that, and his expression, like hers earlier, was unfeigned, if a little frayed around the edges.

"Martha, my good lady wife, she used to say the exact same thing."

"Oh. Sorry," Miss Cady said.

"Don't fret none. She's been gone some years now. Scar still hurts, but the wound is done festering."

He sighed.

"I mean it though, ma'am. Looks like you got yourself home first try, or a lot closer to it than I ever did. Perhaps you should consider hopping off the train here. You've given me some pointers about how to use this thing." He patted the watch in his pocket. "I'm sure I could work it out from here. And as you have seen now, the olden days aren't always the best."

"What about the future?" she asked, and her eyes flickered with a small but undeniably bright flame of curiosity. "You've seen that too, right?"

"Some," he conceded, without giving more away.

She turned from him, staring up the road where two bright lamps were gliding through the darkness toward them.

The carriage she had summoned.

"You're a good guy, Marshal. And you're right, I might be better off here."

She turned back to him and he was surprised by how low his spirits sank when he realized that she was considering his offer.

"I can't promise to retrace your entire journey with you. In fact, there's no way I'm doing that. But, look, I won't send you off without at least working out some basic instructions for the watch. That might mean staying here for a couple of days, collecting more data. You know, sitting down, taking you through where and when you've been and the parameters of each jump. I'm pretty sure, given how well this one went, even with Chumley, that I can show you how to rewind."

"Fair enough," he said, although it was a heavy weight to pick up. She seemed to be quickly adapting to the demise of her London friends. Was she still thinking of "restarting their level?" Perhaps not, now. Smith lowered his gaze, ostensibly because the lamplights of their approaching carriage were uncomfortably bright to look at, but mostly so as Miss Cady would not see that he was discomfited by the prospect of their impending separation.

They had only been partnered up for a day, and Smith was surprised by how much he had come to rely on her, at least as far as understanding the watch was concerned. It had been a comfort as well, he had to admit, having somebody to whom he might turn and share his thoughts about the whole thundering mess.

*   *   *

The motorized hansom cab was a wonder. Not the first he had seen, of course. The last few weeks, Marshal Smith had witnessed such things as most men could only marvel at. But he'd tended to keep his distance and his head down. This was the first time he had been in any conveyance more newfangled than a stream train. He was no rube, of course. He understood that the "car" was no more the work of wizards or deviltry than the subways of New York, or the elevated rail of Chicago, both of which he had ridden on during the twentieth century.

But it was still a powerfully confounding experience to crawl into a stage coach without horses and light out across the landscape. Or, he corrected himself, along the road that ran through the landscape. As efficacious and well-appointed as this engine-driven cab undoubtedly was, Smith doubted it could keep up with a simple Conestoga wagon away from the paved roads on which it traveled.

Their driver—he was pleased to hear they retained the terminology of the wagon era—was a silent fellow who sat up front, while Miss Cady and he remained in the rear seats. They were more luxurious than even the finest coach in which he'd traveled before his misadventures. Although to be fair, he was not one given to wasting money on pointless luxuries.

Their baggage stowed in the trunk of the cab, Miss Cady and he shared most of the ride in silence. A strange and terrible noise filled the cabin of the vehicle, and it was some few moments before the marshal realized it was music. His companion occupied herself craning around, taking in the sights. One would have thought that she was the tenderfoot here, not him.

"Seems a little different," she said as they rode into the city proper. Smith was well past goggling at the architectural mysteries of any particular era. He had seen cities great and small now. He had seen them at the height of their power, and lying in ruins.

Miss Cady's lodgings were situated near the waterfront, a hazard-ous place for a young woman in almost any period of history, although in this, her native time, the docks and neighboring districts of this metropolis seemed strangely quiet. Smith could see that great earthworks and engineering feats were underway here. Whole blocks appeared to have been razed, and enormous mechan-ical cranes stood sentry over the open pits. Much of the construc-tion appeared to be the work of a company called 'Trump'.

"Ha. I guess he went on a tear after Hillary handed him his ass," said Miss Cady, without explaining further for Smith's benefit. He took it to be some local reference. "I was worried they would've knocked this place down," she said as they drew up to a large brick warehouse. It was framed in scaffolding and dressed with a motley drapery of ragged tarpaulins. But it was standing and in one piece. "Not sure why they didn't."

"Ivanka wants it for her new casino," the cab driver said over his shoulder. Also without explanation. Miss Cady didn't ask for one.

"Whole thing's tied up in court," he explained anyway. "Hell of a fight."

They exited and she paid the driver with cash money as he hauled their baggage from the trunk. She'd been frowning at her building, as though perturbed by what the driver said, but she soon found something else to vex her.

"Whoa. Seriously?" Miss Cady said as she handed over the bank-notes, and Smith thought for a moment that perhaps the carriage driver had tried to stiff them on the fare. "You're carrying?"

The man smiled. A happy grin.

"Yeah, it's pretty cool isn't it? You folks been away for a while, I gather."

The man pulled back the jacket he wore to display a pistol holster under his armpit. Smith tensed for an instant, and then relaxed.

"Haven't had a fare jumper since they changed the law," explained the cab driver.

Smith had not been expecting the man to display a sidearm, but he'd had enough guns pulled on him over the years to know that this fellow was simply showing off his piece. Men who did not really have to use a weapon as a tool of their trade were forever doing that.

"Your gentleman has a fine looking piece there, too," the driver said, nodding at the gun Smith wore at his hip. "Real old-school."

"Gets the job done," said Smith.

"I'll bet it does. What is that, like a .45 six-shooter or something? Looks like a real John Wayne antique."

"It is almost as new," Smith explained. "It's not my original sidearm, though. I had to replace—"

"You think we could leave the reciprocal genital inspection for later, boys?"

Miss Cady was standing by the bags, looking tired and unamused.

"Hoo boy, that's a cranky one you got there, buddy. Good luck with that," said the driver, and winked. He climbed back into his carriage and drove away.

"Jesus Christ," said Cady, causing Smith to wince. "My Twitter trolls and the Second Amendment. A fuckin' winning combination."

She shook her head, dismissing the man, and searched in her pockets. She found a single key and used it to open the main door of the building.

"No power," she announced, flicking a switch just inside the door to no effect.

Smith began to lower the bags, intending to hunt out a packet of matches, but she surprised him by pulling that small rectangle of glass from her back pocket and somehow causing it to throw out a bright cone of light. He had seen people obsessively worrying away at these gizmos in a number of different times and places, and had been naturally curious about what they could possibly be doing besides sending telegrams to each other. Cady somehow fashioning a lantern out of the thing gave him to understand that there was probably all sorts of utility he would never reckon out, packed away inside the darned things.

"Sorry, Marshal. But I'm up on the top floor and there is no elevator," she said. "Not that it'd be working with the power out anyway."

She moved up the staircase, leaving him to follow, carrying both bags. Smith said nothing to her, but he was quietly relieved to discover she lived in a normal building and not some strange floating bubble on top of a giant needle or suchlike. The warehouse felt cold and desolate, as though life had departed this place a long time ago. There was no sign of recent habitation, and every sign that the building was returning to a state of nature. Dust on the floor. Rat droppings. Spiderwebs everywhere.

"This doesn't look too bad," said Cady. "They must have a caretaker come in or something."

Her boots thumped up the steps in front of him, and he had to avert his eyes from her derrière, lest he find himself staring at it in absent-minded rapture. It had been many years since he had known the comfort of a woman. Not since sweet Martha had departed the world. Her memory made him blush at his wanton urges. Shame was no little part of the heat that burned at his cheeks, and Smith was grateful for the darkness.

"Now, one last boss battle," Miss Cady announced, as she wrestled with her key in the lock. "Damn thing always sticks," she said, jiggling the key so fiercely that Smith feared it might break off.

The latch clicked open, and she pushed a shoulder against the heavy steel door. It slowly gave way on squeaky runners. Smith laid a heavy hand on the cold steel and put some of his own considerable weight into the effort of shifting it

"Jeez, I hope someone looked after the cat," said Cady. No starving feline attacked them, and her domicile smelled musty and close, but it did not reek of dead animal. She flicked at another switch on the wall, again without luck. The room stayed dark.

It was not as pitch black as the staircase had been, however. Some light came in through the tall windows, even though they were too opaque to offer a clear picture of the outside world.

"Looks like the cops were here," she said, waving her makeshift torch around. "Maybe my parents, too, and Georgia. Looking for me, I suppose. Man, I didn't think I'd see this place again."

Smith could hear the regret in her voice at the hurt she must have caused her family and friends through more than two years unexplained absence. He took the burden of blame upon himself, for it was he who had given her to disappear.

"I'm gonna crash out," she announced, in a voice so unexpectedly free of guilt and contrition that for a moment he thought there must be a third person in the room.

But, no.

Miss Cady had simply moved on from whatever contemplation of regret she must have been entertaining.

"Sorry, Smith. My cot sleeps one and we're not bunk buddies," she said. "You mind sleeping in the armchair? You can put your feet up on the coffee table if that helps."

He dropped the two sacks with all their luggage to the floor.

"Ma'am," he said, "I could just lay my bedroll out on your hard floor there, and it'd be a princely comfort compared to some places I've dossed down before. But if'n you don't mind, I might just sit a while and keep watch. Until I know we ain't been tracked by Chumley or his ilk."

She measured him with a level stare.

"Nice bedtime thoughts, buddy. Thanks for that. Yeah. You can totally stand watch."

CHAPTER EIGHTEEN

She woke him the next morning with coffee and a sweet roll so sweet that it set his teeth on edge.

"Doughnuts," she breezily informed him. "That's how you know you've made it back to civilization, Marshal. Doughnuts and coffee."

Cady handed him a white cup, which appeared to be made of stiffened wax paper. Smith couldn't help but be skeptical of its beverage-holding abilities. He sat up in his chair and followed her example in sipping the coffee through a lid. It was black and unsweetened. Not as he preferred it, but as he was used to. Life on the back of a horse did not allow for luxuries such as cream or chicory.

Smith felt a momentary pulse of sadness pass through him at the thought of poor old Chester, lost somewhere on the ebb and flow of years.

He sighed, and the sigh turned into a yawn, and he realized, as he started to wake up, that he had fallen deeply asleep, in spite of his best intentions. He was seated in a surprisingly comfortable armchair, big and deep, and covered in old, cracked leather. He had meant to keep a look out for the apprentices, it being his experience that, if they were going to find you at any particular time, they tended to do so quickly, or right at the end of a stay, just before a feller jumped out of that little square on the calendar, usually with his six-gun blazing.

"You fell asleep," she said. "Figured you might like some sugar and caffeine to kickstart your heart."

"I do appreciate the thought, ma'am," he croaked, his voice still rough.

"Back to ma'am, are we?"

"It's only good manners."

"Would have been better manners not to snore so loud you knocked the dust from the rafters."

"Oh. My apologies, Miss Cady," he said, but she cut him off.

"*Ms.*," she insisted. "You're gonna stand out a hell of a lot more here than you did in London, Smith. Be a good idea not to draw attention to yourself with . . ."

She appeared to struggle to find her words, eventually shrugging in exasperation.

"Look, it's just good manners to call women "Ms." here. Anyone young enough that you'd feel comfortable giving them a piggyback ride around a pillow fort, you can call Miss. The rest of us prefer Ms."

Smith doubted that, but he was not inclined to argue. He was of a mind that Miss Cady definitely preferred "Ms.," but he would not take her word for every woman he might encounter. He'd had reason to converse with women born many years after *Ms.* Cady McCall, and they'd not come the high hat with him over his manners. But perhaps Wu's diabolical timepiece simply translated everything he said into whatever they needed to hear. Everyone except this little snapdragon.

"Got it," he answered. "Ms."

Cady sat herself down on the edge of her cot. She hadn't been lying or using some strange terminology about that. She had slept on the sort of fold up bed—a couple of crossed slats and a length of canvas—that you often saw in half-settled frontier areas like mining camps, where folks'd had time to attend to some of the basic amenities, but not so closely that everyone was sleeping under silken canopies in four poster beds.

"You sleep alright?" she asked. "I've crashed a few times in that chair. It's cool for naps but it's hell on your back if you spend a whole night there."

"I'm sorry I dozed off," he said. "And sorry I snored up such a storm. Been a while since I had anyone to complain."

She waved her doughnut at him, dismissing the apology, or rather the need for one.

"You and me both, Marshall. I been hacking away at my game up here, all on my lonesome, as you'd say, for about two years now."

She stopped, as if in mid thought.

"Four and half years," she said, shaking her head. "It's now four and half years ago that I wrote the first line of code."

She looked back at him.

"That seems weirder than having been in London yesterday. To me, anyway."

"Probably feels more real," he said. "London felt real to me. Real enough that if I'd been only two years off the mark, like you are now, I mighta stayed. Made my way home and found my little girl. She'd-a been young enough that I could've picked everything up again, I reckon."

Cady nodded slowly, as though measuring his words and finding them honestly spoke.

"You think I should stay here?" she asked.

In truth, he did. There were hazards in prospect that she could not yet fathom. But that's not what he advised.

"*Ms.* Cady," Smith said, "you got to make that choice yourself."

She smiled around a sip of coffee.

"You can actually get by without the "Ms.," too, if you like. It's gonna make you stand out just as much. Let's just roll with Cady."

"Cady," he said, trying it on for size. It fit. "Well, Cady. To answer your question, I don't rightly know what to tell you. You been gone a long while from home. That might be no never mind where I came from, and people were always moving around, disappearing into the frontier and such, but I would guess you have people here who were worried, and then frantic. To them, you been gone for years."

She looked around the small room where she had lived just yesterday, and many years ago. It was crowded with all manner of machines that Smith did not recognize or understand, but also with simple things that he did. The cot. The chair. A set of dresser drawers. Pictures on the wall. Books on a shelf. A bottle of whiskey. A leather satchel. And what he assumed were children's toys. For a full grown woman, she seemed to have a lot of little play figures scattered about her working desk. He knew the thing on the desk was called a computer, too. He'd learned that elsewhen.

"You sound like you think I should jump again," she said.

"I don't presume to think anything about what you should do, ma'am," he said, before quickly correcting himself. "I mean, Cady."

"Well, you're probably not wrong about peeps being pissed that I went dark. My folks must think I'm dead or something. And, man, Georgia. I gotta call her as soon as."

Smith took a long draw on his coffee. It was waking him up.

"I am your servant in this . . . Cady. You just tell me what you want to do, and we'll get it done."

"First thing, we got to clean ourselves up. There's a gym down the street. Was still there when we drove past last night. We can get day passes, use the showers and stuff. There's no hot water or power here."

"And then? After this gymnasium?"

"And then we go find out how much trouble I'm in."

*   *   *

The gymnasium was a strange place, frequented by even stranger people. There were some who had muscled themselves up into the form of human bison, all grotesquely oversized shoulders and chests and enormous gorilla arms, and that was just the womenfolk. The men were even more fantastical and mutated.

Titanic Smith's name was not to be taken ironically, however. He was a large man by anyone's reckoning, and he found himself having to endure the attentions of an obnoxiously fruity fellow at the counter who fussed about him like a giddy idiot. Miss Cady seemed to find a good deal of amusement in his discomfort at this, but she did eventually intervene to assure the dandy that he was wasting his time.

"Dude, forget it, he's straight. And he sleeps in his socks. His *unwashed* socks."

"Eww! Alrighty then. Showers down the hall to the left."

Smith was not the bashful sort, but he took his towel into the shower stall and closed the door behind him, locking it securely. There were people here, men and women and some sorts in between, who could have been mistook for buck naked, so poorly did their apparel hide their natural shame. The hot water was nevertheless a joy, and he wore down a bar of soap cleaning the trail scum and the years off of his hide, but he kept his clothes on a hook inside the stall and dried off and dressed in there, where none of the enormous fruits or muscle women could see him.

He met up with Cady in the entry foyer. She had changed into a fresh set of clothes, but looked almost exactly as she had before. The same color and style of form fitting blue denim trousers, the same undershirt worn on the outside, except with some very peculiar words stenciled on this one. CODE MONKEY LIKE FRITOS. Her leather jacket and boots.

Practical clothes, but not feminine in any way that Smith could credit, even though the outfit did show off her curves to good effect.

He admonished himself not to stare.

She was not his woman to be staring at. His woman was long gone and the daughter she had borne him was lost beyond oceans of time. Smith could have but one desire now, to cross those oceans back to his little one.

"You smell better, but your clothes are still rank," Cady adjudged without preemption. "We'll get your duds sorted later. Right now, we're taking an Uber to go see my friend, Georgia. She's cool. She's my bestie. She totally won't believe me when I tell her what happened, but she won't kick me to the curb, either. She puts up with a lot."

This last was delivered with an apologetic shrug and smile that was notable for its manifest lack of remorse. Miss Georgia, Smith surmised, would be putting up with more than her usual lot from Cady in the next little while.

The Uber was just another form of carriage for hire. The driver was another man with a gun who was appreciably chattier than the previous night's chauffeur. He wore a cap emblazoned with the words "WE'RE MAKING AMERICA GREAT AGAIN," and was in a fever to discuss some game of ball that had just occurred and was the occasion of a grave injustice done to a hapless company calling themselves the Hawks.

"Goddamn refs must've left their seeing eye dogs in the locker room. Could've at least bought us dinner before fucking us."

Smith ground his jaws together with the effort of not upbraiding this hooligan to watch his language around a lady, but while Cady would not engage with him, she seemed less vexed by his cussing than she was by his sidearm, which he wore in a holster strapped to his upper thigh. She stared openly at it, as though she had never seen such thing, even though she had just recently seen Smith firing his Colt at Chumley, and Smith had espied more than a few fellers and even some womenfolk getting about the town with their shooting irons on open display. The marshal did frown at the odd holster arrangement, adjudging the man's thigh to be a poor place to seat a weapon. He would struggle to unship the gun in the confines of the Uber, and the firing line into the passenger seats was all wrong. Presumably he had armed himself against his passengers, less'n his intention was to pop off the occasional shot through the window at passersby who did not share his affection for these luckless Hawks.

Of course, the weapon may have been worn simply to dissuade his poor customers from lodging complaints, because this feller thought nothing of them and only of his running ball game, on which he offered ceaseless narration and review. It did not matter to him that neither of his customers were in the least bit interested.

"Their secondary couldn't have been tired," the man continued. "They rode the Hawks receivers' backs the whole game. Just look at the replay. That back's knee was down a yard before the goal. That wasn't a touchdown. Not even fucking close! That was a bullshit interference call at the end. I wonder how much money the ref had on the game. Probably needed to cover the over under."

Cady ignored him after a few minutes, attempting some trick on her phone, but without success. Her expression grew darker, her brow more furrowed as they rolled through the city streets. It was early, and the traffic was much lighter than London's, but comparisons were pointless, thought Smith. This city was an entirely different creature to the one they had left behind. Larger, or at least taller, the way the buildings climbed into the heavens, and immeasurably more orderly. It was a clean place. They rode behind sealed windows but he fancied that if he could somehow open the aperture and put his head into the wind it would smell as fresh as any meadow, save for the persistent metallic tang that he could taste in the air of all of the cities he had visited after his own time.

"Her service got suspended," Cady said quietly, after a few minutes. "That's what it says. Not cut off. Suspended. By Homeland Security. For irresponsible intent. What the hell does that even mean?"

It took him, or the watch, a moment to intuit that this homeland thing was an instrument of the federals in Washington. Like Cady, he had no idea what "irresponsible intent" might mean. He had never tracked a man for any such offense.

"Hey, buddy," she said, riding in over the driver's extended monologue, "what's irresponsible intent?"

It brought him up speechless for the first time since they had entered his conveyance.

"What? You serious, lady?"

"Yeah," she said. "I got a message my friend's cell has been suspended because of irresponsible intent. What's that . . ."

Smith was thrown forward in his seat as the car screeched and stopped. It was like the driver had pulled the reins on a horse, but hellaciously more effective.

"You need to get out. Now," he said.

"But we're not even half way there," Cady protested.

He was not interesting in dickering.

"No charge. No problem. I won't report you. Just get out."

"I'm not doing anything until you tell me what's going on."

"Okay. Fine. I'm calling the cops," he said. "They can tell you what's going on."

"*You what?*"

Cady's voice was angry and confused. Smith suspected she was about to unleash one of her long streaks of foul language. He laid a hand on her arm and squeezed ever so gentle.

"We can walk. Or catch the omnibus. Let's go. Now."

They did not need to tangle with the local law. That sort of thing was almost certain to bring the apprentices. To the driver, he spoke in a louder voice.

"I'm sorry for your inconvenience, sir. We've been away on travel for some time. Please excuse our ignorance of your local customs and bylaws. I am sorry for the poor showing of your Hawks. They were undoubtedly robbed."

The man was sweating now. Smith had seen that look on any number of felons over the years. The driver was scared. Of being caught at something. Of the hard consequences that would follow.

"Come on, Ms. Cady," he said.

Smith struggled to open his door. The mechanism was unfamiliar to him. Cady did swear then, angrily wrenching her door open and barking at the driver to let her into the trunk. They had bags there; the bright pink valise she had taken to the gymnasium with all of her clothes, and a smaller pack she called a "go bag." It was essentially the possibles bag they had put together in London, reduced to the most essential items. The marshal slid over and followed Cady out of her door. The driver did not get out. He sped away as soon as Smith closed the back door.

The metal trunk in which they'd stored their luggage was still open.

"Well, that's a hell of a thing," Smith said.

"Something's wrong," said Cady.

"I don't imagine they'll be handing out any prizes for that observation."

"No, Smith. I mean it. Something is really seriously wrong. It's not just that guy, or Georgia. I don't know what's going on, but I'm starting to think we shouldn't be here."

They were standing by the side of the road in a quiet part of the city. A few cars drove past in each direction, but there were greater numbers of commercial vehicles carrying merchandise and stock. The city waking up, getting ready for the day. The buildings were tall here, at least to his eye, but they were not the soaring towers that reached up to the heavens from the center of the metropolis.

"Do you know where we are?" he asked.

"Yeah, we're good. Even if he'd dropped us somewhere I didn't know, I got the phone."

She turned a half circle, taking in their surroundings.

"We're miles away from Georgia's office, but her old apartment is only about a twenty-minute walk from here. Since I can't raise her on the phone, and there's definitely something going on, I think we should head over there. Check it out. She owned her place. Well, she had a mortgage on it. So there's a good chance she hasn't moved, you know, unless this irresponsible intent crap is . . ." She trailed off. "I don't know what it is."

"Nice enough morning for a stroll," Smith offered hoping to lighten her mood.

And it was. They had blue sky for a change, and although the air was brisk, it was dry with no promise of rain on the slight breeze. Felt that way to him, anyhow. He wasn't familiar with the local weather. It might change, but for now it was just fine.

"I guess so," Cady conceded. She tossed the small leather go-bag over one shoulder. "Could you carry this?"

She tapped the toe of her boot against the other bag, the bright pink one.

"Certainly," Smith said, wondering why she seemed reluctant to ask. Some of the heavier equipment was in that bag, along with her dirty clothes. Maybe that was it. She thought he'd be squeamish about carrying her unmentionables around.

"Lead on, McCall," he said, "and you can tell me why you've suddenly gone all squirrelly on this place."

They walked for a quarter of an hour, never leaving the outskirts of the city behind, but passing from a quarter which had been given over almost entirely to commercial enterprise into a neighborhood where many more people than businesses were domiciled. He smelt coffee everywhere, and sowbelly and frying eggs, all wafting out of the open doors of cafeteria and hash houses. The footpath soon filled up with men and women hurrying off to work, or strolling to their breakfast. They did not look so different from people of his own time, save for their unusual dress. The beards on the younger fellers would not have been out of place on the California diggings.

"I guess you didn't notice," she said, "because you're used to it."

It was a strange thing for her to say about her own time and place, and Smith wondered where she could be going with her thoughts.

"But both the cab driver and the Uber guy were, like, open carry Nimrods. Like you, you know, walking around with a gun strapped to the hip, except you're a cowboy and a marshal and that's cool. Those guys going around with all that artillery? Not cool, Smith. Not cool at all. And not even legal, I don't think. Or at least it wasn't when I was here two years ago."

"You're right," he said. "I didn't really cotton to it. In my day, and most other days, it seems to me, it's natural for men to get around armed. Truth to tell, it's kind of dangerous not to. So that ain't the case here?"

"Not in Seattle, it isn't no. But, I don't know. Maybe there was another shooting or something. Maybe the law changed."

She seemed more unsettled than would be justified by having seen a man with a gun. She hadn't blinked at his Colt, nor had she protested when he bought the rifle back in London. It was hidden away in her big pink valise, wrapped in a towel. They'd had to use the biggest locker at the gymnasium just to fit it in and the stock protruded from the handy zipper fastening even now. But there was no denying that Miss Cady was upset, maybe even on a deeper level than she had been by Chumley's attack. She had suffered a shock and understandable distress over the fate of her new friends. This current malady of hers seemed rooted much deeper. He supposed he did understand it. She had thought she was home. But maybe she wasn't.

He found the idea pretty damned unsettling himself.

"Anything else?" Smith asked, letting his eyes track over the street, scanning the faces for any sign of someone paying them undue attention. As unfamiliar as early 21st century Seattle was to him, it did not seem to offer any immediate threats.

"Well, the thing with Georgia," said Cady, as if that explained it, "and my apartment building. I don't know what's going on there, but it should have been knocked over or completely renovated by now. But there's something else too, something . . . I just . . . I don't know. Something's . . . missing."

They had reached an intersection, busy with pedestrians and motorized vehicles. Every second shopfront seemed to offer food and beverages. Other storekeepers were opening up for the day, readying their wares for the shoppers who would come in the next hour or so. Some of the businesses, he understood. A dealer in plumbing fixtures. A frock shop for the ladies. A bookstore inexplicably named "Amazon." Others, as with so many places, were utterly unfathomable to him. What in tarnation was a Sapphic Memes Dispensary?

Cady paid no heed to their surroundings. She attempted to contact her friend on the pocket phone again, but again, she shut down the device and jammed it away in her dungarees when it did not give her satisfaction.

"Still not getting through. Just the same stupid message."

"You want to go somewhere, sit down, try to figure it out? Perhaps there's a lending library in this town. Somewhere with a newspaper. You could study them. Surely if something has gone awry, there will have been reports."

She smiled at him, but it was a sad expression, almost pitying, and Smith found he did not care for it.

"I doubt there's any newspapers left, Marshal. Not real ones. You know, on paper."

What other sort would there be?

"But you're right. We'll have to do some research. First we find Georgia, though. Figure out what's up with her and maybe see if I can help. I got all this money to spend after all. It sounds like she might need a lawyer."

"Hope not," said Smith. "In my experience, needing a lawyer is one step removed from needing the undertaker to measure you up for a pine box."

He saw the pained expression on her face.

"My apologies," he said. "I did not mean for that to come out the way that it sounded."

"It's okay." She squeezed his upper arm. It felt like she was doing so more for her own reassurance. "I know you didn't. You're just being you, Smith. Come on. That Uber douche dropped us in the ass end of nowhere, but we're almost at her place now. We might get lucky and find her home. She didn't used to start work until mid-morning most days, anyhow."

He could tell that Cady was talking herself into believing everything would be okay. He let her have at it. Better that she convinced herself than that he fail in trying.

"And if she's not home," she went on, "we'll find a library or an Internet café, if they still have them, and do some research. I could do some on the phone, but the bigger screen would be better."

He let all of that sail past him, wondering how much of it he would have understood were he not in possession of the watch. Just the words, he concluded, not their meaning. He was learning that the meaning of words changed with the seasons.

Smith picked up Cady's bag and tugged at the brim of his hat to indicate that she should lead the way.

CHAPTER NINETEEN

Miss Georgia Eliadis lived in a much smaller, more agreeable tenement block than Cady. This was a real street, full of people's homes, not the industrial wasteland and waterfront construction site favored by his traveling companion. Although, to be fair, maybe the state of her neighborhood was one of the things that had unsettled Miss Cady. The longer they were in Seattle, the more anxious she became. She would not talk about it with him, preferring to remain alone with her thoughts, but her agitation was plain to see.

Her friend lived in a three-story brick building. It looked somehow new. That is, it looked new to him. To the people of this time, it was probably something of a relic, but a relic which had been lovingly maintained or restored. Moving up and down the years was powerfully confusing like that. The place had the air of a residence about it, with small pots of flowers and greenery hanging from window boxes, and a number of impressive velocipedes chained to a wrought iron fence at ground level. To Smith's eye they looked as though they might be faster than a horse at the gallop, and he could not be sure, indeed, that they were not. He had borne witness to stranger things. Peeking in through the windows behind the balustrade afforded him a glimpse into the domestic lives of the building's occupants.

A man was leaving as they arrived, and Cady hurried up the front steps to reach the main entrance before it closed behind him.

"Just going up to see Georgia in 4A," she said, when the man stared at her. He seemed to be searching his memory for her face. His surprise when he found it was obvious, and he opened his mouth to say something, but she had already brushed past him into the hallway.

"I'm with her," Smith said as he followed her into the building, leaving the man out on the stoop, gulping fresh air.

He could hear Cady knocking on a door just one floor up.

"Georgia it's me. Are you home?"

Smith arrived just as the door opened.

He saw an attractive young woman, dark hair, olive skin, a few inches shorter than Cady, her face a shifting mask of irritation, confusion, and finally, of shock. Then it looked as though someone had pulled her bath plug, draining her completely.

She swore softly, and her eyes rolled back into her head as she started to faint away and collapse toward the wall.

"Whoa. Down she goes!"

Smith pushed past, managing to catch the falling woman before she could hit the ground and crack her head. He almost knocked Cady off her feet in doing so, but she had the good grace not to chastise him for it.

"Oh, my God, she fainted! Georgia never faints. She could drop acid and watch a slasher flick marathon without batting an eyelid."

She was babbling. Letting her feelings gush out of her in words that weren't really meant to be attended on. They were just a blast of steam she was letting off. Smith carried the unconscious woman down a short, narrow corridor into an airy sitting room. Morning sunshine poured in through giant windows, taller even than he, throwing long shadows across the wooden floorboards. He laid her gently on a couch that was bigger than some beds he'd slept in. She was already stirring.

Cady appeared with a glass of water, familiar enough with the apartment to have fetched it without delay. Georgia's eyelids flickered open, and Smith stood back, allowing the young lady to see her friend first. She did not need to come to and be confronted by the sight of a giant stranger in her home. If she didn't faint away again, she would probably start screaming.

She almost did just that.

The poor girl drew in a sharp breath, gave out an involuntary moan, and actually scuttled into the corner of the couch, away from Cady.

Smith could not blame her. After all, she had just seen a ghost.

"Georgia, It's me. It's just me."

"Omigod, Cady. What the . . .? Who? No." And then she started hitting her friend, and crying, and then the two women were both crying and hugging, and Smith frowned, feeling uncomfortable at intruding on what should have been a private moment. He quietly slipped away to stand by the window, taking the opportunity to spy out the land. The streets below were unchanged. Perhaps a few more people were out, making their way into the day.

He wanted to give the young women some space and privacy, but did not feel comfortable removing himself from the room. He was certain Miss Georgia would not want some strange feller prowling through her apartment. And so he was required to stand vigil while they embraced and blubbered and said nothing of any note other than a condensed babble of apologies and recriminations and the peculiarly feminine nonsense of talking in circles.

"Where have you been? Where have you *been*, Cady? We thought you were gone. Your parents. Oh, my God, your parents thought you were dead. They prayed you were alive. Where did you go? Where?"

Cady wore another cuffing for the thoughtlessness of not letting everyone know she was alive, but it was a half-hearted kitten slap of a thing and she wore it without requital.

"Oh, this is Smith," she said, without warning, as though the little tap had only just shook free the memory of his being there.

"This guy?"

He felt obliged then to reintroduce himself into their circle.

"Titanic Smith, ma'am. Deputy US Marshal."

"My God, Cady, are you in witness protection or something? Wait. What? Titanic? Is that a real name?"

He had already turned out his lapel to show her his badge, and was about to crank up the same old explanation he always seemed required to provide anywhere but home, when Cady stepped in to forestall him.

"Yes. It's his name. He is a US Marshal, and we will get to all of that, I promise, Georgia. But I need to know what's going on with you. What's that creepy message on your phone about and what's this thing and . . . and what the actual fuck is up with everything. Seriously?"

That last was as much an exclamation as a question.

Smith watched as Miss Georgia gently fended off Cady, who was trying to touch her necklace. He had thought nothing of it at first, having seen so many wildly various types of adornment in his recent excursions that only the most unusual were like to catch his eye now. But there was something about how she touched it . . .

"Where have you been?" the young woman asked a third time, with frank incredulity. She was holding the thing around her neck in a way that caused a dread sensation to steal over Titanic Smith. He had seen men and women carefully worry at bands around their necks in just that fashion more than once: in the South, during the war, when his cavalry unit had come upon and liberated a band of negro slaves, of late absconded from their masters' plantation; and once during his enforced travels in a hot desert place, where brown-skinned men made slaves of their black-skinned brothers. He had not even attempted to liberate those poor souls, and his conscious failure to do so still gnawed at him.

Cady reached for the necklace again. For the collar, he corrected himself. Given the expression of shame and loathing that twisted Miss Georgia's face Smith had no doubt now that it was no lady's fancy, but rather a mark of punishment.

"Cady," she asked in a soft and shaking voice, "God, where have you been?"

It was her fourth attempt at having the answer from her. Cady turned to him, her face as marked by hesitation as was her friend's by humiliation.

"Ms. Eliadis," Smith ventured carefully, "Ms. McCall has been helping me with a delicate and dangerous matter. I'm afraid I'm not yet at liberty to explain further."

A second passed, and then another.

Smith did not know if the ruse would hold. He searched for a phrase he'd heard Cady use just that morning, appending it quickly when the words came back to him. "We had to go dark."

The young woman regarded him with suspicion, if not open hostility.

"Well, why don't you tell her what I did, Marshal? I'm sure you've got all the details at your fingertips. You people always do."

Her surprising animus forced Smith to move even further away from the literal truth of things.

"Ma'am, I can honestly assure you, I have no interest in your case. I do not know what alleged offense has brought you to this pass, or what circumstances might be raised in mitigation, but I am sure you must have had good cause for whatever it was you done. Your friend here assures me of your integrity," he nodded at Cady, "and for what it's worth, I am not blind to the faults of the law. I see them every working day."

It was not a speech he'd have wasted breath on for ruffians like the Buford twins. For them and their ilk, Marshal Smith had a short rope and a high branch. But Miss Georgia was not of his day, and whatever conviction had seen that odd collar snapped around her neck was no concern of his.

Her demeanor was defiant, right up until the moment when her face cracked and she started crying again. More feminine exchanges of hugs and embracement ensued, but this time Smith did not feel as though it was necessary to absent himself. He was, after all, the cause of her distress. He had to stand there and sup his medicine.

It took some time for the squall to pass, as it can with the lady folk, but when Miss Georgia was done a-wailing, she wiped the tears from her eyes and visibly gathered the reins of her emotions in hand.

She took a deep breath.

"Thank you, Marshal," she sniffled.

Cady squeezed her shoulder.

"Tell me what happened. What I can do?"

"I . . . I don't even know where to start. Everyone lost their shit when you went missing. You were on the news. You were trending on Twitter for like two days."

Cady interrupted her, but gently. "Yeah. I figured. It must have sold a lot of games. But tell us what happened to you."

"Well . . . they're sort of connected," she said haltingly.

"How?"

"It was Matt. He was . . . he *is* such a great guy, Cady. He never gave up looking for you. He kept your story running for months, but then they sent him to the wall, because he was writing things, and the government was getting angrier and angrier, and even Trump was tweeting at him at, like, three in morning, so you know he had his crazy on, and saying they were coming for him and—"

"Whoa," said Cady, as though trying to calm a bolting horse. "Just back up. What wall and what the hell does Trump—you mean *that* Trump, right?—What does . . ."

But her friend was staring at her as though she was genuinely crazy.

"Cady. Where have . . ."

Miss Georgia caught herself before she could ask the same thing a fifth time. Instead she turned to Smith.

"You went dark? How far off the grid did you go? How can she even be asking these things?"

"Ms. McCall has not been in correspondence with anyone for some time," Smith answered carefully. "She may not be as well informed of current doings or a-goings-on as you would rightly think."

Georgia stared at both of them then, looking as though she had awoken at last to discover mental patients loose in her home.

"Who is this guy? What's going on here? Is this a joke, Cady? Because you've pulled some pretty sick shit over the years, but this is not cool."

Cady leaned over as though to hug her friend in reassurance again, but this time Georgia pulled away. Cady made a face.

"Georgia, you would not believe me if I told you."

"Try me."

Smith wondered if they were about to get chased out into the street with a broom, but Cady surprised him by lying with all the polished sincerity of a New York carpetbagger.

"You remember the hacks on the Democrats? The Russian hack on Hillary Clinton's campaign? I got caught up in that. That's why I've been missing. They had to hide me from the KGB or FSB or whatever it's called now."

The extravagant lie—not even sprinkled with a light dusting of truth—served only to confuse the other woman. It did not do much for Smith's ability to follow along, either.

"But why would the marshals do that? Clinton's in jail. Both of them. Trump's not interested in getting to the truth of that."

Smith had been but a short while in the company of Cady, but he could tell she was reeling under invisible hammer blows. Although he understood in a literal sense what Miss Georgia was saying, he did not share a history with these two young women and could not say why this conversation should be so distressing.

"Trump?" Cady said carefully. "Trump is president?"

Georgia regarded her with frank disbelief.

"Well, duh."

"And the wall? He built his stupid wall?"

Georgia's face betrayed very real confusion and frustration at having to explain. Smith felt he should step in before this got out of hand. Cady, who had proved herself so much better at understanding the mechanics of the watch than he, was nonetheless having a harder time adjusting to the reality of what it did.

"He tried to build it," Miss Georgia went on, "but you know, that was always a . . ."

Somebody hammered at the door and a harsh voice yelled out, "Homeland. Open up! Now!"

Miss Georgia let out a terrible cry.

"*Oh, no!* I forgot. I forgot."

Smith reached for his pistol, and lunged for the pink valise where his rifle was wrapped up.

"No! Smith, don't," Cady shouted. "They'll kill you."

The door of Miss Georgia's apartment crashed inwards, and at least six or seven men charged in, all of them dressed in black overalls and helmets, their faces hidden by goggles. They were armed with weapons Marshal Smith knew to be far more deadly than his own, and they were all shouting at the three of them to get down and place their hands behind their heads.

He had kicked in a few doors himself over the years, and he knew he had a good chance of getting shot in the next two seconds.

CHAPTER TWENTY

Smith dropped to the floor, adding his own voice to those of the raiders.

"Get down," he called out.

He could not see whether Cady and Georgia did as they were told. One heavy boot came down on the back of his neck, crushing his face into the hard wooden floor.

"Armed. This one is armed," a man's voice yelled, just behind his head. Smith felt his arms expertly locked up, and his wrists shackled. The metal handcuffs bit deeply into his skin and more than one fist pounded into his ribs and lower back while somebody removed his gun from its holster. It was like being caught under the hoofs of a stampede.

He could hear the women screaming and men yelling abuse at them, swearing with unbridled profanity. He felt the heat of the angry offence he took at that burning through him, wanting to explode outwards, but he forced himself to lay still under the blows and the abuse. There weren't no call for using language like that against these women, but there weren't no point in getting killed over it neither.

He was pulled painfully to his feet. Somebody gave him a couple of kicks as incentive on the way up.

"Christ, this one is huge," somebody said.

Smith was no sooner to his feet when he felt the back of his knee kicked out. A solid blow propelled him toward the couch where Cady and Georgia were also trussed up like tiny Thanksgiving turkeys. Of the two, Georgia probably looked the more frightened and Cady the more furious, but her eyes were also wide with fear and shock. They were both shaking.

The violence of the break-in receded as the raiders assured themselves they had their quarry under control. Smith rolled his shoulders to work out some of the tension and impacted rage, and he flexed his wrists within the steel restraints that secured them behind his back. There would be no breaking out of the cuffs.

Half a dozen long guns were still pointed at them, mostly at him, and mostly at his face. A tall man, solidly built, removed his helmet and pushed the unusual-looking eye protectors up onto his forehead. They left a mark around the top half of his face.

He handed his weapon to another man.

No, it was a woman, Smith realized.

Now that he had some time to inspect the party at his leisure he could see that there were seven of them, two of whom were ladies. Not so long ago he would have been astounded by such a thing. Now, he mused, it was not even the second or third most surprising development he had encountered of late. Smith expected the boss man to address him, and was mildly taken aback when he directed his first comments to Miss Georgia.

"Ms. Eliadis, you are in violation of your detention agreement. You are not entitled to receive visitors without authorization from either the local police department or from your Homeland Security caseworker. Do you have a legitimate reason for breaching this condition?"

Georgia began to babble.

"I'm sorry, I'm so sorry. I didn't . . . I forgot. I just . . . I'm sorry, I forgot. It's just my friend . . . she's been gone, and I forgot . . ."

The official cut her off with a chopping gesture of his hand.

"Not good enough. You enjoy a lot of privileges under your sponsored detention agreement. Not the least of which is the ability to earn a living and remain in your own home. I am afraid you will be breached for this, and if it turns out you have been harboring other fugitives, your agreement will be revoked."

His words had a galvanic effect on the young woman. She let out a terrible, animalistic sort of sound that cycled up into a high-pitched screech. The officer winced and directed the other female in his posse, the one who wasn't carrying his weapon, to escort Georgia out of the room.

"I can't even hear myself think," he said. "If you can't keep her quiet, at least keep her out of here while I interrogate this pair."

He turned his attention back to Smith and Cady.

"ID cards," he said holding out his hand and snapping his fingers.

Cady jutted her chin at him defiantly.

"You handcuffed us, you idiot," she said, shrugging extravagantly to emphasize her inability to comply with his order.

The man stepped in and calmly backhanded her across the face. It was not a knockout blow, but it sounded like a stinger. Cady cried out as her head snapped back. Without thinking Smith launched himself up out of the couch. Or at least he tried to. He didn't have much leverage with his hands secured behind him, and the female officer who was holding her commander's rifle moved with much greater speed than he could manage.

She kicked him in the chest, fair driving him back into the depths of the couch, which scraped back a few inches on the wooden floor.

One of the other raiders—they had heretofore only identified themselves by the unusual name of Homeland—moved to unshackle Cady, presumably so she could produce these so-called cards. Smith had no idea what sort of document they wanted.

None of this struck him as being regular or reasonable. Since when did lawmen go around demanding the personal documents of citizens who had been doing nothing but visiting company in the privacy of their own homes?

Since sometime between his own day and this present one, he supposed.

Cady took her wallet from a back pocket and passed it to the commander with an unsteady hand. He looked at it, his face rearranging itself to convey an even greater measure of unhappiness at the offering, before he said, "What the hell is this?"

"My driver's license."

"I can see that," he shot back. "That's not what I asked for. Where's your liberty card? You know? The one with the chip?"

He spoke as if to an idiot child.

Cady caught Smith's eye. There was more fear and incertitude in that brief glance than he had seen from her in all of the previous day. She looked even more distressed, if that were possible, than when they had landed here with Chumley's murderous visage still dancing in their memory. The man turned to Smith.

"What about you?"

"Ain't got no card nor paper or nothing," he answered honestly. His marshal's badge, pinned to the underside of his coat lapel, seemed to be growing heavier by the second. Smith did not fancy having to account for it to this tyrant and his lackeys.

Cady tried to interpose herself between the two men.

"Georgia is my friend," she said. "I've been away. I just wanted to see her, is all."

The man laughed. A couple of his outriders chuckled along with him.

"Have you been living on the moon or something, little girl?" he said. "If she is your friend, you would know how much trouble she's in and how much worse you just made it for her."

"But I don't," Cady protested. "I don't know any of that. I don't understand. I don't know what's happening."

He smiled, but his eyes were cold.

"I can tell you what's happening," he said. "You're coming with us. Both of you."

Smith got to ride in another horseless carriage, but this one had none of the amenity of the last two. In a strange way, it reminded him of the stage coaches with which he was familiar. A big, black crate of a thing, it was obviously designed to carry a large number of passengers within its ugly, angular confines. They were rail-roaded out of the apartment, down onto the street and into the back of the six-wheeled vehicle in less than a minute.

Or at least, he and Cady were.

Miss Georgia was taken away separately. To what end, he could not imagine and did not care to.

He desperately wanted to reach into the pocket of his waistcoat to satisfy himself he still had the watch, but his hands remained chained behind him. He twisted about once or twice, trying to feel the weight of the chronometer, but a black-clad Homelander cuffed him hard upon the side of his head and warned him not to mess around; although, he used much stronger language than that.

Cady was trussed up a couple of places down from him, with two officers separating them, preventing any exchange of intelligence or even reassurance. The seating arrangement recalled the omnibus they had ridden in London, except here the passengers lined the walls and faced inwards. The Homelanders talked quietly among themselves on the ride to the jug—he assumed that's where they were headed—but Smith gleaned nothing useful from their exchanges. Mostly they seemed fixated on the same game of running ball as the Uber man had been earlier.

The marshal found himself quietly pleased that their team had lost.

The journey was no less comfortable than a coach in his own era, save for the pressing sense of confinement. The Homelanders' steel omnibus enjoyed only two small windows on the rear doorway, and they were protected by some manner of iron grillwork. Outside, the city rolled on with its business.

The trip came to an end inside the basement of a building. He felt them descend a series of inclines just before the vehicle drew up and a Homelander threw wide the rear doors. Strong hands gripped his upper arms and pushed him out. He looked around hoping to take a fix on their location but could see nothing but the grey concrete walls and low ceiling of whatever guardhouse now held them. He tried to talk with Cady, but got a baton in the guts for his trouble.

"Just sit tight, Smith. I'll get us out of this," she said and it sounded like the greatest of all the lies she had been forced to utter that morning. Her bold claim occasioned some hilarity among their captors.

They were quickly separated and he found himself at a counter, where a rotund, pasty-faced fellow relieved him of all his goods.

The deputies, if that's what they were, patted him down.

They found his Marshal's badge, and one of them bellowed directly in his face.

"What the hell is this?"

Before Smith could answer somebody whipped him on the back of his legs with a heavy baton. He had taken some whuppins over the years, and he was ready for this one. He did not go all the way down, which may have been unwise.

It encouraged one of the men to jab him fiercely with the end of his club, just below the rib cage.

That doubled him over with a loud "oof" even if it still didn't drop him all the way to the floor.

Smith would be damned if he was gonna roll in the dirt for these varmints.

"Impersonating a law officer? Oh, you are neck deep in the wet brown now, big feller."

They did not pummel him as he expected. Instead, one of the deputies grabbed a handful of his hair to haul him back upright. He was pushed into the edge of the counter, like a drunk with no credit being run out of a bar.

A Homelander deposited Ms. Cady's bright pink bag on the counter.

"Careful," he said. There's a loaded rifle wrapped in a towel, and the towel is really fucking rank."

His chums all laughed.

A deputy unlocked his manacles and Smith rolled his shoulders in relief and rubbed at the chaffing on his wrists. It was a fierce temptation to haul off and throw some punches around, but he kept his own counsel and thanked the good lord for an excellent opportunity to practice his saintly forbearance.

The pale-faced functionary slid a piece of paper across the counter and a large buff-colored envelope.

"Small personal items in the envelope, including your belt and any jewelry. Watches, rings that sort of thing. They all go in here."

Smith stiffened at the mention of his watch.

"All of it," the clerk insisted. "You'll get it back on release. You will be searched. Any contraband will be confiscated and a note of your noncompliance made to the court."

Smith did as he was told, but slowly, wondering the whole time if he might get away with holding on to Wu's chronometer. It was not like these fellers were familiar with pocket watches. They wore their timepiece on the wrist if they wore one at all.

He decided to hand it over. The bookkeeper here appeared to be making an honest record of his possessions. And as bad as it felt giving up the watch of his own volition, he could not contemplate losing it as contraband.

Smith took the small, golden circle out of his waistcoat and dropped it into the brown paper envelope.

It felt like letting go of a safeline in flood waters.

"Sign here," said the clerk.

He scratched out his John Hancock.

The man pulled a gizmo out from under the counter. It looked like a much larger version of the phone Cady was using.

"Place your hands on the scanner one at a time," he said.

Smith did as he was told. The window lit up with a bar of blue light and he snatched his hand away, earning him a rebuke from the clerk and another quick baton-whuppin from the Homeland deputies.

"Please leave your hand in place until the scan is complete, sir."

He complied with some reluctance. It would hurt a lot less than a billy club to the kidneys.

The clerk then produced a tiny white stick and told him to open his mouth for the purposes of collecting his saliva!

"The hell I will. I ain't no droolin' lackwit."

One of the deputies spoke up. "Open your mouth, or I'll fucking tase you, and we'll take the swab anyway."

Without the watch, he did not understand what they meant by "tase," but he did not seem well situated to make inquiries.

Smith opened his mouth. The clerk pulled on a pair of thin rubber gloves and swabbed the inside of his cheeks.

And it was done.

They had taken everything. His weapons. Supplies.

And the watch.

His heart slowed, then sped up as he looked on helplessly while it disappeared with the clerk and the rest of his other things.

In all of his misadventures, he had never once lost control of Mr. Wu's chronometer.

Icy fingers traced a delicate dance up his spine.

The deputies were not of a mind to have him standing around contemplating his lot, however. Smith soon found himself hurried along. In less than a minute, he was sitting at a table in a plain, boxlike room, three bare walls and a large mirror wherein he could watch himself be chained to a steel hoop affixed to the metal tabletop.

"There you go, Buffalo Bill," one of them joked. Or Smith assumed he was joking. "All trussed up for the slaughter pen."

Both of the Homelanders laughed.

Of the many low places he had fetched up since losing his way, this felt like one of the worst.

The men who secured him did not stay. Smith was left to stew in his own juices, but that did not much bother him, as they had surely calculated it must. He was awake to that game.

No, he was much more concerned at losing the watch, at least to begin with.

Granted, he had not lost it as such, and they had the better part of the day left to reclaim it, but at 9:45 in the evening it would pass from its current inert state into something akin to a loaded gun with the hammer cocked. Just one squeeze on the trigger and whoever was holding that thing would be gone, along with his only way back to little Elspeth.

If Smith allowed himself to dwell on that circumstance, it was quite possible that he would go quickly and quietly mad. So, as difficult as it was, he tried to empty his head of such thoughts and waited instead for the questions he knew were coming. He needed to convince these people he was no lawbreaker.

He did wonder whether he would understand them, given that he had lost the watch and with it the translation of all that was said to him. But, "tasing" aside, he took some comfort from the relative ease with which Miss Cady had conversed with the natives of old London.

Smith snorted softly and shook his head at that.

He had readily taken to thinking of it as "old", adopting her perspective, when in fact, to him, the London of the late 1880's had been a marvel of the future, with industries and conveniences almost impossible to imagine out on the wild frontier of America.

There was no accounting for how much he'd had to adjust his thinking since this began. Sometimes it felt like trying to hit a mirage with a rifle you just knew did not have the range anyway. Sometimes he just gave up and waited. More'n once he'd landed somewhere with fair shelter and clean water, with hard tack and salt meat in his viands bag, and no earthly idea of where or when he'd fetched up, and so he waited for the watch to run down its twenty-four hours.

This helpless passage felt akin to that, but without the prospect of resolution at the end. It was a miserable interlude, but there weren't nothing to be done but the enduring of it.

And so he waited.

And he waited.

And he waited some more.

Eventually Smith had been so long in waiting that he desperately needed to relieve himself, but he was chained to a table in a room with no facilities for a man to make his water.

This, too, he thought likely a stratagem by his captors, and as much as he thought ill of them for the low cunning of if, he had to admit to its effectiveness. He was getting to bursting point and could see only two ways forward. Either he wet his britches, or he cried out for help.

The discomfort had become real pain by the time he folded.

"Hey!" he yelled out, and was surprised by how loud his voice was in this small, bare box of a room. "Hey! A feller could use some relief in here. Less'n you want to have to mop up after him. And believe me, you don't."

Nothing.

Another minute passed. A minute which convinced him he was not far from shaming himself.

"HEY!" he shouted.

The door opened.

It was not the man who had arrested them. This one was dressed in a civilian suit, not too remarkably different from the duds a Philadelphia dandy might wear. He was followed into the room by a woman, dressed in a similar fashion to Cady.

The man tossed something at him, getting a reaction from Smith, who flinched.

It was his badge.

It landed on the table top with a harsh, metallic ring.

"So, Marshal Smith, is it?"

He summoned up what dignity he could, vowing to himself that he would not be chivvied into reaction.

"John Titanic Smith, sir," he said, his eyes watering with the terrible pressure of his need for relief.

"Titanic? Really? And you're sticking with that?"

"Goddamn you," Smith snapped. "You need to bring me a bucket or take me to the outhouse, but you need to do it now, less'n our accommodations here are to get filled to the brim with my waters."

The woman seemed amused.

Her offsider merely nodded, as though happy to have proven something to himself. He produced a small key and unchained Smith while the lady stood back, her hand ostentatiously laid on the grip of her pistol.

"Come with me," the man said.

Smith did not need telling twice.

There were a couple of uniformed fellers waiting in the corridor outside. They escorted him to a bathroom that was just two doors down and watched on while he stood at a steel trough and let loose a geyser.

Never had he known such a merciful release. He groaned with the dizzy pleasure of unleashing the flood torrent of his own personal Mississippi.

After washing and drying his hands, he was returned to his cell and refastened to the table. Smith was not inclined to protest. He was grateful for not having been forced to wet himself, especially in front of a woman.

She scraped a chair across the floor and set herself down opposite him when he was fixed to his restraints again.

"So," said the woman. "Marshal John Smith. Is that who you say you are? John Smith? Seriously?"

"That is my name. It is no nevermind to me if you do not care for it."

The man did not sit down in the empty chair next to his colleague. He leaned over the table. Loomed over it, to be entirely accurate.

"I'm Special Agent Brubaker," he said, "and this is Special Agent Forsyth, and for what it's worth, no we don't care for it, Mr. Smith. And Homeland Security especially does not care for people like you putting themselves about as officers of the law."

Smith held on to his temper. He was still feeling oddly well-disposed to them after his toilet visit, but he did not take well to having his integrity questioned. It was not his way to take any man's insolence without a due and dispassionate reckoning.

He uncurled his fingers, which had started to bunch into fists.

"I do not recall representing myself as a peace officer to you or to any of your hired janissaries," he said. His voice was low, and he took a breath and attempted to sound less like a mountain bear woken hungry from its hibernation. "Do they allege that I did?"

The question seemed to bring them up short. But Smith had a bad moment when he remembered he had indeed introduced himself to Miss Georgia as a marshal. Had they spoken to her yet? They must have. It had been hours since their arrest. Had he just stepped into a trap of his own setting?

He tried to stop his fears running off with his reason. Chasing down their own panicked thoughts was what brought most men undone when answering to the law.

"We have the badge," Brubaker said nodding to where it lay on the tabletop. Smith did not attempt to pick it up. Had he not been restrained, he still would not have done so. The less connection between him and his badge, the better it seemed, at least for now.

"It is a genuine antique," he improvised, "from the western district of Arkansas. Somewhere round the 1870s according to the feller I bought it from. If you were even halfway competent investigators, you would know that. But from what I've seen of your operations this morning y'all ain't much better than bandits."

It was rank foolishness baiting them like that, but it felt like a cool drink of water in the Arizona Badlands. Got a response, too. The lines of Forsyth's already sharp features seemed drawn just a little deeper, and Brubaker's eyes darkened with such malevolent intent that Smith thought it entirely likely he was about to get himself severely beaten.

"Do you know how many John Smith's there are in America right now?" Brubaker asked. He answered his own question almost immediately. "Just a touch over seventy-four thousand," he said. "None of them are federal marshals though. There was a special agent John Smith of the FBI, but he retired. Probably a whole heap of them over at the CIA. And here and there we got a couple on this or that local police department. Patrolmen, detectives. Nothing special. But no John *Titanic* Smith in the US Federal Marshals. In fact, no John *Titanic* Smith anywhere. Seventy-four thousand John Smiths to choose from, and you aren't any one of them. You aren't anybody as far as we can tell. So, you wanna tell us who the hell you really are. My colleagues will have it out of your accomplices before I sit down to dinner tonight, so best you just give it up."

Smith wasn't sure what was happening here but he did not like the tone of this man or the description of Cady and Georgia as accomplices.

"I have told you my name," he said. "I don't have any others to give you."

Brubaker looked as though he'd be more'n happy to pick away at this particular mystery for hours, but his colleague Forsyth decide to shake the pan.

"All right then, Smith. What were you doing at Ms. Eliadis's place this morning?"

"T'weren't doing nothing," he said. "Miss Cady and she are friends. Real wheel horses, they are. Ain't seen each other for a while, though. It was just a courtesy call, was all."

"What are you, Cletus the slack-jawed sheriff of Yokeltown or something?" said Brubaker. "Ain't nobody done talk like that no more, *pardner*. So lay off the audition."

He leaned in over the table to emphasize the gravity of his intent.

"You were detained at the address of a known political felon, a serial offender convicted of multiple counts under the Gowdy-Chabot Act and of criminal trespass on a Federal security reserve, and while there of aiding the attempted escape of a declared alien descendant, one Matthew Aleveda. The only reason Ms. Eliadis isn't back down in Texas helping Señor Aleveda build the wall is that her employers made a strong case to the community sentencing panel that a crucial commercial project would be unduly disrupted were they to lose her services."

"Hence her home detention," said Forsyth, as though that explained everything.

"And hence you are in a world of hurt for breaching that detention agreement without written permission or clear and present justification," said Brubaker.

So, thought Smith, turns out old Wu's watch has indeed been doing a powerful job of translating the gibberish these people speak. He had a bit less than half of no idea what in hell they were talking about. His blank expression served only to further inflame Brubaker's rage.

"And to add to all of this, you not only breached a federal security agreement, but you did so in the company of a woman who has been missing, presumed dead for over two years."

Cady.

Smith felt as though solid ground was slipping out from beneath his feet. This did not feel like an encounter that was going to end with them pointing him to the edge of town and giving him a warning not to come back.

"Well, I only just met Miss Eliadis," he offered, hating the weasely sound of it as the words came out of his mouth.

He was starting to wish he'd gone for his guns back at the apartment building. Seemed to him he might've had more chance of shooting his way out of this trouble than he did of talking his way through it.

"Why don't you let us help you," said the woman, Forsyth. "Just help us and we can help you."

Her tone and manner were much softer than Brubaker's. But while she seemed more reasonable than her colleague, there was something of the rattler about her, Smith thought.

"I would like to help you," he said. "But I don't know what you want. You asked my name and I told you. You didn't take to that, but it's the only name I got. You asked me what business I had with Miss Eliadis. I'm telling you I had none. I did not know her or even know of her until this morning."

"And the other girl," snapped Brubaker, "the one you kidnapped?"

"The hell I did," Smith said, his voice much louder than he'd intended.

Without knowing why, Brubaker had struck a raw nerve. Fact was, Smith had been feeling guilty about having got Miss Cady caught up in his problems.

Hell fire.

How long could it be now a'fore those apprentice sons of whores showed up? He half-expected Chumley to walk in through the door at any second with a cold smile, a new suit, and a long knife.

"Is that what happened, John?" Forsyth asked gently. She gave no hint of having been upset by his outburst. "Did you take Cadence two years ago? Have you only surfaced now because you could finally trust her not to run away?"

Smith looked at her as though snakes were slithering out of her mouth. Where did she get these plumb crazy notions?

"You stash her away somewhere off the grid?" Brubaker asked, his tone a good deal more confronting. "Is that why you're a ghost, Smith? What are you? Really? Political? Ex-military? Alt-Right Militia? It'll go better for you if you just tell us now. Maybe you should think about the shit we'll dig up when we really start looking into your history."

Titanic Smith laughed then.

A rich, peeling baritone burst of laughter at the absurdity of his situation. It was his interrogators' turn to look as though they were the ones stuck in a room with a crazy man.

"History," he said. "You have no idea."

Special Agent Forsyth leaned toward him and held his eyes with hers. It was quite the trick. She must have been practicing it for years.

"Then help us understand, John," she said. "Tell us what we don't know."

The only door to the room opened while she was speaking.

A man entered. Another civilian. Not one Smith had seen before.

"What I know," said the stranger, "is that this interview is over."

CHAPTER TWENTY-ONE

Until now, the appearance of a lawyer in his life had never been cause for celebration. Even the county prosecutors with whom he had dealings in the course of his marshaling duties were as like as not to occasion vexation. They were forever demanding to know why he had shot some rascal instead of bringin' him to court, or why he'd brought some other ruffian a'fore the bench when, on the paucity of evidence, it might have been better to just shoot him and be done with it.

There was never pleasing a lawyer.

But this one was definitely in the way of pleasing Smith, if only because of the instant look of peptic displeasure his arrival elicited from Agent Brubaker. Even the charming Miss Forsyth appeared more than somewhat irked by his sudden appearance.

"Mr. Smith, my name is Thomas Calvino, and I have been retained by Ms. McCall in the matter of your unlawful arrest. I will take instructions from you in that matter right now, and we can discuss the settlement you will receive from Homeland Security when we sue them in due course."

Smith wasn't entirely sure what this Calvino character meant by all that, but he could see that Brubaker and Forsyth understood, and they did not enjoy it at all.

Calvino strode up to the table and banged a leather briefcase down on top of it, before turning his attention to the Homelanders.

"Undo the cuffs and either charge or release my client immediately. You've had your fun. Playtime is over."

"Your client has questions to answer, Calvino," Brubaker shot back. "He's impersonated a Federal agent. Probably kidnapped a young woman. Breached a security agreement. And he's a ghost. He doesn't have an identity card. He doesn't have an identity!"

Calvino smiled.

"I am advised that Mr. Smith is a professional cosplayer and collector of western antiques. He did not represent himself to your officers as a federal agent, and neither Ms. McCall nor Ms. Eliadis have made any such allegations. They will not be doing so. Ever. The alleged breach was a minor infringement and we both know that with my clients' spotless records and unimpeachable skin color, you will get nowhere with it. As to Mr. Smith's identity, it is not yet a crime to go without an identity card, merely an inconvenience. So, release him or charge him. By all means, I would welcome the opportunity to seek vastly aggravated damages from your department when we litigate the civil case with all dispatch."

It sounded like lawyers had lost none of their taste for codswallop and gobbledygook since Smith had last dealt with one, but in this case, the lawyer's mouthing off was all for his benefit. Smith merely sat back and smiled.

He guessed that it had been nearly four or five hours since he'd been chained to this table and, unlike him, Cady had obviously been busy. He did not care to contemplate how this encounter would have played out for him had he not been allied with someone who knew what she was doing.

And had the wherewithal to do it, he added to himself.

Calvino did not look like the sort to work for charity. His suit was immaculate, his shoes highly polished. Everything about him reeked of money and connection. Smith would normally have hated him on sight, but he felt quite warmly toward the feller right now.

Brubaker did not.

His face looked like a bowl of egg custard gone rotten in the sun.

He dug out a small set of keys and tossed them across the steel tabletop where they fetched up against the thick metal hoop to which Smith was chained.

"Do it yourself, *Marshal.* You should know how."

Miss Forsyth's caring and helpful persona, Smith noted, did not extend to helping him with the awkward task of undoing the manacles while still fastened securely by them.

Calvino actually rolled his eyes.

"You're not helping your case, agents," he said, and shooed Smith away from his efforts to free himself. He leaned over the table to pick up the key. It slid into the lock and with a quick turn the cuffs fell open.

The most noteworthy aspect of the whole exchange was how extravagantly perfumed the lawyer was. Titanic Smith had never smelled so fine a feller in his whole life. It was like he'd been dipped in a bath of exotic spices, and Smith could only wonder what he made of the reek emanating from his client.

Or at least from his client's trail-worn clothes.

At least he'd been able to scrub himself at the gymnasium this morning, another tick in Miss Cady's column.

"They took all my things," he said to Calvino.

"Standard processing," the lawyer assured him. "But if there is a problem, please do not hesitate to call my office."

He turned on the Homelanders.

"I'm certain the department's legendary administrative efficiency will not fail you, Mr. Smith. I would be most surprised to find otherwise."

It sounded like a threat.

Chair legs scraped as Forsyth pushed back from the table and stood up. Brubaker was already halfway to the door.

"Enjoy it while you can, Calvino," he said over his shoulder. "My personal hero, the US Attorney General, is about three weeks away from putting you fags out of work."

Smith did not know what the agent was talking about, but for a man who had just been convincingly bested, he did seem to be recovering his mood.

Calvino, on the other hand, appeared quite somber, now the agents were leaving.

"Come on," he said. "I don't like to spend any more time here than is absolutely necessary. And I have to get back to my office. Ms. McCall wants me to file on behalf of Ms. Eliadis's fiancé. That won't be easy. Once they go to the wall, they rarely come back."

The words, as had been the case from the moment he lost the watch, made only a simple kind of sense. He understood them, but not whatever deeper story they were meant to tell.

"I thank you for your efforts, Mr. Calvino," Smith said as they left the small room. "You did a fine job of work on old Brubaker there, chipping his horns. But I really need to get my possibles back. And I'd like to find Miss McCall and Miss Eliadis as quick as I might."

Calvino examined him, his eyes crinkling.

"Miss Eliadis was processed out two hours ago. She should be home by now, working. She needs to meet her KPIs to maintain her detention agreement. It's the only thing keeping her off the Wall. I would strongly advise you not to approach her again, and if you could emphasize the importance of that to Ms. McCall I would be grateful."

He paused, and a rueful shadow passed over his face.

"It really is as though she's been living on another planet for the past two years."

"I can set with that," Smith agreed. "So. No talking to Miss Georgia."

"You can communicate with her via my office. But her personal communications are monitored, and if you breach the order a second time I'm afraid I won't be able to spring you as easily."

"Right you are then," said Smith. "And Miss Cady?"

"Should be waiting for you in reception. Your personal items will be returned to you there, although you should expect them to take their time about it. They can be unbelievably petty."

They walked down a short hallway, almost as featureless as the room in which he'd been questioned, passing by Homelanders, uniformed and not, who saw Calvino and mostly ignored him. A couple did favor them with hard looks and unpleasant regard.

It meant nothing to Smith, who'd run his own lock up for long enough to be used to such ridiculous displays of plumage.

Calvino pressed a button in the wall at the end of the corridor, causing two doors to slide open onto an elevator room—an arrangement not unlike the mule driven cages he had seen miners ride up and down in the Kentucky coal diggings.

"I understand your reluctance to carry an ID card, Mr. Smith," Calvino said, as they rode up. "They are an abomination. But I would advise that it's only going to get harder to do without one. Especially for someone like you who is in the system now. I'm afraid they've got your number, along with your DNA and hand prints."

"I'll consider it," Smith said, knowing he'd do nothing of the sort. He guessed they had a picture of his hand in that infernal machine he'd been forced to touch earlier in the day. What good that would do them, he did not know. And this "dee-en-ay" was likewise a mystery he did not care to look into. At a guess, Calvino appeared to be advocating that he register himself with the government less'n he be harassed over his preference for privacy; an outrageous idea at any time. But given his intention to quit this time and place as soon as possible, Smith did not mind leaving the lawyer with the impression that he would play along.

All he wanted was to get gone with his watch and Cady, assuming she was of a mind to tag along.

Turned out she was. Cady McCall was waiting for them in the anteroom of the Homeland barracks, a grim little space cut-off from the rest of the building by design. She sat on a concrete bench, her hands clasped between her knees, which were bouncing up and down as she tried to work off her nerves.

"Ms. McCall, I hope you haven't been put to any further inconvenience," Calvino said as soon as he saw her. She looked up, and her expression brightened just a little, but it was a candle flickering in a long night of high wind.

"Haven't been hassled, if that's what you mean," she said, "but they wouldn't tell me where you guys were, and they won't say what's happened to Georgia. I'm worried about her, Tom. I just wanted to help."

Calvino silenced her with a shake of his head.

"My job is to help. Leave it to me. Ms. Eliadis is safe at home, and my colleagues at the firm are already working on her case. We'll make all of this go away," he promised, seeming to take in the entire edifice of the Homeland building.

Smith doubted anything like that would be happening quickly, but Calvino's promise went some way toward lifting the pall which had settled over his traveling companion. The confidence and hope which had illuminated Cady when she'd woken him with a sweet roll and a cup of coffee, was entirely gone. In its place Smith found a haggard vision of a woman on the first step of the gallows.

"Thanks," she said. "I really appreciate that. Did you get the retainer? Did that money go through? I don't want there to be any problems."

"You are not to worry about that, Ms. McCall," Calvino said. "My firm has been in contact with your bank and explained that you have returned from a long trip and that they can expect renewed activity on your accounts. We have further informed them that we now act for you, and that should any federal agency attempt to place any lien or caveat over your assets, we are to be informed immediately. I have also given them to understand that we will seek punitive redress for any action they take in such matters without such notification and without our written consent."

His manner softened, just a little bit.

"We might be losing our rights, but the administration still respects the rights and privileges of money, and you have plenty of that."

Buoyed by her lawyer's fighting words, Cady gathered her resolve and pushed herself up off the cold concrete block which did for public seating in this place.

"So, we just wait here for our personals?" Smith asked. He could see that, like him, Cady had not had her bag or other possessions returned. Calvino looked pained.

"I'm afraid so," he said. "There's not much I can do about that. It's just one of the stupid little games they like to play with people."

He looked at his watch. Smith would have bet good folding money that it was made out of gold. He wondered how much Cady was paying this man and his law firm.

"I can stay with you if you would prefer that," Calvino offered, "but I honestly think they might drag the whole process out a lot longer if I did. And I can be of more help to you back at my office."

"That's okay," said Cady. "You go, Tom. I don't have my phone back yet, but there's a 7-11 down the street. I can just get a burner from there if I have to call you. If I think they're jerking us around," she added.

"Please do, and quickly," he said, offering her a professional smile and a handshake before turning to Smith. A thought occurred to him. "You'll need money for a phone and incidentals, maybe a cup of coffee, if they decide to keep you waiting. Here, take this."

Calvino produced a money clip and peeled off some bills. Cady did not even bother with making a show of demurring.

"Thanks," she said.

"Mr. Smith, I won't say it's been a pleasure. These things never are, but be assured that Dexter and Calvino have your back."

As long as she's paying you, Smith thought, watching Cady out of the corner of his eye. It would be churlish to say so, however, and he shook Calvino's hand in good faith. Maybe this guy was different, he thought, as he watched the man stride away. Maybe lawyers had changed since his day. After all, most everything else had.

"Let's go outside while we wait for our stuff," said Cady. "This place is probably bugged. I mean, they're probably listening to us. Outside is better."

Smith did not feel confident leaving the building because it meant putting even more distance between the watch and themselves, but Cady was already moving toward the door with a determined tread and a set to her jaw that told him she was in no mood to be second-guessed. He followed her out and down the steps onto a small grassed area shaded by a large conifer.

"We've got to get out of here," she whispered fiercely as soon as she judged them safe from eavesdroppers.

"I would not disagree," Smith said, "but we can't leave without our baggage."

Cady looked as though she had misunderstood him, but then she shook off that annoyance.

"No. I meant this whole timeline. It's wrong. It's messed up, Smith. It wasn't meant to happen and we shouldn't be here."

For somebody who'd just escaped a good long stay in the jug, she leaned more toward hysterical than relieved. Cady paced about in a tight circle, oblivious to the scene around them. By the light and shadows, it seemed they had lost most of the day. Seattle folk went about their business, giving the crazy lady a wide berth, and, he thought, steering as clear of the footpath and grounds outside the Homeland barracks as possible.

He could understand that. The place looked like a fortification from the Civil War, except on the grand and brutal scale that engineers did everything here. To his eyes, the Homeland Security forces looked dug into the sort of massive concrete bunker in which you stored a whole army's supply of gunpowder against the chance of a stray spark. There were just a few tiny windows looking out over the city it was presumably supposed to safeguard, and armed guards stalked around at ground level, like trigger men standing watch over a bandit hideout. But none of that seemed to agitate Cady as much as the doubts and fears swirling around inside her own pretty little head.

"You need to slow down," he said, "catch your breath and your thoughts, and explain it to me like I don't understand nothin' about this place, because frankly I don't."

She stood in front of him, her arms folded, her shoulders hunched, looking as though she were stood atop a barrel full of dynamite that she needed to jump off, but couldn't because she was afeared any sudden movement might cause the thing to blow.

"Miss Cady," he said, "you figured out the watch. You can figure this too. I couldn't, but you can. Just tell me what you're thinking, and we can work out what to do."

She did take that breath then. Closed her eyes, breathed in deeply through her nose, and let it out through her mouth like a sprinter getting ready for a big race.

"Okay," she said. "Where to start? Fucking quantum theory. Bubble universes. Schrodinger's fucking dead cat in a box. Maybe—"

"Maybe with less cussing and somewhere I got half a chance of understanding," he said, taking her gently by the elbow as he tried to lead her away from the dark whirlpool of her thoughts. "Why don't you tell me about your friend Georgia. Did you find out what happened to her?"

She nodded, and having that one real thing to explain seemed to calm her down. Her eyes narrowed as she looked to the Homeland bunker, perhaps still suspicious that the occupants might somehow be listening in. How they could do that with no windows to speak of, Smith was not sure. But he knew now that almost anything was possible.

"Do you want to get a little bit further away from them?" he asked. He truly did not want to stray much further afield, not while they still had his watch, but he felt obliged to ask. She was in such obvious distress.

Cady nodded and cast around for a bolt hole. He knew she'd found her place when her eyes fixed on a storefront across the street and her features hardened, losing their fearful and despondent cast.

"Over there," she said. "I want to check a few things online."

Smith followed, weaving through the light traffic and into a shop which sold the sort of machines he had seen on the work bench back at her apartment. They shared a feature with her phone—an illuminated screen—but these were much larger. The store was crowded, and the attendants stood out because they were all dressed in the same colored undershirts as each other.

Smith did not concern himself with trying to archeologize the future; he did not need to know what she was doing. It was enough that, whatever Cady had planned, it had distracted her from their troubles. She now proceeded with the native resolve of a carnival wrestler, climbing through the ropes, determined to win or to give at least as good as she got.

Smith was forced to hide a smile. He was warming to her spirit, and that unexpected connection left him just ever so slightly agog. It had been a long time since any woman had engaged his regard. Not since Martha had passed. He jammed his hands into his pockets and stood back from Miss Cady, who was invested in hammering away at what looked like the alphabet keys of a letter typing machine. Smith had seen one in his own time, in a bank. It had given him the impression of being a diabolical trial to maintain, not at all as convenient as a humble quill and ink. But there was no denying the speed and alacrity with which Cady's fingers clickety-clacked over the little pellets with all the letters of the alphabet stenciled on them.

As she worked, Smith saw the machine's window glass flickering and changing as though it offered a real window into a real and busy world. Images appeared there and screeds of typography. It likely would have unhinged him a few weeks ago, but he had seen stranger mechanical artifacts in other times and places. He had avoided entanglement with them, and was just as happy to leave this operation to his . . .

He paused to ponder what she was to him, this strange young woman.

It seemed they were abroad on an adventure together, so perhaps she was his . . . bestie? Was that the term? He wondered how she would take to being described as such, and then admonished himself for a fool. She was a beautiful girl, but Miss Cady McCall weren't no buckle bunny, that was for damned sure. There was no riding the long way around her being three or four professors smarter than him. That there was a fact as large and immovable as the Rocky Mountains themselves. She sat, furiously staring and glaring into the magic window of the computational machine, her jaws grinding away as she executed whatever scheme had occurred to her. Smith attempted to hide his own awakening attachment to her, indeed to deny such a thing was even at issue. He kept his face a mask of detachment, occasionally breaking away from her to walk over to the window and spy out the Homeland building across the way. Nothing had changed over there. Once or twice the store clerks in the brightly colored undershirts attempted conversation with him, but he did not respond in kind.

It was on the third or fourth return leg of a trip to the window that Cady suddenly arose from her machine. She had lost track of him, and he was touched to see she looked a little flustered, even alarmed, until she was able to pick him out of the crowd in the shop. The relief on her face was a wellspring of solace to him, too.

"Did you get whatever you were after?" he asked.

"Yeah. Sort of. Let's step outside. We need to get back and get our stuff, or start making trouble about it."

"Why?"

"I'll tell you outside. Come on."

Her demeanor had changed. She no longer affected the helpless air of a woman in peril, but the change was not entirely for the good. Her mood was, if anything, darker. Smith said nothing as they left the store and nothing while they walked a short distance to a park bench in a small patch of open ground with a view of the Homeland barracks.

"Better sit down," said Cady. "This is gonna take some explaining."

"And I don't have the watch," he reminded her.

"No," she agreed. "And more than anything else, we need that thing back."

"Because?" he said carefully. "Besides being my only way home."

"Our only way home," Cady corrected him.

Smith furrowed his brows.

"I'm already losing the trail."

"This isn't my home," she said, "and we haven't been time traveling."

CHAPTER TWENTY-TWO

It wasn't the gravest shock he'd been forced to accommodate, but it made less sense than some of the more recent insanities.

"I don't understand," he said. "We were just in London in 1888."

"Yeah, we were," she said, "and now we're here and you've been to Christ knows how many places and time zones since you first double-clicked the watch."

"But you're saying that weren't time travel?" he said, feeling his moorings beginning to slip.

"Yes. But, no," she sighed heavily, more exasperated with herself than by him. "This is hard because you have no reference points. No cultural . . ." Cady waved her hands about as if hoping to pluck the right words from the air. "No . . . context. Mark Twain hadn't even written his King Arthur book yet when we were in London. I checked. You first jumped in 1876. Twain didn't publish *A Connecticut Yankee in King Arthur's Court* for another decade or so. I'll put a copy on my phone, by the way. You should probably read it, and the H. G. Wells time travel book, and some others. I'll get you to read them all and maybe watch some movies when we get the hell out of this neo-fascist alterworld."

Smith had been barely following up until that point, but as Cady talked, she sped up, and her explanation pulled away from his comprehension and galloped off over the hills.

"Whoa, just layoff the stirrups, missy. You're right. I got no, whatever you called it, no culture or context, for this. I'm guessing you mean that'd be like you trying to make your way in a Comanche camp or a Pennsylvania Dutch village. You can't begin to understand the big things because you ain't even got a carrying handle on the little ones."

She stared at him for a second and then a smile rose on her face like a new dawn.

"It's a shame you only got a primary school education, Smith. I think there's a very smart guy under all that bristle and bullshit."

There were a couple of ways he could choose to take umbrage at that, but Smith decided to let them float past. Instead he rode along on the compliment she had just sort of paid him.

"Thanks, I think," he deadpanned. "Why don't you slow down and see if you're smart enough to explain your complicated postulations to this wooden-headed cowboy."

"I'll try my best," she said. Another quiet, frail smile. "I think what's happening is that every time we use the watch it doesn't just move us up and down a fixed timeline. It couldn't. You'd eventually encounter a grandfather paradox."

Cady frowned as if the necessity of having to explain such a thing was more than she should have to bear.

"Long story short, you can't invent a time machine to go back and kill your grandfather because then you'd never be born to invent the time machine. You see?"

Smith snorted.

"I reckon you'd have a whole heap of other problems before you got anywhere near of that one," he said, "but go on. I understand so far."

Cady nodded. She took a few seconds to compose her next thoughts, probably not wanting to get too far ahead of her plodding student. Smith followed her gaze, taking in the late afternoon strollers. Aside from superficial differences like their clothing, the people themselves looked quite commonplace to him. A costume change here and there, a proper bonnet and modest skirt on the ladies, say, and a decent town hat for the menfolk, and they could have walked down any street from his day.

"So," Cady went on slowly, choosing each word now as though searching for gold flecks in a stream. "I think every time you jump, or every time we've jumped now, that a . . . let's see . . ."

She made a face, squinting in concentration.

". . . that the watch . . . builds a whole new timeline, a new history if you like. What I'd call an alternate history, or an expanding quantum bubble universe. But I won't, because you wouldn't understand. I think this place . . ." she gestured to take in the world around them. "I don't think it is the world two years after I disappeared. My world, I mean. I think it's an alternative to that. A whole new reality."

Smith could not help but be troubled by this fantastical line of argument.

"But what happened to our rightful time?" he said, fearing her answer. He'd always assumed he could eventually get himself back to Elspeth. Cady had all but promised him as much. Now she was pulling that rug out from under his boots.

"They're still there," she said. "Be cool. Don't worry. Your daughter is waiting for you, and if we do everything right you will be able to get back to her."

Smith closed his eyes. At that precise moment he believed that nobody had ever said anything which meant more to him. He wanted to kiss her. But he didn't, of course, because he had been raised a gentleman, and also, he had not shaved properly in a long while.

Cady seemed to sense both his torment and relief and she took his hands and squeezed them. They were shaking but he made no effort to pull away.

"She's still there," she said again. "My time, too. And I'm pretty sure, or at least I hope, that we can get back to them. But we need the watch."

"I guess we'd better go get it then," he said, opening his eyes and letting out a breath he had not realized he was holding inside.

"I guess so," she agreed.

She was still holding his hands and neither seemed inclined to let go first.

"Better go," he said.

"Better had."

And finally they did.

It were but a short stroll back to the ugly fortress of the Homeland Security, and Cady tried to explain as much as she could while they walked, but there was a fair tale to tell, and she had to pull him up on the grass outside to finish it.

As Smith had the telling of it from her, there was simply no way their current reality—that's what she called it, the "current reality"—was possible. It could not have come to pass in the short time she had been away. Her principal objection seemed to be political. There was a feller sitting in the White House of whom she did not approve. He almost bellowed with laughter at that, despite the obnoxious character of the situation. Or perhaps because of it. He had seen men laughing like loons as the hangman slipped the noose around the neck.

"Miss Cady, if'n I thought the whole world had gone wrong just because some lickspittle chancer I did not care for parked his derriere in George Washington's rockin' chair, the world would never be right."

"That's not what I mean," she said, mashing her eyebrows together in a fierce display of feminine disapproval at being told better.

"Then I apologize. Please do tell me what you did mean and I will do my best to comprehend, notwithstanding all of my bristles and bull . . . well, all the rest of it."

There was a moment where Smith was uncertain whether she'd be able to unmash those eyebrows and get back to her explainifying, but she did.

"Look. You don't understand. This guy," she said, slowly, in a tone of voice that all but dared him to interrupt. "This man, Trump. There is no way he could be president. Okay, just take my word for it. It was never going to happen."

Try as he might, Smith could not keep the skeptical look off his face. Miss Cady, however, seemed ready for that.

"Okay, I get it," she said. "A guy like you, you're the whole reason they invented the southern strategy. But it's not just Trump and the wall and the whole weird-ass Aryan Nation vibe I've been picking up on since this morning and, you know, since we got picked up by the gestapo."

She had lost him, but Smith decided to let her get through whatever was giving her such conniptions. It'd be the same with Martha. When the storm blew up, best just to close the shutters and let it blow itself out. He arranged his face in a mask of polite interest and waited until she said something that made sense.

"They wouldn't let me talk to Georgia," she said, "but they couldn't stop Calvino and his guys carrying messages between us. What I know is, our personal history here checks out right up until I left that dinner with Georgia and Matt, the BuzzFeed guy. Then I go missing. They end up together. And everything goes sideways. Not because they got together. That was probably always going to happen, even if it was just a one-night stand. But Trump wins the election, and he does exactly what he promised to do, or at least he tries to. Turns out building a giant wall halfway across a continent is not so fucking easy. Deporting ten

million people, likewise. So this idiot savant starts rounding up
the ten million and sending them down to build his stupid wall,
and it's like the most insane, the most destructive, the most hated,
and the most popular thing he's ever done. And that's why Georgia
is locked up in her own apartment. Home arrest. With a little
indentured servitude to her corporate sponsor to sweeten the
deal."

As she spoke, the color rose in her cheeks and the words started
to shoot out of her like bullets from a repeating rifle. Finally, Cady
saw how perplexed he was and threw up her hands in surrender.

"Okay, Okay. I got it. My bad and I'll slow down. Just . . . just
forget all of that. It means nothing to you. It's only important to
me."

"I'll do my best to make it important to me," he said. "But yes,
it would be a mercy if you could slow down some."

"I'm sorry," she said, and he could see the energy running out of
her. "Look. True fact, it's impossible. When I left, the voters were
gonna murder Trump and dump his body down a mine shaft. But
not here. In this place, the race was neck and neck. And he won."

She waved away his objections before he could voice them.

"Well, maybe he won fair-n-square."

"No way!"

"But what was he promising? What's this wall of his for?"

"To keep out Mexican rapists."

Smith was really confused now.

"But, Cady, nobody wants rapists in town, Mexican or not.
Lord knows I've put a few fellers in the ground for that and less. I
just don't see a problem here."

"Gah! That *is* the problem. Men like *you* are the problem . . .
Look. Fine. We won't talk politics. How about history? I looked
up Gracie and Bertie on some genealogy sites. I just wanted to see
if I could find them. I did."

She did not look happy with whatever she had found.

"They're part of history now."

"Well, yeah, I suppose so."

"No. You don't understand. Actual history. They're famous. They've been studied for over a hundred years. They were the only victims of Jack the Ripper who didn't match the profile."

Smith could see that was supposed to mean something, but he shrugged, apologetically, because to him it didn't.

Cady closed her eyes and counted to three.

"Sorry," she said. "Again. My bad. So, context. Jack the Ripper was a famous murderer. The first celebrity serial killer. That's like a murderer who goes from one victim to the next, and just doesn't get caught until he's stacked the bodies so high they tumble down on top of him or something. Anyway, Jack didn't. Get caught, I mean. He killed half a dozen women, prostitutes in London, at the same time we were there. And now Gracie and Bertie. And people have been arguing about why them ever since."

Understanding was starting to dawn on him.

"And this Jack Ripper, he didn't do for them originally? That's only happened since we was there?"

Cady looked inconsolably sad.

"Yes," she said.

"I see," he muttered, but he didn't. Not clearly. "Are you implying that Chumley was this Jack feller? Not one of my apprentices?"

"I don't know what I'm saying," she said, sounding defeated. "None of this makes any sense. It's insane. All of it."

Smith felt the need of dragging her back onto a sunlit path before she became utterly lost in her melancholy.

"Was there anything else got you to pondering this new idea of yours?"

He saw her consciously pick up her sadness and put it to one side. It was still there, but she'd pushed it out of the way where it wouldn't stop her moving forward.

"A few things," she said. "I'd need a couple of hours of access to really nail it down, and I was never much of a history student anyway, but I'm pretty sure World War II ended in 1945, not 1946. And Australia doesn't speak French."

Smith didn't know about that world war business. He knew about his own war, of course, and he'd seen a couple of nasty ones on his travels. But he did know that they didn't speak the frog tongue in the antipodes. He'd once hung a man who'd dug for gold down there, and he had kept Smith awake the whole night before his appointment with the drop, telling his life story. Weren't no Frenchies in it.

"Yeah," he conceded. "Don't seem like we could be responsible for that."

"No" said Cady, and a glint of steel entered her voice. "But we are responsible for doing something about this."

Smith did not like the sound of that.

"What do you mean?"

"I mean, Marshal, I'm fixing to break my friend out of this hoosegow."

Smith knew she was gently mocking his manner of speech. But he didn't care. It was but gentle mockery after all, the sort of thing old friends might do between each other.

"You want to take her with us?"

"If she wants to come."

He didn't know what to make of that. He didn't even know whether it was possible for three people to step through the years together.

"Well, I suppose together you still don't weigh as much as Chester. And he had four legs. And you . . ."

Smith trailed off.

"I'm doing it," she said. "Or at least I'm going to give her the chance to say no."

"You'll have to explain everything," he said. "What odds she'll believe you?"

Cady turned the question over while they stood in front of the massive grey fortress of the Homeland Security.

"I don't know," she admitted, "but I do know we need that watch back."

"That's the first thing you've said that I truly understood," Smith said.

First thing you've said that I truly agreed with, too, he added, but only to himself.

The Homeland Security was not a welcoming place. There was the counter in the foyer, presumably for visitors to announce themselves, but who ever worked at it was hidden behind solid steel shutters. They were still closed. After banging on them without luck, Cady addressed herself to a device hanging from the ceiling, a little box that put Smith in mind of a tiny daguerreotype.

She swore up a storm at that thing with no more luck than she'd had banging on the shutters. Eventually, she advised that they would be best served by staking out the perfidious Homelanders while threatening apocalyptic retribution from the law firm of Dexter and Calvino. Without her phone, however, she had no way of putting the legal hounds on to them. So they set to waiting out the 'gestapo', as Cady now preferred to call them.

Smith had no idea who these 'gestapo' fellers were—Mexican soup cooks maybe?—but they had surely done Cady McCall some grievous injustice at one time or other. She hated those fellers.

"We're not leaving until we get our shit back," she yelled at the daguerreotype.

They were another hour delayed and inconvenienced by this initial hoo-haa. Another hour closer to Wu's gold watch cocking the firing hammer again. The shadows lengthened outside, and three parties entered and left the barracks, none of them inclined to make inquires on their behalf. One group ignored them completely. Another character, all on his lonesome, begged their pardon in a put upon fashion as he brushed them off and hurried away. The third one merely cussed at them. It was only when Cady informed Smith, loudly, that she was going to buy a phone, call her lawyers and commence proceedings, that the shutters rattled open and an older, tired-looking functionary pushed their belongings across the counter along with a couple of forms and one of the ink pencils you found in many of the time periods Smith thought of as 'later.'

"Sign here," he said without emotion or energy.

"How about we check nothing's missing first," Cady said in a voice that could have scratched a deep furrow into the steel shutter behind which this character had been hiding.

She quickly collected her phone and wallet and the go-bag with her notebooks and food bars and other small items in it. Smith ignored the pink valise, instead tearing open the buff colored envelope and tipping out the contents. His marshal's badge clattered out first, followed by sundry coins and banknotes, and a small stainless steel fire lighter he had acquired in a German city sometime in the 20th century.

But he saw no watch. His heart slowed down. Almost stopped.

He shook the envelope, opened it wide, peered inside, and eventually tore it apart.

"That's government property, sir," said the clerk.

His heart restarted and tried to gallop away out of his chest.

"Smith?" Cady said, her voice sharp with anxiety.

"It's not here," he snapped. "They took it."

He glared at the clerk, who stepped back from the counter and dropped a hand toward the pistol holstered at his hip.

"There was a gold pocket watch in here," Smith said. "I gave it up and I signed for it downstairs. They told me it would be returned. You better return it right now, mister, or there will be blood, I guarantee it."

The clerk was not much impressed by the promise of violence in Titanic Smith's voice. Smith adjudged that was due less to the man being armed than it was to this not being the first time he and his colleagues had connived at a dodge such as this. Smith had been given occasion to lock up two of his own deputies for stealing from prisoners. He knew how it went.

"If you have a complaint, sir, you will have to fill out and sign the complaint form."

Smith was getting himself set to roar murder into this charlatan's face when Cady interceded in an altogether quieter and decidedly more intimidating manner.

"The only thing we'll be signing is a check to my lawyers to fund their extravagantly punishing pursuit of you, personally, if you don't return his watch," she said.

"You got it, or your fat little friend downstairs got it," said Smith. "I don't care who gives it up. But I will have satisfaction and have it now."

The hours they had left until the watch could travel again seemed suddenly much shorter.

Cady began stabbing her finger at the little glass window of her phone.

"I'm calling them," she said. "I'm telling them to go after you. Not Homeland. You."

The clerk was undisputedly more dismayed by her threats than by Smith's. His eyes darted from side to side, flicking up at the tiny daguerreotype more than once.

"I don't have it," he said. "Miller took it. It's always him."

"That the fat little saphead downstairs?" Smith asked.

The clerk's noggin bobbed up and down nervously.

"Then best you go get him," said Smith.

"No, just get the watch," Cady countered. "We don't care about Miller. Or you. Just bring us the watch. Now!"

She raised her phone as if showing him the blade by which she would take off his manhood if he tested her.

"I can't," the man wheedled. His bravado had collapsed in on itself like an old tree stump eaten out by the termites. "He's finished for the day. He's gone. He worked the early shift."

Smith's head was spinning. Visions of this Miller riding away with Mr. Wu's chronometer left him sicker than a fevered hog. He wanted to reach across the counter, grab this scallawag by the scruff of the neck, and bounce him off a few walls until he gave up what they needed. But he stayed his hand with great forbearance. They were already caught up in exactly the flavor of local entanglement as was almost certain to bring the apprentices. And again, it was Cady who knew best how to play it out.

She spoke clearly and quietly, without any of the imminent threat of violence. "I think you'd better get him on the phone and get him back in here with my friend's property. Don't you?"

The nameless clerk, looking very nervous now, muttered that yes, of course, he would get right on it.

"You do that," said Cady. "I'm going to call my lawyer anyway. He was in here earlier today. Embarrassing your superiors. Making them and their superiors look like idiots. I'm sure they'll remember him fondly. I'm going to call him and tell him your friend Miller has given him a chance to double down on his fun. Whether he has that fun with Miller, with you, with your bosses, that's all down to you. There's a bar across the street. We'll wait over there."

She turned and walked for the glass door.

Smith leaned over the counter.

"We'll be back," he growled.

CHAPTER TWENTY-THREE

Cady swore up a storm as they stomped out of the barracks, down the steps, and across the street into the saloon. She cursed with such extravagant vehemence that not only was Smith offended to the point of moral harm, but every passerby she horrified with her crude prolixity veered away as though fearing a physical assault would surely follow the verbal.

Smith let her wear out the raging bull of her distemper. He knew from waiting out Martha's rare but scarifying tirades that this was for the best. And indeed, Cady did not stop cussing as she stormed into the saloon, but she did quieten down some. By the time she had reached the bar she was breathing heavily, but the air was no longer glowing a deep and profane shade of blue around her.

"Troubles?" the barkeep, another lady, asked.

"Two Bulleits's worth," Cady said shortly, "and whatever he wants."

She jerked a thumb at Smith as he laid the pink valise on the floor and took a good look around. This quiet dram shop was the front parlor of heaven compared with the drinking establishments they'd visited in London. Were it not for the hundreds of bottles behind the lady barkeep, all of them different colors and shapes, and all artfully illuminated from below, he might not have realized it was a saloon. The barkeep was a vision of loveliness and Smith wondered if the clientele here were limited to one shot of liquor lest riot and tumult ensue. He would not reckon her good odds of going unmolested in even the swankiest saloon with which he was familiar.

"You want some food?" she asked. "Kitchen just opened for dinner."

Cady ordered something called "buffalo wings," which did not sound at all enticing. Although contemporary Americans were gifted in the arts and sciences, he did not imagine that even they had figured a method of growing edible wings on a buffalo.

Turns out they had.

For tiny little buffalo, anyways.

Cady slammed the first bourbon down like a hardrock miner come out of the earth at the end of a long week, resolved to put a real hurtin' on the bottle. The second took only marginally longer. Smith nursed his drink. A bourbon, like hers, but only one. He needed his wits about him, and the loss of the watch and that encounter with Chumley inclined him to discretion.

It was a fine libation, nonetheless, and he felt the better for having it inside him. Cady breathed out and laid her hands flat on the bar. They were shaking, but she looked as though her fit of profanity might be over.

"We gotta get that fucking watch back, Smith, or we are right-eously fucked in the ass."

Nope. Still going strong.

"And we will," he said, assuring her of something he was not at all sure of himself. "You put the fear of God into that bunko steerer back in the Homeland. He won't want to take the fall for his light-fingered compadre. No honor among the thieving classes, Miss Cady, I guarantee it."

"Thanks," she said. "That'd be reassuring if we hadn't fetched up in a protofascist RPG with a giant rapey baboon in an orange fucking fright wig as the final boss."

Smith took another sip and stared at her.

Finally, he said, "Nope. Didn't understand a dang word."

She laughed at that, the tiniest silver thimble of a laugh, but he felt the yoke lift from his shoulders, just a touch. Their pretty barkeep returned with a bowl of winged buffalo pieces. To Smith's back-country palate, they tasted remarkably like chicken.

"Here you go, cowboy. You want a beer to wash them down?"

"I surely do, ma'am," said Smith, "but that pleasure will have to wait on my seeing to my responsibilities first."

She cooed and winked at Cady. "Ooh, this one's a keeper."

"I guess he is," she conceded. "Especially if he's gonna leave all the froths for me."

"So you'd like a beer?"

"Yeah. Beer me good. And a glass of ice water for my responsible friend here."

The barkeep pulled a long glass of the amber for Cady, and Smith marveled at the small beads of condensation which quickly formed on the outside. It must have been a surpassingly cold brew to do that. That was almost cause enough for him to question his responsibilities.

Almost, but not quite.

"So, this Miller dude," he said around licking Buffalo wing spices from his fingers, "how long do we give his accomplice to cough him up? Given that we are on the clock, so to speak."

Cady lips quirked in a small, fragile grin.

"I'm guessing "dude" doesn't mean the same to you as it does to me."

"It does if you mean it to describe a small, pustulant boil on the derrière," Smith explained. "Why? It mean something different now?"

She thought it over.

"No," she concluded. "Not so much. And no, we don't trust that other shifty-eyed motherfucker to do the—"

Smith dropped his shot glass to the bar harder than he'd intended. It sounded like a small gunshot when it struck the polished wood.

He threw up his hands.

"Whoa! That's enough. I been inclined to hold back my counsel, Miss Cady. One thing I have learned of late is that my ways are not the ways of others. But I got to tell you that I find it surpassing difficult to hear such language. That word you just spoke! That was a cuss too far."

She laughed again, and a scoffing hoot it was, too.

"What? From a lady, you mean?"

"From anyone," he said forcefully. "It's wrong, is all, and I would be right grateful if you could just accept that I find it so."

She regarded him with such cool reserve that for a moment he thought he had said something more offensive than the grotesque obscenity she had just uttered. Was this one of those context things, he wondered.

Then she shrugged and said, "You're sweet, for a killer who smells bad. And we have bigger problems. So, sure, I'll try not to drop so many F-bombs on you."

Then she pinned him with that level stare again.

"Unless some motherfucker really fucking needs it," she added.

He closed his eyes and drew in a deep, calming breath. "Fair enough then."

Impatience got the better of Cady after a few minutes. She pushed away her beer and stood up from the bar.

"Smith," she said, "I don't think we can just sit here waiting for this guy to get back to us or not."

"I don't disagree," he said, "but what do you have in mind?"

She took out her wallet and gave him a couple of banknotes. Twenties.

"I need you to sit here and wait, just in case he turns up. Especially if he turns up with this Miller douchebag. If he does that, get the watch, and come get me. I will be just down the street in that shop we went in earlier. You remember it?"

Smith did. The place that sold the machines she had used to study up on her time travel theories.

"I'm just gonna go get some equipment," Cady explained. "Stuff we can use to find Miller and . . . well, just stuff we can use. I'll be gone at least half an hour, but not much more than that okay?"

He had to trust her. They were in this together now.

"I can set with that," he said.

"Thanks," said Cady. She turned to go, and had even moved away a couple of steps before she halted and hurried back, giving him a quick hug and a promise.

"We're going to be okay. We're going to get home."

She left for real then, almost jogging out of the bar.

The lady barkeep returned presently to see if he wanted more food or something else to drink.

"Perhaps a cup of coffee," Smith suggested.

"Filter or latte?" she asked.

"Just a big old coffee with a dash of milk and maybe a spoonful of sugar, if'n you run to the little luxuries here," he said.

She poured him a mug from a glass jar that was brewing at the other end of the bar. The place was beginning to fill up with customers, probably in for their supper at the end of the day. The barkeep returned with Smith's coffee and a cookie.

"On the house," she said. "Your girlfriend is cute. Are you guys from around here? I'm pretty sure I've seen her somewhere."

"I'm from out of town," said Smith. "Cady is a local girl, but we been away."

Not having immediately corrected the woman's mistake about Cady being his sweetheart, Smith found he was not inclined to do so at all.

He sipped at his coffee, watching the street outside for Cady's return or for the appearance of the Homelanders with his property. As the minutes ticked away, becoming half an hour, and then three quarters of an hour, he became convinced that she was right, that they could not rely on that front office clerk to do the right thing. And then as even more time leaked away, he started to worry that something had happened to Cady. The bar was growing very busy and he was just about ready to abandon his post and search for her out on the street when she reappeared carrying two armfuls of shopping bags. And a long roll of gift wrapping paper.

Consarn it!

Were there no circumstances under which a woman would not go shopping?

She headed toward the last empty booth with a clear view of the entrance, indicating to Smith that he should follow her. Whatever she had been up to, it had lifted her mood. She was no longer afflicted with the air of one who could not help themselves.

"Take this," she said. "It's a phone. I've loaded it with my new number. We'll be able to stay in contact. At least while we have self-service. I put a couple of other things on there which might help. I'll show you how it works later."

Smith took the black rectangle she passed over to him. The window on the front lit up, displaying a picture of the stars at night and what he assumed was the time.

6:07 PM.

Nonplussed at what she expected him to do with a piece of machinery he did not know how to work, Smith put the thing away in his coat pocket. Miss Cady had bought three of the things. Hers was a slightly different shade of black. Shinier. The third remained in a white box.

Most of her attention was focused on the typing machine she had also purchased. He could not see the glowing window, only the grey sheet of metal into which it was embedded. That was emblazoned with the shape of an apple with a bite taken out of it. The significance of the totem was lost on Smith.

"Keep an eye out for Miller's buddy, just in case he does come looking for us," Cady said, "but we gotta assume the worst. They're probably gonna get rid of the watch and pretend it was lost, or we're lying, or something."

Smith considered that. Cady was right. It seemed the most likely course that events would take. Those varmints would not care to explain to their superiors what they had been up to, and time was getting short.

"I called Calvino," said Cady. "Told him what happened. He wasn't surprised and said he'd do what he could to get the watch back, but he didn't sound very confident. I told him it was a family heirloom. Something from your wife, I'm sorry. Still didn't make any difference."

"No need to apologize," said Smith. "Martha would likely approve of your scheme. She would want me to get back to Elspeth."

Cady looked up from the typing board at which she had been so furiously tapping away.

"Yeah," she said without further elucidation.

"So what's the plan?" Smith asked.

Cady kept at her typewriting.

"I could explain, but even with the watch, you might have trouble following."

She did not seem to intend offense. The look of deep concentration on her face spoke of someone invested so fully in their work that they could not spare their attention for the niceties of conversation.

"Long story short, Smith," she went on, "I'm shaking the trees here. We know enough about this guy to find him ourselves. His name is Miller, he works for Homeland Security, and he lives in Seattle. There are people who could serve up his severed fucking head on a platter in about two f . . ." She caught herself in the obscenity, glancing up at him and actually looking abashed. "Sorry. My bad. Anyway, they'd be able to tag him and bag him in just a few minutes with those data points. Might take me ten or fifteen. You think you could order up some more food or something? I'm guessing you don't have mad gift wrapping skills, or I'd get you to do that last phone for me."

"I'll see to the vittles," Smith said. He had no idea what she was doing with that machine or the wrapping paper, but she did appear to have every confidence it would lead them to Miller. And when it did, Titanic Smith would have a chance to employ his particular expertise in settling up with him.

Cady had estimated it might take her a quarter of an hour to locate Miller. As it transpired, she got her man before she got her vittles.

CHAPTER TWENTY-FOUR

Cady McCall, it seemed, had some mastery of the criminal arts, too. Having obtained an address for the crooked receiving clerk, she arranged transport for them, but not to his front door. Instead, the posse of two made their way to Miller's neighborhood by way of an Uber carriage, but they did not directly alight at the thief's domicile. Smith was both impressed and a little taken aback by this nefarious cunning. Furthermore, she did not have the driver terminate their journey at some random place. Rather he was instructed to drop them at another hash house selling strange Italian pies, collectively known as pizza.

They tarried at the Italian pie shop for a few moments while Cady negotiated with the manager to deliver a surprise birthday present to her "bestie." Some culinary atrocity she referred to as "a pepperoni and pineapple meal deal." And a phone, the third of the magical little telegraph machines she had purchased while Smith waited in the saloon.

"End to end encryption," she said, by way of explanation. "We'll see whether the NSA has cracked that bitch yet. My money's on Apple."

It wasn't much of an explanation, thought Smith.

"If they're watching her, they'll be watching for us," she went on, "not a pizza guy who could be delivering to anyone in that block."

The third phone, now hidden in gift wrap, she gave to the manager with precise instructions and two banknotes, each of one hundred dollars in value. One for him, and one for his best delivery boy to make the surprise delivery with a sealed birthday note from Cady.

"You know," said Smith, "that manager is almost certain to pocket the two hundred himself."

"As long as he makes the delivery, I don't care," said Cady. "Let's keep going. We're on the clock. Or the watch, you know."

She slung the little go-bag over her shoulder and walked briskly out into the night. It was colder this evening than it had been when they arrived, possibly because there was no cloud cover to trap any warm air over the city. Smith craned his head up at the stars as they proceeded on foot, although there weren't many stars to see.

"Light pollution," Cady explained. "It's like trying to look from light into dark. In the middle of a city, it's almost never dark enough to see the sky now."

"I consider that a grave loss," Smith said, and he meant it. "Oftentimes the stars have been my only companion."

"Out in the wilderness, maybe," said Cady. "But in a city, you're surrounded by people."

"You can be surrounded by people and still be alone," said Smith.

She was a moment in replying.

"Guess so," she said in the end.

The streets they walked to reach Miller were the meanest he had yet seen in this place. Unfamiliar with how a town should present itself in this epoch, Smith nevertheless thought this neighborhood suffered poorly in comparison with Miss Georgia's and even with Cady's, which was not looking to be judged on its residential amenity. Here he could see overgrown gardens, windows covered with paper and black sheeting which crackled in the light breeze. Some of the cars at the side of the road rested on deflated rubber wheels. Some were clearly rusted out, while others simply looked beaten down and unloved.

There was no pride here. No love, he thought.

That was good. Smith understood people like this. He had been dealing with them ever since he took up a lawman's badge and gun.

They made a left turn and then a right, fetching up in a dead-end street, half of its length given over to small manufactory and warehouse operations, and the rest to vacant, weed-choked lots or even meaner little houses than the increasingly poor and tumble-down cottages they had passed on the way here.

A dog started barking, and then another, and another.

"If we are to do this, best we be done quick," Smith said.

"Suppose you're right," Cady said, but her voice was nervous.

Having brought them to the line, she was no longer certain of what waited for them on the other side.

Smith was.

He shucked the big pink valise off his shoulder and removed the Winchester.

"If I might offer some advice," he said. "You might be better situated a safe distance away from what I'm about to do. Do you think it likely they will be armed?"

"What do you mean 'they?'"

"Cady, I assume the worst and dare the fates to disappoint me," he said. "This Miller might not be our choice of a companion, but in my experience, low company has no trouble seeking out its own kind. There will likely be others inside. Do you expect they will be armed? I would say yes, but this is not my time."

The dogs' barking grew louder, and somewhere nearby he heard a woman's voice cursing at them to shut up.

"I don't think so," Cady said, but without conviction. "There's probably guns in the house. They seem to be everywhere now. But they're probably not wearing them, like in holsters or anything. They're probably watching pornos or playing Xbox."

"I see," Smith said. "This pornos and Xbox, is it dangerous?"

The question delighted her, which he had not expected. They were standing under a scraggly evergreen tree of some sort. The branches were mostly bare, allowing the meagre street lamps to light up her face.

She smiled.

"No. Not dangerous. Not to you," Cady said.

If Smith were not mistaken, she said so with a trace of real affection.

"Fair enough, then," he said, somewhat more brusquely than he had intended. "You wait here. If this goes wrong . . . well, let's hope it don't. But if it does, get yourself away and lay low."

"It won't," she said. And then she surprised him by standing on tip-a-toe and kissing him lightly on the cheek.

He wished she hadn't done that. Helluva thing, distracting a man in such a fashion just a'fore he has to face off with some varmints. Smith tried to set it aside, with a measure of success, but his short walk to Miller's front path was yet a struggle.

He wasn't much concerned about kicking down this door, but his conscience gave him a terrible time about the memory of his good lady wife and, twisting the knife, his continued separation from Elspeth.

Titanic Smith had not journeyed here to dally with some pretty girl. He had but one purpose: to return safe home to his daughter.

He was so angry with himself for losing sight of that—for thrilling to the brief and probably meaningless peck on the cheek from Cady, for not telling that barmaid that they were not together—that by the time he pushed through the creaking, rusted gate which did nothing to guard the entrance to the Miller homestead, his blood was up and he was fit to be tied.

The path through the untended front garden was strewn with rubbish and even broken glass, which crunched under his boot heels. He hammered at the door rather than knocking on it, forgetting to stand to one side as was his custom, less'n he be greeted with a bellyful of buckshot. When the door opened, a shirtless young man covered in tattoos greeted him with an obscene question.

"What the fuck do you want?"

The marshal was in no mood to shilly-shally. He smashed the butt of his rifle directly into the nose of Miller's companion, knocking him out cold.

The man collapsed with a gurgling moan before unconsciousness claimed him. His body hit the floor with a mighty thud and Smith cursed his own ineptitude and impulsive foolishness. Miller would now be alerted and waiting on him in ambush.

He brought the rifle up to a firing position, forcibly reminding himself that he could not shoot to kill. They needed to secure the watch from this man, or at the very least, to learn its whereabouts.

Miller's shack was even more miserable on the inside than it had seemed from the street. It smelled of stewed farts and hung meat gone bad. The entry corridor was strewn with more refuse than the front path, almost as though they had brought in their garbage, rather than taking it out. The residence was poorly lit; a single light source flickering around the corner up ahead.

He heard a laugh, then a curse, followed by another laugh, a full-throated almost maniacal cackling it were. It fair raised every hackle that Smith had to raise. He could not think of any reason other than congenital lunacy why a man would laugh and curse like that. He advanced with even greater caution, reminding himself with every step, *Do not kill him, do not kill him.*

He found Miller, and Miller alone, in what he took to be the sitting parlor. He was certainly sitting. The receiving clerk was stretched out in a giant armchair, his stockinged feet resting on a low table full of even more rubbish. Miller was reclined in front of a gigantic sort of moving picture window, similar in effect to Cady's phone and typing machine, but much, much bigger. Smith could not tell what was happening inside the window, but it looked very colorful.

Miller's settee had been furnished with an ice cooler, which hung in a sort of basket on one side. It was full of ice and beer bottles. Or at least Smith assumed they were beer bottles. Drops of cold water ran down the side of the bucket and dropped to the floor.

Miller was holding a beer in his left hand while he juggled some other unfamiliar device in his right. For a wonder, on his head he wore earmuffs.

It was not a warm evening by any stretch of the imagination, but not cold enough inside for earmuffs, Smith thought. Still, he did not complain. The uncomfortable-looking things had obviously prevented Miller from hearing his bunkmate cry out or his carcass dropping heavily to the floorboards.

Smith grinned without warmth.

He ghosted up behind his quarry, being careful to lower the hammer on the Winchester. No sense in blowing this idiot's head off now. Not when he had made it so easy for them.

When he was close enough, Smith swiped the earmuffs off of Miller's head and dug the muzzle of his rifle in behind the man's ear, breaking the skin and drawing a little blood. Tinny noises came out of the earmuffs, possibly explaining Miller's temporary deafness.

The look on his face when he espied Smith standing there would have puckered a hog's butt.

"I believe you have something of mine," said Titanic Smith.

Miller squealed and flinched away. Smith whacked him in the face with the barrel of the Winchester, doing no real damage, but earning an agreeably girlish scream for the effort. He moved around where he could keep an eye on the hallway where the other occupant of the house still lay unconscious.

"I'll be having my watch back now, thank you, Mr. Miller."

They both heard the front door close, and Smith dug the gun muzzle into Miller's neck, ready to use him as a hostage if needs be.

It did not prove necessary.

"Smith, we cool?"

It was Cady's voice.

"You were supposed to wait outside," he called back to her.

Her head appeared around the corner.

"Sorry," she said. "It was starting to feel more dangerous out there than in here. Just hold on a second would you?"

Smith heard her fussing about with something heavy in the hallway, before she reappeared about a minute later with their bags.

"Thought I'd better tie up that other guy. I used his belt. He's out of it. But, you know, in the movie he'd totally wake up and get the drop on you or something."

"Thanks . . . I think," said Smith. "But I'm pretty sure I knocked him out colder than Montana in January."

"Oh my God," cried Miller, "you two are going down so hard for this. And your friend too, McCall. You can't do this."

"We just did," Smith reminded him. "Now, give us the watch and we'll be gone."

"I don't have it," Miller whined.

Smith whacked him in the face again. This time he aimed to break the man's nose, and he did not miss. Miller screamed and the claret flowed.

"The watch," Smith said calmly. "Now."

Miller was holding his face in his hands, blood running through his fingers. He started to cry.

"Hey, Miller," Cady said over the noise of his blubbering. "Look at me."

Before he complied, she had to repeat the instruction, walking over and giving him a little kick in the shins for emphasis.

"Look at me. I need you to know something. You're going to give us the watch back."

She cleared a space on the low table by simply sweeping all the rubbish aside with her boot. Then she sat down and took one of his beers, twisting the top off with her bare hand. Smith had no idea she was so strong, or that her hands were so uncommonly leathery.

"I tell you why you'll give us the watch back," she said. "Because if you don't, we're going to torture you."

Smith almost reared up to protest that. He had no intention of doing any such thing, but a warning look from Cady stayed his objection. Miller saw nothing of the exchange. He was still hiding behind his fingers like a frightened child. Cady took a sip of the beer she had stolen and gently pried one of Miller's hands away from his face. She grimaced a little, but not at the blood. The long strands of snot that came away stuck to his fingers were much worse.

"Look at me, Miller," she said quietly, and he did for the first time. She winked at him, tipping the beer in his direction in an utterly innocent gesture. *Hail fellow well met*, she seemed to be saying with her sparkling eyes. "Thing is, you can trust that we'll torture you. Do you know why?"

He shook his head. "But I don't have the watch," he protested weakly.

She shushed him like a small boy caught out in a little white lie.

"Miller, please. I'm trying to explain the torture. See, you're in a bad way here. My friend, Smith? The guy who broke your nose? He's a time traveler."

It was all Smith could do to maintain his poker face. Where in tarnation was she going with this? Did she truly intend to torture this feller? He was suddenly worried that he had no idea.

"And me," she continued, "I'm not so much from another time as I am from another reality."

Well, she certainly had Miller's attention now. His eyes were wide, with disbelief, with fear, with denial. Cady McCall seemed pleased with that. Her eyes sparkled.

"I'm afraid I can't explain how it all works, but I can assure you that I'm not lying. Smith here, he looks like a cowboy because that's what he is. An honest-to-goddamn cowboy. And me, I came from another world where Trump isn't president, Hillary isn't in jail, and you're probably still sitting here playing *Titanfall*, but without the broken nose or the looming prospect of being tortured because you're too stupid to give up the watch that you stole."

"But I haven't . . ."

Cady smashed the beer bottle on the edge of the little table, causing both Miller and Smith to jump. Beer frothed everywhere. She held up the jagged tooth of glass she had made of the bottle, inviting him to consider it. In spite of the sudden violence, her voice did not change. She still sounded the very acme of moderation and restraint.

"Come now, Miller. We both know that's not true. So, you can give it back to us, or you can spend the next hour or two screaming while we torture it out of you, because you only have two options. Either I'm completely bananas, in which case you get tortured because, you know, bananas. Or I'm telling the truth, in which case you're getting tortured because your existence means nothing to me. This whole world means nothing to me. You mean less than to me than some bullet magnet NPC in *Grand Theft Auto*."

She twirled the bottle around and raised it high as though to stab it deeply into the meat of his leg.

"No!" barked Smith.

"BUT I DON'T HAVE THE FUCKING THING," Miller wailed. "I sold it," he blubbered. "I t-tried to tell you. I already s-s-sold it."

He fell apart then, giving into his cowardice and shame. Cady closed her eyes and pressed her lips together, looking like she was fighting off the grandfather of all headaches.

"Awesome," she said. "That's just awesome."

Still worried that she might actually start carving him up, Smith hauled Miller's limp, blubbering deadweight out of the chair.

"Who did you sell it to?" he said. "Will they still have it?"

"The payday loan place," he snuffled miserably.

Smith was pushing the man toward the entry hallway, partly to get him away from Cady, partly because time was running out and he had no intention of letting Miller get away until he had laid hands on Mr. Wu's chronometer again.

He heard glass break as Cady tossed the bottle away.

"Can you carry the bags?" Smith asked her. He was busy with Miller, but he also thought it might be a good idea to give her something to do with her hands, lest the devil find work for them.

"Sure," she said, sounding tired. "You got a car, Miller?"

"No, b-b-but Johnny does."

"That your b-b-boyfriend on the floor out there?"

"No, I mean yes, I mean . . ."

"Just get the fucking keys."

CHAPTER TWENTY-FIVE

Johnny's car was a half-open wagon. Smith thought it would make a useful conveyance on a homestead. It was in much better shape than the house where Miller and his buddy lived. There were two rows of seating. He rode in back with their captive while Miss Cady drove.

They traveled at quite remarkable speeds through the streets of the borough. Miller and Smith were thrown into each other once or twice when she took the wagon around a tight corner. Smith raised no objection to the wild ride. They had less than an hour to go before the watch bestirred itself into life again.

"Clean him up," Cady ordered from the front seat. "We don't need any more trouble with the cops when we get to this place."

"Better do as she says, Miller," Smith said. "I do believe she spoke true back at your cabin. She will take your scalp if you steer us bad."

Miller used his undershirt to wipe away most of the snot, blood and tears. His face looked sick, nigh on malarial, under the glow of the street lamps.

"Is she crazy?" he asked in a whisper. "All that stuff she said? That can't be true."

"Then I guess she's crazy," said Smith. "Either way, you don't want no trouble with her."

Miller fell silent at that, leaving Smith with his own thoughts as they raced through the night.

They were not happy thoughts.

He had known Cady McCall for the shortest while, and had come to respect her during that brief time. She was whipcrack sharp, no doubt of it. Brave enough to die standin' up, too.

But hell fire, she had him convinced of her malign intentions back at Miller's place.

Was she some sorta Broadway calico? A natural actress who never found her way to the stage?

Or did she speak true when she threatened torture on this blubbering lickspittle?

He honestly could not say.

"We're here," she announced, pulling Johnny's wagon over to the side of the road out front of a blockhouse with a large, well-lit signage touting itself as a provider of "Payday Loan$" at "Supalow interest." Every window and door were protected by bars. The premises to either side offered "Best Cheap Tattoos" and "Live Sexxx." Both businesses looked to be doing loud and boisterous trade.

"Leave your rifle, Smith," said Cady. "Take the six-shooter, but keep it holstered. Oh, and maybe wear the badge out so they can see it."

"I thought we agreed it to be a poor idea for me to be putting myself about as a marshal here," he said.

Miller started whimpering and cussing under his breath at that. "Oh, man. You guys are in so much trouble."

Cady opened Smith's door and he climbed down out of the cabin, watching Miller the whole time.

"Come on, Miller. Let's just get the watch and get gone."

The fat man shuffled across the width of the seat and stepped out unsteadily.

"But what if they already sold it?" he said, sounding just as worried about that as Smith felt.

"You better pray not," Cady told him.

They left their baggage in the wagon, which Cady locked with a magical totem that she squeezed between thumb and forefinger. However fraught their circumstances, Smith could not help but marvel at small wonders like that. There were other things to contemplate, though.

The tattoo shop appeared to double as a saloon for a gang of desperados all tricked out in black leathers and—here was a helluva thing—bright cloth patches announcing these fellers as . . . *Desperados!*

"What in the Sam Hill?" Smith muttered to himself as they hustled on by. There were maybe eight or nine of these layabouts, just layin' about, and a working majority fixed him with the evil eye as he happened past. They had seen his badge, and he would wager good folding money they were not well disposed toward the US Marshals Service.

Smith was afeared this would not end well as Cady led them into the payday loans place. He fixed his attention on her and Miller rather than the Aladdin's Cave of stolen goods into which they had stumbled. For there could be no doubt that the business here was the receiving and conversion of merchandise taken by thieves. After all, they had purchased his watch from Miller without need of a receipt or any other proof of ownership. He wondered if the tattooed desperadoes next door had a commercial interest in the operation.

Cady was already engaged in conversation with the storekeeper when Smith rolled up with Miller in harness.

"So, I'm sorry but we need my grandad's watch back," she explained.

The feller behind the counter seemed less interested in her than he was in Smith and Miller, in that order. Or perhaps to be more accurate, it was Smith's badge that caught his eye. He looked even more a thief than he did a customer of thieves. Tall and hollow cheeked, his face was scarred by the pox. A drooping mustache gave his mournful appearance an even more funereal aspect.

"Don't know what you're talking about," he told Cady, while looking directly at Miller with knives in his eyes.

"Oh, come on, man," cried Miller. "Just give them the watch. Seriously. I made a mistake. They need it back."

The man turned his eyes on Smith. It was like attracting the attention of a snake.

"Never seen this man," he said, nodding at Miller. "Never bought nothing off him."

"This is bullshit," Cady snapped. She took out her wallet and removed a fat wad of currency throwing it on the glass counter-top. It sat suspended above a motley collection of pilfered jewelry.

And watches.

Including Wu's timepiece. Smith could see it in there. He was certain.

For maybe half a second, Cady had the man's attention. But his eyes flicked back to Smith's badge and he shook his head.

"We don't deal in stolen goods here," he said.

"Bullshit," said Smith, causing Cady to spin around.

She had never heard him cuss a single word a'fore.

"Got a warrant, pig?"

"I got what you need right here," Smith growled. He hauled out his Colt .45 and pistol whipped this lying scuzzler without warning or remorse, dropping him like a bag full of Idaho spuds. Then he brought the gun down on the glass of the counter, shattering it with an enormous crash.

Miller cried out.

Cady swore.

And Smith calmly reached in and retrieved his watch.

They had fifteen minutes until they could jump again.

They also had company.

"Yo. Pig."

He turned, gun still in hand, and found himself facing off with the bandit crew from next door. Perhaps they were concerned citizens. More likely, his guess about their investment in this place had proved right.

One of the men was carrying a shotgun, and as he raised it toward Smith, the marshal snapped off two shots, drilling him though the heart and the head.

All kinds of hell broke over them at that.

He heard Cady yell out his name and turned for her, only to find the storekeeper climbing back to his feet, unsteadily waving his own shortened shotgun in the general direction of Smith and Miller. He fired, and poor sniveling Miller caught most of the blast in the face. Smith was sprayed with bits of the clerk and a few stray, stinging pellets of shot.

Before the storekeep could get off another blast, Cady laid him out with a baseball bat she had retrieved from Lord only knew where. It was a shiny metal thing and it met this feller's melon with a sickening *CLONK*. Down he went.

"RUN," Smith bellowed at Cady, who did not require a second telling.

They headed for the door, where at least two of the Desperadoes had taken poor cover to fire on them. Shots cracked and bullets zipped past, and rather than running as Smith had so strongly advised his partner, he stopped dead still, took the time to lay his sights on one Desperado, then the next, and he sent them both down to Hell with two pulls of the trigger.

Then he got to running again.

In Smith's experience, the fight did not always go to the quickest, the strongest, or even the meanest, although you should never discount those particularities in any man intent on killing you. Nope. In his experience, the fight went to the man who held his nerve and kept his wits about him.

He told Cady to run, and he himself moved with all dispatch toward the exit, but he did not panic, and he did not fire wildly about him. He held onto the watch. He killed those men who needed killin', and he made sure to interpose his considerable bulk between Miss Cady and any of the desperadoes who had not cleared out at the first shot.

Thankfully, that appeared to be most of them.

Again, in Smith's experience, men like that were strong in a pack, but once you broke the pack apart by blowing the heads off one or two of their number, they tended to scatter like curs.

He emerged from the payday loans ready to put the last of his bullets into any man who stood in their way, but it was not necessary. They had a clear path to the wagon.

Cady was swearing. The same crude word over and over again, and Smith could not bring himself to think ill of her for it. The devil had got the better of his tongue back in the store when he could see that they were being gulled by the villain who ran the place. And now that everything had turned to blood and chaos, he found himself tempted to vent his own choler in the strongest of language.

The strange exaltation of the spirit that can make the quickest and most violent action pass in a slow, dreamlike state was clearing like morning mist. Smith piled clumsily into the wagon as Cady struggled to start the combustion engine. She let out one, huge scream.

"*FUCK!*"

Exhaled all of her breath.

And laid her hands lightly on the steerage wheel as though they had no business more pressing than a buggy ride to a picnic.

Unable to operate the wagon, Smith had to place his faith in her.

She reached calmly for whatever mechanism stoked the boilers on this thing, and with one simple turn, brought it to life.

Her sangfroid was tested when two bullets struck the metal frame of the wagon like hammer blows, and she did effect such a sudden acceleration and wrenching turn that Smith's head was slammed into the window, filling his vision with stars. But he was just glad the glass did not shatter and cut him.

"How long?" Cady asked, her voice sounding jagged and sharp, like a rusted butcher's knife.

"The watch?" he asked, and suffered a second of blind terror when he could not find it.

"*Yes! The watch! How long until it's live again? Come on, Smith! I'm driving.*"

His heart slowed down some when he felt the small golden circle in the same pocket where he'd stashed the phone she had given him. He took it out and checked.

It was hard to say without a minute hand to parse the exact moment, but he thought they were coming up on a quarter of ten.

"Maybe five or six minutes. Maybe less."

She swore again, and punched the steerage wheel.

"We'll never make it."

"Then we lay low and try again tomorrow," he said as she barreled down the road away from the mayhem they had unleashed.

"Are you fucking kidding me? You think we're going to just hole up in some canyon or gully and wait for the posse to ride on past? That's not how it works here, man."

Her voice was a plaintive wail.

Smith himself was beset by an unfamiliar keenness of sentiment and, try as he might, he could not shake it.

He felt that he had done the wrong thing.

There was no questioning each individual decision he had made, each separate action he had taken since arriving here. They had all been justified and necessary in the particular.

But in the general?

He could not shake the feeling that they had done wrong, and now they would be, quite rightfully, the subject of pursuit by men such as he had once been.

Cady pulled off the road, made a couple of apparently random turns and stopped under the spreading arms of an ancient evergreen. They were in a quiet street. A neighborhood of small residences. Lights burned in windows, but nobody appeared to question their presence or bonafides.

"I have to think," she said. "I just need a moment."

"Then take it," said Smith.

She breathed in deeply, held it for a few seconds, and breathed out, taking twice as long. Cady sat, doing this like some oriental mystic, for what felt like a very long time, but which really only delayed them a minute.

Smith wished he had a real drink to hand.

"I need to call Georgia," she said at last.

"That is not a good idea," he cautioned. "The Homelanders, the sheriffs, they'd be watching her anyway. They said as much. And after tonight . . ."

"After tonight we won't be here," she said, cutting him off. "We have to get out of here, Smith. We have to go now, or as soon as we can. And I have to at least give Georgia the chance to come with us. Don't you see?"

To be honest, he did not.

"You had no chance to explain your circumstances to her this morning, Cady. You won't get one now. When the local law rides out from that shambles back at the Payday, her place is gonna be one of their first calls. I saw them little daguerreotype boxes every-where. The ones you were yelling at back at the Homeland, like someone was watching from them. Well someone woulda been watching us stroll in with Miller, and they'd a seen things turn bloody. Won't take them long to pin it on us, I don't reckon."

"All the more reason to go and get her out, Smith." Cady's voice was still shaky but her resolve seemed rock solid. "They will *bury* her after this. When they can't find us, they'll make do with her. And it's my fault. It's all my fault."

He thought she might come apart then, but although her eyes teared up a little, she sniffed and rubbed them dry and jutted her chin out as if daring him to take a swing.

He felt more exhausted than at any time since he'd lost his way.

"Miss Cady."

"Gah! Ms!"

"Sorry," he said. "Cady. I cannot judge you because I do not share your judgment. You did not ask to be drug into all this. That was my doing and I am sorry for that. But because that fault lies with me, I know how much worse it could be for you if'n you drugged Miss Georgia out of her home year. Yes. It's bad here. But it can get so much worse."

She paid him his due. She listened and he could see her dili-gently turning it all over. But in the end she was unmoved.

"Titanic . . . hmm, no, that just sounds weird. Smith, I have to do this. I *have* to. She's my friend and I've put her in real danger. Took a bad situation and made it infinitely worse. I have to at least try get her out of it."

By way of an answer he shrugged, "Well, you're not driving now. You should check that phone of yours. You set something like an hourglass on it, as I recall."

She had forgotten. The surprise and remembrance were written plainly on her face.

"Oh, yeah!"

Cady pulled the device out of a pocket in her leather jacket. Not for the first time, was he struck by the incongruity of her wardrobe choice. She was dressed in a similar style to the Desperadoes back at the payday loans.

"We're too late," she said. "Three minutes too late, and counting. The watch is live."

Cady drove with more care and much less haste for the next leg of their trip. Smith reloaded. She pulled up in Miss Georgia's street, but a goodly distance from the apartment building itself. Cady insisted they sit and "scope out the scene."

Smith reflected again on just how remarkably adept she was at this sort of caper. It occurred to him then that he did not really know what she did for a living.

For the nine million dollars and change sitting in her bank account.

She worked at her magic window and did . . . something.

She'd never explained exactly what.

"What is it you do?" he asked, as they waited in the dark.

She continued to "scope out the scene."

"What d'you mean?"

"I mean your job. Your line of work? You never told me what you do. It must be unusual, less'n it's normal for folk to be paid millions of dollars for laboring and such like."

She snorted in amusement.

"No, Smith. It's not. I'm a game developer. I wrote a game, an app. It sold a fuck ton of copies."

He understood the words, even the unusual swearing, but not the meaning. She discerned his perplexity.

"And this is why I didn't bother trying to explain," she said. "I build games," she said. "People play them on their phones."

"And you got ten million dollars for this?" he asked. Frankly, he was stunned.

"Yup," she said, still carefully watching the street. It remained quiet. "But I would probably have made less if I hadn't disappeared and become a mystery girl for months."

She bit her lip. Something was worrying her.

"I guess Matt helped with that."

"Miss Georgia's feller?"

"Yeah."

"The one you plan to leave behind here?"

He could see her lips pressed to together with irritation, but she said nothing. The silence between them grew heavy, like a weight held at arm's length.

"My apologies," he said at last. "That was unworthy. I understand you have instructed the lawyer Calvino to attend to his case. I imagine nine million dollars will be more than sufficient to buy his freedom from this wall."

"I hope so," she said and her voice sounded small.

She came to a decision then, fetching the phone out of her jacket.

She held a thumb to it and the front window glass lit up.

A finger dance followed and she put the device to her ear. After a moment she spoke in a low voice.

"Georgia," she said, "it's me. So, you got your birthday pizza?"

Cady listened to whatever her friend said before she spoke again.

"I know it's not your birthday. It's a fucking ruse, bitch."

Smith could not fathom the way they spoke to each other in this way. It seemed they should come to blows but never did.

"Babe, I'm sorry about today," said Cady. "Like, really. I didn't know, I just . . ."

She went quiet while Georgia spoke, but Smith could not hear what passed between them. The conversation proceeded in this lopsided fashion for another minute until Cady got to her point.

"Georgia, I need you to do something. I need you to trust me. I'm gonna get you out of this. I promise."

Another pause.

"No. I don't mean that. The lawyers will look after Matt. I've set that up. I mean you, babe. I can get you out of this. Out of the country. Completely gone and free. But you have to trust me. And you have to come, right now."

More quiet as Georgia undoubtedly sought further and better particulars.

Cady did not provide them.

"Babe," she said, her voice hushed and sincere, "all I can tell you is you wouldn't believe me. And I'm serious about Calvino. He will get Matt out, no matter what happens with us. With you. He has instructions and money. That's all a lawyer needs. I can get you out, but you can't come back. You have to understand that. We'll leave and we'll never come back here. But it has to be now. And it has to be forever."

There was another pause, but not a long one.

"Okay. Don't worry about the collar. I can fix that."

She fell quiet again before saying.

"With bitcoins. Use the phone to find us. See you soon. Move quickly."

Cady cut their telegraphic connection, but did not return the phone to her pocket. Instead she did the little finger dance again. The phone made some funny noises and then she did put it away.

"She's coming now. And we're getting the hell out of here."

"They'll be watching for her," Smith warned.

"They'll be watching for her collar," Cady replied, "and I just paid a guy in Latvia about a hundred thousand dollars to deal with that. As far as Homeland or the NSA or anyone but us knows, she's still at home, eating pizza and watching the Bachelor."

"I'll not inquire further," said Smith.

"Best you don't."

Everything that happened then, happened very quickly. Not at first. There were a few minutes of waiting before a wedge of light spilled out into the darkness of the street from the front stoop of Miss Georgia's apartment building.

She appeared wearing a hooded jacket and holding the phone Cady had given her. Smith could see the bright beacon of its illuminated glass. The hooded figure appeared to consult the glass and compare it to the street before stepping quickly in their direction.

"I do not feel right about this, Miss Cady," said Smith. "She has no idea what she's agreed to."

"I'll explain while we drive over to the jump point," said Cady. "Once she's committed, she won't turn back. She can't. And we'll jump tonight. I know it's not the plan, but . . ."

She trailed off.

"But you want to get gone," said Smith. "Fair enough. Won't be the first time I've tucked my tail between my legs on this trip."

They watched as Georgia hastened toward them, looking from side to side and back over her shoulder the whole way. Cady opened the door and hopped out.

Smith did too, coming around to doff his hat. It was simply a matter of courtesy.

They waited in the shadows of the street while Georgia approached. Smith found himself nervous, expecting Homelanders or Desperados to leap from the shadows at any moment.

They didn't. Not then.

They waited until Cady and Georgia had embraced.

Then the very night itself seemed to split apart in a shrieking riot of light and sound and color and noise. Giant voices roared from all around.

"HOMELAND SECURITY. GET ON THE GROUND. FACE DOWN. HANDS BEHIND YOUR HEADS."

And Smith leapt, diving for Cady and Georgia, enfolding them within his arms and clicking the crown of the watch twice as soon as he had them within his embrace.

It was a difficult venture, all told, and in the chaotic moment of action, his thumb slipped.

CHAPTER TWENTY-SIX
INTERLUDE

He remembered the feeling of placing his hand on her throat. It would have been so easy to finish her then. She had even taunted him to strangle her.

But of course, he could not do that.

Not with so many witnesses.

Not with the other one watching. That one was well armed and had proven himself more than willing to offer resistance, more than ready to generate yet another complication.

So far, the man called Smith was uniquely responsible for twenty-six complications. With the woman, McCall, he had created a further two; now three, the senior apprentice supposed. But she was the greater danger. From the moment of her involvement, the potential complications multiplied in fractal complexity and amplitude. The Watchmaker viewed her as uniquely disruptive.

The senior apprentice strode through the small huddles of men and women nervously circling the place from which the three fugitives had left. There was nothing to mark the spot, not even the faint, metallic burning smell which often lingered at such transit points. It had already dissipated.

"Hey, Bowers, you believe this shit?"

The question was for him, but his name was not really Bowers.

Bowers was an alternance, carefully inserted into the mechanism of this complication by the Watchmaker himself.

"No, I don't," the apprentice said, speaking in the mild tone he had chosen for this character. "Please check the sewers. They could have dropped down into the pipes. And keep canvassing the neighborhood. Eliadis lived here. She'll have friends who'd take her in. Even now. Especially now."

The local law enforcement officer did nothing to hide his low opinion of that suggestion, but the man who was not really Bowers did not care. He was done with this time and place. The elusives were gone and the seven months he'd invested in the identity of Mike Bowers had been wasted.

Just like the two months spent waiting in London, one hundred and thirty years ago.

That was so often how it went.

The Watchmaker had studied this complication when it arose and determined that the best chance of intercepting the elusives was to be had when the woman attempted to make contact with her family. But McCall had not done that. She had behaved erratically.

For all of the precision engineering that went into a crafting a timepiece, the weave of time itself was coarse-grained and dishearteningly inexact. People were the problem. They were always the problem. Time would lose nothing without them to mark its passage. The man who was not Bowers had seen time described as an arrow, which was laughably wrong. He'd also heard it compared to a raging river, beset with treacherous eddies and whirlpools, which was better, but not by much. Most interestingly, he had once read of the cosmos in all of its epochs as a library. In this last metaphor, time was an infinitely vast world constructed of hexagonal rooms, each lined with shelves, and upon those shelves, random volumes written in every possible ordering of 25 characters; twenty-two letters and three punctuation marks. Because of the infinite number of rooms and books, most volumes contained utter gibberish, but there also existed on those shelves every book that ever had been or ever would be written in every language, and somewhere, lost on some far away shelf, or maybe just across the room, there was a perfect index which would bring order to the whole collection.

The man who was not Bowers, who had no name other than "Apprentice," liked this metaphor most of all. It whispered to him of the unbounded futility of time; of moving through it, or attempting to bring order to the infinite.

Each book he imagined as a complication. Smith, and now McCall and this other woman, were writing new volumes, adding them to the infinite collection. But of course, he conceded with some melancholy, time was not a library either.

The senior apprentice examined the scene.

The truck's engine had been running when they left, but was not now. There were two bags in the cabin; a large pink sports bag in the rear, loaded with food stuffs, weapons, ammunition, survival equipment, and wet gym clothes. A second, smaller bag lay in the front, on the passenger seat. It contained a water bottle —half-full— protein bars, a cheap cellphone, and notebooks.

The man known as Bowers examined the notes. Nobody attempted to stop him. Nobody offered to help. Bowers' clearance was rumored to be so far above theirs they'd need a telescope to find it.

This Bowers was an unremarkable man. You could sit beside him in a briefing at Homeland, or the FBI, or at any one of a dozen inter-agency taskforces, and two minutes after the meeting adjourned, you would be unable to recall a thing about him.

The notebooks in the truck would disappear, but nobody would question the disappearance.

It had been . . . that guy.

The one from . . . Washington.

He'd secured them.

They'd be in the system . . . somewhere.

The senior apprentice quickly scanned three pages of handwritten notes. It seemed the woman McCall had written them. The vernacular was early twenty-first century American. The technical knowledge and cultural paradigms spoke to a greater familiarity, if not understanding, of the chronological arts and sciences than Smith had yet demonstrated.

The marshal had been difficult enough to hunt and, so far, impossible to erase.

She was going to be worse.

The senior apprentice placed the notebooks into a plastic evidence bag. None of these people would ever see them again.

He left the vehicle and walked up the street toward the apartment where Eliadis had lived. It was unlikely there would be anything of interest there for him, but he had his procedures.

He would spend some time familiarizing himself with her, the latest elusive. Then Mike Bowers would take his leave of this world. He would not be missed.

PART THREE

CHAPTER TWENTY-SEVEN

The warmth and sweetness of the air was not the first thing she noticed. First was Smith crash-tackling her to the ground.

Then the soft grass where they landed.

Not the hard road surface of the street outside Georgia's apartment.

Then Georgia.

She was with them.

She had escaped.

They had all escaped, and now they rolled on soft grass under a warm sun and Smith was apologizing and Georgia was swearing and Cady was laughing even though she had no idea where or when they'd landed. All she knew was they were free and gone from the nightmare of that broken future.

"Dang, but I'm sorry, ladies," said Smith as he rolled to one side and climbed to his feet. "But I did not see no other way."

"It's cool," Cady assured him as she stood up and took in the view. A green and lovely countryside, shot through with rivers of bright yellow and red flowers, dotted here and there with small white buildings tied together with winding, unmarked country roads. "It's all good," she said.

"FUCK!" shouted Georgia, who remained on the ground, shaking like a small dog shitting razor blades.

Cady took a second to enjoy the sun on her face, closing her eyes and telling herself it would get better, but for now this was pretty damn good.

And then she looked to her best friend who was, understandably, freaking the hell out and peeling off one WTF after another, each louder and more plaintive than the last.

"Ma'am, please," said Smith.

"Georgia, it's cool," Cady said, as Smith wiped grass and dirt from his butt and scowled at their surroundings as though they hadn't just escaped a fascist clusterfuckturducken of epic scale and infinite suckage.

Cady held out her hand and Georgia took it, finally getting to her feet with Cady's help. She was still shaking as Cady hugged her and rubbed her back, shushing her like a child.

"It's okay, baby. We're good. We're safe. I promise. You're safe."

"Where . . . w-where . . ."

"Where are we?" Cady finished for her. She turned to Smith. "Marshal?"

He looked deeply unhappy.

"Looks like a few places I been," he said, but he kept any further thoughts to himself.

"Well, it looks a helluva lot better than those cells at Homeland," declared Cady, as if that settled everything.

Georgia pushed her away so fiercely that she tripped and fell on her ass. The ground was soft and the grass thick, but it still hurt. She jarred her arms trying to break the fall. Pins and needles shot up from her hands.

"Georgia. Quit it!"

"What have you done?" she shouted. "Where am I? What the fuck is this?"

Her fear was palpable, but anger was catching up with it.

"Ma'am," said Smith. "If'n you'll hush, I can explain, and probably should, since this is my fault."

Cady decided to stay seated for the time travel lecture. She shaded her eyes to scope out more of the countryside. Gentle plains, divided into large fields of irregular shapes and different colors, rolled away in all directions. A line of dark mountains shimmered in a heat haze far to the north.

"I can't say exactly where we fetched up, Miss Georgia," Smith explained, "but it's not your home. Nowhere nearby from the look of the land hereabouts."

"No shit!" Georgia spat back, and Cady waited for Smith to give her his stump speech about profanity and womanly virtues. She was a bit surprised and perhaps a little put out when he didn't.

"Can I ask you to believe something?" Smith asked, sounding as though he regretted the necessity of asking.

Georgia was turning around, first one way and then back in a small circle, shaking her head, but not at him.

"Go on," she said.

He held up Wu's golden watch. Passed it to her.

"Hey," she said, mildly.

It had probably just cleared up her nausea and headache. Cady felt fine, unlike her first time. Another data point?

Smith took the watch back.

"This here device is not as it would seem at first, ma'am. It has carried us away from hazard in your time and place, and delivered us into uncertainty. Where, I do not yet know. But I can tell you that you are not in Seattle, and this is not your time."

Color flushed into Georgia's face. She looked first to Smith and then to Cady, who finally climbed back to her feet.

"We time traveled, Georgia. How cool is that? We slipped those Homeland assholes like a bad Tinder date."

The bright pink flush which had colored her friend's cheeks, drained away and her eyes rolled back in their sockets.

"Whoa, look sharp," Smith called out. "She's a-gonna swoon."

"No way," Cady protested, but Smith ignored her and swept Georgia into his arms for a second time, saving her from another fall to the ground.

He laid her down gently and shaded her face with his hat.

"Some water . . ." he started to say, and then "Damn it!"

Cady was surprised, as she always was when Smith uttered even the mildest curse, but then it struck her too. They had no water. They had no food. They had nothing. Not even the contents of the little go-bag. She'd left that in the pick-up, back in Seattle. Her oversized pink gym bag, which she'd so enjoyed making Smith carry around, was back there too.

And in it, every piece of carefully chosen equipment they had bought in London. Including his rifle and ammo.

The clean light of this new day did not seem quite so delightful after all. She could feel it burning her exposed skin, baking her in the cold climate outfit she wore. Her mouth was dry and her nostrils itchy with the dust of an unfamiliar land.

None of those little white buildings looked like they had a drive-thru.

She knelt down next to Smith, who was fanning Georgia with his hat.

"We don't have any water," she said.

The look he gave her was a frontier version of, *Well, duh.*

But he said, "I hear some nearby. And we need to get off this ridge." He squinted as his eyes traversed the landscape, looking for threats.

"Come on," said Smith.

He picked up Georgia again and carried her, at a crouch, over the small hilltop, down a gentle slope into a gully shaded by a stand of trees. The trees, Cady saw with relief, spread their branches over a small stream. Georgia was stirring when Smith lay her down in the shade, making a pillow for her head with his jacket, just as he had done for Cady back in London.

Georgia's eyes fluttered open, she groaned, leaned to one side and vomited into the grass.

The pizza Cady had sent with an iPhone.

Because Cady McCall was such a 007 bad-ass bitch and, like, totally three moves ahead of those idiots from Homeland. The idiots who'd chased them here.

She felt her head begin to spin and she stumbled down to the stream where she fell to her knees, leaned down and splashed shockingly cold water over her face.

She stayed there, kneeling by the brook, shame burning her cheeks, despite the icy kiss of the fresh water. She didn't move, because when she did, she was going to have to go back to her friend and explain what she'd done. And why she had done it.

Even though Smith had been the one who . . .

"*No.*"

"What?" Smith said from behind her.

"Nothing," Cady said, forcing herself to stand up and return to them. She carried a little water cupped in her hands, and sprinkled it on Georgia's brow. None of this was Smith's fault. He'd defended her from those muggers or apprentices, or whatever they'd been, back at the start of all this. He'd just saved them being fed into a Trump-brand gulag. At best, they'd have ended up with Matt on the Wall. Even more likely, they'd have been dropped into a black cell and spent the next fifteen years explaining to a bunch of agencies and acronyms that didn't officially exist what the hell they'd been doing the previous twenty-four hours.

No. This wasn't Smith's fault. It was hers.

Cady walked back to where her friend lay on the grass. Georgia watched her through slow blinking eyes. She was still having trouble coming to terms with everything.

"I'm sorry, Georgia. I'm so sorry. I just didn't know what to do. I thought we'd screwed things up for you. I'd screwed things up for you. And I just wanted to help. I just wanted my friend back."

Smith kept fanning Georgia with the hat. He said nothing. His face was unreadable.

"Is this where you were?" she asked. "All that time? We thought you were dead, Cady."

She shook her head.

"Not here, no. We were in London. Late 19th century London. Sherlock Holmes, Queen Victoria, Jack the Ripper. That London."

Georgia started to deny it, but the evidence of her own eyes told her Cady was not lying. Or at least that they had passed out of the world of real things and into a Twilight Zone of possibilities.

"But you were gone more than two years. Your parents . . . God, Cady. I mean . . . they never gave up on you, but—"

Cady waved her hand at Georgia, wordlessly begging her to stop talking. That'd be why she could still access her bank accounts. Her dad probably. He'd have fought every day to keep the idea of her alive. He'd have made sure she could get to that money if she needed it.

And she hadn't even called him.

She fell silent.

Nobody spoke. Light breeze whispered through the leaves, dappling them with shade. The stream water gurgled and birds sang unfamiliar songs in the branches above.

"How? How did this happen?"

Smith and Cady swapped a look.

"Some guys attacked me, after the dinner with you and Matt. The marshal stepped in. He saved me, but we ended up . . ." she waved her hands helplessly. "In London. In the 1880s."

"I believe the men who attacked your friend were looking for me, ma'am," said Smith. "But for their own reasons they turned their attentions on her. Can't say as to why."

"Two years, Cady."

Georgia said it quietly, like a whispered accusation.

"It were only twenty-four hours to us, ma'am," Smith said, making Cady wince. He was trying to help, but he was making it worse. He didn't know her friend.

Georgia fixed her with a chilling stare. Colder than the icy water she had just splashed on her face.

"One day? You were gone one day?" Her voice grew louder. "You took a fucking daytrip? Watched a little History Channel, picked up a cowboy, and wandered back two years later to fuck everyone up all over again? Because it wasn't enough that you were lost, you were dead to everyone who loved you for all that time? Oh no! *Cady McCall had to have it her way.*"

The last few words she shouted, her voice so piercing and shrill that Smith reached over and gently but firmly clamped his giant hand over her mouth. Georgia's eyes flew wide open at that and she tried to tear herself out of his grip. But she was a tiny sparrow in the paws of a grizzly.

He shushed her again and shook his head mournfully.

"Best you don't go a-hollerin' like that, ma'am," Smith warned. "We don't know nothing about this place. Could be we rolled a natural seven. Could be we got snake eyes. I would just as soon not bet the farm until we see how the bones come out."

Georgia's eyes darted back to Cady, who shrugged.

"He says things like that."

Smith carefully took away his hand. Georgia was breathing heavily, but she did not cry out again. Instead she took a series of deep breaths, composing herself. "How bad is it?" she said at last.

Cady and Smith exchanged a whole conversation in a single glance. She answered for both of them.

"Like the marshal said, we don't know yet . . . Oh!"

She pulled out her phone. Her new phone.

"No signal. So, I'd guess not just out of range. We've probably jumped back in time. Smith?"

He looked very uncomfortable. She set a timer. Twenty-three hours and fifty minutes. Enough to give them a little wiggle room. Then she turned the phone off again. This didn't look like the sort of place she could recharge, and the timer would run anyway, even with the phone off.

"I did give the little crown thing a good tweak as I grabbed y'all up," Smith explained. "I'm afraid we did not get to try your experiment, Miss Cady."

"Smith, please."

He went from uncomfortable to abashed. "Sorry, I mean Cady. I think I might have nudged us a good deal further back than the one minute you was intending to try."

She tried to sound conciliatory. "Well, it's not like we jumped under controlled conditions."

"Nope."

Georgia spoke up again, but kept her volume in check this time. "What are you talking about?"

"We're trying to work out the control scheme for the watch."

"You don't know how it works?"

Her voice was climbing again and Cady had to make hasty a placating gesture.

"I've got some ideas," she said.

"Ideas?"

Georgia was losing her temper for real now. Cady, who never did like to be second-guessed, was drawn into her spiral.

"Look, I've only done this once or twice, and never under ideal circumstances."

"Omigod!"

"Look. Just shut up would you. It's . . ."

"Ladies," warned Smith.

"No, you shut up."

"Ladies."

"I'll work this out, Georgia. I can get us home. And not to that bunk-ass alterna-fucked timeline you were locked up in."

"Ladies!" Smith shouted.

He got to his feet with surprising speed for a man of his size.

He drew his gun even quicker.

CHAPTER TWENTY-EIGHT

Smith shot down the man who rode at them with a spear raised. He killed another wielding some sort of axe. Three more riders veered away from the report of his pistol, but they did not flee. More men appeared over the next ridge, arrayed on foot. They were armed with a motley collection of edged metal and blunt clubs, and dressed in short smocks which showed off their bare legs.

They were shouting, but too far away for him to be able to make anything out. It was undoubtedly the same old thing as always. Throw down your weapons, put up your hands, we got you surrounded. Smith tried to reload his gun, which was empty now, but more riders appeared, this time they came over the hill down which he'd just carried Miss Georgia.

She was struck dumb, perhaps even shocked into catatonia. Cady, he noted was casting about for a weapon, which he supposed was admirable, but as like to get her run through as not. The marshal faced the hard truth of it and holstered his gun, raising his hands in surrender and stepping to put himself between the nearest of the riders and the two young women. No sense their getting speared because he'd just plugged some fellers.

"Smith? What's happening?" said Cady, her voice frightened and unsteady.

"Dunno," he admitted. "But I'd say we're goin' in the bag. Ain't got the bullets or the time to pick off so many targets."

A first rider drew up in a shower of pebbles and mud from the banks of the little stream.

"Who are you to trespass on the estates of Lentulus Batiatus?" he demanded to know.

Smith could tell from the blank incomprehension of Cady and Georgia that they did not understand a word of it. To Smith's ear the man's voice sounded harsh, but devoid of any accent.

More riders made the bank of the stream, and behind them came the men on foot, all brandishing their spears and swords and clubs.

"Well, I do beg pardon," Smith said, "But we're travelers. Merchants," he improvised. In his experience, merchants tended to go wherever there was a dollar to be had. That were as true in times when men wore dresses and sandals as it were when they covered their heads with fish bowls and flew off to the stars.

"He is dead!" a new voice called out.

Merchants did not tend to go ventilating fellers with .45 pistols, though.

He was saved the inconvenience of explaining away the corpses he had just made of their comrades by the blow to his head which sent him down into darkness.

He awoke in chains, lying on the cold flagstone floor of a prison cell.

It was mighty surprising to be alive.

Smith's head throbbed pitifully from the knockout blow, and his stomach heaved and flipped over with the sickness of it. He held down his gorge with great effort.

"Smith?"

It took him a moment to recognize Cady's voice.

"Smith are you okay?"

He blinked away his blurred double vision and pushed himself up off the floor.

"Still breathing," he grunted.

As his eyesight came back into focus, he took inventory. Apart from the lump on his head and his roiling guts, he was unhurt. He'd taken worse falls from horses over the years, been hit harder from behind in more'n one bar fight. He had suffered no broken bones, and had been spared the inconvenience of waking up to find pieces of himself missing.

His scalp remained firmly attached to his head.

All in all, not much to complain about, then. The headache was ferocious, but unless they'd knocked his brains loose, it would pass.

"Marshal, your jacket," said another voice. He blinked and squinted and found Miss Georgia pushing his coat through the gaps between the iron bars separating his cell from theirs. They were imprisoned. Widening his attention from his own woes to the larger question of what the devil had just happened, he found himself secured in a small cell, flanked on both sides by identical lock-ups. He could see bright sunlight, so at least they were not confined in some dungeon.

Smith rubbed his eyes, and at last his vision cleared completely. He could see now that their penitentiary took an unusual form. It was constructed in a circle, with the cells all looking out through shaded cloisters onto a large grassed area. The sun shone fiercely out there, where half naked men engaged in physical training. Some wrestled. Others fought each other with sticks. He could hear the dull crack of wood on wood. The sun looked as though he might've been out for hours, occasioning a moment of free-falling terror when Smith reached for the watch and realized he was not wearing his jacket.

"Marshal," Miss Georgia said again. "Here, take your jacket and use it as a pillow. You're hurt."

He remembered, then, the watch was in his waistcoat, not his jacket. He found it and checked the local time. The watch always knew that.

Late morning. Just after eleven.

"Thank you, ma'am," he said, shuffling over to the bars separating him from his companions. Georgia still wore the Homeland collar. She and Cady looked scared but unmolested, for which he was profoundly relieved. It was his experience that there were few places and times that women, let alone captive women, could be assured of their safety and honor without the strong hand of a male protector to safeguard them. That, or ready access to a loaded shotgun.

Cady and Georgia had had neither while he was down for the count.

"Any idea where we ended up?" he asked. "They said something about us trespassing on some feller's land, but whoever knocked me out done knocked that memory right out of my head, too."

"I think we're in ancient Greece or Rome," said Cady. "All the dudes are wearing dresses and sandals and swords and shit."

"We're definitely somewhere around the Mediterranean," said Georgia. "The landscape looks right to me." Her voice was tight with anxiety, but the shock and confusion which had undone her upon their arrival had passed. She'd probably had time to talk with Cady. "I can't understand a word they're saying, but every now and then it sounds familiar," she added.

"I got the watch," Smith said. "So I could understand. They said we were on somebody's land, and then, bang, they put out my lights."

"You are on the estate of Lentulus Batiatus, friend."

Smith turned towards this new voice, a man's. He found the feller standing on the far side of his cell, behind the same sort of iron bars that separated him from the ladies. This man was of medium height, but broad and powerful through the shoulders.

His skin had the deep brown tan of someone who worked out of doors, rather than the naturally dark pigment of a Mexican or a mulatto.

Smith raised his eyebrows at Cady and Georgia, as if they might have some information about their fellow prisoner, but they just shrugged and shook their heads, reminding him that they did not have the advantage of holding the watch. They couldn't converse with anyone here.

"My name is Smith," he said turning to face the man. "John Smith."

He walked across the breadth of his cell, covering the distance in three careful strides, holding his hand out in greeting. It was a gesture he found to be nearly universal.

"And I am Gannicus of Salluvi."

This Gannicus took his hand through the bars and shook it. Smith remained alive to the possibility of a ploy, and was ready to turn and snap the man's arm at the elbow, but his gesture of greeting was returned without trickery.

"I hear tell of your prowess in combat, Smith John Smith," he said. "I hear that you slayed a mounted retainer of Lentulus at bow shot distance, and brought down another, but neither with a bow."

Smith remained guarded with him. It was possible, more than probable even, that this Gannicus was no friend, but rather a jailhouse snitch.

"We're merchants," he said, falling back on the first lie he had chosen.

"What's he saying, Smith?" Cady called across the cell.

"Just getting acquainted," he replied without turning around.

"Do you sell these women?" Gannicus asked.

"Oh, hell no," Smith said, insulted at the very thought. "The buying and selling of people ain't my line of business, sir. They're my partners, I suppose you would say."

The man seemed to consider this, eventually nodding as if he approved.

"And how did you end up here, friend?" Smith asked pointedly.

"The Romans overran my village when I was fourteen years old," he said. "I killed two of their legionnaires and would have been killed myself save for Batiatus, who bought me as a slave for his school."

"A slave? His school?" Smith was not certain he understood. Perhaps the watch had not translated well. His skin prickled uncomfortably.

"You are here," Gannicus said, as though it should be obvious. "Lentulus Batiatus runs the largest gladiator school in Capua."

The dozen or so men training in mock combat out under the high sun suddenly made sense. Of a sort.

"Excuse me, Gannicus," he said. "I'll be right back."

He returned to Cady and Georgia.

"This feller says we're being held by some slaver called Lentulus. Reckons he runs a school for gladiators. That's like professional fighters in olden days Rome, right? He also reckons the Romans took his village. Made slaves of everyone."

"I guess that tells us where we are," said Cady.

"But not when," said Georgia. "Could be the Roman Republic, the Roman Empire, could be East or West. Did he say anything else?"

They all looked back over Smith's shoulder at their fellow captive. He did not look like a prisoner. He seemed well fed and strong. Fit. He watched them curiously, but without obvious enmity.

"Said this slave owner was based in . . . Capua, I think."

Cady looked to Georgia, who shrugged. "Never been there, but I know the name. I think it's near Rome, but north or south I couldn't say. And near for us doesn't mean the same thing for these guys, remember. They don't have Uber or hyperloop."

"Okay," said Smith. "I'm gonna talk to this Gannicus feller a bit more. See if I can spy out the land."

He shucked on his jacket, feeling a little more settled in the old familiar coat, despite the heat of the day outside.

"This Lentulus, he gonna be reasonable? For a big bug?" Smith asked Gannicus.

The man laughed, but not with any pleasure. "He is no bug. He is a pig."

"Oh. Well I meant boss, not a bug in the exact meaning of the word. An overseer. Is he reasonable as an overseer?"

He could not bring himself to say 'owner'.

"Do not imagine you can reason with him Smith John Smith."

"Just Smith will do."

"Smith." The gladiator considered the word as if it were a gift. "Good," he pronounced at last. "You cannot reason with him, Smith. Even before you killed his man, you were on his estate. For Lentulus, you became his property the moment you set foot upon his land."

Something twisted inside Smith.

"The hell I did," he said.

"Then I hope you can repeat your trick of killing a man without laying a hand upon him," said Gannicus. He looked suspiciously around him, as though fearing eavesdroppers. Then he leaned forward and whispered fiercely.

"Do this, Smith, and we will stand with you and all of your band."

"What do you mean?" Smith asked, but before the gladiator could answer, he turned away, muttering out the side of his mouth, "Beware, the pig itself approaches."

CHAPTER TWENTY-NINE

Smith heard them before he could see them. Sounded like four or five men, crunching through a gravel pit. They appeared through an arch in the cloisters three cells down from Gannicus.

"Look sharp ladies, I think this is *el jefe*," Smith warned.

He expected Cady and Georgia to inconspicuously hide themselves away in the corner of their cell, but instead they pushed right up against the bars, seeking a vantage point from which they might better glimpse who was coming.

A fat man in a bed sheet, attended by his thugs, that's who.

You stripped away all the costuming and theatrical props, and that's what you got. Smith had seen their ilk many times before. He'd stretched the necks of men like this, and shot more than a few who proved unwilling to face a jury of their peers.

There was no question which of the crew was Mr. Batiatus. He stood front and center, holding Smith's gun and Bowie knife. One his underlings carried a phone. Presumably Cady's.

"Hey, that's my phone, asshole!" She protested.

It did not appear she would be making herself as inconspicuous as possible.

"Shut up," Miss Georgia hissed at her. "Seriously, Cady, if you were ever, for once in your life, just going to shut the fuck up, now would be the time to do it."

Lentulus Batiatus regarded them with a sneer, but he directed his first question at Smith.

"Where do you hail from?"

"Purdue County," he said, not feeling the need of bending the truth just yet. "But lately from all around."

"And your women? None of my household recognizes their tongue."

"They ain't my women. I don't own 'em, and they come from even further away than I did."

Batiatus walked a few steps beyond Smith's cell, to get a better look at Cady and Georgia.

"Are you a sorceress?" he asked Cady.

She looked to Smith for a translation.

"I think he wants to know if you're a witch," he said.

She answered Batiatus directly.

"If I was, you'd be a fucking blob fish by now. You're halfway there already."

None of it registered on the slave owner's face. Not a word of it made any sense to him.

"She explains that she is a merchant, sir, just like myself. We are traveling salespeople, and I'm sorry if we lost our way and wandered onto your property, but . . ."

"Take him and beat him," Batiatus ordered.

"Whoa! Ain't no call for that."

Two of the guards stood forward and handed off their weapons. They were not about to give him a chance to arm himself.

"Smith? What are they doing?" Cady asked anxiously.

"Get on your knees," Gannicus hissed at him. "Take the beating. It will go easier."

"I think not," Smith replied as the guards unlocked his cage door and came at him, fast.

They were good fighters. He could see that from the way they carried themselves, the way they split up and came at him separately. The cell gate clanged shut behind them, too. Nope. You could not fault these fellers for their jailhouse technique.

But Smith had survived on the frontier. He had not yet encountered the fighter to best him. He knew not to wait and get swarmed. He faked a dodge away from the closer man, before pivoting and driving his boot into the attacker's knee cap. It shattered with a wet crumblin' sound and he went down screaming. The other guard was on him in a blink, but there was a whole lotta of Titanic Smith to be getting on with. This one was a wrestler, and he snaked all of his limbs around the marshal, tied him up in human knots.

Didn't matter none.

Smith simply toppled to the flagstones liked a redwood felled by the axeman. His enormous bulk crashed down on top of the smaller man, crushing him, breaking any number of bones large and small, and cracking his head like an egg on the stone floor. Smith heard one or maybe both of the girls screaming, and what sounded like Gannicus roaring out encouragement.

He dug an elbow into the broken man's sternum, using it to lever himself back to his feet where he waited for the next attackers to come charging in through the gate.

Instead, he found that Batiatus stood directly in front of him, just on the other side of the bars, two of his goons to either shoulder, both of them holding spears long enough to find Smith even if he retreated into the furthest corner.

"Coarse, but effective," said the slave master, nodding his appreciation.

He seemed not the least bit concerned about his men, one of whom, the one Smith had crushed under his own mass, was twitching and gagging like a spastic in a fit. The other cried and moaned, clutching at his broken knee, the leg bent impossibly back against itself.

"You did not just wander into my holdings," Batiatus said, as though the violent hiatus had not taken place. "You were found in the middle of my estate. You appeared through sorcery, and you killed one of my men and injured another through foul magic. And now you have put me to the inconvenient loss of two more of my bondsmen. You are no merchant."

Smith did not reply immediately. What was there to say? It had been a thin tissue of a lie behind which to hide, and it required no real effort from Batiatus to rip it asunder.

"What's he saying, Marshal?" Georgia asked.

"Well," said Smith, stepping away from the fallen men, "I tried to tell him we were but traveling salesfolk. But he ain't buying that, I'm afraid, Miss Georgia."

Batiatus turned to the goon standing on his right.

"Kill the woman who just spoke," he said.

"Whoa!" Smith cried out. "Hold on there!"

Not knowing what was happening, but guessing that it weren't likely to finish sunny-side up for them, the girls beat a hasty retreat into the rear of the cell, adding their own protests to Smith's.

The slave master let his head fall to one side, examining Smith the way a man might consider his next move in a game of checkers.

He snapped his fingers and the goon returned to his side. The man's face did not change. Smith recognized him as one of those hirelings who would kill on command without so much as blinking. If he enjoyed it, he would not show it. He was the weapon, not the man carrying the weapon. Smith found himself grateful he'd not had to face that one in close combat.

Batiatus held up the pistol as the man with the fractured skull stopped moving and making any noise at all.

"My men tell me you pointed this at them and two of their number were struck down by thunder."

Feeling his uncomfortable proximity to those glistening spear tips, Smith got ready to dodge the points for as long as he might. Vowing that he would grab the first spear that came through the bars at him and take as many of these varmints as possible, he stood erect, his chin jutting out at Batiatus, his knees flexing ever so slightly, just in case he had to move with any haste.

"Your men were fixing to do us in," he said. "The first one I killed was just about to let loose with a spear. The second man I shot when he did not break off his attack. I'm sorry they're dead," he lied, "but a man has a right to defend himself and his own."

All through this speech in his defense, Smith was aware of Gannicus listening in the next cell over. The gladiator had retreated a safe distance from the bars, but he did not pretend any lack of interest in the exchange.

The moaning of the guard with the broken leg, meanwhile, was growing louder and more distracting.

"You will show me how to perform this sorcery," said Batiatus. It was neither an invitation, nor a threat. It was an uncomplicated statement of fact. "Do this now, and your women will live. Lie to me, defy me, vex me in any fashion, and I will give them to my gladiators as practice dolls while you watch on. I will have your eyelids cut off to ensure you miss nothing."

"Smith?" Cady asked, intuiting that she and Georgia were the subject of this conversation, even though she could have no idea of what the men were saying to each other.

"Just dickering' some, Miss Cady," he said out the corner of his mouth. "Best you let me be."

To Batiatus he hurried on.

"If'n you were good enough to give me the gun I'll be happy to show you how it works," he said.

The man smiled for the first time. His grin cracked open and rich, deep laughter spilled out of his corpulent frame, making his giant belly jiggle like a jellied dessert.

Some of his strong-arm chumps braved a chuckle along with the bossman. They seemed no more concerned by the loss of their comrades than was their master.

"That will not be necessary, *merchant*," Batiatus informed him. "I am the principal of the finest gladiator school in the Republic. You will tell me how to use your magical weapon, and I am certain I will be able to follow your instructions."

Smith hesitated.

It was bad enough that they had become so deeply and disastrously entangled in the affairs of this local potentate. That in itself was probably enough to attract the attention of the apprentices. But showing this man how to load and fire a pistol? He would not be surprised if Chumley or one of his comrades suddenly appeared striding down the cloisters a bare minute later.

"Kill the women," Batiatus said, to his nearest lieutenant.

"No, that won't be necessary. I can tell you," Smith said quickly. Without really intending to, he stepped sideways, moving a little closer to Cady and Georgia, as if to defend them. It was an empty gesture. If Batiatus wanted them dead, Smith did not see what he could do about it.

"You need to load the gun," he said. "I already done fired off the last of the ammunition in it."

"So it is like a bow, then?" Batiatus said. "And there are tiny arrows or darts perhaps that must be equipped somehow?"

He turned the weapon over in his hands, occasionally looking straight down the barrel. Smith cursed silently. If only he'd not shot off the last bullet, this fat fool was a good chance of blowing his own dang head off.

Maybe . . .

He removed a bullet from his gun belt and carefully passed it through the bars. Still toying with the pistol, Batiatus did not take the slug. One of his men stepped forward and plucked it from Smith's fingers.

"You need to make sure the hammer ain't cocked," Smith said, and immediately he could see that this was not something Mr. Wu's chronometer could easily translate.

"The hammer?" said Batiatus.

"That crooked little dingus at the end there," he said pointing at it. "Okay, look, it's where it should be anyway. So forget it. Now you have to hold the grip, the handle, without putting your finger inside that trigger guard there. No. I said don't put your finger in there. You cup the weapon with your other hand . . ."

"Smith, is this really such a good idea?" Cady asked.

"Oh, believe me, you'd think it was if it was you havin' this conversation," he said before hastily returning to his instructions. "Yeah, that looks right, or close enough as makes no never mind. Now use your thumb, no your other thumb, to push on the cylinder latch, no, not that part . . ."

It took a good deal longer than it should have, but eventually they did manage to seat a single bullet in the cylinder. Batiatus then proved himself to be less than a complete idiot by snapping his fingers again and demanding more bullets from Smith.

"They go in these other holes, is that so?"

The Marshal reluctantly plucked out five more rounds from his belt and handed them through the bars. He was aware of the intense attention focused on him; from the ladies, from the gladiator in the cell next to his, and from other men in other cells leading away around the odd circular jailhouse. Only the fighters training out in the hot sun seemed not to be following along. Oh, and that moaning feller with the broken leg a-laying there on the floor. Smith was beginning to think Batiatus had forgotten all about him.

After another frustrating minute, the slave master was able to snap the cylinder back in place. He now had a loaded gun.

What the hell have I done? Smith asked himself.

"The thunder. Where does the thunder come from?"

"It comes out of the hole at the end of the long tube there," Smith explained, hoping that Batiatus would be enough of a dumb corn cracker to look down the barrel.

He weren't.

He waved the gun around, causing Smith to flinch away. He saw Cady and Georgia doing the same. None of the guards seemed to understand the hazard. Batiatus certainly didn't.

And then the pistol went off.

In the confined space of the cells, the roar of the single round sounded many times louder than the shots he'd fired out in the hills of the estate.

Everyone jumped.

The bullet ricocheted away.

Maybe it hit someone, maybe not. There were so many cries of alarm and terror that no single cry of pain could possibly stand out. The guards around Batiatus looked thoroughly spooked, but the slave master recovered quickly.

He laughed again. Louder this time. A long, peeling church bell of a laugh.

"This is magnificent," he crowed.

Without preamble he pointed the pistol at the man who still lay on the floor next to Smith, clutching at his broken limb, and he shot him.

Once. Twice. Three times.

CHAPTER THIRTY

The noise of the gunshots was enormous and terrible in Cady's ears, but the effect was worse. The guard Smith had crippled died screaming as pieces of him sprayed everywhere. Cady was screaming. Georgia was screaming. Even Smith was shouting obscenities, or what passed for obscenities from him.

Cady and Georgia held on to each other, cowering away in the corner of their cell. Georgia was shaking, her whole body wracked by tremors. Cady cradled her friend as best she could, rocking her back and forth, but she wasn't much better herself. Even the guards, who had earlier closed around their boss like a fist, now shied away. One ran out into the sun, babbling like a child.

The fat guy in the toga just kept laughing. He was like a super-sized Joker or something, getting off on his own lunatic bad-mofo act.

It seemed to take forever, but eventually the situation calmed down. Toga bro ordered his minions to do something, presumably to get Smith out of his cell. The three who remained approached the task with extreme prejudice. They all entered leveling swords and spears at him, barking orders which even she could understand. The words were foreign, but the meaning was clear.

Come with us or die.

Smith backed himself up against the bars separating his cell from theirs.

"Cady," he said in a low voice, "take it."

Still paralyzed by shock, she remained frozen in place for a moment, until Smith spoke again with more urgency. "You'll need it. Take it."

She realized then that he held the watch in his massive hands. He had palmed it. She quickly stood up and ran over to the bars, reaching her arms through as though to hug him.

"John, don't go, oh, please don't go," she said, in a terrible attempt at role-playing. Smith looked at her as though she'd gone mad, but he nodded when she slipped the watch out of his hands and retreated away from the bars, back to Georgia.

The guards led Smith away.

And they were alone.

Servants came to clean up Smith's jail cell, carrying away the bodies.

No, not servants, Cady reminded herself. Slaves. Anybody who was not a master here was almost certainly a slave, one way or another. She and Georgia spoke quietly, both of them tense, as the slave crew worked.

"Where are they taking him?" Georgia asked.

"Why would I know?" Cady shot back.

"Oh, I don't know, because you're the time travel girl, and I'm just the redshirt who got beamed down to the planet with you."

"Oh, you mean when I rescued you from the fucking Fourth Reich run by an angry Cheetos demon and its talking peehole?"

They glared at each other, both ready to blow, but when they did the release came in the form of hysterical laughter. There was no lightening of the mood. It was simply a release of the unbearable tension. The manic laughter became hitching cries and then they were both bawling their eyes out, hugging each other fiercely.

"Oh, my God, Georgia, I am so sorry I got you into this. I am so sorry. I just . . ."

"It's okay, it'll be all right, it'll be fine. We just have to get out of this. We have to think our way out, Cady. We're smarter than these guys."

"And we're girls. So they totally won't see it coming."

Whether it was crazy talk or crazy brave, they needed it. They had to talk each other into believing they could survive.

"You two. Hey. Can you hear me? Do you understand? It is said you are witches and that you speak an alien tongue."

"What's he saying?" Georgia asked. The watch was tucked away in the front pocket of Cady's jeans.

The man Smith had been talking to, the gladiator, was still in his cell, and now he was trying to get their attention.

Cady checked up and down the cloisters before she spoke. There was no sign of any guards. Out on the training field, in the center of the great circular court, gladiators or trainee gladiators or whatever the hell they were, hacked and pounded at each other with practice weapons.

"Where did they take Smith?" Cady asked when she was confident they weren't being watched.

"Your man?"

"Not even close," she said as Georgia appeared at her elbow.

"Hey, hold my hand," said Cady, taking the watch from her pocket. "I want to try something."

Georgia looked slightly baffled but did as she asked, closing her hand around the watch. Now they both held it, their fingers entwined.

"Ask him something," said Cady. "See if he understands you."

"How far away is Rome?" Georgia asked, surprising Cady just a little with this level headed request. One thing about Georgia, she got her shit sorted quickly when she had to.

It seemed she had surprised the gladiator as well.

"Your man, Smith John Smith, said you were merchants. How do you not know how to find Rome? All roads lead there."

"We got lost," Cady shrugged.

"Couldn't get a GPS fix," Georgia said.

The gladiator regarded them as though they might be unhinged, but only because he understood the words they had said, and it still made no sense.

"Your man fights well, for a merchant," he went on.

"He's not our man," said Georgia.

"I already told him that," said Cady, before addressing the gladiator again. "So, my name is Cady and this is my friend Georgia. And we were wondering if you'd like to help a couple of gals break out of this festering hellhole."

"I am Gannicus of Salluvi, and yes, every man and woman who struggles under the heel of Lentulus Batiatus yearns for their freedom."

"Awesome," said Cady. "So, this breaking out thing. Ideas? Suggestions? Cunning plans?"

Gannicus of Salluvi looked troubled. "If your band has more of these weapons hidden somewhere, a cache that you have kept from Batiatus, we could use them to strike off our chains."

"We're not in a band and no, we don't have any more weapons. Got any other ideas?"

"So the thunderbolt of Smith John Smith is unique?"

"There can be only one," said Georgia.

"Where have they taken him?" Cady asked.

"Batiatus will put him in the fighting pits," said Gannicus. "When your man has been broken there, he will give the pig everything he asks for."

The gladiator looked them up and down.

"Including you," he said.

"Oh, man, you *so* don't know Smith John Smith," said Cady.

Gannicus suddenly turned away from them, and she wondered if she'd said something to offend him, but she soon heard footsteps crunching over gravel. Two guards arrived at their cell door, and behind them, two women; some raven-haired fox from the Golden Years of Hollywood and an old witch who looked like she'd fallen off el Diablo's charm bracelet. Bent-backed and sour-faced, she struck one of the guards with a long wooden cane, motioning for him to unlock their cage. The man, who was at least three times bigger than her, leapt to the task. Even so, she continued to whip him with the cane, absentmindedly, almost as though she had nothing better to do.

He flinched under each bow, muttering apologies for his tardiness, his stupidity, his unworthiness.

The younger woman watched Cady and Georgia, her eyes giving nothing away.

"Shut up and open the gate," the older one growled. "Lentulus Batiatus would have me judge them."

Crack!

"Yes, madam. At once, madam."

Crack!

"A thousand pardons, madam."

Crack!

Cady and Georgia flinched almost as much as the victim of this flogging. She was raising welts with every stroke of the cane.

"Jesus Christ," muttered Cady. "She's like Judge Judy on steroids and bath salts."

"Looks more like Joan Rivers," said Georgia, "but, you know, as a snarly fucking zombie or something."

The cage door creaked open and the guards muscled in ahead of the old biddy and her PA to secure their entrance. They needn't have bothered.

No way was Cady crossing this crazy bitch.

"Strip," the hag ordered, and when they didn't she whipped Cady on the arm with the cane.

"Ow! Bitch, that really hurt!"

"Ah. So it speaks," crowed the woman. "I had it from Lentulus Batiatus himself that you were mute. Now strip!"

She raised the cane again and Georgia put her hands up in the pretense-weak position Cady recognized from their self-defense classes. She looked like she was flinching from the anticipated blow, when in fact she was getting ready to close with the old crone and stick that cane right up her ass.

"Georgia, no!" Cady said. "It's alright. Just . . . just do it."

She let go of her friend's hand and started to undo her jeans, using the move to slip the watch back into her pocket.

"It'll be okay. They're just checking out the merch. Roll with it, for now."

They undressed in front of the audience.

The old woman considered them like grocery items from an untrustworthy bodega. Her assistant stared into the middle distance, the way a shop girl would when you put in your PIN at the checkout.

Nothing to see here.

At one point, unable to bear looking at their captors anymore, Cady glanced across at Gannicus and was strangely comforted to see he had turned his back and folded his arms. He was steadfast in his refusal to look on, unlike the guards who were so pleased with the show they forgot themselves, earning a couple more lashes of the cane.

"They belong to Batiatus now," Judge Judy snapped at them. "Let neither your hands nor your eyes defile his property, lest I take your eyes in settlement."

They dropped their gaze and did not look upon the two young women again.

"Pussy-whipped much, boys?" Cady taunted them, earning her another stroke of the cane, but also a secret smile and the faintest nod from the silent woman behind the crone.

Cady sensed the connection immediately. This one, like Gannicus, was a slave of Batiatus, not a servant or ally. Whatever thoughts she might have had about that, however, fell away as ol' Judy leaned in to take a good long sniff of her crotch.

"Hey! That's not cool, you old vaginasaur!"

Cady scored an arthritic but stinging bitch slap for that, which delayed Georgia's genital inspection and sniff test for all of one second.

"They are clean," the old woman declared. "Not virgins, but not riddled with the pox. They can serve in the bedchamber."

"No way!" Cady spluttered.

"What?" Georgia asked. She had lost translation service when they stopped holding hands.

"This old hag thinks we're gonna do the nasty with Jabba the Hutt."

"Wait, what? No way!"

Judge Judy measured them with her dark little eyes. She smiled and Cady saw that her teeth were rotten, adding to the whole Walking Dead effect.

"You will serve your master in the bedchamber, and you will please him, or I will leave you to these men."

She inclined her head toward the nearest guard.

The man did not dare look at her now, but Cady thought she could sense his anticipation.

"We can cook," Georgia said, without warning.

The crone did not understand, but Cady followed up immediately.

"Oh, hell, yeah. And I make a kick ass margarita," she improvised. "You don't want to go wasting our five star skills in the flophouse, Granny. We're like Masterchefs. Your boy, Bashy? He's got a bad dose of the permanent munchies, right? Well, we could invent waffles for him. He's gonna love waffles, believe me. And he's gonna love you for plating them up."

To Georgia, she said out the side of her mouth, "You know how to make waffles, right?"

"I've eaten waffles."

The crone narrowed her eyes.

"These waffles of which you speak. Tell me more."

CHAPTER THIRTY-ONE

Smith had never truly been lost before. He understood that now. When he palmed the watch to Cady he'd known what he was giving up. That was why he gave it up. Cady McCall was smarter than him. Her friend, Miss Georgia, might be smarter again. But none of those smarts were going to do them any good if they were lost in the Tower of Babel. Smith knew he was not likely to fight his way out of this. If they were to survive and escape, it would be because those girls were able to outthink Batiatus and his goons. He had faith in them. He had to.

But right now he had to live with the consequences of that faith. Right now he was the one lost in Babel.

From the moment Cady had closed her fist around Wu's timepiece, Smith had been plunged into an ocean of strange sounds and meaningless gabble. It started with Batiatus, of course. The slaver was talking as his goons marched Smith away from the cells. Away from his friends. There was really no point attending to the man's words. Without the chronometer they were utterly senseless. It was all Greek to Smith. Or Roman, he supposed.

But of course, Batiatus was not a man used to having his words ignored and it soon blew up between them. They were striding around the edge of the circular courtyard, keeping to the shadowed cloisters, staying out of the sun. Batiatus was waving Smith's gun around. Only the devil knew what he was saying, but Smith did understand that it was all for his benefit. When the slave master grew irritated at not receiving the replies he obviously sought, Smith finally sighed and brought on his fate.

"You can keep jabbering away all you want in your heathen tongue, my fat friend. None of it will ever make a lick of sense to me. Just as not a word I say will ever penetrate your thick skull."

Batiatus and his entourage stopped.

They had reached a tunnel leading away from the circular prison. The cells here were empty. Perhaps their occupants were out in the sun, having at each other with wooden staves and swords. The man in the bed sheet said something to him again, possibly repeating his last statement or question, and Smith smiled like a man who has just played his last chip at poker, and lost.

"If I thought I had a chance to grab that gun off you and blow your head off, rest assured the wind would be whistling between your ears already. But I know your janissaries here will turn me into a human pincushion if I try. Heck, they might do it anyway. And I need to keep breathing, because there's a chance my two young lady friends will reverse our fortunes and remove the yoke you have placed upon our necks."

All of his captors exchanged baffled looks. Smith could understand that, even sympathize some. They had even less idea than he did of what was afoot.

Batiatus said something, and Smith replied in a level tone, "Sorry, didn't catch that."

Color was rising in the man's face. His cheeks turned a florid pink and then purple. It was just possible, thought Smith, that his heart might give out. That would be a jolly caper. He might just have a go at grabbing that gun then, and seeing how many of these spear carriers he could put down before they got to him with their steel. Three, at most; the number of bullets left.

Batiatus shouted at him.

Smith's mother had taught him that if he ever got to thinking he was a person of some influence, that he should try ordering somebody else's dog around.

He fixed his eyes on Batiatus, who fumed at him.

"I ain't your dog," Smith said quietly.

The slave master had a man-sized conniption, screaming and waving his arms around, spittle flying from his lips. He jammed the gun up under Smith's jawline and Smith got ready to take his leave of the world.

"Our Father, who art in heaven . . ."

The Lord's Prayer did nothing to soothe the troubled soul of Lentulus Batiatus, but he was not so far gone in his outrage that he pulled the trigger. Instead, he smashed the gun into Smith's face, breaking his nose and drawing blood. The big man staggered back under the blow, into the arms of a guard behind him. He took a shot in the kidney, someone kicked out his legs, and then he went down under a threshing machine of kicks and punches.

He might have fought back. There are ways to defend yourself even in dire and forlorn straits such as that. But much as he longed to account for himself, rational forbearance won out.

He was very close to dying here. All these men needed was a reason to stop punching and to start hacking and stabbing and cutting. So Smith did something he had never done, not once in his life. He curled himself into a ball and endured the loathsome experience of taking a beating without retribution. It was his only path back to his daughter, and he held tight to the memory of little Elspeth as he tried to roll with the punches and the kicks. The blows came so quickly and from so many directions, that the only form of resistance left open to him was to deny them the pleasure of his pain. Marshal John Titanic Smith gritted his teeth and received the attack in silence, while yearning for his little girl.

Eventually, the furious tide ebbed and the last blow fell.

He groaned then, allowing himself that one indulgence. He could not see his attackers. His eyes were filled with blood. He expected to hear Batiatus cursing him, perhaps ordering someone to count coup on his sorry carcass. But the killing blow did not come. Instead, he was hauled to his feet, kicked in the rear end, and sent down the long tunnel surrounded by guards who were all panting with the effort of beating him down. Of Lentulus Batiatus, he could hear and see nothing.

Smith stumbled and fell twice in the tunnel, before emerging into another bright, open space. He was so discombobulated by the beating that he didn't realize, until he was blinking and squinting in the sun, that he'd picked up a couple of pals in the tunnel. Two men in chains.

Both tried to talk to him, but he could no more understand them than he could Batiatus. When he lost his footing a third time, however, they took him by the elbows and supported him until he could find his feet again. Their grip was firm but gentle. They could not be guards. They had to be slaves, like him.

They helped him out of the tunnel to stand at the edge of a great court, maybe three or four times larger than the practice ground enclosed by the prison cells. This looked like a stadium where big city teams might play the final game in a baseball season. Stands climbed away from the field, providing seating for many hundreds, if there had been that many to watch. Today the stands were mostly empty. Through his blood-dimmed vision, Smith could make out a few scattered figures, all of them dressed like Batiatus, in long flowing robes.

Masters, then.

He allowed the men at his elbows to half-carry him under a shaded awning. They gave him a bladder of something to drink. He assumed it to be water, but after a couple of gulps and gagging on the unexpectedly strong, sweet taste, Smith realized it was a medicinal blend of water and wine. Mostly wine. A woman in a simple, home-spun tunic fussed and mopped at his sweat and blood with a damp cloth. It felt like a kiss on his ruined face.

Smith imagined at first that the guards had abandoned him to his new companions, but he soon realized that they had simply dispersed, joining the ranks who stood at ease around the circumference of this coliseum. There were dozens of fighters under training here, many times the number he'd seen back in the prison. The training looked to be more intense, too. Here they fought with metal weapons. He could see them glinting under the sun and hear the clash of steel.

Unable to converse with him, the two men from the tunnels—gladiators like Gannicus he supposed—left him to the care of the nurse, or whatever she was. She spoke to him while she tended to his bruises and bumps, twittering along in a singsong voice as she cleaned out a cut on his cheek.

"I am mighty grateful for the consideration, ma'am," he said, "but I'm afraid I have no way of telling you that."

She paused in her ministrations, as if she expected him to say something she might understand. Smith attempted a smile and inclined his head in thanks. She returned the gesture and took up her one-sided discourse again.

He had not felt so lonesome since those first days with Chester, when he'd understood even less of what had befallen him. But at least then, he'd not had to deal with the perfidy of other men. At least then, he'd thought himself honestly lost, not cast adrift on the eons by sorcery.

As his wits returned to him, Smith asked himself what Cady would make of all this. Why did these men, trained fighters all of them, not rise up against their oppressor? He estimated there to be more than a hundred gladiators under tutelage in this larger arena. They outnumbered the guards four or five to one. Why did they not just stand up?

"Why don't you?" he muttered to himself, unable to keep recrimination from his voice.

His nursemaid twittered something at him, which of course he did not understand.

"My apologies, young lady," he said. "Please, I think you've done enough. From the looks of it, there's fellers out there will need your care more than I. I just took a beat down, is all. Weren't my first. Won't be the last, God willing."

He gently pushed her hands away and smiled. Then he inclined his head towards the training grounds, and made a shooing gesture with his hands.

"Thank you," he said.

She smiled, uncertainly, but in the end she seemed to take heed of his meaning. When she left, two guards took up station outside the shade cloth.

So why don't you just stand up, Marshal? Smith asked himself. *If'n you're so fired up for these other fellers to throw themselves onto the spear points, perhaps you should lead by example.*

He sat nursing his wounds and his dark mood until more guards arrived and began yammering at him in their heathen tongue. He deduced that he was to go with them. He felt every blow of that late beating all over again as he climbed to his feet. His clothes were torn and covered in blood. He thought of the big pink valise back in Cady's home year, sitting uselessly in the rear seat of the wagon where he'd left it.

If only he'd had a mind to pick it up.

The guards started shouting at him, and like a broken man, he did as he was told. Or as he assumed they were telling him. Smith shuffled out of the tent and fell in between his captors.

They walked him around the edge of the stadium, giving him a chance to marvel at the array of bizarre weapons and fighting styles. Men fought with nets, tridents, and all manner of arms that made no sense at all to him. Although they were training, they did so in earnest, and he was constantly assailed by the sort of screaming and shouting he'd not heard up close since his own time in the war. Once or twice he saw men destroyed.

He could only hope he'd done the right thing in giving Cady that watch. He didn't know if these pagan savages had even heard the Good Word. It was more'n possible, he supposed, that baby Jesus had not yet turned up in that manger. But a man had to have faith, and so Titanic Smith sent the only prayers he had to the only God that mattered.

"Yea though I walk through the valley of the shadow of death . . ."

At the far end of the stadium, he found himself confronting that shadow.

Batiatus sat on a small throne surrounded by licksplittles and toadies, all of them dressed like him in their bedsheets. The slave master was saying something important. You could tell from the air of grand significance that surrounded him as he stood forth and orated. Smith was actually glad of not having the watch. He didn't much need to hear any more hot air from this pompous goose.

As Batiatus performed, another man appeared next to Smith. He turned his head and thought for the merest second that he recognized one of the gladiators who had helped him from the tunnel.

"Hello, John Smith."

"Goddamn!"

Smith jumped away like a jack rabbit on a hot griddle.

"Chumley!"

It must've looked right comical to anybody watching on, and sure enough, the toady circle around Batiatus did start braying with laughter.

Chumley smiled, an empty sort of expression.

"My name is Apprentice."

Hot blood and jumping beans roiled up inside Smith. The las
time he'd laid eyes on this verminous character, two innocents had
died. His aches and pains and deep melancholy of the soul suddenly
seemed less hurtful. Smith bunched up his fists and made ready fo.
the man who had murdered poor Gracie and Bertie.

There could be no doubt he had done so.

The Chumley they'd met in London was gone, his nervousness
and incertitude replaced by cold calculation in the face of the
stone killer standing in front of Smith.

"So, you're one-a-them," said Smith, his voice low and accus-
ing. "An apprentice. I figured as much."

"And you are an elusive," said Chumley, calmer. Almost reserved.

He looked so different from the last time Smith had seen him a
day ago, and some thousands of years from now. Maybe twenty
pounds heavier. His skin burnished bronze by the sun hereabouts.
And scarred. The man was a relief map of scar tissue.

"We have been searching for you, John Smith. And I have been
waiting for you," Chumley said. "You understand that this must
end now. You cannot go on."

His voice had changed too. He'd sounded like all of the other
Londoners before. Now he sounded like no one. It was a voice
without accent or shade of dialect.

In the stands above them, Batiatus finished with a flourish and
sat down, waving one pudgy hand in their direction. Chumley
turned towards the slave master and performed some type of
salute, before striding away, putting a good ten yards or so between
himself and Smith.

"You can go to hell," Smith shouted up at Batiatus and his
hangers on. He offered no salute, and refused to move, drawing
scandalized gasps and glares from the small audience.

Chumley watched him closely, both wary and curious.

"They think you a stranger, John Smith, and they are right. You do not belong here."

"You seem plenty settled in, Chumley."

"To these people I am *il Scissore*. I arrived here some time ago. I will depart when my work is done, and I will soon be forgotten, as will you."

A guard jogged up carrying two swords. When he threw them to the ground, Smith saw that one of the swords was his Bowie knife. The other was a wicked sharp-looking length of steel, maybe half a foot longer.

He felt the old ice water trickling into his guts. He felt the pain that was on him already, and the pain that might be coming down the trail real soon.

This weren't no practice.

These ghouls intended for them to die under the high sun, purely for their amusement. And Chumley aimed to kill him for some reason known best to himself.

A drum began to beat and a trumpet sounded. It weren't no bugle call that Smith knew from his cavalry days, but the effect was the same. Across the stadium grounds men stopped and answered to the call. Those closest walked over, but briskly. The gladiators and guards farther away came at a trot. In less than a minute a crowd of more than a hundred had gathered in a loose circle around them.

The guards formed an inner ring, their spears and shields separating Smith and Chumley or *il Scissore*—from the onlookers.

He looked at the man he was supposed to fight.

Strangely, there was no more animosity in Chumley's demeanor than a surgeon might feel toward a tumor. About as much mercy, too.

"You ain't some savage, Chumley," Smith said over the clamor of the gathering mob. "Don't see as why we have to cut into each other for the merriment of that infernal cur."

He jerked a thumb in the direction of Lentulus Batiatus.

Chumley did not bother to follow the gesture.

"Batiatus is a minor escapement," he said. "If it were not through him, we would make the adjustment somewhere else."

"Adjustment?" Smith called out. The noise of the crowd forced him to raise his voice.

"You caused this complication to arise, John Smith, this and twenty-eight more. You cannot be allowed to create further disorder."

Chumley stepped forward and picked up his sword.

He stood back and nodded at Smith's Bowie knife.

"You are expected to defend yourself," he explained.

"And if'n I don't."

"I cannot strike you down on my own initiative. But have no doubt Lentulus Batiatus will order your death if you refuse the contest."

Smith spat in disgust.

"This ain't a contest, you idiot. It's an abomination, and the devil has a fire pit set aside for the likes of Batiatus."

"No," said Chumley. He did not shout but he somehow projected his voice over the growing uproar. "In three days, Lentulus Batiatus will die at the hands of his own slaves and chattels, but that is all that will happen to him."

Smith staggered forward, kicked from behind by somebody, occasioning a great eruption of laughter among the crowd.

He turned to confront whoever had done it, but found two guardsmen with spears leveled at him.

They seemed to think he should pick up his knife.

CHAPTER THIRTY-TWO

The waffle plan was not working out.

"Jesus, Cady, I can't make waffles here," Georgia said, "and you promised them waffles. You promised the original redneckulous murder-chubby a feast of sugary hi-carb goodness. What the forgetful fuck were you thinking?"

"Oh, I don't know," snarked Cady, "that maybe you'd prefer to spend this evening doing something other than blowing a duet on his nasty little meat whistle?"

They bitched and argued with each other in a relatively quiet corner of the kitchens, which were huge, much larger than either of them were expecting. But that made sense. The women here, and it was mostly women, weren't just cooking for Batiatus. They had a couple of hundred gladiators and guardsmen and even more slaves to feed. This place probably ran 24/7, and it did everything with log fires and artisanal hand-drawn hipster water.

"Shut up! The two of you just shut up and cook, now!"

Their supervisor—some sort of Old Testament sous chef—had a cane just like Judge Judy's. It was almost as though she was hoping to grow up into a vicious old hag herself, one day. She whipped at them both with the thin wooden rod. It stung like a bitch.

"Ow!" Cady cried out.

Georgia just swore and dodged away from the next blow, infuriating the woman who lashed Cady even harder on the backswing.

"Fuck!"

Cady tried to avoid the blows like Georgia but only flinched and stumbled into a stack of cooking pots which went crashing to the flagstone floor, further enraging their latest tormentor.

Before shuffling off to whip and thrash random kitchen hands, old Jude had given Cady and Georgia over to this would-be troll. The problems started when they couldn't keep up the pretend-lesbian hand-holding routine to give Georgia access to the universal translator. Cady, whose mad kitchen skills began and ended with pop tarts and microwaved cookie dough, was not well suited to mediating the increasingly fraught exchanges between the Georgia and their latest tormentor.

"Do you two even know how to cook?" the woman snarled. "I should send you to the barracks right now. You can spread your legs there. It will not matter to them that you are so useless. To them you are just a cooze anyway."

She looked ready to lash Cady with her cane again, raising it on high for a scarifying blow, when her expression changed and she tumbled over backwards, crying out in alarm.

The younger woman who had shadowed Judge Judy down in the prison cells, stood behind her, smiling enigmatically.

"Drusilla, you must be more careful in the kitchens. The floor is slippery and dangerous. Look how you have fallen."

Drusilla fixed their savior with a glare, but said nothing. Cady could tell there were layers of meaning to the exchange that were completely beyond the power of the watch to translate.

"I will supervise them. You can attend to the skinning of the eels."

It seemed as though Drusilla might object, but another of those unreadable, unspoken exchanges changed her mind, and she butt-scuttled away, only getting to her feet when she was well beyond reach.

"I am Calista, prophetess of Antioch," the woman said, turning to Cady and Georgia as though Drusilla did not exist and had not just been humiliated.

"Thanks," Cady said, a little warily. "I'm Cady, programmer of iOS. This is my friend, Georgia, maven of Bungie. We shouldn't be here."

Calista smiled. "Nobody should be here."

"Cady, what's going on now?" Georgia asked. "What's Wonder Woman after?"

"Dunno. Gimme a second and I'll find out."

The businesses of the kitchens went on around them, uninterrupted by the small drama in the furthest corner. Pots and pans rattled. Oven fires burned. Cleavers chopped through meat and bone and bit deeply into wooden butchers' blocks.

Calista seemed little interested in their waffle-making venture. She kept glancing back over her shoulder as though watching out for someone.

Judge Judy maybe?

"I have heard of your feats this morning, that you arrived by sorcery, and by even greater sorcery you slew four dogs of Batiatus before they took you in chains."

Cady gave Georgia a slightly pained look.

"Er, I think they think we're like masters of the dark arts or something, and we laid a bunch of Voldemort curses on those dudes those morning."

"The ones Smith shot?"

"Yep."

"Awesome," Georgia deadpanned.

Cady took a bet on Calista not being a narc.

"So, it was two guys, not four," she said, "and it was our friend Smith who killed them, not us. But otherwise, yeah, you got our number."

Calista narrowed her eyes. "Excellent. And this Wizard Smith? He can bring more of this magic?"

Cady blew her cheeks out. How to tell her that Batiatus now wielded the magic six-shooter? Probably straight up.

"He doesn't have his magic wand anymore. The fat guy has it."

"I see," said Calista. "And the spell you cast to travel here. Why have you not left by the same magic?"

"I wish we could," Cady said, keenly aware of the watch tucked away in her jeans. If these assholes got hold of that, too, they were screwed with a capital F. "We travel by the stars and they are not in alignment," she improvised. "But you're like a kickass prophetess, right? You already knew that."

Calista of Antioch nodded sagely.

"I understand," she said, not pleased, but accepting of the fates. Her stars and fates probably weren't in tiptop alignment either.

"How about you ask her what's going down here?" Georgia suggested. "What's her gig? Chief executive troublemaker would be my guess. Be nice to know for whom."

"Good point. So, er, Calista. We're not from around here. We seem to have got on everyone's bad side. Is there some way we could, you know, not be enslaved or anything?"

"You seek your freedom?" the woman asked, her tone sharp, but not accusatory. She doubled her watchfulness.

Yep.

Troublemaker.

"Yeah. Freedom rocks," Cady said, trusting the watch to make to make the translation.

"Then we are allies," Calista whispered fiercely. "You will stand with us when the time comes?"

"Mmm . . . sure. Why not?"

She clasped Cady's forearm, and then Georgia's.

"For now," she said, "tend to your waffles."

"So, what the hell is going on?" Georgia asked as soon as they were alone again.

Cady carefully scoped out the room. It was chaos, but organized in a way that was just beyond her ability to understand.

"I'm not sure," she said, "but I think we've come under the protection of the maximum kitchen dyke. She has magic powers, and I think she wants to overthrow the system."

"Great," said Georgia, clearly unimpressed. "So now we have to be time-travelling lesbians?"

"You wish."

They were quiet for a moment.

"Cady, what are we gonna do? I can't make waffles. I can't be a lesbian. Ruby Rose really scares me. And not even sexy scare. She just terrifies me, all those tattoos and that haircut."

Cady put her arm around her friend and gave her a reassuring hug.

"We have a way out," she said quietly, "or we will, soon."

Georgia pushed back out of the embrace. "How?"

"The watch," Cady explained. "It resets every twenty-four hours. I told you that, right?"

"Jeez, I dunno, maybe. It's been a bit crazed since you got back, you know."

"Fair call. Anyway, look. They took my phone, with the timer, but tomorrow as soon as the watch ticks over a full day here, it reboots or goes live or whatever. We can jump away, just like we jumped away from Seattle. We just have to be in physical contact with each other."

Georgia was quiet for a few seconds.

"What about Marshal Smith?" she said.

"He gave me the watch."

"So?"

"I think he wanted us to use it."

"Cady! We can't leave him here."

"Georgia, he could be dead."

"You're reaching," her friend said sharply.

"And you're in denial," Cady shot back

"No, you're being cruel and unusual."

"Oh, don't make me roll my eyes."

The rapid fire back and forth came to a halt with each of them glaring at the other.

"No, Cady," Georgia said at last. "Don't make me hate you, again. You're just being a selfish bitch. Again. And you know it. We can't leave without him."

Cady wanted to say something cutting, to pull her friend down off that high horse. But in that perverse way the human mind at full gallop can leap from one thought to another, hers went from the idea of "high horse" to "Smith"—because "high horse" was totally the sort of old-school bullshit he would've come up with—and from Smith to Chester, the horse he'd left behind in the vast wastes of time. She thought of how quietly, grievously wounded Smith had been by the loss of that old friend, by that abandonment, however unintended.

And her face started to burn with shame.

Georgia smiled, her eyes lighting up. "There it is. Your conscience. I knew that feeble, pussy ass little bitch was in there somewhere."

"God, I hate my stupid conscience," Cady mumbled. "It's always getting in the way."

Georgia returned the hug that Cady had given her a few moments earlier.

"No, baby," she said gently. "Trust me. Your conscience almost never gets in the way. Unless I'm around to give it a push."

"Fuck you."

"And you."

They were hugging it out when Drusilla returned.

Perhaps things might have gone differently if Drusilla hadn't snuck up like that. Maybe if she'd stayed in character and started screeching like a harpy as she ran at them with her little whacking stick, they might have had a chance to prepare themselves.

But the first either of them knew she was there was when she whipped Georgia across the back and screeched some old timey curse about Medusa's pubes turning into snakes or something, raising the cane for another blow.

Georgia cried out in shock and pain, and before Cady really understood what had happened, or what was about to happen, her friend snapped out a side kick that took Drusilla in the sweet spot and folded her up like a cheap, Chinese umbrella. The girls stood looking at each other dumbly, unsure what to do next. Drusilla made the decision for them, screaming a banshee curse and raising the cane as if to whip them both in the face. Georgia yelled her own war-shout and busted out some high level *aiki-jutsu* move which broke the woman's arm in all sorts of places and sent her flying across the nearest table. Pottery jars went flying and crashing everywhere.

There was a second, maybe less, of complete silence.

It was like they were on stage and every spotlight had fallen on them. Every actor was in place and all eyes were on the principals.

Cady and Georgia.

In that brief, eternal, suspended moment Cady saw everything. The armed guards, at least eight of them, turning-turning-turning in their direction. The fearsome glare of Judge Judy. Just behind that malignant old hag, Calista, her eyes wide, then narrow, her face morphing and distorting. Slaves, servants, prisoners all, looking to Cady and Georgia, to the guards, to Calista, to the old woman.

And then it began.

The old hag had just started screeching at the guards when something flashed and her head came off. Like, right off, revealing Calista to be holding a heavy, blood-smeared cleaver.

Things got nasty. Kitchens are dangerous places full of sharp edges and hot things. The ordered chaos that Cady had earlier tried and failed to understand exploded into disorder and violence as dozens of captive women took up knives and cleavers and pots of boiling water and oil, and fell upon the guards before they had moved more than a few steps towards the newcomers.

The sudden, caterwauling din of riot and murder was like nothing Cady had ever heard. Not at the largest sports event. Not at the gnarliest rock festival. The screams of the women in revolt were as awful as those of the men they cut down. Loudest of all, because they were closest, were the yells and shrieks of her friend and the woman she was methodically destroying with vicious combinations of kicks and punches and fast-flowing body moves. Cady shrank away from them as Georgia finally threw Drusilla to the ground. The woman was alive, but she had no fight left in her.

Georgia looked up, panting. Cady didn't recognize her. Those eyes did not look in on the soul of Georgia Eliadis. Hellfire and madness burned in there.

"So," said Cady, nervously, "still keeping up the martial arts classes?"

Georgia slowly came back from wherever she'd been, shaking off the fugue state of her killing rage and taking Cady by the arm. Her grip was strong and it hurt.

"We have to go," she breathed heavily. "Now."

They ran, hand in hand, but they had no clear path and soon found themselves channeled into the presence of Calista, who looked like she'd taken off a couple more heads with that big ass bone chopper of hers.

"It is a sign. It is *the* sign, as foretold," proclaimed the crazy prophetess. "The Magi of iOS and Bungie have traveled here to free us, sisters. Lift them up and carry them forth into the day where freedom shall be ours."

And lo, were the reluctant magi lifted up and carried out of the kitchens and into the violent bloodswarm of a slave revolt.

Cady lost contact with Georgia, which was almost as terrifying as the bloody mayhem and confusion of the uprising. Borne aloft against her plea, she crowd-surfed out of the kitchen on the insurgent tide. Mostly she saw only the ceiling of wherever they were headed, generally downwards and into darkness. After a few minutes in which the phalanx of murderous women rolled over all opposition, she found herself back in the cloisters outside the cells surrounding the little practice ground.

As Cady was lowered to her feet, she witnessed the revolt spreading to the gladiators who turned on their less numerous guards and cut them down with kitchen knives. She turned away from the terrible spectacle. Who'd have thought that actual slaughter and horror wasn't nearly as much fun as the innocent virtual murder she'd enabled so many people to enjoy with her cool, little game back in the 21st century.

"Gannicus, where is my husband?" a woman called out.

Calista.

And then Georgia reappeared, looking grateful beyond words to have found Cady again.

The gladiator who had been locked up in the cell next to Smith was free and armed with a short sword he'd taken from a dead guard. It was painted with gore, as was Gannicus.

"He was training in the main stadium, mistress," he said.

"Where's Smith?" Cady shouted over the uproar. "The man we came here with, the one in the cell next to—"

Gannicus cut off her questions with a wave of the bloody sword.

"Your man was also taken to the main training grounds," he said.

"But he's not a gladiator," Cady shouted. The riot seemed to be reaching some new zenith of madness, buffering them in the seething crush and flow of the crowd through the cloisters.

"It does not matter," said Gannicus, leaning in to be heard over the rabble. "He defied Batiatus. I saw him. He was beaten for it, but that will not satisfy the appetite of the pig. The guards said Smith John Smith was to face *il Scissore* for the masters' pleasure."

"Cady, where's Smith," Georgia shouted. She was standing right next to Cady, but had to raise her voice to make herself heard over the din. "I don't have Google translate like you, remember."

"Just wait," Cady said before asking Gannicus, "What's *il Scissore*?"

"The carver!" Calista shouted.

Cady explained to Georgia.

"Smith is fighting some badass called the Carver."

"Really? That doesn't sound good."

"Yeah, I don't think the name's ironic. I don't think they've even invented that yet."

The din around them was easing, just slightly. Everyone in need of being murdered must have been dead now.

"This carving guy," said Cady, "he's not like a wood worker or anything, is he?"

She was hoping maybe the watch had missed some vital nuance in translation.

"No," said Gannicus. "He arrived here three months ago, a free man offering to fight for Batiatus. He has never been bested in single combat."

"All righty then," said Cady. "Do you think we could go find our friend now?"

CHAPTER THIRTY-THREE

If there was a formal signal to begin the duel, it was lost on Titanic Smith. He edged forward to where his Bowie knife lay on the hard-packed dirt.

Chumley backed off a few steps, giving his opponent space to bend down and pick up the weapon.

Smith's back ached, his knees creaked, but his fingers closed around the familiar bone-handle grip with something like satisfaction. It did feel good to have ol' Jim back. He settled into a comfortable stance, or as close as he could manage in his battered state.

"Chumley," he said, "we still a got a path out of this without needing to spill blood."

Privately, Smith was minded to gut this feller like a pig for what he'd done back in London. But Miss Cady would surely say they needed his aptitude with the watch and all its complexities more'n they needed his innards feeding the flies. Chumley seemed able to step in and out of the years like other folk might get on and off a train. They needed to know how he did that.

"I'm sorry if I done the wrong thing with Mr. Wu's timepiece," he said, "or if I have given offense to some rule or charter of your timekeeper's guild, but I would plead both ignorance and innocent motive in mitigation."

The murmuring of the crowd shifted in tone, becoming a touch louder and hard-edged with disapproval. Everybody wanted to get to the slashing and the bloodletting. They didn't come for no debate.

Whether sensing their hunger for the contest or simply wanting to get on with it himself, Chumley stepped carefully towards Smith. His movement was cautious, but unafraid. Smith rolled his shoulders to work out the knots and cramps of his recent pummeling, but he did nothing to bring on the moment from which they could not turn back.

"Your intentions are irrelevant, John Smith," said Chumley, easing just a little to Smith's left, putting himself in a flanking position, moving away from the heavy blade in Smith's right hand.

"Maybe," Smith conceded. He took no steps toward or away from Chumley, but he did pivot, just slightly, on the balls of his feet, keeping the man within his fighting arc. "I understand that ignorance of the law is no justification. But I would beg the chance to make restitution, to right whatever wrong I might have done, and to lift whatever sentence might lie upon my companions, Miss Cady and Miss Georgia, who are entirely innocent."

Chumley paid him the compliment of a glacial smile as he came in cautiously and tried a few experimental swings with his own short sword. It cleaved through the air with a hiss.

"Marshal, you would understand that nobody is ever entirely innocent."

Still, Smith did not move.

The angry buzz of the crowd had dropped back to an expectant murmur now that blood was in the offing.

"In this affair, those young women *are* without sin, damn you," Smith growled. "Any fault lies upon me alone. Since you must know how to pass between the years with alacrity, it would be the decent thing to return them home before all of this happened."

"They cannot simply step back through the golden minutes," Chumley said somewhat cryptically. "The complications are manifest now. They will run on until the end of time."

The apprentice began to circle him, forcing Smith to adjust his footing. He did not consider himself an expert with the blade, but he had spent some time with men who were, and he had applied himself to such lessons as they had offered. He did not present himself square on; to do so simply laid out a smorgasbord of targets for an opponent to choose. Instead, he arrayed himself in a slightly side-on posture, with the heavy steel blade held but lightly in front of him. Smith's knife was larger than the average run of Bowie knives because he was larger than the average run of men. The cross-guard stuck out an inch-and-a-half on each side of the cleaver-like steel. It was a dagger that would do for a man with one thrust.

The crowd was growing restless at the lack of action. The toadies around Batiatus started to shout insults and oaths at the fighters. Or at least, Smith assumed them to be insults from the tenor of their cussing.

Smith did nothing.

Chumley finally launched himself at the outlander. He came in as fast as a Comanche brave, but with the sabre control of a Spanish *hildago*. He would have been a devil to beat, but that was not Smith's ambition. He merely wanted to hold the man out, and to that end, he danced and dodged and parried and blocked. The steels sometimes sparked and clashed, and sometimes whistled through clean air.

The crowd fell quiet, then found their voices, and their anger, when it became obvious what game he was playing. Initially cautious, then frustrated, Chumley increased his tempo, looking to pick apart Smith's defense. But wherever he struck, the Bowie knife flashed out in warding. Within minutes both men were puffing, and each had collected a few slashes and shaving cuts, but neither had suffered a grievous wound.

Chumley retreated a few paces to consider his tactics. His eyes searched Smith's for an answer.

"Free men do not kill each other for the enjoyment of lords," Smith said, during this lull in their dance.

"They do at this time, John Smith, and most others of my experience. You should accept what you have made necessary. If I fail, more will follow. Your fate is settled."

He came in again, feinting and weaving, changing his angles of attack, always looking to unbalance Smith, to force him onto his heels.

The other man would win. Smith knew that. If this went on long enough, he would devise an attack that broke down Smith's defenses.

There was another way, though. Smith fell back under a sustained assault, and left himself open to a straight thrust. Frustrated and even baffled by an opponent who would not attack in defense, Chumley leapt at the simple finishing move.

Smith suddenly transferred his balance from one foot to the other, performed a little sidestep that would've wowed all the ladies at the Purdue County Harvest Moon Ball, and kicked the devil's legs out from under him.

A roar erupted from the crowd.

In a mortal contest, Smith would have been on him then, hacking off his sword arm and holding down his screaming enemy while he delivered the killing stroke. Instead he kicked the sword out of the man's hand and stood back.

He turned to the party gathered around Batiatus.

"One drop of this man's blood is more precious than all of your worthless hides stitched together," he called out. The crowd roared again, but not in unity this time. Some of them were outraged, and some were behind Smith. He could feel it. They did not know what he had just said, but they could all see what he had just done.

He reached a hand down to his fallen opponent and lifted him up.

Chumley came to his feet, clasping Smith's forearm.

The apprentice was the picture of confusion.

He had prepared himself to die just a moment back.

The men, and even the womenfolk, around Batiatus looked angry and scared; always a poor combination. They were still shouting and gesticulating wildly. The guardsmen, who in surrounding the fighters had allowed themselves to be surrounded by a hundred more fighters, looked anxiously to their bossman for instruction. Unlike his lackeys and fawners, Lentulus Batiatus, was silent and still, like a snake just before striking.

He climbed to his feet, held out his fist, and stabbed his thumb at his own chest.

A terrible roar went up and the guardsmen drew their weapons.

Smith felt the grip on his arm tighten, drawing his attention back to the gladiator he had spared, all to bring on this very moment.

Chumley was holding a blade.

He thrust the stiletto at Smith's unprotected side, but the marshal had the benefit of many years' experience with the lowest and most vicious curs. He had hoped Chumley might take the proffered hand of peace, but he was ready to break the man's arm if not, and he did so, turning on one foot to dodge the strike, pulling Chumley off balance by his wrist, and slamming his hip into the vulnerable elbow. Weren't no amount of muscle or scar tissue you could build up to protect that particular joint.

It came apart with a sickening crunch and a cry of shock and pain from Chumley.

The guardsmen were not to be put off the execution of the master's order, though. They came on behind shields with spear points lowered. The crowd was now baying like Satan's own pack of monster dogs, heaving and pushing against each other and against the inner ring of guards.

Smith heard the unmistakable crack of a pistol shot over the uproar, and was pulled off balance himself when Chumley, still screaming, drove a fist into the side of his knee. The last thing he saw as he toppled over was a single spear tip coming at his face.

CHAPTER THIRTY-FOUR

Not wanting to be separated again, Cady and Georgia held hands as they ran into the main stadium amidst the snowballing riot of mutinous slaves. Cady was wired and jittery, expecting to be cut down at any second. Her friend seemed less fearful. In fact, for the first time since arriving here, Georgia seemed to have found herself. In violent action.

Thousands of hours of training in a martial art that was thousands of years old probably helped with that.

Cady, unfortunately, was finding that her mad skills at coding digital violence for hi-res smartphone screens wasn't nearly as useful. She did her best to stay somewhere near the middle of the fast moving pack, even though she desperately wanted to catch some glimpse of Smith.

The main stadium was much grander than the little training ground surrounded by the prison cells. It was easily as big as a high school football ground. The sunlight was harsh after the subterranean tunnel from the prison, and she squinted against the glare. The light was different here. Not just in this part of the world, she thought, but at this point in history.

The noise in the tunnel had been oppressive—the screams and stamping of feet, the clash of metal on metal—but there was an even greater uproar out here in the open. For a second she was scared that it might be a crowd celebrating the murder of Marshal Smith. But as they ran onto the hard packed earth and the tight knot of bodies loosened up and spread out, she could see they were hurrying from one mad slaughter into another.

Hundreds of men hacked and bashed at each other. More combatants poured onto the field from the dark mouths of tunnels around the stadium.

"We have to find Smith and get out of here," she shouted at Georgia.

But Georgia didn't reply. She pulled Cady to one side with a violent tug, saving her from injury at the hands of some half-naked man wielding a heavy pole. Hard to believe she'd missed him. Dude looked like an unhinged leather fetishist as he swung the giant length of hardwood around, raising it on high as though he meant to smash Cady's head in. Georgia didn't give him a chance. Shrieking as loudly and savagely as any of the crazy people around them, she threw herself at the attacker, scissoring her legs around his midriff and using the impact of her body mass to jackknife him in half. She rolled quickly to one side, and before the man could regain his feet, Gannicus ran him through with a sword.

Cady was beyond screaming. She'd had her fill of horror and imagined there was nothing more to shock or terrorize her.

The cavalry charge proved her wrong.

Four men came thundering out of the darkened maw of a tunnel on the far side of the stadium, riding directly at the slaves. They swung swords and spears and weapons of a design Cady had never seen before. The first horse crashed into the crowd and bodies flew through the air.

Cady saw Georgia dive to take what cover she could find rolled up in a ball next to the man she and Gannicus had just killed. The gladiator, however, stood his ground. He waited for the next rider, resolute, as though challenging him to a game of chicken. Man and horse came on and it seemed that Gannicus would be mowed down until, at the last second, he deftly twirled aside like a matador avoiding the bull's horns. He turned in a complete circle, hacking the rear leg of the poor horse clean off.

Well, maybe not so clean . . .

The shrieking of the injured animal only added to the insane furor and turmoil. It crashed down in a three-legged heap, crushing half a dozen people and creating a barrier that tripped up the horse directly behind it. Screaming Georgia's name, Cady ran to pull her friend out of the jumble of bodies. She had lost track of the fourth horse and rider, but they were gone, maybe fled, maybe pulled down and hacked to pieces by the mob.

"GEORGIA!"

And then her friend was there, appearing through the chaos like a conjurer's trick. She was breathing heavily and covered in blood, but she pulled her lips back from carnivore teeth and ran to Cady.

"We have to find Smith," they both said in unison.

They'd lost contact with Gannicus, with Calista, with anybody who might have helped. There was no sense to the boiling cauldron of violence. Men and women raked at each other with animal ferocity. There had to be some order to it, Cady thought—slave versus master, the oppressed and their oppressors—but she could not sort one from the other.

Georgia armed herself with a sword.

"Pick up a club, something, anything," she yelled. "Kill anybody who even looks halfway wrong."

Cady wasted a few seconds casting about for a weapon until she patted at the zippered pockets of her leather jacket, searching for a memory. She found it in there: a can of mace.

She shouted at Georgia holding up the artifact of a long lost future time. "Good enough?"

"It'll do," yelled Georgia. "Let's go. He'll be in there somewhere."

She pointed her sword at the dense, roiling mass of murder and anarchy at the far end of the stadium.

That was the last place Cady wanted to go.

They set off at a run.

Calista, flanked by two gladiators, caught up with them just before they entered the depths of the ferment. Cady thought they might hack and slash their way in, but instead, they began pulling people apart. She realized then that they had passed through the worst of the violence. This was something more akin to a mosh pit.

"Come!" Calista called back over her shoulder. "Come with us. Crixus says your man is up here. He safeguards *il Scissore* from the mob. Hurry now."

Georgia, shuddering, threw down the sword, as though discovering she was disgusted by it. Cady held onto her can of Mace, but kept it discreetly tucked away in one palm. They fell in behind Calista and her bodyguards, slowly forcing an advance through the crowd. The earthen floor of the stadium was muddy with blood. Once or twice Cady tripped on bodies or body pieces.

The whole thing was totally gross.

They emerged into a small clearing where Smith stood over a man, presumably this Carver asshole. Cady saw immediately that the marshal was not guarding him to prevent escape, but rather to stop the mob from tearing him apart. He looked badly cut up. Even with the benefit of the watch to translate for her, she had trouble understanding.

Was this *il Scissore?*

"Cady! Miss Georgia!" Smith whipped off his hat and mopped at his brow. He was a mess. "Ain't this a hog killin' time, and ain't you a sight for the sorriest eyes? You recognize our friend here?"

Cady wasn't quite sure what he meant. Why would she . . .

"Holy shit! That's Chumley!"

"Who?" Georgia asked.

"Chumley," Cady said, unhelpfully. "Oh, sorry, he's . . . well, he's like us. He shouldn't be here."

"What? He's like a time traveler, too?"

"My name is Apprentice," Chumley croaked, barely audible over the noise. He was drenched in blood and one of his arms was grotesquely swollen. "You should not be here."

"Yeah, he will not let go of that particular bone," Smith said.

The marshal looked like he'd been tied to a horse and dragged backwards through the worst part of Texas. He was covered in blood, his clothes torn, one eye was swollen, and livid bruises stood out all over him. Chumley looked worse. Cady guessed that the mob had tried to tear him apart and had been about half way done with that before Smith put a halt to it.

Cady ran forward and threw her arms around the cowboy.

He staggered back under the impact, which told her how badly hurt he must be. Running into Titanic Smith would normally be like head-butting a tank.

Calista and her sword-and-sandal twins loomed over Chumley looking like they couldn't understand why he was still drawing breath. The taller gladiator, standing protectively close to her, pointed his sword at Chumley and announced, "This one has no honor."

Smith eyed the new arrivals.

"Cady, could you tell these folk that I'm right grateful for their help earlier' in the tunnel, but I will not have this man lynched. Already had to see to a few folk decided to poke holes in him."

"You can tell him yourself," she said and knelt down to Chumley.

"Best be careful," Smith warned.

The apprentice tried to push her away, so Cady maced him. He cried out and raked at his eyes with one bloodied hand.

"Hey," Smith protested. "He's my prisoner."

"He had it coming," said Cady. "For Gracie. Besides, I need him distracted."

She looked Chumley up and down.

He was not the thin and unimpressive specimen they'd met in London. He looked musclebound and scarred. There was no way to affect that sort of transformation in two days.

Another data point.

Cady found what she was looking for at his hip; a small pouch, tied to his belt. He tried to stop her when she tugged at it, and Cady punched him on the nose, drawing another rebuke but no further action from Smith.

Chumley was half blind and weak from blood loss and injury, and it made Cady feel good to hit him, even though it sort of hurt her knuckles.

"I need a knife," she announced, and Gannicus appeared beside her.

"You know of *il Scissore*?" he asked, passing her a small, nasty-looking hooked blade. Like every other piece of edged metal she'd seen today, it was sticky with blood. She used it to cut away the pouch.

"I know him from another place," she said. "He killed two friends of mine."

Gannicus nodded.

"Mine too," he said. "Shall I kill him now?"

She almost said, "Sure, why not," but Smith had obviously kept him alive for a reason. Hopefully not just because he was a better person than her.

"Maybe later. Just, you know, keep an eye on him."

"Here," she said, tossing Smith a gold pocket watch, just like the one in her jeans pocket. Cady had a moment of fleeting panic, then, thinking she may have dropped it, but a quick pat reassured her it was still there.

Smith took the second timepiece, as Georgia attempted to get a good look at it.

"Is this it? Is this how you do it?"

"I reckon as much," Smith confirmed, taking in the faces of the crowd. Cady could tell he was listening to them now, and he could understand what they were saying.

"We must seize this day," the man standing by Calista announced. "We cannot remain here. The legions will come from Capua. If we defeat them, more will come from Rome. We must be gone when they arrive."

"Us, too," Cady said, climbing back to her feet.

Calista took Cady in her arms.

"You should come with us. The stars are not in their heavens for you now, but your arrival here set the constellations in place for us. Come with us. You have led us to freedom. My husband will lead us to a safe place, where that freedom can never be taken from us again."

"Thanks," said Cady, "but, you know, we should probably be going."

The guy who had to be Calista's old man saluted Smith with his sword and bowed to Cady and Georgia.

"Your names will forever be remembered, Smith John Smith, Cady of iOS, and Georgia of Bungie," he said to each in turn.

"You know what, you should probably just keep us out of it," said Cady. "Good luck with your slave revolt and everything, though."

"We are no longer slaves; praise be to you."

"Awesome. You be you then . . . err . . . Gladiator Maximus. Sorry, I met Gannicus and Calista, but I didn't get your name."

The freed man stood a few inches taller.

"I am Spartacus."

CHAPTER THIRTY-FIVE

Gannicus helped Smith carry the apprentice to a shaded tent where the same young woman who had tended to him after his beating now cleaned out Chumley's wounds.

Chumley's watch was not an exact replica of Wu's. It had a minute and a second hand, for starters, and two crowns. But it afforded the same convenient translation of all that was said around him, and for now Smith was content with that.

"If Chumley's somehow been here for a couple of months, his watch will be live," Cady warned. "You double-click that thing, and you're gone, Smith. We can still use this one to get out of here tomorrow," she said, holding up the original chronometer, "but we'd be on our own, and the chances of finding you again would be zero. Probably less."

He took the warning to heart, looping a thin leather strap around the crown in such a way that it could not be easily depressed. It meant Smith couldn't activate the watch quickly if he got himself into a tight corner, but he didn't want to leave here without them, so that was no consideration at all.

He thanked his little nurse, whose name was Lyvia, for her earlier kindness, and was glad of the opportunity to do so. Smith did not care for being unable to offer his gratitude when he'd been the recipient of such benevolence. Had Lyvia not tended his wounds so well, he might have been unable to hold out Chumley's attacks.

It were a dang close run thing, that fight.

They sat with Chumley until he passed, a vigil of some three hours. Ms. Cady was inclined to offer him no comfort at all, until Smith reminded her that the apprentice was the only one of them with any knowledge of how to properly use the watch, or watches. She only grudgingly acknowledged that, but she did admit to it in the end.

"I can't even look at him without thinking of what he did to Gracie," she said. "You didn't read the stuff I did, Smith. You don't know."

"They were already dead," Chumley coughed, spitting up a small gobbet of dark blood. It did not endear him to Cady. "Drowned," he added, cryptically.

"You can say hello when you meet them, douchebag."

Smith simply got on with the job of trying to interrogate the dying apprentice. Miss Georgia was a help, lacking her friend's investment in so much personal animus towards Chumley.

Smith would have preferred that Cady swallowed her resentment and took part. After all, she was more familiar with their circumstances and had done some real professorial thinking on the matter of time travel. It did not reflect well on her that she could find no Christian charity within herself for a man who, as far as Smith could tell, had simply been going about his work.

Granted, it seemed that he worked for the devil, but Chumley did not appear to hold any personal feelings about the "elusives" he pursued. Indeed, he didn't seem to hold personal feelings about anything, except maybe dying. And on that, he had one more surprise for them.

"I was born near here, you know," he said in a rare moment of lucidity, shortly before he passed. Most of the final hours they spent with him, he was unable to string together a coherent thought. Despite the best efforts of Miss Georgia to engage him,

Chumley remained out of reach, mumbling and babbling and occasionally passing out as his life bled away.

"That so?" Smith asked.

"I was to return one day. At the end of my service. Such is our due and reward."

Georgia moved in closer too. It was a rare thing, hearing sense from Chumley by that point.

Cady paid him some heed, but she mostly watched the last of the freed slaves and fighters as they looted the property of Lentulus Batiatus and prepared to flee. Many had already lit out on their own, striking out across the countryside singly or in twos and threes. Smith did not doubt that most of them would quickly be hunted down. More interesting was the caravan this Spartacus feller put together under a lowering sun. Seventy or eighty fighting men like him, and whomsoever cared to join up with their party.

They reminded Smith of settlers in company heading west.

"I was born in Pompeii," Chumley said softly, "in the house of Julius Polybius."

"If you wanted to go there," Georgia said almost as softly, "if you wanted to go home, we could take you, but you'd have to tell us how, Apprentice."

"I would have gone home. One day," he said. "But now, I cannot return. I have failed."

Cady left her post, watching over the preparations for the wagon train, and joined them with Chumley. Her expression was still dark, but she'd heard enough to catch her interest.

"How were you going to get back if you hadn't failed, Chumley?" she said.

He closed his eyes and shook his head, going quiet for so long that Smith thought he may have slipped the mortal coil. The sounds of looting and departure reached them faintly.

Georgia brought him back, stroking his hand.

"Apprentice. You were telling us how you were going home," she said. "Remember?"

Chumley frowned and coughed. Another small spot of blood flew from his mouth and Georgia wiped it away.

"I was born into the house of Julius Polybius," he repeated.

Cady kneeled down next to him, and Smith was surprised by the tenderness in her voice.

"And you can return there, Apprentice. Tell us how."

He opened his eyes and smiled at her.

His teeth were stained with blood.

"We all go home. But I have failed," he said. "You should not be here."

"I know," Cady nodded. "Tell us how, and we'll make it right. You can go home. We can go home."

His eyelids fluttered closed.

". . . Can go . . . can go back . . . in one golden minute," he whispered.

Chumley did not open his eyes again.

CHAPTER THIRTY-SIX

Smith would have buried the man. It was the decent thing to do. But there were so many dead men that, in the end, they threw his body on a funeral pyre of slaves and masters alike. Cady insisted on searching the body in case he was carrying anything else which may have been of use to them, but they found nothing.

"So what now?" said Georgia as dusk fell and the wagon train of freed slaves and fighting men departed.

"I guess we could probably jump right now, using Chumley's watch," Cady suggested. "But I don't think we should. It's a different model, different UI, probably a different UX as well."

Smith frowned.

"Is it the case you think we shouldn't use Chumley's timepiece because we know even less about it than Mr. Wu's?"

Cady nodded. "Got it in one, Marshal. We don't know where he came from, when he was last there, or how he managed to hang out here for months when we saw him only a day ago, give or take."

Georgia grinned as though the answer was obvious. "Cady, he's a time traveler."

"So are we, babe, and yeah, sure, Chumley had some mad Timelord skills, but I just don't understand why he inserted himself into this timeline to wait for us. If he knew we were coming here, why not just be standing on that hill ready for us with a net or a phaser or something?"

They walked aimlessly around the grounds of the estate. There were only a few people left now. Fires burned here and there, and the occasional shout drifted to them on the early evening breeze. Smith did not mind admitting the whole thing gave him the shivers. Felt like the place was haunted before its time.

"Sometimes," he said, "I might get word a fugitive is going to be someplace at some time, but that word ain't gospel. Often times you would set up to surprise a feller and he'd already be gone long a'fore you even set the trap for him. Or he wasn't in this town, he was in that town, one over. Tracking a man is never simple. I don't know how he found us here. I don't know why circumstances were such that he had to burrow in for such a long while to wait us out. Can't even begin to contemplate how he did that. But it don't matter. He's dead and we're not, and if these apprentices are anything like marshals, another one will be along shortly. Chumley promised as much."

They climbed a set of steps leading up to a villa. The white marble looked pink in the sunset. Smith drew his Bowie knife, just in case. He missed the reassuring weight of a pistol on his hip.

"Do you think we should bug out like Calista and the others?" Cady asked.

Smith did not.

"Batiatus was a slaver. His estate is gonna be surrounded by more slavers. Most of those what run are gonna be back in chains a'fore nightfall tomorrow. That big caravan with Gannicus and the others, they got a chance, but they'll have to fight their way through. It'll be just as bad as it was here today. You don't want to get mixed up in that do you?"

"No," both girls agreed at once.

"Then I suggest we hole up here," said Smith. "Find a hiding place if we need one, but otherwise lay low and get gone as soon as ol' Mr. Wu allows."

They reached the top of the steps into the villa and took a moment on the stone porch out front. It afforded them a fine view of the gladiator school and the lands beyond. Would've made a fine spot for a rocking chair.

"You ladies best wait here while I scout this place out. Miss Georgia, you might profitably equip yourself with a weapon. Plenty to be picked up, just laying around."

"Hey," Cady objected. "I'm not the damsel in distress here. I kicked some ass today, you know."

"In your own way, yes you did," Smith allowed. "But I heard from Gannicus how Miss Georgia put down three fellers, all of them armed, and did so with her empty hands and true grit."

"Why sheriff, I'm blushing," grinned Georgia, before teasing her friend. "You hear that, Cady? I have true grit."

Smith picked up a short sword that lay near a bloody sandal and gave it to Cady, who did not take to being teased. "Okay then, Jim Bowie, you take this. I don't doubt you got the sand to stick it in someone if the need should arise. Miss Georgia, you okay to look after yourself?"

"You know what?" she said. "After today, I think I am."

Smith spied out the villa, which had been thoroughly ransacked. He took a few minutes to drag away the three bodies he found, dumping them in a small garden out back. There was no hiding the thick blood smears they left on the polished stone floors, but he was confident the ladies had seen enough of the red stuff spilled by now that they weren't like to come over all faint and a-flutter.

The villa sat on top of a small hill, giving them a long view of the road down which he expected the authorities to arrive sometime on the morrow. Hopefully, long after they had decamped. He fetched Cady and Miss Georgia in when he was happy the place was secure.

"It's like a museum," Cady said, boggling at the surrounds.

"That got looted," Miss Georgia qualified.

"There's a sitting parlor out back which weren't too badly messed up," Smith said. "No blood, anyways. I vote we rest up there, post a guard, and head out to the little creek in the morning to make our departure."

"Damn," said Cady. "My phone. I set a timer. I still want us to leave as close to the top of the clock as we can, but without that phone, we're just guessing."

"Not so much," said Smith. "I did check on Wu's pocket watch when we arrived. It put us here at about a quarter past nine in the morning."

"That's great," said Cady, sounding like she did not think so at all, then she caught herself using that less-than-agreeable tone and apologized. "I'm sorry," she said. "I just really want to do this the right way."

"What is the right way?" asked Georgia as they sidestepped one of the blood trails without so much as a grimace.

"I don't know, that's the problem. I was working this idea that if we controlled the time and spatial coordinates, you know, if we jumped as close to the minute, even the second we arrived, that . . ."

"Oh, my!" said Smith.

They both stopped to look at him, intrigued rather than alarmed.

"When I was talking to Chumley before we had to fight, he said something about a "golden minute." Stepping back through the golden minute, or some such. I thought it was just preacher talk, was all. You know how they do love their fancy rhetoricals. But when he was dying, he said it again. I adjudged him delirious then, but now maybe not."

"What'd you mean?" Cady asked.

"He said he was born around these parts," Smith recalled.

"That's right," Georgia confirmed. "In Pompeii. I remember."

"What?" said Cady. "Near the volcano?"

"Yeah. Vesuvius."

"Chumley said he was born there and he was supposed to return one day," Smith continued. "Said something about going back in the golden minute. I didn't pay it much heed, what with him bleeding out and all so . . ."

"Omigod! That has to be it," Cady said, almost squealing. "Don't you see? That has to be it. That's how you can step back. It has to be."

She all but jumped out of her own hide she was so excited. Miss Georgia seemed more reserved. Smith could tell from her expression that she had not quite bought this particular bill of goods.

"What else did he say?" Cady asked. "Can you think of anything, no matter how odd or even innocent?"

"Weren't like I were taking notes for court," he frowned.

"I know, I know, but try to remember as much as you can."

He furrowed his brow.

"Well, he called me an elusive, I recall that. Not just elusive, like hard to find, but *an* elusive, like it were a proper name."

Both girls were fixed in their attendance on him now. The light was fading fast and Smith thought they'd need to find candles, but Cady fetched a small black tube out of her pocket and made a bright light shine from it.

"Go on," she said.

"Okay," Smith said without much confidence. "Let's see. He said he was an apprentice. No surprise there. Said they'd been a-looking for us. Again, no prizes for picking the winner of that one-hoss race."

He focused hard on trying to recall every detail of the moments before they'd had at each other with steel.

"He said this had to stop, we didn't belong here, we couldn't go on. He called Batiatus something odd. An escarpment or something."

The girls exchanged a baffled look.

"Yeah, I couldn't make no head nor tail of that, neither."

"Did you say anything to him? Anything he reacted to?" Georgia asked.

"I told him we didn't have to kill each for the amusement of some slaver. That's when he said Batiatus was an . . . an escape. Nope, an escapement, that's it. Strange word. It mean anything to y'all?"

It didn't.

The shadows of the villa closed in around them as Cady's little hand-held lamp grew brighter in the dusk.

"He told me I'd given rise to complications, twenty-eight of them, and I must confess I remember that because it seemed so strangely exact."

"Twenty-eight?" Cady asked.

"Yep."

She mulled it over.

"Maybe he's talking about the number of times you jumped, Smith. You've been gone a month or more, right?"

He nodded in the gloom.

"Yep."

"But some places you stayed more than a single day."

"I did, but I did not think to make a note of them. Not until you suggested we do so in London."

"What are you thinking, Cady?" Georgia asked.

"Let's go sit down and talk it through," she said, leading off and lighting the way. "This way, Smith?"

"To the end of the hall and then to the right," he confirmed.

"When I was in Seattle, your Seattle, Georgia . . ."

"And yours."

"No, I don't think so. There were historical details that were totally wrong. It wasn't just finding Gracie and Bertie on Jack the Ripper's wiki page. I figure Chumley did that to cover his tracks or something. Or maybe, I dunno, maybe just having two bodies turn up then meant they got pulled into the narrative. It doesn't matter, because there were other details that we couldn't have effected. Like Australia speaking French."

"You mean *Australie?*" Georgia said, as though to correct her.

"No, I don't," Cady insisted. "I mean Australia, the once-upon-a-time British penal colony."

"No, I'm pretty sure it was a French colony," said Georgia. "You know, that's why they speak French."

"Not where I come from, babe," Cady replied, and she sounded a little sad, just for a moment. She turned to Smith as they walked on.

"I think the complications Chumley was talking about were bubble universes which inflated every time you jumped outside of this golden minute. It's just a theory, but I think to move up and down a timeline, you have to leave and enter it precisely. Maybe within one minute of the watch going live again. Any other time you jump, like we have twice now, you create an alternate timeline, a complication on the face of time itself. I think that's why they're chasing us. If they're time keepers, we're fucking everything up for them."

They stopped in the dark.

"Cady," whispered Georgia. "I've got goosebumps."

"Me too," said Cady.

Georgia giggled nervously. Then she laughed out loud.

"I think you might be onto something," she said.

Just before she died.

CHAPTER THIRTY-SEVEN

The thunder was enormous in that confined space, with those hard stone walls and marble floors. The flash and roar so close together and so unexpected that Cady jumped and screamed, not in fear, but surprise. She hadn't noticed a storm brewing up. There'd been no clouds or threat of rain, no distant grumble of thunder and lightning through the dusk.

There had been none, because there was no storm.

There was only Batiatus, standing at the end of the corridor, awkwardly waving Smith's handgun at them, screaming curses and invoking his gods and pulling the trigger until the hammer fell on empty chambers.

And Georgia fell at Cady's feet, her mouth forming an O as she tried to gasp, her chest hitching as she tried to breathe, blood bubbling up out of the bullet wounds there.

Cady screamed and Smith roared, but she was the closer to Batiatus. She ran at him without understanding what she was doing. She carved and slashed at him with the sword Smith had given her, and he screamed and wailed and fell under the attack.

She heard someone telling her to stop, someone yelling, "No," over and over again, but it was some time before she realized that it was her own voice and her throat was raw.

She was on the floor, in Smith's arms, her head buried in his shoulder, his hands gently patting her on the back as he rocked her like an infant in a crib.

Cady came back to herself, suddenly dropping back into the world from wherever she had been. She tried to push away from Smith, to get to her friend, to save Georgia. To make everything right again. But the marshal's arms enfolded her like the limbs of a giant tree which had grown up around her while she was gone. There was no escaping them.

"She's gone, Cady. She's gone," he said, almost as though he was crooning a lullaby.

"Nooooo . . ." she wailed and tried again to escape him, but there was no strength left in her. No hope. All of that had died with Georgia.

She couldn't even see her friend.

They weren't in the hallway where Batiatus had appeared from the shadows like an evil jack-in-the-box. There was no sign of the Roman and none of the young woman he had murdered.

"Wh . . . where . . ." she choked out.

Smith's voice was low and powerful, but not as steady as she had grown used to.

"I laid Miss Georgia out on a bed, Cady," he said, continuing to rock her back and forth. "I tended to her as best I could, but she did not come good. I'm sorry. This is my fault."

She pushed him away.

"No," she said fiercely. "It's mine. I brought her here. I didn't tell her what I was doing. I just did it because I wanted her with me and I was selfish and I didn't think and I never fucking think of anyone but me and now, and n-n-now . . ."

But she could talk no more because she was crying again.

She cried for hours and at some point, she supposed, she must have fallen asleep.

She experienced the terrible vertigo of having the whole world go sideways and drop away from you, when you wake up and it takes a second or two for your memory to fire. You could be at home in bed, a few weeks away from being rich and famous and all over BuzzFeed. But you're not. You're lost in some ancient version of hell and your friend is dead because you dragged her there.

Cady swore and pushed herself up off the bed where Smith had left her. Free falling panic followed when she could not see him.

"Smith!" she cried out.

"I'm here," he replied and appeared at the door. "Sorry. I was just keeping a look out."

Silence fell between them.

"How are you?" Smith eventually asked.

"How do you think?" Cady mumbled, but she felt even worse for being such a bitch, that she apologized. "Sorry. I'm just . . . you know."

"I do," he said. "I got this off Batiatus. He was wearing it like jewelry. A pendant or such like."

It took her a moment to recognize her iPhone, the one Batiatus had taken. It was wrapped in leather thongs from which crystals or jewels now dangled. They glinted in the morning light. The screen was cracked and it was sticky.

"I did try to clean it off for you," said Smith. "But I didn't want to fuss with it overly in case I broke it anymore."

Cady's head felt numb but heavy. The world seemed far away, as though she was not part of it. She took the phone without expectation, held down the power button.

The home screen came to life, which should have been a surprise, even a pleasant one. But she was inured to any sense of pleasure or anticipation, of hope, of anything.

"Where's Georgia?" she asked.

"I sat with her, while I kept look out," Smith said. "She is next door if you would like to visit, perhaps say something for her. I did a few rounds of the rosary on her behalf."

Cady didn't understand him at first. She thought he said "rose-mary." But then she realized that Smith had sat up and prayed over her dead friend while she had slept.

Cady did not respond to his invitation to visit with Georgia.

To sit with a corpse.

Nausea rolled through her at the thought and she clamped her jaws together.

"Did I kill Batiatus?" she asked.

"Yep," Smith confirmed. "You did for him, if'n that helps. Never does, in my experience."

Smith was right. It did not.

Cady had trouble with the touch interface. The cracked screen was flaky and unresponsive, but she did eventually bring up the timer she'd set.

An hour and ten minutes until the watch powered up again.

She started to cry.

Smith did not exactly insist that she say her goodbyes to Georgia before they left, but he did not make it easy to leave before she'd done so.

Cady was freaked beyond imagining by coming upon her friend in state. That's what they said in the olden days, wasn't it? Dead people lay "in state."

She'd hoped that maybe Georgia would look like she was sleeping, but death did not spare her with that illusion. Cady took a deep, shuddering breath and, with a trembling hand, pulled back the sheet Smith had draped over her. Her best friend looked dead.

Some far away part of her understood he must've put the shroud on fresh. It wasn't stained with blood. Cady closed her eyes. The color had drained from Georgia's face and there was a dread sense of weight to her, as though she was so heavy in death she might fall back into the earth.

"I'm sorry, Georgia," she whispered, struggling not to cry again. "I'm sorry, and I will make this right. I promise. I don't care how long it takes. I don't care if I have to erase this entire fucking timeline. You are not going to die here. I promise."

It sounded mad and empty, all at the same time.

Her overweening confidence of yesterday, that she'd figured it all out, had deserted her.

"Best we be going, Miss Cady," Smith said from the door. "I have directions from Gannicus to the spot where we arrived. I can see some riders moving around on the horizon, too. Don't imagine they're freed men. They'd all be gone by now."

"Bye," she whispered and turned and walked out of the room, weighed down by something vast and invisible.

Smith wore his gun belt and pistol again and had rigged up a scabbard for the Bowie knife. He offered her a hunk of cheese and some stale bread, but she was not hungry.

They walked through the baking heat of the morning, the stench of rot and smoke staying with them until they'd left the main campus of the gladiator school well behind.

"You got bullets?" she asked him, her voice empty of feeling.

"Yep," he confirmed.

That was it for conversation. Smith seemed to understand she wanted to be left alone.

The road from the estate took them most of the way to the stream, at which point they left the cobblestones and tramped across rolling fields, climbing ever so gently towards a ridge line dotted with olive trees. She assumed they were olive trees anyway. Not that it mattered.

A rider crested the ridge when they were almost there, but Smith fired one round into the sky, and he galloped away. No more appeared.

They arrived with a few minutes to spare. Her thoughts were slow and heavy, and she had trouble moving them around.

"We should, ah . . ." she started.

"We should what?" Smith asked when she trailed off.

"I had an idea. About the special minute."

"The golden minute."

"Yeah. That one. So we don't miss it."

Smith said nothing. He waited for her to go on, and she thought, bizarrely, inappropriately, how unusual that was; for a man to wait for her to speak.

Be a shame to waste such a rare opportunity.

If only she could remember what the hell she'd been . . .

"Oh, yeah," she said without animation. "I thought if we held hands and, you know, double-clicked every thirty seconds leading up to the twenty-four-hour mark, we should be right. We'll trigger the jump in the first minute."

Smith nodded. He didn't smile, but he did seem pleased.

"Cady, if that's what you think we should do, then by God, that is what will happen."

They stood atop the small hill where they'd arrived. The weather was nearly identical. A scorching day, the sky unmarred with clouds. According to the timer, they had a few minutes to spare, but Cady suggested they start trying as soon as they stood in the spot where both agreed they had appeared.

They held hands.

She did not look back.

On the third attempt, they jumped.

CHAPTER THIRTY-EIGHT

They arrived before themselves. The same spot by the quiet road in the woods outside the city. The same gas station, lit up in the dark, about ten minutes' walk away.

"You did it," Smith said. "I think we're back, Cady. Back to Seattle, yours or Georgia's."

Cady should have been excited, but she couldn't crawl out from under the heavy, suffocating blanket of sadness that'd lain over her since Georgia died.

"Yeah," she said, and started to walk. She took out her iPhone and thumbed the home button. The screen lit up and the phone searched for a signal.

Two bars, but no service.

Both watches were synchronized to the local time zone. 9:47 p.m. by Chumley's watch. It was much easier to read to the minute.

Smith was right. They were back. Maybe.

She felt her heart beat a little faster at that. Her phone, she remembered, would not be registered with AT&T yet. The SIM was tapping the network, but flaking out because her account didn't exist and would not until tomorrow.

"Shit," she muttered, before absently apologizing to Smith for swearing.

"It's okay," he said. "Don't matter. Just keep doing whatever you're doing."

She put the phone away and resumed the trek towards the gas station.

Could it be that they had a handle on this now? It did seem they were having an actual Groundhog Day moment this time around. Everything looked the same; the time on the watches, give or take a few minutes; the weather; the familiar skyline on the horizon.

Cady picked up her pace and crunched along the wet gravel at the side of the road, intent on getting to the Texaco and making the call she dreaded more than anything in the world.

There was one difference, though. She picked it out of the night sounds, when she heard the voices reach them on the breeze.

"Hey! Hey you two!"

"Look," Smith said, his voice hushed with almost religious awe. "Cady, just stop and look."

She turned around.

There they stood, waving to themselves, calling out. Too far away to be certain in the dark, unless you knew who they were.

John Titanic Smith and Cady McCall. Newly arrived from London.

Her whole body crawled with gooseflesh.

She shivered and turned away as the spectral figures faded out of existence.

"That was us," Smith whispered, the timbre of his voice that of a man who has not just seen a ghost, but has seen his *own* ghost.

"Quantum shadows," Cady said. "Come on."

She double-timed it all the way to the gas station, occasionally checking behind them to see if they were being followed. By themselves.

But they were alone.

She tried not to think about what it meant. She knew little enough of the technology or magic that had done all of this and she was learning not to make assumptions. Not to be so fucking arrogant.

But it was hard not to let her excitement grow. It was a dark flower inside, budding and growing and blooming at 10x speed as they hurried towards the lights.

Cady ran across the wet concrete tarmac of the Texaco. She could already see the clerk behind the counter, the same Indian guy who'd been working the till when they last arrived. A bell over the door rang as she hurried in. He looked up, but he did not recognize her or Smith. And Smith was not a character you forgot.

His eyes did go wide momentarily, but then he dropped his gaze and Cady realized just how much dried blood covered her tee shirt and jeans. Smith looked like he'd been in a car accident.

The cash machine sat exactly where it had before. The same junk food and porno mags lined the aisle leading to the rear of the shop. Smith did not recoil in fright from the skin mags this time. He stuck to her heels, following her through the little convenience store.

Cady's hand was shaking as she grabbed her wallet and took out the plastic. The machine gobbled it up. She was so jittery she messed up the PIN code twice.

"I don't exactly know what you're trying to do," Smith said, "but I can see you need to take a breath and come at it a little slower."

She resisted the urge to say something harsh and stupid. He was right. Smith was always right. It could be annoying, but she would have to get used to it. They were going to be spending some time together.

Three deep breaths, and a few seconds with her eyes closed to clear her mind.

She entered the PIN for her business account and requested a balance.

Nine and a half million dollars.

The tremor in her hands spread to her whole body.

"It's there, Smith," she said. "It's all there. It's like we haven't been here yet."

"That's good, Cady. So, what next?"

"This," she said.

She withdrew $200, the maximum she could take in one hit from this machine. Then she hit it again, twice. She didn't buy a burner phone this time. Instead she picked up a $50 micro SIM for the iPhone. Her fingers were numb, and her hands were shaking so much that she had to ask the clerk to switch out the simcards for her.

"Man," he said, "you're lucky. This is our last one of the old SIMs. Gotta sell the new ones now. With the backdoor."

She giggled nervously at that. Laughing inappropriately, she paid him for the card and tipped him another fifty bucks. He was stunned and then a little suspicious. She noticed for the first time that his ID tag was not issued by Texaco. It had come from Homeland Security.

"Don't worry," she said, "we just had a big win. Thanks."

She virtually dragged Smith out of the store so she could make the call.

"You getting one of them Ubers?" he asked.

"In a minute," she said. "But first I have to call . . ."

She trailed off unable to finish.

"Miss Georgia?" Smith asked gently.

She couldn't speak around the lump in her throat so she just nodded.

"I just need a minute," she said, and walked away from him. Smith did not follow.

Cady walked into the dark. She wanted fresh air, but all she could smell were petrochemicals. She didn't know what would happen when she rang her friend. Would Georgia be here? Would she be lying dead back in the villa? If she did answer the phone, did that mean that their whole sword-and-sandal adventure had never happened? That could be, but they were still covered in blood and bruises.

And what of those quantum shadows? An echo of things which had not happened yet?

There was no way to know what would happen until it happened, even when you could travel in time.

Cady calmed herself as best she could. She walked back to Smith who waited patiently for her by the pumps.

"We can't make a call here," she said. "Mythbusters proved it was bullshit, but people still think cell phones will blow up a gas station."

He didn't ask what she meant by that. He was learning to roll with it. They both were. They walked a few yards away to the spot where she'd previously called up a taxi to take her back to her apartment.

She entered Georgia's number from memory, her landline this time. One of only handful she knew by heart. Her own and her parents were the others. They'd shut down Georgia's cell phone, but she had to have some way of contacting work, didn't she? And her prison guards, of course.

It was after ten o'clock now and she wondered if Georgia would be awake. If she would be alive. The phone rang and rang. No voicemail cut in. When nobody picked up, Cady's heart sank. She could feel the heavy darkness of spirit creeping back upon her.

She'd been wrong.

She'd fucked up again.

And she'd left her best friend behind, shot dead in some villa two thousand years ago.

"Hello. Georgia Eliadis."

Cady gasped.

And hung up.

They did not return to her apartment. Not this time. Instead they caught a cab to the Alexis Hotel after she'd grabbed a couple of adjoining rooms on Expedia.

"It was her?" Smith said in the back of the cab.

"It was," Cady said, still giddy with relief half an hour after she'd heard Georgia's voice.

"But you didn't talk to her?"

Cady shook her head slowly.

"I didn't want to get her in trouble. Not after what happened last time."

"But you intend on talking to her?"

"Not about what happened, no. But yes, tomorrow. I'll talk to Georgia. Call my parents, maybe. But first I need to get a lawyer."

"Well, you are in luck, ma'am. It just so happens I met a good one last time I was here in Seattle," Smith joked. "I could give you his name if you so wished."

She squeezed his arm. The sleeve of his rawhide jacket was stiff with dried blood, but she did not pull her hand away.

"That's very kind of you. First thing in the morning, then. But right now, I want a deep bath and a soft bed."

They had both at the hotel.

Cady rang the concierge to warn them they'd be checking in late, and that they had suffered a minor car accident. Their luggage had been trashed. They looked a little rough around the edges. The staff shouldn't worry, but they might need to buy some clothes in the morning. Was that something the concierge could arrange?

It was. Indeed, if they had no objection, he could provide them with clothes from the lost property room as soon as they arrived.

The hotel held on to such items for a month, before sending them to charity.

Smith worried about Chumley.

"If Georgia is alive, shouldn't he be, too?" He asked over a late snack and a drink in the bar of the hotel. Cady had a crab sandwich. Smith ate two bowls of fries and a cheeseburger, washed down with a couple of bottles of beer. They were clean and reasonably presentable, having taken the concierge up on his offer of dipping into the lost property bin. They wore tourist outfits while their own clothes were being laundered. Cady had told the concierge she'd pay whatever it took to get them back by morning. In the meantime, she found a reasonable pair of jeans and a black T-shirt, which was one size too large. Smith wore a loud red and white tracksuit left behind by a visiting Welsh rugby player. It was the only thing that fit him.

"He could be here," she conceded, "but I'm hoping not. I'm really hoping that, because he was independent of this reality, because he wasn't native to this timeline, like we're not, that he can't be rebooted or overwritten or whatever. He was playing hard-core, like us. Dead is dead."

"But you don't know for sure," said Smith around a mouthful of cheeseburger.

"No, I don't," she admitted. "I don't know a lot about how this is going to work out, Smith. But I do know that we're a lot closer to getting home, both of us, then we were when you rescued me from those guys."

He looked troubled at that.

"Yeah," he said. "I still don't rightly cotton to what happened there. That pair were apprentices, no question of it. They'd been tracking me for hours. But when you came walking down the street, it was like they were a couple of wolves got the scent of new blood. They went after you, not me, Cady."

She smiled and leaned forward as if to impart a secret.

"Maybe they saw the future," she said. "Maybe they saw just how badly I'm gonna kick their asses."

Smith raised his drink to that.

They retired to their rooms, but she was pretty sure he did not sleep. Not for long. She found him in the morning, sitting in an armchair in her room, his pistol on the coffee table in front of him. He had been watching over her. Guarding her.

Three days ago she'd have freaked.

Now, she found a warm unfamiliar feeling curling deep inside her chest when she woke and saw him there. It was possible, she thought, that she might be falling in love with this huge, hairy brute of a man.

Possible, but impossible, too.

They came from different times, and neither would ever wish to live in the other's world. Not forever. Nor, it seemed, would they be allowed to.

She got out of bed, careful not to wake him, showered, dressed and ordered breakfast. Their laundered clothes arrived with the coffee and eggs. Smith's jacket was permanently stained and Cady's jeans had lost color to multiple bleaching rounds. Neither cared.

"How long do you think we should stay here?" Smith asked when the meal was finished. "Even if Chumley stays dead, he said more would come, and I believe him."

Cady sipped the last of her coffee.

"We won't stay long," she said. "We should get back to London. Make sure Gracie and Bertie are cool."

"All right, and then?"

He did not ask the question that obviously weighed so heavily on him.

"Then we drop into my home year. I'll let people know I'm going to take a little time off because I need it after releasing the game, and we find a way back to your daughter, Smith."

He said nothing, but his eyes held hers for what could have been an uncomfortably long time.

It wasn't uncomfortable, though, and Cady could happily have let the moment go on much longer.

"Thank you," he said quietly, "but what about you?"

"Smith, if I can get you home to Elspeth, I can retrace my steps to Seattle. To Georgia and Matt and my parents and my home."

"On your own?" he asked.

She smiled. "Only if you weren't minded to ride that trail back with me, pardner."

The apprentices did not find them, not this time. Doubtless they were looking, using all of the arcane technologies and methods at their disposal, on behalf of whatever master they served.

For time itself?

For the great watchmaker?

Who knew?

Cady's only immediate concern was to protect those closest to her, and to get gone, as Smith would say. She paid cash at the hotel. If they had to stay another night or two or even three, they would not return there. They were fugitives now. But Smith was a man who had hunted fugitives, and he knew how to remain inconspicuous, how to move without drawing the unwanted eye. Cady would learn from him. After all, he had been willing to learn from her.

They visited the law firm of Dexter and Calvino, where one of the senior partners, Mr. Thomas Calvino, assured them that the firm would gladly take on the cases of Mr. Matthew Aleveda and Ms. Georgia Eliadis. Mr. Calvino did not question Cady's instructions that Georgia be given power of attorney and control of Cady's assets, which principally consisted of nine and a half million dollars in a checking account.

Mr. Calvino also promised to personally deliver a handwritten note from Cady to her parents, explaining that she could not come home, but that they were not to worry about her. She thanked them for never losing faith in her and told them that she would always love them, now and for all time.

But she had to go.

She did not call Georgia again.

Mr. Calvino strongly recommended that all contact with Ms. Eliadis be channeled through his office.

"They'll probably put down your call last night to a wrong number or a cold caller, but she is being monitored and it could adversely affect her sentencing agreement if she's found to have made unauthorized contact with anyone."

They thanked Calvino, organized his payment, and were done with this world before lunch time.

Cady did not feel the need to explore it, like she had with London. The longer she was here, the more it disturbed her. She could understand why Smith did not see things the same way. To him, this looked a perfectly reasonable time and place. Pleasant and prosperous, even.

But he didn't see what she did.

People were missing.

Lots of them.

Had they gone to the Wall, or somewhere else?

She didn't know, and she found that she did not want to know. She just wanted to get gone.

"You don't want to see your ma and pa?" Smith asked as they sat in a coffee shop, passing the hours.

It was a painful question for him, and she could see it hurt to ask. He must have been contemplating his own daughter, from whom he had been gone a month, and many, many years. Would she refuse contact with him when they were reunited?

"I do want to see them," she said, "but they're not my parents. Or, they are, but, you know, they're . . . not. Chumley was right, Smith. We don't belong here. We have one place, one time we belong. And we should be getting back."

They spent the afternoon shopping discretely, picking up some camping supplies, survival equipment, weapons. Just in case. But most of the day they stayed low and kept away from other people.

After all, they did not belong here.

At 9:47 that night, they were back standing by the side of the road where they had stepped into the future. Or this version of it, anyway.

They held hands.

"Are you ready?" Smith asked.

"Always," said Cady.

Together, they jumped.

AFTERWORD

A Girl in Time is finished, but I can't help feeling Smith and Cady will be back. If you'd like a heads up, and a big discount on the next adventure, you can get both by joining my bookclub at

jbismymasternow.com

Oh, and there's plenty of free stuff waiting there for you, too.

ACKNOWLEDGMENTS

As always, first thanks go to you, the readers. I'm not being precious. My first editors are my readers, specifically those long time friends who serve as my alpha crew, and beyond them, my blog regulars, who are always willing to tell me exactly what they think.

The production team for *A Girl in Time* went above and beyond, as they always do.

Jen Wadsworth, for editing.

William Heavey, artwork.

Alicia Wanstall-Burke, proofreading.